THE FIRE THIS TIME

The Fire This Time

A novel
by

S. FREDERIC LISS

Adelaide Books
New York / Lisbon
2020

THE FIRE THIS TIME
A novel
By S. Frederic Liss

Published by Adelaide Books, New York / Lisbon
adelaidebooks.org

Editor-in-Chief
Stevan V. Nikolic

For any information, please address Adelaide Books
at info@adelaidebooks.org

or write to:

Adelaide Books
244 Fifth Ave. Suite D27
New York, NY, 10001

ISBN: 978-1-952570-88-9

Printed in the United States of America

For A, J, and J
with the prayer the world they grow up into
will not be the world depicted in this novel

Contents

Oh, maybe then you all shock a little too easily. Jews are heirs to greater shocks than I can possibly deliver with a story . . .

Nathan Zuckerman as quoted by
Philip Roth, *The Ghost Writer*,
Fawcett Crest Books,
New York, 1979, p. 134

PART I

MADDIE DEVLIN

Prologue

April, 1981

That venomous spring a massive high pressure system stalled over Georges Bank and Canada's Maritime Provinces lifting the jet stream north of the Saint Lawrence River, trapping a five-hundred-year heat wave over the northeast United States, a heat wave that lingered like a fever incubating a last illness. In Boston, a radio station ran a contest—first prize central air conditioning—to the listener who found the sidewalk that fried an egg the fastest.

The contest was a sham. No sidewalk ever got hot enough to fry an egg. Experiments in Death Valley where such heat was as common as a carpet of flowers after an early spring rain had proven that. There would be no winners. But, there were losers. Victims of heat stroke backlogged hospital emergency rooms, overflowed mortuary embalming tables, or braved the pollution of Boston's beaches.

Many blamed the heat for the events of that miasmal April recounted here. Others blamed God or Satan. Boston's Jews blamed the city's mayor, Charles F. Sullivan, Jr. The city's Irish blamed the Jews; its African-Americans blamed the whites. Everyone blamed somebody; nobody blamed themselves.

Chapter 1

Friday, April 10, 1981

-1-

Attorney Mary Ann Devlin, Maddie to everyone but the judges before whom she appeared every day, tried to persuade herself it was too hot to do her daily calisthenics, Royal Canadian Air Force Exercises, Level 5, on the three or four days a week she did not run five fast miles along the Charles River, outrunning the druggies and derelicts who often showed up on her client list in the Criminal Session of the Boston Municipal Court.

Maddie's salary as a public defender with Suffolk County Legal Services did not allow the luxury of membership in an athletic club with state-of-the-art equipment, autocrats masquerading as exercise leaders, and a swimming pool to stretch the long muscles of her back and legs. Dues at the YWCA, as low as they were, were also out of reach. She purchased her running shoes, factory seconds of the brands worn by the Boston Marathon's elite runners, on the grey market from a pushcart hidden among the produce stalls in Haymarket. At her age, halfway between thirty and forty, she was thin, but softly firm, with her mother's auburn hair, an oak leaf in autumn which had just peaked. If beauty lay in the genes, hers–like Trish Devlin Sullivan's, like Katie Devlin's, like all the Devlin women's–was her birthright. Her beauty, however, did not extend to her voice. Aged by circumstance, it was shrill and shaky like that of an opera singer no longer able to hit her notes; a voice so perfect in the courtroom, so mood breaking in the bedroom.

Maddie dug the TV remote out from the pile of unread magazines beneath her night table–*The New Yorker, The Economist, Vogue*–to feed her craving for things not found in the world she grew up in, and clicked on the morning news. Framed in black bunting, nine-year-old Bumper Sullivan's boyish face filled the screen, a school photo, wearing a white shirt and clip-on tie that sagged from one collar. His hair swooped across his forehead; his smile was a shade shy of a smirk. In a halting voice, the announcer recounted how Bumper's bloodless body had been found by his father, Mayor Charles Sullivan, in the library of the Capablanca Chess Club the previous evening.

"According to high-level sources in the police department," the announcer continued," a skull cap belonging to Avram Levy, also a member of the Club, had been found near the body. Levy is in custody and his arraignment is scheduled for this afternoon."

Maddie gasped. Her lungs felt on fire. Ever since her daughter's death thirteen Aprils ago, April had been her cruelest month. Now it would be Trish Sullivan's as well. Elizabeth Devlin Gloucester, Bumper Devlin Sullivan, never cousins in life because of their age difference, now cousins in death. She counted to ten, then counted to ten again. At last, her heart rate moderated and she breathed more easily.

She removed the mouth guard she wore so she would not grind her teeth in her sleep–hundreds of dollars to keep perfect a smile she rarely had occasion to use. She picked up the phone. The dial tone jarred her and she hung up. Trish had not called when Elizabeth died, had not attended her wake or funeral. Bumper's death tempered Maddie's grudge, but not the realization that Trish would not welcome her call. The sins of generations past victimized them both, making present day sins unnecessary.

A photo of Avram Levy's skull cap replaced Bumper's picture on the TV screen. Maddie applied her lawyer's mind to the scant information offered by the report. She rummaged through her bag of defense attorney tricks and treats to make sense of what she had just seen, had just heard. She played these mind games because an ancient litigator whose nose and ears bristled with the hair of experience once told her visualization was the key to being a successful trial lawyer. It worked in her professional life, if not her personal.

Leaking this information–Levy's name, the photo of the skull cap–to the press was not the style of the Suffolk County District Attorney. He held his cards so close to the vest the dirt on his hands and fingers smudged his white dress shirt. Mayor Charlie was too calculating to finger Levy before the public had processed the murder of his son and none of his underlings had the balls to do something like this on their own. Jewish votes and Jewish money were essential to Charlie's U.S. Senate campaign. High-level sources in the police department, the news anchor had said. It had to be the highest, Police Commissioner Dante Ugolino. But, why?

Maddie ticked off potential explanations on her fingers, each a negative. Ugolino wouldn't do it to scare off the defense bar because the best made their reputations and fortunes winning high-profile unwinnable cases. Nor to calm the community because the disclosure was too inflammatory. Nor to incite anti-Semitism, even though it would. A mistake? Ugolino was too foresighted, too farsighted.

Maddie stopped counting on her fingers as two possible explanations came into focus. Ugolino was laying the foundation for justifying a cursory police investigation of Bumper's murder. The police had their man, so why bother? Maddie could offer a multitude of reasons why the police should bother—the possibility Levy didn't act alone being the most obvious, the possibility the skull cap was a plant by the killer to mislead the police the second most obvious. Or, Ugolino was generating pretrial publicity that would make it impossible to impanel an impartial jury in Boston, sucker-punching the average defense attorney to move for a change of venue.

Maddie had tried cases in rural Massachusetts, Franklin and Berkshire Counties, and Worcester County north of the city. Jews were scarce in those parts of the state. Blue-collar workers, farmers, older people with traditional values and strong bonds to their ethnic communities as well as their churches—older people who had been brought up to believe Jews were responsible for the Crucifixion—filled the jury pools. Those people would focus on the obvious—the skull cap beside the body—and ignore whatever smoke defense counsel would blow. The case would be decided, the guilty verdict rendered, before the lunch break on the first day of deliberations.

Years of trying cases in the Criminal Session of Suffolk County Superior Court had taught her that Levy needed a Boston jury drawn from a pool large enough to include liberal Democrats, the college educated, a white-collar jury with teachers, engineers, business owners, accountants, people who would listen and assess the evidence rather than be swayed by emotion or prejudice. It only took one, one out of twelve. Her trial experience also made it clear to her that Ugolino had outfoxed the defense bar. He wanted to deep-six a thorough police investigation to force the defense to do the police's job on the defense's nickel. He wanted the change of venue and he was doing his best to finesse the defense into requesting it.

But, why? The prosecution's case must have a weakness. A set of fingerprints that didn't match Levy's. A break in the chain of custody. A piece of physical evidence "lost" in the police department evidence room. Or, planted at the crime scene. Ugolino was not beneath corrupting a crime scene, something every experienced defense attorney knew but could never muster sufficient evidence to prove. Too obvious, these weaknesses. Pre-trial discovery would alert defense counsel to them. No, it had to be something so subtle, yet so fatal, only one in a thousand defense lawyers would figure it out. It was the kind of challenge she thrived on and succeeded at more often than not.

Maddie tried to infer what the weakness was. Less than twelve hours had elapsed since Bumper's murder, since Mayor Charlie had found Bumper's body. Logic said it had to be tied into something Charlie did before the police arrived, before the police tape cordoning off the crime scene went up. Corrupting the crime scene was one explanation; removing evidence another. With or without consulting Ugolino first? Maddie loved conspiracies. The more implausible, the more she loved them. Her secret vice, alien abductions.

No, as much as this was her kind of case, she wouldn't represent Levy, if asked. She never represented homicide defendants accused of killing a child or any defendants accused of abusing a child, a preference the director of Suffolk County Legal Services had respected to date when assigning cases.

The camera zoomed in on Avram Levy's name embroidered in the lining of the skull cap. The spidery stitching reminded

Maddie of the way her ma had embroidered her name in her church dresses. Ma had mothballed those dresses for the grand-daughter she yearned for, but Maddie had unpicked the embroidery and donated the dresses to a charity which shipped used clothing to missions in Africa. At the time, Maddie thought seeing her dresses walking down the street would decimate whatever remnant of her fragile psyche had survived Elizabeth's death; but, now, years later, she regretted acting in such haste. She rolled to her side, her head resting on an arm. Hair covered her cheek. On the television, the newscaster, now perky, moved on to a story about the possible postponement of the Boston Marathon if the heat did not moderate.

Maddie clicked off the television, eased out of bed, and rested her elbows on the window sill. The street was quiet, empty except for the heat waves rising off the pavement. The streetlight opposite her bedroom window hummed softly like a fluorescent light beginning to wear down. It was six in the morning. After Elizabeth's death, it had taken months, years, for her to reset her internal alarm clock, seven months before she first slept through the night rather than awaken for the 3:00 AM bottle, two years before she slept through it regularly. Habits and routines were another form of grieving; giving them up, a way of letting go. Which was not the same as forgetting. Or forgiving.

-2-

The phone rang as Maddie washed her breakfast dishes. Half a pink grapefruit. A slice of whole wheat toast, dry. A cup of coffee, black, French Press brewed fresh each morning, coarse ground Kenyan coffee beans, the one luxury she allowed herself. On this morning, she sought solace in a second cup. Since her da had passed, calls before work were rare, usually a solicitation on behalf of a police or fire relief fund where most of the money went to the company raising it and a penny or two trickled down to the widows and children desperate for money. She thought about letting the phone ring, but she had been trained to answer a ringing phone just like dogs had been trained to respond to a bell by that Russian whose name she didn't remember. In college, she had taken a psychology course to satisfy a science distribution requirement and hated every minute of it. Now, after eight years in the courtroom, she knew more about ins and outs of the human mind than Professor Whatever-His-or-Her-Name-Was.

"Maddie," George Harriman said. "Bumper . . . "

"I know, Uncle George. I saw it on TV."

Detective George Harriman. An uncle by affection, not blood, who had always been there for Maddie. Her da's best friend, their friendship originating in catechism class at St. Dymphna Catholic Church and forged on the beaches of Guadalcanal during World War II, a friendship so strong it survived George's moving back and forth between the two branches of the estranged Devlin family, an envoy with diplomatic immunity, a friendship which in spite of its strength was unable to reunite what had cleaved asunder two generations before. And, so, he had stopped trying.

"Was Ugolino the high police source?" Maddie asked.

"You should go to Bumper's wake," Harriman said.

"Why does he want a change of venue? Did Charlie corrupt the crime scene? Was the skull cap a plant?"

"Trish needs your help."

"Ugolino's as obvious as the fat hanging over his belt."

"Maddie!" Harriman's voice had the snap of a frustrated beat cop trying to control an unruly crowd. "Trish needs you."

"She wasn't there for me when Elizabeth died. She wasn't there for me when I asked Charlie to add the Elizabeth Fund to the list of charities city employees could contribute to through a payroll deduction and he told me to go fuck myself. She wasn't there for me when Ugolino vetoed Boston cops taking the Elizabeth Fund's course in child abuse prevention and you and the union forced him to approve it. So, why should I be there for her?"

To honor her daughter's memory, shortly after her death Maddie had founded the Elizabeth Fund, a charity to provide support to victims of child abuse and to educate the public on the problem, a problem that received little or no attention in the press. Michelle Furey, an attorney recommended by a law school classmate of Maddie's, had donated her services to form a charitable corporation under Massachusetts law and to qualify it as a charity under the Internal Revenue Code so that contributions were tax deductible. Furey had declined an invitation to join the board of directors. Maddie had not believed Furey's "standard policy" explanation and replaced her as the Fund's attorney.

"You've been through it," Harriman said.

"What about Father Curry? I'm not her savior."

"Talk to her. For her sake and yours."

"I tried. Bumper's First Communion. I reached out to her. You know what happened."

Aunt Katie Devlin had happened. Katie had imported the Devlin blood feud from Dublin to Boston and enforced it with the enthusiasm of a nun sowing the fear of God in the minds of impressionable children.

"Maybe," Maddie said, "if there's a time Katie's not there."

"That's the same as saying no."

"It's the best I can do."

"No, it's all you're willing to do."

"You have a nice day, too."

It would serve Trish right, Maddie thought as she dried her breakfast dishes, if I represented Levy. Still, she had made a promise to Elizabeth's memory, a promise more important to her than payback to Trish's side of the family.

-3-

While commuters crawling along the Southeast Expressway listened to radio talk shows whose ratings fluctuated with how inflammatory the hosts and callers were, three men drenched the Passover matzoh offered for sale by a West Roxbury supermarket with pig's blood. The Boston Superintendent of Schools locked down the high school in Roslindale after fights broke out between Catholic and Jewish students, Catholic and Jewish teachers. Everywhere, people heard footsteps; yet, when they looked over their shoulders they saw only shadows.

Later that morning, Rabbi Isaac ben Reuben, the rabbi of the Chelsea synagogue where Levy *davened*, absorbed the arrhythmic pulse of the city as he crossed City Hall Plaza. The heat and humidity of the canicular weather gnawed at his knuckles. Although he had no memory of it, Nazi hammers had fractured and re-fractured those knuckles as if they were rocks being split apart. Now they bulged from the back of his hands like cancerous tumors whose cells had never stopped dividing. An amateur boxer who fought several fights too many was his explanation when people asked.

After the war, the rabbi healed himself by cocooning certain of his memories of the Nazi era to create an amnesia so selective that although he did not forget the Nazi era from an historical perspective, he had no memory of his having lived through it, no memory of his personal experiences. These memories did not exist for him, but they had enough of a presence in his subconscious to influence his life. He never married. He did not share the naive belief so common among American clergy, especially rabbis, that a benevolent God would somehow make things right. Nor did he question how God could permit such an evil as Adolf Hitler. For Rabbi ben Reuben, men of unspeakable evil were as much a part of the history of the Jewish people as the Covenant.

Now, the rabbi weaved between the lines of people on City Hall Plaza queued up at the pushcarts offering hot dogs and sauerkraut, gyros and Greek salads, meat pies, and cold soda, pushcarts whose prices for cold drinks rose in lockstep with the temperature. The lunch hour rush had begun, but the *knish* and *latke* vendor's space was vacant. Snatches of conversation curled above the pushcarts. "His blood was drained," a woman waiting for a gyro said. "I told the wife not to let the kids out of her sight," a construction worker told the hot dog vendor.

Levy's call to ben Reuben had come shortly after sunrise in time for the rabbi to turn on the news and hear a phrase he thought he had forever left behind in Europe: blood libel. "It's not true," he screamed at the announcer, but she repeated the phrase twice before moving on to a commercial for a breakfast pastry that could be heated in a toaster.

Pain detonated inside the rabbi's skull. He staggered to his desk and collapsed into the desk chair. Blood libel. Sparks darted along the neural pathways of his brain tracing white lines against the pinkish hue of his brain tissue as shocking as the bolts of lightning discharged from the Van de Graaff generator at Boston's Museum of Science. The white lines roamed freely until they reached an island of black engulfing the hippocampus, a barrier that dead-ended the neural pathways. The sparks piled up against this barrier like medieval soldiers against a castle wall they could not breach. As suddenly as it appeared, the pain in his skull vanished. A thought lingered in the rabbi's mind. Something unknown lay dormant within that castle.

Later, in the synagogue, as he and Jacob Moskovitzky waited for a *minyan* to assemble for *Shacharit*, the rabbi repeated the words he had screamed at the television announcer. "It's not true."

"Not here, not in Europe," Moskovitzky replied.

Aged and elderly, they gathered each day in the Chelsea *shul* with other refugees from Nazis or Stalinists, Bolsheviks or Communists, pogroms or inquisitions as virulent and violent as centuries earlier when Spain exiled its civilization. The slander was not true, Moskovitzky and ben Reuben agreed, but they knew it did not have to be true to be "true." It was the nature of this peculiar and indelible slander against Jews that the truth was in the slandering regardless of the inveterate inaccuracy of what was said. After a long wait for a tenth congregant, the rabbi asked *Yod. Heh. Vav. Heh.*'s forgiveness and began the service with nine. *Yod. Heh. Vav. Heh,* the name of God expressed as a tetragrammaton since His name was too sacred to be spoken.

"I will call my grandson," Moskovitzky said after the benediction. Moskovitzky had founded Boston's preeminent Jewish law firm, its name sanitized as Mosca, Baruch and Cohen. On his ninetieth birthday, leadership of the firm devolved upon his grandson, Jeffrey Mosca.

"They refuse," Moskovitzky said after completing the call. "Jeffrey says they are not criminal lawyers."

"He's afraid, Jacob. In Europe fear made us brave. Here it makes us cowards."

"Jews have it too easy in this country," Moskovitzky said. "We've become complacent. Forgetful of history. Our senses cauterized."

For the remainder of the morning, Moskovitzky continued to seek legal counsel for Levy. Boston's principal civil liberties firm, Ginsberg, Levin, and Katz, begged off, confessing that they depended on Jewish contributions to balance their budget and they feared those contributions would cease or be substantially reduced. Other firms demanded substantial cash retainers or quoted high hourly rates. One or two admitted they depended on the good will of City Hall to represent their clients effectively. Soliciting contributions to a defense fund failed. Jews who raised millions of dollars for Israel in a morning shunned Levy as if he were *traif*. The rabbis of wealthy suburban congregations refused to return Moskovitzky's phone calls.

"In the old country, we were not our own enemy," Moskovitzky said.

"Who defends the undefended?" The rabbi chewed aspirin to relieve the pain in his joints.

"Suffolk County Legal Services."

"What do they know of blood libels?"

The rabbi went into the kitchen for water to wash down the aspirin grit coating his tongue. Curling his fingers around a plastic child's cup with an oversized handle and four large finger notches, he struggled to line it up with the stream of water flowing from the faucet. Water cascaded around his wrist, soaking the cuff of his shirt sleeve. He leaned on the edge of the sink to steady his arm. Slowly, too slowly, the cup filled with water. Cartoon characters decorated this child's cup, three large dogs with eye patches chasing a puppy holding a bone. As recently as yesterday, these characters had amused him; but on this morning, he could only think that somewhere there must be a cup where the puppy was caught and ripped asunder by the dogs. He raised the cup to his lips and drank, swishing the water around his mouth before swallowing it. The aspirin particles felt like crushed stone sluicing down his throat.

Now, under a midday sun hotter than the wrath of *Yod. Heh. Vav. Heh.* at the golden calf, Rabbi ben Reuben hobbled across a crowded brick plaza fronting Boston's city hall that festered with the talk of blood libel. The air was so thick with heat that breathing seared his nasal passages and lungs. The stench of greasy pushcart food, intensified by the heat, made him nauseous.

He wondered whether he had smelled a similar stench before. Where? When? He did not remember. He dismissed the thought as a by-product of the heat, worrying instead that at his age, prone to heat stroke, he might not make it to the other side of the plaza.

He gagged, then dry-heaved, and leaned against the outer wall of the entrance to the Government Center subway station to catch his breath. He sucked on a mint to cleanse the funny taste in his mouth. His mind felt like a 1,000-piece jigsaw puzzle that had been dumped from its box onto the table, several hundred spilling onto the floor. After several minutes, he pressed on across the plaza.

In the office of Steve Frohling, Director of Suffolk County Legal Services, the rabbi shivered in the draft of the air conditioner. "Sit. Please."

That was the same invitation the agent of the Immigration and Naturalization Service had issued to the rabbi when his turn finally came for the interview that would determine whether he would be allowed to enter the United States. Many hours he had waited in a large room which smelled of hundreds of unbathed people, the sweat of his hands staining the paper with the interview number that has been assigned to him. New York. 1946 or 1947. The rabbi did not remember which.

The nameplate on the agent's desk identified him as Mr. Minzhe and he resembled the waiters in the Chinese restaurant across the street from the docks in London. The rabbi did not eat in that restaurant even though he was hungry because neither the food nor the kitchen was kosher. On the boat, during the long ocean voyage, he had no choice but to eat. To absolve himself, the rabbi invoked the doctrine of *Pikuach Nefesh*, the principle in Jewish law that the preservation of human life overrides the restrictions of *Kashrut*, the Jewish dietary laws mandating what observant Jews could and could not eat. Perhaps, he would have survived the voyage without eating, but he had heard the INS turned away people who were sick. In his mind, *Pikuac Nefesh* applied.

"The early 1930's," he had replied when Mr. Minzhe asked him when he had been ordained as a rabbi. "I came to the rabbinate later in life than most."

"And then?" Minzhe had asked.

"Now, I am here?"

"From then to now?"

The rabbi paused. "I don't remember."

Minzhe eyed him with the look of a judge being told by a recidivist that he would not do it again if given probation rather than a jail sentence. "Recite the *Shema*," he said.

"The *Shema*? You know this prayer?"

"It was drilled into my head in Hebrew school."

Because of Minzhe's sallow skin tone and Chinese features, the rabbi assumed he was not Jewish. The rabbi knew the presence of Jews in China had been documented as early as the seventh or eighth centuries. He knew the history of the Jewish community in Kaifeng in the Henan province, a Chinese community that practiced Judaism. But, he had never met nor seen photos of any Chinese Jews. To him, they were as exotic as the black Jews of Ethiopia.

After the rabbi finished, Minzhe said, "Now, the *Amidah*." Again, the rabbi did so.

"The blessing before and after reading the *Haftarah*."

"You know this blessing?" the rabbi asked.

"You fake it at your own peril," Minzhe said. After the rabbi complied, Minzhe conceded he was a rabbi. "Normally, your memory gap would disqualify you from entry into the United States, but I will use a generic description of a typical Jewish experience during the Nazi era to answer the personal history question."

"You will make up my history?" the rabbi asked.

"If I don't, you're on the next boat back to Europe."

Using carbon paper, Minzhe made a simultaneous copy of the statement he entered on the rabbi's immigration form and gave the copy to the rabbi to memorize in the event the INS called him in for further questioning. "Welcome to the United States." Minzhe stood and offered his hand in friendship.

Now, accounting sheets covered Frohling's desk, sickly yellow, sickly green, many stained with brown coffee rings. Numbers filled the columns, some written over, others blemished by erasures made by dirty erasers. "Next year's budget," Frohling said. "Every dollar has to do the work of twenty." In the fluorescent light, Frohling's skin was sickly and slack.

Frohling listened between bites of prune Danish and slurps of coffee as the rabbi explained Levy's predicament. Crumbs gathered on the bulge of his stomach. He gulped the last of his coffee and pushed the final bite of Danish into his mouth, then brushed the crumbs away, crushed his cup, and balled the wax paper from his Danish, tossing both into the waste basket. "I thought you people took care of your own."

Rabbi ben Reuben squirmed in his chair.

Frohling continued, "We don't get many Jewish lawyers here. They're too clever and amscray as soon as they figure out the way to the courthouse. The one we got now, Larry Gingold, we're his last resort. B & E, A & B, larceny under, fine; but a capital case, never." He tapped a cigarette against his thumb nail, then lit it. Its tip glowed with each inhale. Each exhale looked like a plume of smoke from a chimney. "Levy's little hat under the chair, you don't need a law degree to know how damning that piece of evidence is."

"I apologize for wasting your time."

"We're prisoners of the law here, obliged to represent indigent defendants. All indigent defendants. No picking, no choosing. If Pol Pot walked through that door and proved he was penniless, we'd have to defend him."

"Pol Pot?"

"Cambodia's Hitler." Frohling tapped the ash off his cigarette. "I know the perfect attorney for Levy," he continued, "someone here who has a better than even chance getting him off, the best defense attorney in the city, public or private. Maddie Devlin. Bad news is, she won't defend him. She's as Irish as green beer on St. Paddy's Day and comes with more baggage than all the skycaps at Logan."

Devlin, the rabbi said to himself. Maddie Devlin. A spark of recognition smoldered in his memory. Several years ago, he recalled, she contacted him to solicit a contribution from his congregation to a charity she had founded to provide support to victims of child abuse. The Elizabeth Fund. "We are a poor congregation," he had told her, "but I will mention it at Friday night services." That was his standard reply to solicitations from outside the Jewish community. He didn't remember whether the congregation made a contribution to the Elizabeth Fund and, if it did, how much.

Frohling blew smoke rings at the air conditioner. In the rush of frigid air, they twisted and turned and tore apart. "A man in your line of work must have a pretty good read on human nature. What are your top five motivators, the five things that really make people tick tock? Maddie brings two of them to Levy's defense. First, hatred, or more precisely, its stepsister, revenge; second, greed." He leaned across his desk. "Bumper Sullivan's mother's a Devlin. There's a blood feud between the two sides of the family what goes back to the old country. Getting Levy off would wreak a lot of revenge for her. As for greed, she's been lusting for a break-out case since the day she got here, something to rescue her from the poverty of legal aid. Sounds good, you say? Not so fast. She never defends anyone whose victim's a kid because once upon a time her kid was the victim and her ex-husband walked when his attorney out-lawyered the prosecution."

Frohling brushed a cigarette ash from the budget papers. "And she's got a chip on her shoulder bigger than an Egyptian pyramid. She thinks she's been blackballed by Boston's white-shoe law firms 'cause she's a woman, Irish, divorced. Truth is they won't go near her 'cause they think she's a bit touched." He tapped the side of his head with his finger. "Unhinged. They're afraid she'll drop off the deep end any time."

"You're not?"

"I am, big time; but here we take what we can get and thank God for it."

The rabbi bit his tongue as pain radiated from his knuckles throughout his hands. "You would ask her?"

"We'd be collateral damage. I fight for every paper clip and, Constitution be damned, I never have the money to defend as zealously as possible everyone entitled to free legal counsel. If Levy's indigent, I'm stuck, even if it means blowing the whole year's budget on one case. And next year come budget time Beacon Hill will punish us big time. Fifty cents on the dollar if we're lucky. One thin dime if we're not."

The rabbi gazed at the water tank on the roof of the adjacent building. Its copper sheathing, once shiny, was crusted with the turquoise of age. He had, he realized, as much free will as that copper sheathing had in choosing whether to be oxidized or not.

Talk of Avram Levy and Bumper Sullivan still suppurated from the bricks of City Hall Plaza, but the lines at the pushcarts were shorter and the rabbi's passage through the stench faster. "Hey, mister," they gyro vendor shouted. "The lamb she is tender." The rabbi quickened his step. There was a vague familiarity to the wisps of smoke rising from the charcoal, but he couldn't place it.

-4-

Maddie Devlin joined Suffolk County Legal Services after graduating law school. Eight years later, it had become a sinkhole, swallowing her whole, then closing over her, fossilizing her, bringing her to the edge of petrifaction. The sinkhole opened the week she was sworn in as a member of the bar, the reward for winning her first case, a verdict of Not Delinquent for a juvenile charged with B & E. Flustered at finding him under the bed in the master bedroom, the arresting officer forgot to Miranda him. Three years later, Maddie plea bargained that juvenile, now an adult, down from kidnapping to unlawful restraint, ten years to three, eighteen months to be served, eighteen months suspended. Over the years, he became one of her steadiest clients until a judge who actually read the pre-sentence report brushed aside her argument of mitigating circumstances, a broken home, an abuse victim as a child, a below-average IQ, and sentenced him to twenty years, ten to be served before being eligible for parole, for aggravated assault and armed robbery. One less file on her desk, one less predator on the streets of Boston.

After winning her first capital case by attacking the scientific validity of the fingerprint evidence, Maddie submitted résumés to Boston's Mayflower law firms which years earlier had awakened to the fact that defending people charged with white-collar crimes such as stock fraud, tax evasion, criminal antitrust violations, currency manipulation, and other business misdeeds was lucrative and did not besmirch their images. We don't handle homicides, one human resources director told her. Two years later when one of her murder cases rated thirty seconds on the evening news, she sent out another set of résumés. Four firms invited her for interviews; one offered her a job, indexing depositions and document discovery in complex civil litigation cases, a dead end that at best would relegate her to staff attorney status, a permanent associate never to be elevated to a partnership, never to see the inside of a courtroom. Preferring to try cases, she remained with legal aid.

Boston Municipal Court one day, Roxbury District Court the next, she toured the courts of Suffolk County like a hamster running on a treadmill: Dorchester District Court, Boston Juvenile Court, South Boston District Court, West Roxbury District Court, Charlestown District Court, East Boston District Court, Brighton District Court, and occasionally courts in Middlesex and Norfolk Counties, now and then one or two in Essex. She visited them all, some more than once, in the course of a routine month.

To an employment lawyer who specialized in employee discrimination cases, Maddie railed against Boston's hidebound legal community for discriminating against her for being Irish, female, and divorced, not the profile of the type of women attorneys these firms preferred to display. When she demanded the employment lawyer file a complaint with the Massachusetts Commission Against Discrimination or the Equal Employment Opportunity Commission claiming discrimination based on gender and national origin, the lawyer had advised her it would be impossible to prove a case even with the lower burden of proof required in civil law suits. The evidence is too circumstantial, the lawyer explained. There's no smoking gun. Maddie knew the lawyer was right.

"The power of visualization is the key to success," advised a mentor and visualize Maddie did. First, her case on the front-page of *The New York Times*; then on the network news. She visualized herself surrounded by a horde of cameras, mobs of reporters competing for her every word. She saw herself in a corner office on a high floor in one of Boston's office towers earning a high-six-figure salary, picking and choosing clients, the way she picked and chose a pearl necklace or diamond choker during one of her many imaginary shopping sprees at Tiffany and Company. She visualized while waiting in court for her cases to be called, while working out, while on the subway when she tired of the book she was reading, at home waiting for her dinner to heat or in a restaurant waiting for it to be served, while stuck on the Central Artery during rush hour, in the theater, at the ballet, on dates with men for whom she was one or two rungs higher on society's ladder, in the bleachers of Fenway Park or the nosebleed seats at Boston Garden, whenever, wherever, her mind drifted; but for all her visualizations she still wallowed in the depths of her private sinkhole defending people whose names she banished from her memory before the courtroom door closed behind her.

Instead, she numbed her pain by transferring it to the victims of her clients, people she also quickly forgot. The shopkeeper whose store was robbed was a blank face in a white apron. The rape victim was a statistic, a rape kit, a lab test, a woman who should have known better than to be where she was when she was with whom she was. Widows were women dressed in black, widowers men in black suits. Winning cases, freeing the guilty, salved her conscience, her dark secret never talked about. To anyone who asked why she did not become a prosecutor after her ex-husband's acquittal of homicide in connection with the death of their daughter, Elizabeth, she offered well-rehearsed cant about *Powell v. Alabama* and *Gideon v. Wainwright* and the right to legal counsel. She wore her nobility the way a leper wore his skin and felt equally isolated, quarantined, diseased.

To assuage her guilt and to honor her daughter's memory, Maddie devoted herself to the Elizabeth Fund. She personally visited every church and synagogue in greater Boston soliciting either donations or for them to sponsor fundraisers. One of the mental health professionals she occasionally used as an expert witness in her criminal cases designed a short one-session course to educate the law enforcement community. With George Harriman's help, the Boston Police Patrolmen's

Association, over Mayor Charlie's opposition, forced Chief Ugolino to mandate it as part of its neighborhood policing program. This created a cascading effect as more and more police departments in the greater Boston area included it as part of their training. A law school classmate whose father was president of the Massachusetts Bar Association arranged for the MBA to add the seminar to its continuing legal education curriculum. At the urging of the Chief Justice of the Boston Municipal Court who presided over child abuse cases with a depressing regularity, the Massachusetts Judicial Conference offered the seminar as part of its training program for new judges. For sitting judges, it was optional. After several visits and much nagging, the United Fund of Boston added the Elizabeth Fund to its list of approved charities and provided small annual grants.

Yet, for all the personal satisfaction the Elizabeth Fund provided her, for all the contacts she made, for all the praise she received, for reasons Maddie did not understand, she could not escape Suffolk County Legal Services. Once a leper, she told herself, always a leper.

She led a bifurcated life, defending the scum of the earth in court, defending the most vulnerable victims of that scum out-side of court. She had little time for a social life. Her occasional dates provided no emotional satisfaction and little physical gratification. When she needed to relax, to unwind, she drank a Guinness and used a vibrator she had mail-ordered from a store in New York City that specialized in sex toys. It was a life, not the worst of all possible lives, but also not the life she had anticipated. She did not have a Panglossian view of the world.

Now, the office door had not closed behind her when Carmelita Delgado, receptionist and fetcher of Frohling's daily prune Danish and coffee, told her the boss had been screaming for her all morning and she better have a damn good explanation for being so late. Maddie barged into Frohling's office.

"Remind me, Maddie, what a closed door means."

"I just did."

"I need you to cover an arraignment. Judge Spodapoulos. Third Session. Two fifteen."

"One of the third-years can handle it."

"Avram Levy. His rabbi came to see me this morning."

"It's a frame. The skull cap's a plant."

"How so?"

"It's the only logical explanation for Ugolino's TV special."

"If he's innocent, defending him won't violate your golden rule." Frohling tapped his watch. "Spodapoulos won't wait. He'll appoint someone else. Maybe that piece of shit Ed Hornstein." Frohling shifted his attention to a file on his desk, thumbing through the papers with the interest of a schoolboy being forced to conjugate Latin verbs. He knew mentioning that name, Hornstein, would keep Maddie under his thumb.

"Drink after work?" Frohling asked.

"Fuck you."

"Your place or mine?"

Running to the Old Court-House, Maddie dodged cabs, busses, bike couriers, and the tourist trolley. Pedestrians she ran over. Frohling being Frohling, she thought. He acted that way toward everyone in the office, men and women alike; but his pathetic efforts at seduction were laughed at, spit upon, too comical, too inane, to warrant a sexual harassment complaint. As she crossed Tremont Street and jumped the steps two at a time between One Beacon and Center Plaza, half-moons of sweat accumulated under her arms and stained the front of her blouse. Hotter than hell, someone complained, and she laughed. Hell, the nuns had preached, was a dry heat.

-5-

The lobby of the Old Court-House in Boston's Pemberton Square ascended four stories from a ground-level floor littered with cigarette butts, candy wrappers, cardboard coffee cups, half-eaten sandwiches whose bread was as stale as the excuses offered by defendants to judges who had heard it all already, and tissues soggy with the tears of mothers, wives, or children as their sons, husbands, fathers were led away in handcuffs to the Charles Street Jail or one of the many houses of correction or state prisons maintained by the Commonwealth of Massachusetts for the betterment of its misbehaving citizens. Arching over the lobby floor at a height of four stories was a domed ceiling caked with more than one hundred years of the blighted hopes and betrayed illusions of people having business before the courts of the Commonwealth of Massachusetts. At one time, when the wall between Church and State was neither high nor solid, domes had been a popular architectural feature of court-houses, a feature borrowed from churches in the expectation the resemblance between church and courthouse would lead people to believe when they stood before the judge they were standing before God. Experienced trial attorneys knew better.

Cavernous and dimly lit, the lobby was like the central chamber of an uncharted cave inhabited by creatures of the dark: attorneys, shape-shifters camouflaged into invisibility nodding with feigned sincerity, and clients, creeping and crawling across its floor like moles searching for grubs, the luciferous glow of their anger lighting the way, clients squat with hairy faces, lupine eyes, and venomous voices snarling with bravado.

Waiting for an elevator, Attorney Maddie Devlin sipped grapefruit juice purchased at the food concession operated by the Massachusetts Commission for the Blind. Its acidic tartness matched her mood. She centered herself between the four elevators, two on each side of the lobby, so she could run to the first that arrived. According to courthouse myth, the elderly operators came with the elevators as an accessory installed by the manufacturer. Maddie respected courthouse myths no matter how silly and greeted the operators upon entry, thanked them upon exiting. They, in turn, never closed the door in her face. In obeisance to another myth, she always skipped over the brass engravings set in the brick plaza outside the building as if they were cracks in the sidewalk, one plaque commemorating each of the rights guaranteed by the Bill of Rights. According to the myth, an attorney who trampled the Bill of Rights would lose his case. Someday she'd put it to scientific proof.

"May your Irish eyes always smile, Maddie."

"Top of the afternoon to you, C. J."

Claudius J. Antenor, Esq., C. J. Ant to bar and bench alike, chewed on an unlit cigar that accented the roundness of his face the way a curlicue turns an O into a Q. He had a fisherman's face, sun dark and lined with an ocean of wrinkles; yet his hands were smooth and soft like the hands of a male model who appeared in magazine ads for Swiss watches or Italian leather gloves.

Maddie had interned for C. J. Ant the summer after her second year of law school, attracted by the opportunity of hands-on legal experience and the chance to see how the law functioned outside the classroom. During that internship, she had plea bargained Jim Ed Wallaca—one of the few out of the scores of names, the scores of cases, she remembered because he was the first case C. J. Ant allowed her to present to the court herself—out of a prison sentence and into the Marines and Vietnam; yet what had become of him she neither knew nor cared. Without this obdurate armor she would be as vulnerable as a crustacean without its shell.

C. J. Ant specialized in defending snatch-and-grabbers, street hookers, bookies and their runners, low-level mob enforcers who were not "made" men, drunks, disorderlies, and petty criminals picked up at the arraignment session or assigned to him by judges he knew from law school. At summer's end, C. J. Ant put Maddie on the payroll paying her enough to cover her third-year tuition and retire some of her student loans. When she graduated, C. J. Ant offered her a job; but she declined, accepting a position with legal aid because she naively believed it would provide a better chance for professional growth. Now, years later, ensnared at legal aid, cancerous was the way she described that growth.

"What brings you to paradise?" Maddie asked.

"To watch my favorite protégé in action."

C. J. Ant stepped aside to let Maddie enter the elevator. She smiled at Lorenzo, the elderly operator, who usually replied with a cheery *buon giorno* but this time lowered his eyes as if he was avoiding looking at something so sinful to see it would turn him to stone. Maddie opened her mouth, but closed it when C. J. Ant shook his head. The elevator lurched upward. The cable groaned. The fluorescent fixture buzzed. Residue from the stink of C. J. Ant's cigars scented the air. Lorenzo stared at his hands.

"Someone tipped Hornstein," C. J. Ant said. "He tipped the world."

"Fucking Frohling."

Maddie leaned against the back wall of the elevator. If she were superstitious, she would consider Hornstein an omen, but she didn't believe in omens. No, Hornstein wasn't a sign from God or the work of Satan. He was a pain in the ass, insincere, greedy, so self-righteous he sputtered outrage at attorney jokes. If he were a car, he'd be a VW bug with a Rolls-Royce grill, a Chevrolet Corvair with a rear spoiler, a Ford Pinto with a Mustang scoop in the hood; but he wasn't a car, he was an asshole who bartered her ex-husband's legal fees for race track tips and maintained his active status as a lawyer only to preserve the prestige of being an esquire.

"For shame, Maddie. For shame." Joe Daley, the court officer assigned to the courtroom of Judge Alexander Spodapoulos, held the door for her. A veteran of the Korean War, he was slim enough to wear his Marine uniform on Veterans Day and fit enough to still answer his country's call. He was always kinder to her than he had to be and she reciprocated with a small gift at Christmas—a tin of his favorite pipe tobacco—until the Commission on Judicial Corruption promulgated a rule banning attorneys from giving gifts to judges, court officers, and employees in the offices of the Clerks of Court. Now, Daley looked at her with the eyes of a person mourning the death of a close friend.

Maddie sank into a chair at the defense counsel table. C. J. Ant sat directly behind her on the first bench outside the bar enclosure. She had outgrown her mentor, but his presence comforted her. She jotted the date and name of the judge on the top line of her legal pad, the name of the case and docket number on the second line. She had handled so many arraignments she could do them in her sleep: Waive the reading of the charges. Enter a plea of not guilty. Request Suffolk County Legal Services be appointed. The judge would ask if she wanted to schedule a bail hearing and she would select a date which allowed sufficient time to prepare. Five minutes, maybe fewer, and her client would not have to say a word. She scribbled some numbers on her legal pad. For those few minutes, she would accrue fifteen cents of her weekly salary. Private counsel would charge $100.00 and not handle it as well. She ripped the page off her pad and crushed it into a ball.

Four court officers, double the usual complement, positioned themselves on either side of the door. They wore their guns outside their jackets. As people entered single file, one searched their briefcases and handbags while a second frisked them. The other two were as attentive to their surroundings as Secret Service agents guarding the president. The level of security surprised Maddie. Since the courthouse bombings a few years earlier, a metal detector had been installed at the entrance to the building. Everyone emptied their pockets and passed through it. She had herself. An X-ray machine more sensitive than those used at airports scanned bags, pocket books, and briefcases.

The hands of the court officers rested lightly on the butts of their guns. Their fingers twitched. Maddie sensed they would rather administer justice themselves than leave it in the hands of the judicial system and attorneys like her. She nodded greetings to members of the defense bar as well as prosecutors she had tried cases against. Some nodded back; most looked away. A few mouthed obscenities. To her dismay, Levy's arraignment had become a busman's holiday. Hornstein cleared security and sat beside C. J. Ant. She smelled his lunch on his breath, a tuna fish sandwich and dill pickle. She squared her shoulders and straightened her back and pressed her knees together, posture that would have made the nuns of her childhood proud.

The door to the holding cell opened and Levy entered flanked by court officers. He looked soft and pudgy as if he had not shed his baby fat. At Walpole he'd be another bitch to be fought over by the gangs who controlled the cell blocks. His hands were cuffed and anchored by chains to a steel belt which girded his waist. Ankle cuffs connected his feet, the chain so short he could not climb into the prisoner's dock without leaning on someone as he stepped up. Across the courtroom, Maddie could not read his mood, perhaps equal parts fear and fascination, the reaction of most first-timers, her preference to the icy contempt of recidivists. She searched his body language, the slumping head, the sagging shoulders, the fidgeting fingers, for clues of guilt or innocence; but she saw neither. Ciphers made the worst clients.

The session clerk, Vilda Mikus, entered from the judge's chambers followed by the judge. Weeks from mandatory retirement on his 70th birthday, Spodapoulos was marking time in the arraignment session. His eyes twinkled with the light at the end of the tunnel. Soon, the only judging he would be doing was the amount of break on his putts or which fly to cast. After Mikus entreated God to save the Commonwealth of Massachusetts, the arraignment proceeded like every other until the question of appointing legal counsel. Spodapoulos accepted Probation's determination of Levy's indigence, then said, "I assume, Attorney Devlin, Suffolk County Legal Services will appear for him."

"We will, Your Honor."

"May I be heard?" Ed Hornstein stepped inside the bar. Sweat moistened the back of his neck and darkened the collar of his shirt. A moustache of sweat glazed the skin above his upper lip. "Edward Hornstein, Judge. My firm Hornstein and Shapiro will represent Mr. Levy pro bono. Ms. Devlin has a conflict of interest. She's Beatrice Sullivan's cousin."

"We are second cousins, Your Honor. Our grandfathers were brothers." Over the whispers that sissed through the courtroom, Maddie continued, "It is well known in the Irish community that there is an ongoing civil war between Mrs. Sullivan's side of the Devlin family and my side which goes back two generations to certain events that occurred in Dublin in connection with the Easter Rising against the British. If you were to ask Mrs. Sullivan, I am confident she would say my involvement in this case is only the latest battle in this war and that I would work twice as hard on Mr. Levy's behalf than if the victim were not her son."

"So, Ms. Devlin," Judge Spodapoulos said, "your aver there is no conflict of interest."

"Correct, Your Honor. I would add that Rabbi Isaac ben Reuben, who is the rabbi at Mr. Levy's synagogue, requested SCLS represent Mr. Levy. If Rabbi ben Reuben feels Mr. Levy's interests are not being served, he can engage private counsel and SCLS will withdraw. As for Mr. Hornstein, he's not one-tenth the attorney I am."

"Does this rabbi know of your relationship with the mayor and his wife?" the judge asked.

"No, Your Honor, but if the rabbi objects, I will recuse myself and Mr. Frohling can assign someone else."

"Have you spoken to this rabbi?" Spodapoulos asked Hornstein.

"I volunteered my services to Attorney Jacob Moskovitzky who is assisting him."

"This is just an arraignment," Spodapoulos said. "I will appoint SCLS to represent Mr. Levy. If Mr. Frohling assigns this case to you, Ms. Devlin, I will require Mr. Levy to file his written consent with the court; otherwise, I will disqualify you in favor of another SCLS attorney." Spodapoulos scribbled an entry on the case file. "I assume you will enter a plea of not guilty, Ms. Devlin."

"Yes, Your Honor."

Hornstein objected. "Mr. Levy lacks the capacity to make this decision without independent legal advice."

"You represented to the court Mr. Levy has the assistance of Attorney Jacob Moskovitzky." The judge turned to Levy. "Is that correct, Mr. Levy?"

Hornstein interrupted. "Attorney Moskovitzky is impaired by age."

"Mr. Levy?" Spodapoulos said. "Do you wish to be heard?"

Levy's chains jangled. His expression darkened to one Maddie easily read because she had seen it so often. He wanted to say something, but had been instructed not to, an important piece of information no one had shared with her. His squint, his sneer, told her he didn't want her to represent him. It was as obvious as the locks of hair covering the sideburns on either side of his face. She glanced at the judge who had either ignored or missed the cues.

"Mr. Levy?" Spodapoulos repeated.

Levy paused, then said, "Rabbi ben Reuben knows best."

"The hearing on defendant's application for bail will be Friday next at 10 a.m." Spodapoulos rapped his gavel. "This matter stands adjourned."

Court officers escorted Levy to the holding cell. In the hall outside the courtroom, reporters scrummed for position. Maddie slipped her notepad into her briefcase.

"Sneak us out the back way," C. J. Ant said to Joe Daley who hesitated. "Please."

"For you," Daley replied.

-6-

Frohling had just opened his mouth to eat another prune Danish when Maddie burst into his office with the single-mindedness of a cop kicking in the door of a drug-house raid. "Thanks for the heads up to Hornstein," she said. Anger imprisoned in courtroom decorum now animated her. "It was my ex-husband's trial all over again."

In her mind's eye, she visualized herself smashing the prune Danish across Frohling's face, laughing as he scraped the gooey frosting off his lips, nose, and cheeks. Impacted rage, Maddie's therapist had once told her, it's your full-time job. It's a colloquial name, the therapist had explained, for a manifestation of a psychiatric disorder classified as Intermittent Explosive Disorder. At its worst, a person with IED was the equivalent of an EF-5 tornado in human form.

Three incidents within a month of Elizabeth's death had landed Maddie on the therapist's couch. The first occurred after Maddie had bought an ice cream cone, frozen pudding. Eating it as she walked, she stubbed her toe on uneven pavement and momentarily lost her balance, dropping the ice cream from the cone. Crushing the cone in her fist, she threw it at the nearest parking meter; then, screamed uncontrollably at the lump of ice cream on the sidewalk, hurling every curse word she knew at it as if she herself were sprawled on the pavement, the victim of a purse-snatcher who had kicked her legs out from under her as he grabbed her pocketbook.

The second occurred a few days later. Frohling had complimented her blouse, but said she would look a lot better if she undid a button or two. Swearing, she had grabbed a scissors off his desk and cut off his necktie just below the knot. Frohling had managed to swat it from her hand before she was ab le to shred his shirt.

The third occurred in court the next day. Arguing against her motion to suppress evidence in an assault and battery case, the prosecutor did not address the merits of her position but rather launched an *ad hominem* attack, accusing her of misstating the facts to intentionally mislead the court. Maddie swept the prosecutor's file off the table and kicked his papers across the floor of the bar enclosure. The judge called her and her alone into chambers, assuring the prosecutor that the assault and battery case would not be the subject of their conversation. In chambers, the judge told Maddie he was familiar with her behavior because his son also had explosive incidents of rage, often accompanied by some form of violence, after returning from combat in Vietnam. The judge recommended a therapist, Dr. Vernon Przystas, who had helped his son control his rage. Either that, the judge said, or a criminal contempt and thirty days to be served.

In appearance, Dr. Przystas had dressed like a clerk in a Robert Hall store, a chain of off-the-rack stores that sold inexpensive men's dress clothes, one of the Boston outlets being the store her father had bought his one and only suit, his one and only sport jacket and dress slacks, his two white dress shirts, his two ties. Maddie was reassured by Przystas's rumpled look. A man wearing expensive tailored suits would have intimidated her. Being several weeks overdue for a haircut contributed to his ordinariness. As nervous as she was about seeing a therapist, Maddie sensed his coming at her with an attitude of superiority would not be an issue.

At their first session, Dr. Przystas explained to her that impacted rage, unlike healthy anger, had a disintegrative effect on physical and mental health. The rage itself and the energy needed to suppress it transformed the body into a pressure cooker with a faulty relief valve. Sooner or later an explosion was inevitable. The strain on the body manifested itself in a variety of ways. In the cardio-vascular system, for example, it aggravated the buildup of fatty plaque in the arteries, damaging the arterial walls. The therapist quoted statistics that people with impacted rage are more likely to die of heart attacks or strokes and at a younger age than people without. Among military veterans who have seen combat, impacted rage, at times with intense guilt, at times without, often resulted in anti-social and self-destructive behavior. Her colleagues at Suffolk County Legal Services had defended a handful of Vietnam veterans with that problem, but Maddie had not.

When Maddie heard the diagnosis, she felt she had been given a death sentence. Don't be so dramatic, Dr. Przystas said. He prescribed Cognitive Relaxation and Coping Skills Therapy or CRCST, both in group and individual settings. CRCST, he explained, was a sequence of twelve or more sessions, some patients needing more sessions than others, beginning with relaxation training, followed by cognitive restructuring, then exposure therapy, concluding with sessions on resisting aggressive impulses and other preventative measures. He favored talk therapy over regimens of psychotropic medications because the drugs had shown limited success.

Maddie soon became an expert on relaxation mechanisms, her favorites being imagining a relaxing experience like listening to Irish folk music while lying in a hammock or counting backward from 100 to whatever number necessary for her anger to dissipate. Her record, as best as she could remember, was somewhere in the seventies. Cognitive restructuring was like a tug-of-war in her psyche between reminding herself that her rage would not make her feel better but would often make her feel worse and her rage boiling over. Logic, persuading herself she was not life's victim, only worked before rage engulfed her as rage often rendered logic illogical. The lawyer in her, her rational side, told her impacted rage was a problem and that if she tried hard enough she would eventually solve it. Dr. Przystas cautioned that the frustration of not finding a solution often exacerbated the problem. All-or-nothing thinking, he warned, was one of impacted rage's best allies. Controlling it will always be a struggle; but if you are disciplined about following the prevention protocols, it should ameliorate over time, he added.

For Maddie, the Elizabeth Fund was the first step toward controlling it. Concentrating on the needs of the Fund was one of the most effective ways to reorient her mind away from the ordinary bumps and bruises of life that triggered her rage. Still, she did not know how long she could keep going without finding the second step.

Now, counting backward to 85 while also taking cleansing breaths, she calmed herself. Why waste a good Danish, she thought, pinching a piece of it and popping it into her mouth. Humor, especially if she made herself the butt of the joke, was another coping mechanism for impacted rage.

"I needed you for the arraignment," Frohling said. "I figured a hand-off to Almeida or Southworth."

"Together they're not worth half me. If there's a hole in the case, they'll never find it. How do I get in touch with Levy's rabbi?"

"In the flap of my blotter. The rabbi's card."

Returning to her office, Maddie phoned Rabbi ben Reuben to request a meeting. As soon as possible, she insisted. Reluctantly because soon it would be the Sabbath and business was not to be transacted on the Sabbath, he agreed to see her after Friday evening services. There were exceptions, he explained, and with Talmudic precision he had found one. Minutes later, the intercom on Maddie's phone buzzed.

"Attorney Michelle Furey, line one," Carmelita Delgado said.

"I'll call back Monday."

"She says it's urgent."

"What's urgent is that I get out of here." Maddie punched the button for line 1. After a few seconds of dead air, Attorney Furey said, "Maddie, how're you doing? How's the Elizabeth Fund?"

Furey's voice was as Maddie remembered it, throaty, not a purr, more a growl, a creepy-crawly voice, titillative, a voice that gave Maddie the cold creeps, as if she had thrust her hand into a bucket of ice water, yet a voice that was alluring, like an artificial fly to a trout or a bird call to a wild turkey. Fearing the lure of that voice, Maddie had limited her contact with Furey after the incorporation of the Elizabeth Fund to small-talk at continuing legal education seminars. Since their law practices had minimal overlap, they rarely attended the same seminars.

Maddie remembered saying the first time she met Furey, "Interesting name, Michelle Furey."

"My dad wanted to name me Molly, but my mom put her foot down so they compromised on Michelle."

"You sound like a Molly." Not a Molly, Maddie thought at the time, but *the* Molly.

"Up and down," Maddie now said in reply to Furey's question about the Elizabeth Fund. "Always too many victims. Never enough money. A lot of the bench is still in the dark ages."

"Sorry to hear that. I called because I represent the Estate of Father Gabriel Finn. He has left you a bequest. We're reading his will in my office tomorrow morning."

Maddie wedged the phone between her jaw and shoulder and rubbed her forearms. She hoped her reaction to Furey's voice was nothing more than a touch of paresthesia explainable by tension, pressure, stress. Slowly, her flesh absorbed her goose bumps.

"Who's Father Gabriel Finn," Maddie asked, "and why would he leave me a bequest?"

"Father Bartell Darcy, a colleague of Father Gabriel, has come from Dublin with both the will and the bequest and he'll explain all." Maddie felt Furey's voice in her bones.

"Courier me the paperwork. C.O.D."

"He says it's essential you be present."

"Or what?"

"Or you forfeit the bequest. Not you alone but the other Boston heirs. The will is very explicit. You must all be present. If anyone is absent, everyone forfeits."

"And those who attend will sue those who don't."

"That would be my conjecture."

Curiosity compelled Maddie, not curiosity about the will or the identity of Father Gabriel, but curiosity about the woman behind the voice on the phone. Her curiosity first surfaced when they worked together on the creation of the Elizabeth Fund. Maddie had suppressed her curiosity over the years. In her stronger moments, she wondered how that voice would play out in a courtroom. Would it mesmerize the judge, the jury, or so alienate them they would rule against her every motion or objection, find against her every client? Maddie voted for "mesmerize." In her weaker moments, she wondered how that voice would play out in the bedroom. She doubted it would be as off-putting as her own voice. Again, Maddie voted for "mesmerize."

"Still at the same address?" Maddie asked.

"Same address."

"I have a full day tomorrow so it better be a short will."

"Only one article relates to the Boston bequest. That's the only one to be read unless someone insists on the boilerplate."

On the way to the synagogue in Chelsea, Maddie felt her impacted rage boiling up within her at being commanded to attend a meeting she did not want to attend. This was a classic example of a trivial event causing a reaction grossly disproportionate to the triviality of the event itself. Maddie felt a tightening in her chest, a twitching in her forearms, the type of bodily symptoms Dr. Przystas had told her often accompanied impacted rage. To battle it, to bottle it up, she distracted herself by wondering what did a Molly sound like? What did *the* Molly sound like? Did Joyce have a woman's voice in mind, a particular woman's voice, when he wrote his famous stream of woman's consciousness soliloquy? His wife's, Nora's, she assumed.

It had been a while since her impacted rage had threatened to flare so explosively, but things had piled up on her like stones on a grave: the incessant heat, Hornstein, being treated as if she had gone orange on St. Patrick's Day, Molly Michelle demanding she show up for the reading of a will. Everything in combination had split her atoms. She felt better for imagining the sound of *the* Molly's voice reading James Joyce's stream-of-conscious soliloquy. The more she imagined, the more it sounded like Michelle Furey's voice and the more it restored her self-control.

-7-

In the synagogue's sanctuary, the evening service for the Sabbath had concluded and Rabbi ben Reuben had wished *Shabbat Shalom* to each member of the *minyan*. Because of Levy's absence, he had had to telephone several people to get the tenth man. Exhausted from the heat, he rested in the front pew.

"That attorney, she is here?" Moskovitzky asked.

"In my study."

THE FIRE THIS TIME

Moskovitzky held out his hand to help the rabbi stand.

"Do you think he did it, Jacob?"

"He's such a *tsadek*, such a *nebbish*."

"Such an *akytor*, maybe. What do we really know of him? A few biographical facts? And we don't even know if those are true. We just assume they are."

Moskovitzky pondered the question as if it were a Talmudic enigma. "Why? Why would he?"

"For him, Masada, not the Wailing Wall, is the holiest place in Israel," Rabbi ben Reuben said. "He has all seven volumes of Josephus's *The Jewish War*, both in English and the Greek translation many scholars say was supervised by Josephus himself. He burns with the fire of Elazar ben Yair. He has committed ben Yair's final oration to memory and recites it as if he were a great leader inciting his followers to martyrdom. 'I cannot but esteem it as a favor that God has granted us, that it is still in our power to die bravely, and in a state of freedom.'"

"He is not under siege by the Romans."

"Perhaps in his imagination or his worldview."

"Are you saying he is insane?"

"I don't know what I'm saying."

-8-

Maddie welcomed the deepening dusk as she waited in the rabbi's study. The sun's descent spread darkness across the face of the room and the sharp edge of the shadows dissipated into fuzziness. She needed fuzziness. When the short April twilight passed into night, she turned on the desk lamp and sought distraction in the bookcases that wallpapered the study, shelves of

55

bindings with foreign letters. Hebrew letters. The few words in English were meaningless: *Mishnah, Midrash, Talmud, Torah.* Her heartbeat quickened. She sat on her hands to stop them from trembling. She felt as if she were trapped in the secret lair of an alien cult.

An eternity later, the door to the study opened with a creak and two men, one old, the other older, entered, the old assisting the older who supported himself on a cane and looked like a paragraph sign in profile. Their frailty, their age and infirmities, gave her a sense of empowerment, a sense of having an advantage, and she no longer felt like a stranger in a strange land.

"Let me help," she offered.

The older one waved her off. "This *mishugenah* cane. May the Lord take me before they put me in a wheelchair." He sat. His shirt ballooned as air inflated his clothes. A child's wristwatch with oversized numbers hung loosely from his wrist. "I'm Jacob Moskovitzky and this is Rabbi Isaac ben Reuben."

"I'm Attorney Mary Ann Devlin from Suffolk County Legal Services. Everyone calls me Maddie."

"The Elizabeth Fund?" the rabbi asked.

Maddie nodded. "I came to see you. You contributed $100.00."

"There are a lot of worthwhile causes to which we cannot afford to contribute but a little."

"The Archdiocese of Boston with its millions of dollars contributed half that. You would think preventing child abuse would be one of its top priorities."

The rabbi placed his hands on the desk. His knuckles cast long shadows across the back of his hands. "If Avram is convicted, what in the old country incited pogroms will come to Boston. If he is acquitted, people will believe his innocence was purchased with a few pieces of silver. Either way, the consequences are the same."

"What is a pogrom?" Maddie asked.

"A pogrom," the rabbi said, "is what King Billy did to your ancestors."

Moskovitzky tapped his cane against the edge of the desk. "At my age, I care more about what will be fifty years from now than I do what will be tomorrow."

"If we don't focus on the business at hand," Maddie said, "Levy will spend those fifty years in jail."

"Frohling says you're legal aid's best attorney," the rabbi said.

"I say you're a minor-league All-Star," Moskovitzky said, "who can't hit big league pitching."

Maddie started to rise. "Good evening, gentlemen."

"Sit," the rabbi said.

"Why?" Maddie replied.

"Sit. Stand," the rabbi said. "It makes no difference."

"Let's get one thing clear," Maddie said. "If you don't think I'm the right attorney for this case, I'm out of here. I don't need the aggravation of shoulder-sitters who think I'm second or third rate."

"Are you?" the rabbi asked.

Before Maddie could reply, Moskovitzky said, "I changed my name to Mosca and lied about my religion to get into Harvard College and Harvard Law School. I opened the legal profession in Boston to Jews. I created a law firm worthy of being mentioned in the same breath as the Solis-Cohen firm in Philadelphia. And what is my legacy? A grandson whose ignorance of the past condemns him to repeat it." He spoke with a firmness that belied his age, his voice steady, lacking the quaver and high pitch of the elderly.

"The only legacy that matters," Maddie said, "is Levy's."

Moskovitzky ignored her. "Fear and ignorance have blinded my grandson to the consequences of the blood libel accusation."

Maddie recognized what she called "set speech syndrome." In court, she often encountered attorneys who arrived with set speeches, determined to give them regardless of what questions the judge might ask. Those attorneys frequently lost their cases. Perhaps, Maddie thought, she could shorten Moskovitzky's set speech with a question. "What is a blood libel?"

"What is a blood libel, she asks." Moskovitzky's voice had that blend of sarcasm and disgust Maddie remembered from her catechism classes when she or one of her classmates asked a question whose answer would have been self-evident to the faithful.

The rabbi answered her question. "For centuries Jews have been accused of draining the blood of Christian boys and using their blood to bake Passover *matzoh*."

Maddie recalled how the kids threatened each other in parochial school, especially around Easter. "I'll sell your blood to the Jews" was the most common threat. She had had nightmares the first time one of her classmates threatened to sell her blood. She didn't know then the threat had a name, blood libel.

Moskovitzky continued. "Who is to say years from now my grandchildren's grandchildren won't again be running from Cossacks?"

Maddie slammed her pen down on her legal pad. "Levy won't have any grandchildren if we don't change the subject."

Moskovitzky and the rabbi glanced at each other, then at her. She saw condemnation in their eyes. Moskovitzky pulled a tissue from his sleeve. "Is it better I lived in America where Jack Mosca went to Harvard or ancient Egypt where Jacob Moskovitzky built pyramids?"

"What does this have to do with Levy?" Maddie said.

The rabbi replied, "Hatred is what this has to do with Avram. Hatred is a spider from whose web few escape. Avram must be defended not only for himself, not only for Jacob's grandchildren's grandchildren, but for your grandchildren's grandchildren as well."

"I don't have the luxury of leading a crusade."

"You wouldn't talk this way if his name were Robert Emmet," the rabbi said.

"I would whether you believe me or not."

Moskovitzky cleared his throat. "Why are you here?"

Feigning social concern would be too transparent. Inviting Moskovitzky to be co-counsel would cede the control she needed to work the case her way. Gutting it out would work if desperation sent them to legal aid. She plucked the doctrine of the excluded middle from her bag of attorney tricks.

"Why do you presume I want to be here? If Frohling orders me to defend Levy and I refuse, he can Section 8 me and have me disbarred, thanks to the Supreme Judicial Court. I bet you didn't know that, Attorney Moskovitzky. It's the law. Look it up. Section 8 of my employment contract requires me to accept any assignment made by the director. In *Board of Bar Overseers v. Podolec*, the Supreme Judicial Court on Frohling's petition upheld a one-year license suspension for an African-American attorney who refused to defend a member of the Klu Klux Klan for inciting a riot at an anti-school busing demonstration. In *dicta*, the SJC suggested a second offense would warrant disbarment. If you want me off the case, tell the judge. Without Levy's consent, I'll be bounced. I don't have time for this inquisition."

The rabbi cringed at her use of that word.

"Point two," Maddie continued. "It is clear to me from Levy's behavior at the arraignment he doesn't want me as his attorney. He wouldn't be the first. So, do I have a client to defend?"

"Levy will be guided by us," the rabbi said. "He will do as we recommend."

"We don't question your legal abilities, Ms. Devlin," Moskovitzky said, "but we have every right to satisfy ourselves about your motivations."

"I have one and only one motivation, to get the best possible result for my client. Subject to the Code of Professional Responsibility I will do what must be done to achieve that result."

"From the days of the patriarchs and matriarchs," Moskovitzky said, "Jews have fought for the right to be Jews whether on top of Masada or in the lobby of the King David Hotel. Never, but never, has a Jew committed the crime of blood libel. Punished for it, yes. Many times." He bowed his head as if his thoughts were too heavy for him. "It has never been a crime in this country to be Jewish; but if Avram is convicted, it will be." The hum of the fluorescent desk lamp sounded like an alarm warning everyone to the bomb shelters. "My grandson, to him a pogrom is something in a history book. I lived that history." He placed the cane between his legs, resting his hands on its crown.

Maddie seized the opening. "Jews don't have a monopoly on being hated. It took Ireland as long to be born as Israel. Irish historians, especially those of the rebellion, see the Irish as another race of Jews. And James Joyce. He made Leopold Bloom, the symbolic father of Stephen Dedalus, Jewish." She spoke in the calm voice of a scholar leading a seminar, one of her favorite closing argument techniques. "Joyce saw the Irish and Jews as two heroic races destined to wander the face of the earth and shed their own blood to attain a homeland and then shed more blood defending it. Joyce understood that the bond between the Jews and the Irish was the bond between Leopold Bloom and Stephen Dedalus, the bond between father and son."

"What of the bond between blood relations?" Moskovitzky spat the question with the disdain of a judge who had dismissed her as fatuous and lacking in credibility, then closed his eyes as if he were unable to bear the sight of her. She glanced at the rabbi who seemed lost in thought.

"Trish Sullivan and me?" Maddie rushed her words out of fear of being silenced. "In 1916, my da's da was executed by an Irish Republican Brotherhood firing squad. Accused of being the informer who tipped the Brits about an IRB raid on a Brit weapons arsenal. Implicated in the death of his brother, Seamus, who led the raid. Convicted on the word of his other brother, Clancy, who bore false witness. Patrick Pearse swore to my grand da's innocence. Produced evidence Clancy sold his birthright for a pint and a bob. But, Pearse was only one vote on the IRB Military Council and the others voted to convict, to execute. Seamus was Trish's grand da. Her side of the family never forgave, never forgot. My side neither."

Moskovitzky opened his eyes, but still looked away. "False witness?"

"Over an inheritance." The words vomited from her mouth. "Their grand da's homestead. Clancy got it in his head Patrick would leave it to him, but Patrick left it to my grand da, who was the oldest. Clancy blamed my grand da for poisoning Patrick against him."

"The mark of Cain," the rabbi said.

"Except my grand da was innocent."

"So you do not seek justice for Avram, but for your grandfather," the rabbi said.

Maddie clenched her jaw. Never had she doubted her grand da's innocence. Her da had said he was innocent and das never lied to their daughters. Now, the skepticism of these ancient Jews created doubt. What-if her grand da did bear the mark of Cain? It would have passed through the generations to her da, to her, to her daughter. Is this why Elizabeth died an infant? Maddie recoiled at the thought her daughter bore the mark of Cain.

"Is there a bathroom I can use?" she asked.

The rabbi pointed to a door bunkered by bookcases.

In the bathroom mirror Maddie saw the mark of Cain staining her face, bold and ugly like a purple birthmark, the devil's mark according to the nuns of her childhood. Maddie did deep-breathing exercises for several minutes to compose herself, then flushed the toilet, ran the cold water, splashed some on her face, and swallowed her emotions because attorneys, especially attorneys in her line of work, could not be subservient to their emotions. Her faith in her grand da's innocence reaffirmed, she returned to the rabbi's study.

The rabbi nodded at Moskovitzky who asked, "What of your vow never to defend someone accused of murdering a child? How did you avoid being disbarred for refusing those cases?"

Maddie felt like a witness caught in a lie on cross-examination. "Those cases were not assigned to me. This one has been because I am the only legal aid attorney capable of handling it."

"It is a terrible thing," the rabbi said, "when a mother buries a daughter, but it is more terrible when after so many years grief still warps the mother. Grief can destabilize a mind from within."

Was her struggle with her impacted rage that obvious, Maddie wondered. Grief had destabilized her from within, but she had wrestled with her grief, sometimes with more success, sometimes with less; but she had channeled her grief so that now her infant daughter lived in her memories and in the Elizabeth Fund. Would she have had my face? My coloring? My temperament? Would she have looked like a Devlin? Or her father? No, the Devlin genes ruled. She had seen that in her daughter's eyes moments after her birth. Now, what remained? Grief and memories in all their fallibility; and, a crusade against child abuse.

"Yes," Maddie said. "A terrible thing. But the director holds Section 8 over me like a death sentence." She cursed herself for the sophistry, the circularity, of her argument.

"So, quit work," Moskovitzky said.

"Hanging out my shingle takes courage, more than I have."

"Yet, you would have us believe you have the courage to defend Levy," Moskovitzky said.

His accusation shredded her composure. She struggled to maintain self-control. Judges who acted as inquisitors were not new to her; nor were judges who dismissed her arguments as lacking foundation in law or fact. On the contrary, judges respected her for being fearless in court, unlike attorneys cowed into subservience by a judge's raised eyebrow or off-the-cuff comment. She counted to three, then said, "Nothing I say will still your doubts."

"Perhaps, Jacob," the rabbi said, "a time such as this requires an act of faith."

"Faith has murdered too many of our people."

"Yes, but without faith, would Abraham have entered into the Covenant? Would Moses have led his people into the Red Sea? Would our people have survived the destruction of the First and Second Temples? The Holocaust?"

"Faith did not win the Six-Day War," Moskovitzky said.

"Without faith there would have been no Israel to fight that war."

"How often does our worst enemy come disguised as a friend?"

"As often as a friend comes disguised as an enemy," the rabbi replied.

Rabbi ben Reuben massaged his knuckles. His entire life had brought him to this moment. *Yod. Heh. Vav. Heh.*, one of the ways pious Jews referred to God, had demanded of Abraham an act of faith. Now *Yod. Heh. Vav. Heh.* demanded the same of him. But what was that act of faith? Blessing Attorney Devlin? Dismissing her? If he acted out of faith, would that prevent him from making the wrong choice? Would *Yod. Heh. Vav. Heh.* ordain his making the wrong choice? He had to believe, he had to have faith, that his choice, whatever it was, was *Yod. Heh. Vav. Heh.*'s choice and that it was the right choice. That was the essence of faith, the essence of belief. He felt so inadequate, so unprepared.

The rabbi looked Maddie in the eye. She did not blink. She did not turn away. Her expression remained unchanged, frozen, her lips pressed together. Moskovitzky rested his chin on the head of his cane, his eyes closed. The rabbi was alone, but not alone. Reason would not guide him. Nor emotion. Only faith. Faith in *Yod. Heh. Vav. Heh.* who had let him down, let His people down, so many times before. An old Jewish folk saying came to mind, one he had used in many sermons over the years: A drowning man will grab even for the blade of a sword. Once again *Yod. Heh. Vav. Heh.* had hurled His people into the raging waters and once again extended to them the blade of a sword. Refuse it and they will surely drown. Accept it and they may be saved. The rabbi closed his eyes to trap the tears he felt forming, then opened them. "Will you represent Avram, Attorney Devlin?"

"If he will have me."

"He will have you," the rabbi replied.

"Do you concur?" Maddie asked Moskovitzky.

"If I do not?"

"You will have to leave," Maddie replied, "as your presence creates a waiver of the attorney-client privilege."

"I feel like Moses at the Red Sea before he stepped into the water." Moskovitzky took a deep breath. The air in his lungs rattled. He looked down at the handle of his cane, then whispered, "I concur."

"Good. Let's get to work. What do you know about Mr. Levy's background?"

Without pausing, the rabbi related how Levy joined the congregation the previous fall after moving from New York, how he was studying *Talmud* and supporting himself by working in a Jewish funeral home, how he held life so sacred he would let the fly flit across his bread rather than swat it.

"I'll visit him in the morning."

"On the Sabbath?" the rabbi said.

"A case like this, every day's a work day."

Rabbi ben Reuben and Moskovitzky glanced at each other. Now they understood why Levy did not want her to represent him. He had intuited this about her, that she would raise the profane above the sacred. He would resist their recommendation, resist her. Levy's future depended on his resistance being overcome. The rabbi nodded. Moskovitzky returned the nod. Maddie rose and shook their hands. She wanted to leave before either or both of them had a change of mind, a change of heart. Good trial lawyers knew better than to overstay their welcome before the jury.

As she walked to her car, Maddie felt trapped inside the past, her past, Ireland's past. Today descended from yesterday in as never-ending torrent of "begets" as any found in the *Holy Bible*. Robert Emmet begat Robert Michael Arthur Devlin, named Devlin rather than Emmet to hide him from the British, Michael and Arthur being two Devlin cousins, both veterans of the Rising of 1798 and the Rising of 1803 which begat the Easter Rising of 1916 which begat the Republic of Ireland. In 1829, Robert begat Brian Winifred Devlin who begat Richard Luke Devlin, who begat Patrick Hugh Devlin, who begat Michael Parnell Devlin, who begat Brian Arthur Devlin, Maddie's da, a poor soul imprisoned in the provenance of his name. Patrick Hugh Devlin also begat Brian's brothers, Clancy Richard Devlin, the informer, and Seamus Emmet Devlin, da of Tommy Devlin, grand da of Beatrice "Trish" Devlin Sullivan, First Lady of Boston, Maddie's second cousin, mother of Charles F. "Bumper" Sullivan, III.

Since ancient times, Finn mac Cumaill lay within an unremembered Irish hillock. Today, Finn mac Cumaill and his band of mercenary warriors marched through the streets of Boston. What of today? What of this infernal April day? And the next day? And the day after that? What of these days? In her name and blood, in her memories and deeds, Maddie had entered upon the burning sands that bridged the chasm between the old and the new, the new and the old, condemned to sift through the grains for the courage to answer the call as so many Devlins had before her. But whose call? God's or the devil's?

Was this the second step to her winning the fight with her impacted rage? She had reached her car before she realized she had crossed her fingers. She laughed at herself for adopting a silly superstition, then remembered that humor, Dr. Przystas had counseled, was one of the coping mechanisms for dealing with impacted rage.

-9-

Later that night, Rabbi ben Reuben brought a kosher dinner to Avram Levy at the Charles Street Jail. The temperature was high enough to boil the moisture in the air and weather forecasts offered no prospect of relief. In the history of weather records for the Boston area, one meteorologist reported, no high-pressure system had been so stationary for so long. The jet stream had a stranglehold on Boston, the northeast, the North Atlantic, with a malevolent anger that put to shame the anger Moses felt upon seeing the golden calf when he descended Mount Sinai with the tablets inscribed with the Ten Commandments. Unable to park near the jail, the rabbi left his car at the foot of Beacon Hill and pulled himself up the staircase of the footbridge that spanned the Charles Street rotary.

In the evening, pedestrian traffic to and from the neighboring hospitals, Massachusetts General Hospital and Massachusetts Eye and Ear, made the walk safe, but visiting hours had ended and he was alone. Age intensified his apprehension as did the incessant talk of blood libel on television and radio, especially talk radio where the ignorance and prejudice of the callers rivaled only that of the hosts, the nationally syndicated shows being more virulent than the local shows. A shard of memory stirred, then vanished before coalescing into something recognizable, another of the tricks his mind now played on him since he first heard the phrase "blood libel" on the television news the morning after the Sullivan boy's blood-drained body had been discovered.

The rabbi struggled to climb the staircase while balancing a Styrofoam plate on his palm, its warmth radiating through the bottom. Since coming to America, the rabbi had prided himself for not falling prey to the debate of why a benevolent

God permitted such evil as the Holocaust. Nor did he believe this benevolent God would correct His mistakes and make everything all right. Many of his colleagues in the rabbinate indicted him for lacking faith.

"What do you really know of faith?" he replied. "Words in a sermon?"

To which those rabbis said, "Where was the *Yod. Heh. Vav. Heh.* who stayed Abraham's hand and parted the Red Sea? Whose fire did not consume the bush? Who handed down the tablets to Moses? Was the Covenant a tease? Or, worse, a bait and switch? Why did His chosen people cower in fetid jail cells while those who would destroy them, annihilate them, enjoy the pleasures of their indulgences? When life itself became the lesson, nothing good follows."

Unbeknownst to the rabbi, his faith had been imprisoned in the same black hole as his memories of his personal experiences during the Nazi era. On the boat crossing the Atlantic, he had flipped the coin of Pascal's wager. Now, years later, he still waited for it to land. Heads or tails? Or, on its edge? He doubted it made a difference.

From the shadows of the overpass, a voice still and small emanated. "Spare some change? Please, mister. I's starving."

A black youth stepped out of the shadows. Dirt streaked his face. He wore a faded tee shirt freckled with bleach stains, over his heart a Trojan horse in silhouette. His pants were rolled up at the cuffs. The soles of his sneakers flapped as he walked.

"Please, mister. I needin' eats bad."

The rabbi's thumb pierced the foil and a wisp of steam escaped. He wished he had two plates. "Wait here. When I come back, I'll buy you something to eat."

"No feedin' bloodsuckers." The boy punched at the plate. The rabbi twisted sideways to deflect the blow, absorbing it in his forearm. The plate tottered and the rabbi grabbed it with his other hand so it wouldn't fall. The boy kicked at the rabbi's shins. The rabbi curved his body over the plate as if it were an infant he was protecting from a sudden storm. The boy made guns out of his fingers and thumbs, then shouted, "Next time, you be wasted." The boy vaulted down the stairs two at a time and jumped into a waiting car.

The rabbi leaned on the railing and recited the *Shema*. It pained him to see so much hatred in someone so young. In an adult, he understood; but to pass it on to an innocent youth was a sin worse than violating the laws of *Kashreit*.

In the visitor's lobby of the Charles Street Jail, he stared at the barred windows. They reminded him of the ticket windows of a train station. After the war, he had traveled by train across Europe to London to catch a boat to New York. The bell to the left of the window reminded him of the clerk who refused to sell him a ticket because he had arrived a minute after the ticket window had closed for the day. The steam hissing out of the radiators reminded him of the locomotive pulling the train he had missed because he didn't have a ticket. But, the hollow voice that growled at him from the speaker mounted on the wall above the lobby door, that voice he had heard before. Where he had heard it, he did not remember. What it had said, he did not remember.

"Identify yourself and state your business."

"Rabbi Isaac ben Reuben with a kosher meal for Avram Levy." A door sprung open and he entered a large room, empty except for a table and one chair. An unshielded bulb bathed the room with a light that burnished the hard metallic surfaces of the table and chair in a hard glare. A second bulb flickered randomly as if it were trying to communicate a message in code.

He placed Avram's dinner on the table and waited. He had waited in a room like this before, an interview room at the Port of New York for questioning by immigration officers while the authenticity of his travel documents was verified. Yet, this room had a vague resemblance to some other room he had once waited in. He closed his eyes, but all he saw was the dark. He wished his mind would stop playing tricks on him.

Finally, a door labeled 'Welcome' opened and two prison guards in drab brown uniforms entered. One searched him while the other, acting as if he expected a bomb, removed the foil from the plate and poked through the food with the stub of a pencil. The boiled chicken, overcooked as the rabbi always prepared it, fell away from the bone and settled on the rice and sweet potato. The challah now had the guard's thumbprint in its center.

"I got the knife and fork," said the guard whose name tag was taped over.

"Strip," said the other. He did not wear a tag.

"Never before. Why now?"

"Strip. Don't strip. I don't give a fuck, but you wanna see the Jew, you strip."

'The Jew', the rabbi thought, as he undressed. First, blood-sucker; now, the Jew. That's how it starts. Turning a person into a thing. He felt chilled in spite of the heat. Now, as he removed his shirt, he started shaking and did not stop while the prison guards, laughing and joking, searched for contraband. In all his previous visits to other inmates never had the search for contraband been anything more than a perfunctory pat-down, fully clothed. Why, he wanted to ask; but he knew what the answer would be.

"Looking for lice," one of the guards said.

Lice. For years, the rabbi had been so paranoid about head lice that he shampooed his hair several times a day, something he still did. Obsessive-compulsive behavior, a psychologist once told him. Where does it come from? he had asked. Something in your past, the psychologist had replied. Nothing that I remember, the rabbi had said. Acting out is a form of remembering without actually remembering, said the psychologist. The rabbi did not ask for an explanation because he knew he would not understand it.

Now the rabbi dressed and both guards, one by his side, the other behind him carrying Levy's dinner, escorted him to the visiting area where he was seated behind a bullet-proof partition that divided the room. The guard with the dinner appeared on the other side. "Five minutes," the guard who remained by his side said. "I'll be here, he'll be there."

"The statutory privilege," Rabbi ben Reuben said, "between clergy and . . . "

"You being here's a fucking privilege."

On the other side of the barrier, Levy entered and sagged into the chair opposite the rabbi. He scooped his dinner with his fingers, eating like a young child breaking the Yom Kippur fast. Kernels of rice and shreds of chicken and bits of sweet potato clung to the stubble of his beard. Watching him eat, the rabbi wanted to ask him if he did it, but he knew better than doing so in the presence of the guards. Their presence nullified the clergy privilege granted by Massachusetts law to conversations between rabbis and their congregants.

"Jacob and I met with Attorney Maddie Devlin."

"She's *traif*."

Levy's vehemence surprised the rabbi. The guard on Levy's side of the partition smirked and shook his head.

"She desecrates the Sabbath." Levy tried to rise, but the guard shoved him back into his chair.

"Try that again," the guard said, "and dinner's kaput."

"She does not dress modestly. She does not wear a wig. She is not my Esther."

"Jacob has tried a few cases in his day. He'll keep an eye on her."

"And if Hashem should strike him blind?"

"Then he will see with his ears."

"*Traif*," Levy repeated.

"Time." The guard put his hand on the rabbi's shoulder.

"I'll come back tomorrow to conduct a *havdalah* service."

"*Yizkor* would be more appropriate."

The Rabbi shivered as he crossed the footbridge over the Charles Street rotary. He searched the street below for the car the boy had jumped into, the shadows for the boy himself. Who's watching me? Why? He knew who; he knew why. He feared for his future, for the future. Fear was the price of being a survivor. No one spied on the defeated or the conquered, the dying or the dead; they spied on the living, on the fighters, on those who refused to concede the struggle. America had dulled his fear, had deadened him. Now, for the first time since he immigrated to America, he felt alive. Now, he knew better. Silently, he offered a toast, *l'chaim*. To life.

Chapter 2

Saturday, April 11, 1981

-1-

Maddie Devlin spread her morning newspaper across the table in the back corner booth at Behan's, a crowded Southie railroad diner that served green eggs and ham on St. Patrick's Day and decorated its walls with prints of Irish heroes of the Risings, Easter 1798, 1867, Easter 1916, the rebellions before and after, those in between. For the children there were drawings of the Lorax and other Dr. Seuss characters with a bit more of the tricolors of the Irish flag than in the original illustrations. Behan's was a neighborhood place where everyone knew everyone, a place where people knew not to wear orange whether on St. Patrick's Day or any other day, a place where Sanka was banished because of the color of its packaging, a place with an unlisted phone number, a place whose neon sign–green, of course–said merely Good Eats Cheap.

On Saturdays and Sundays, people lined up from the door, down the steps to the sidewalk, past the newsstand and candy store, past the Convent of the Sisters of Notre Dame, to the bus stop, and beyond, willing to wait because the line at Behan's was as much a social gathering place as any of Southie's churches, clubs, baseball diamonds, or bars. Brendan, the owner's son, sat singles and doubles European style, claiming credit for more than one introduction that culminated in marriage. He kept an album of wedding pictures by the cash register and celebrated anniversaries, christenings, first communions, with dinner on the house. Those who wanted to eat alone sat at the counter on stools that swiveled a full three hundred sixty degrees. Children played spin the top on those stools and more than one gave back the food he had just eaten. It was one of the many quirks which made Behan's Behan's.

Maddie had taken a counter seat, but when the people on either side carried their breakfasts to other stools, Brendan led her to the back-corner booth, the last booth before the door to the rest rooms. He whispered something in Gaelic which she understood to be a curse she would not be welcome back even though she did not speak the language. On this combustible Saturday, people who on previous Saturdays would have smiled a greeting, welcomed her to join them, or joined her, now looked straight ahead on the way to or from the restrooms as if glancing at her would turn them into pillars of salt or mounds of ash.

Maddie, Charles F. Sullivan, III, and Avram Levy, dominated Saturday's *Boston Globe*, five of the six front-page stories, the odd one devoted to the heat wave, two of the three front-page photographs, the third a heat wave photo. Articles and photos filled three inside pages; on page three, a paparazzi ambush picture taken as she snuck out the service entrance of the courthouse after Levy's arraignment. Her name also monopolized the editorial page, two editorials, one preaching the Constitution created a presumption of innocence and cautioning that "Boston can ill afford another Sacco and Vanzetti,"; and a second urging the public to reserve judgment about the propriety of ". . . Ms. Devlin defending Mr. Levy. Watch her closely," the second editorial admonished, "and judge her by what she does."

"Seat taken?" Detective George Harriman asked.

"Every Saturday still, Uncle George?"

"The usual?" Paula, the morning waitress, asked Harriman. The grime of her breakfast shift greased her apron. The pocket where she hoarded her tips bulged with coins and bills. Her support hose billowed at the knees and buckled around the ankles; yet, on St. Patrick's Day, she marched the entire route of the parade, then outlasted everyone line dancing. When Harriman nodded, she shouted to the cook, "Bucket of oats, stallion size." Years of cigarette smoking had toasted her voice and she had the croak of an adolescent on the cusp of puberty.

"It's not the same without your da," Harriman said to Maddie.

Their friendship had been forged, Harriman's and Brian Devlin's, on Guadalcanal as they huddled in a foxhole behind slowly leaking sand bags along the Lunga perimeter. Behind them lay Henderson Field which they had been ordered to defend to the death by some general safely outside the line of fire. They had served together, two boys from Southie tossed by fate into the First Battalion, 7th Marines, both proud to be members of the First Team.

Brian had turned twenty on Guadalcanal. The Marines had taken Henderson and the Japs were coming at them every which way to recapture it. Sea. Air. Ground. Thousands upon thousands for whom dying for emperor and empire was a point of honor. The rounds flying overhead, mortar shells exploding around them, incendiaries making barbecue pits out of foxholes and bunkers, shrapnel shredding flesh. War's violence convinced Brian he would not survive to legal age. He saved his last pack of cigs for his birthday. Luckies. L. S/ M. F. T. Lucky Strike Means Fine Tobacco. A wee bit of home. A wee bit of what he was fighting for. He tossed the pack over to the next foxhole and it went from foxhole to foxhole, everyone taking one until crumpled and crushed and empty, it came back to him. Sixty or so Marines died that afternoon, October 24, 1942. Twenty of them had smoked one of Brian's Luckies, maybe more since Marines shared everything, in life and in death.

The shooting had stopped. Spooked by the quiet of a lull in the combat, Harriman adjusted the chin strap of his helmet, checked his weapon, his supply of ammo. He hated the quiet. In combat, nothing good ever came of quiet. "Brian," he whispered so as not to attract the attention of the Japanese machine gunners and mortar launchers, "I'm out of smokes."

Brian stared at the distant tree line. He squinted, raised his binoculars. "Something moving. At the tree line." He handed them to Harriman.

"Heat currents," Harriman said, "fucking heat currents."

"Hear that?"

"Mosquitoes."

Brian slapped at a mosquito on the back of his hand, smearing the blood it had just gorged on. The sun, hot and fiery, filled the sky and hovered above Guadalcanal as if it had moved several million miles closer to Earth. He could have boiled a cup of tea in his canteen if he had a teabag to dip in it. "Damn, I hate this fucking place." Brian removed his helmet and wiped the sweat from his forehead with his shirtsleeve, then rested his head against a sandbag. He had the troubled look of someone who needed absolution to die a good death.

A second time, Harriman cleaned his weapon, checked his ammo supply, adjusted the chin strap of his helmet, preparing for the next barrage of artillery and mortars, the next wave of soldiers.

They both survived, returning home to Southie, not the same men but in many ways no different than before they had shipped out.

Now, almost forty years after Guadalcanal, these memories saddened Harriman as he sat across from Brian Devlin's daughter in a back booth of Behan's on another morning heat-soaked by a raging sun.

"Beg off this case, Maddie. It's so airtight Ugolino halted the investigation."

"He what? Suppose he's innocent? What-if the real Dracula's still out there?"

"I know your track record, Maddie. If the police made a chain-of-custody mistake, if Charlie corrupted the crime scene, if the crime lab misread the prints, if the M E miscalculated the time of death, you'll sling more shit than all the sheep in Ireland."

"Ugolino wants a change of venue. He wants to make the defense do what he should be doing. Why else his leak to the press? That means he has doubts about Levy's guilt. If he does, why not me? Or you? Or the jury?"

"Stupidity. Ego. Vanity. All make as much sense."

Maddie spread her eggs on a piece of toast. "Ketchup, please." When he didn't pass it, she reached across the table. Slapping the bottom of the bottle, she deposited thick red lines on her eggs, parallel lines like the bars of a jail cell.

Paula brought Harriman his bowl of oatmeal, side dishes of brown sugar and raisins, and a mug of black coffee. He spooned some brown sugar into the oatmeal, then paused before stirring it in. Paula lingered at the table, her teeth bared like a person who wanted to pick a fight. Looking Maddie in the eye, she crossed herself. "What you're doing is blasphemous," she said.

God talk, Maddie thought. She hated God talk. She had had her fill of God talk when her ma died; God talk from the nurses at the hospital who said ma's death was a blessing because it killed her pain; God talk from Father Curry who said ma now walked with God; God talk from Cornelius Moynihan, the director of Moynihan's funeral home, who said ma's serene countenance was a sign she had entered heaven. Everyone talked God talk so they wouldn't have to deal with the grief of a young girl, everyone except Uncle George, this same Uncle George who now God talked to her of abandoning Avram Levy. If God didn't want her to defend Levy, He would strike her dead was her attitude.

Maddie wiped ketchup from her lips. At her ma's wake, this Uncle George had sat with her in a small chapel in the back of Moynihan's, a refuge from the thrum and thrush of conversation, the sobs of close friends, the sounds of mourning. The smell of flowers, too strong for the ventilation system, had infiltrated the chapel and roiled her stomach.

Each year after her da and Harriman returned from Guadalcanal, they celebrated St. Patrick's Day together, marching in the parade with the veterans from World War I, World War II, and, as the years passed, Korea and Vietnam, waving at the children who lined the street, children who in years to come would fight and die in other wars in other places. After the parade, they went to O'Driscoll's where they sang and drank draught after draught of strong, black Guinness, first to the memory of their comrades in arms killed by the Japanese, then to Parnell, Robert Emmet, that Robert Emmet, Wolfe Tone and Fitzgerald, Connolly and Pearse, MacDonagh and Mac-Bride until they had lost count of the rounds, after which they recited Yeats's fated benediction:

> All changed, changed utterly:
> A terrible beauty is born.

At her ma's wake, Maddie had turned to this Uncle George for the consolation her Da seemed unable to provide.

"I don't remember her being sick," she said.

Harriman crossed himself. He had argued with her folks, Maddie found out years later, about their keeping the cancer a secret. Let Maddie grieve in advance, he said. It'll help her when the time comes. At the wake, he wanted to tell her; but how could he? He wasn't her da. Instead, he said, "You'll feel anger for a long time. First, at yourself. You'll remember every little fight, whether it was about staying out late or skipping Mass. And you'll blame yourself for all the unhappiness you think you caused her.

"When you get over that," he continued, "you'll feel anger at your da for all the arguments and disagreements they had. You'll blame him for making her life miserable. That's not the way to grieve. If you do, you'll lose your da in the bargain."

She had rested her head against his shoulder that afternoon in the small chapel in Moynihan's and asked, "Have you picked a reading for the eulogy?" and he said, "*The Stolen Bride*:

> O'Driscoll drove with a song . . . ,
> And never was the piping so sad,
> And never was the piping so gay."

He hugged her that day, that Uncle George, and told her to take good care of her da because she was all he had.

Now, at Behan's, this Uncle George, not that Uncle George, was all she had and she needed his hug more than at her ma's wake, her da's, her daughter's, a hug she knew he would not give, now or ever. In a few days it would be Easter, another Easter; or, in the words of the poetess, *Easter Again*. "Who now cares," the poetess asked, "Whether Guelf or Ghibillin . . . ?" Bobby Sands for one. From Robert Emmet to Bobby Sands. A direct line. From Robert Emmet to Bobby Sands to Mary Ann Devlin. A direct line. She wished she had Bobby Sands's courage, his conviction, his passion, his fearlessness in the face of death. She pushed her plate away.

Harriman finished his oatmeal and started on his coffee. Maddie knew she was invisible to his eyes. "Remember an attorney name of Michelle Furey?"

He shook his head.

"She helped set up the Elizabeth Fund. She says she represents the estate of some Dublin priest. Father Gabriel Finn. Says he left me an inheritance. I'm going to a reading of the will in a bit."

"Father Gabriel Finn?"

Maddie nodded.

"A Gabriel Finn celebrated the Mass at Seamus's funeral, said a few words over your grand da. Long time ago." Harriman finished his coffee and dropped a few dollars on the table. He started to say something, then clenched his jaw and shook his head. A dollop of moisture in one of his eyes trapped the light from the ceiling fixture. He wiped that eye with his knuckle. Standing, he stumbled, regained his balance, and walked quickly away, struggling to contain his tears.

Maddie felt as abandoned as a martyr whose life, whose sacrifice, had been long forgotten. The thought that fate might have cast her to be that martyr frightened her. She couldn't silence the voice inside her head bullying her to defend Levy for her da and grand da, hectoring her that whether Levy was guilty or innocent was as irrelevant as the number of grains of sand on Southie's Carson Beach. Ugolino, her inner voice tormented her, is but a lazy rationalization to conceal your true motive from yourself. Revenge, proclaimed her inner voice as if it were a declaration of independence. But, Trish asked, what was she guilty of? And Katie, a bitter old crone who belonged in a nunnery cracking the knuckles of heretics? Jail runs in our blood, her inner voice scolded, and Clancy, childless Clancy, was the jailer.

Clancy had laid a curse on the children of his two brothers and their children and their children's children if any there be. She and Trish, Elizabeth and Bumper, were its latest victims.

The heat blurred her vision. The letters of her name in the newspaper headlines quivered on the page like the signatures of her namesakes in the Kilmainham register, Dublin's ancient prison to which her da had dragged her years earlier. Jail runs in your blood, her da had said at the time. What she did not understand then, what she did not want to understand then, she now did. Her inner voice cheered.

-2-

Michelle Furey's office was in one of Boston's many office buildings constructed when twelve to fifteen stories was considered a skyscraper and people did not trust the novelty of elevators. Built with gas lights, the building had been retrofitted for electricity twice, first when electric lights replaced gas lights, then again when the demand for electricity caused by the explosion of office equipment overwhelmed the capacity of the original wiring. Clean and reasonably well maintained except for the granite exterior, which had been blackened by more than one hundred years of soot and pollution, it had survived into a charmless old age, its rents a fraction of those in the newer glass-sheathed buildings whose ornate lobbies offered fancy florists, newsstands that sold *The Economist*, and cafés where tuna sandwiches were served on baguettes rather than white bread.

Furey's office shared the sixth floor with a hodgepodge of small businesses whose common feature was that they operated behind outer doors with smoked glass windows reinforced with wire, opaque but translucent, on which the name of the current tenant had been hand stenciled in black, often without sufficient effort to obliterate the names of prior tenants. Common lavatories flanked the elevator, men to the right, women to the left. Incandescent bulbs rather than fluorescents lit the hallway.

"Law Offices of Michelle Furey" proclaimed the door to her suite, the same proclamation when she and Furey first met to discuss the incorporation of the Elizabeth Fund. "Please Enter" read the invitation stenciled in the lower right corner nearest the door knob, the same invitation. At that time, Maddie had paused to imagine such a door proclaiming "Law Offices of Mary Ann Devlin." Or, should it read "Law Offices of Maddie Devlin?" Now, she paused, again imagining a door with her name on it. What was indecision but cowardice in disguise. She envied those who had the courage to fly solo.

Maddie knocked. When no one responded, she entered a small anteroom with a secretary's work station, a Remington manual typewriter rather than an IBM Selectric, three plastic chairs, and a small coffee table covered with magazines that looked abandoned rather than selected. There were three interior doors, two closed, one open revealing a conference room smaller than those at Suffolk County Legal Services, with chairs so closely crowded around a circular table that their occupants rubbed shoulders and knees.

Furey did not look a day older than when Maddie had first met her, still a petite woman with delicate features, her hair in curls and ringlets the color of the night sky, her eyes as green as the Irish countryside in May. Pushing her chair back from the table, Furey bounced into the reception area. "Maddie! It's been way too long." That voice rumbled, again, in Maddie's bones. She still had thin lips, severe, barely peeking out from her mouth, a pair of horizontal parentheses too flesh-less for lipstick. Pale, she looked as if she would scatter like the filaments of a milkweed pod if she were to step into the draft of the window air conditioner. She wore a loose-fitting sleeve-less blouse that made modesty of her breasts. At first meeting, Maddie had guessed their ages were comparable; but, now, Furey glowed with a youthfulness Maddie no longer shared. Judging by the firmness of Furey's upper arms, Maddie thought their workout routines must be similar, though hers, Maddie's, to be less successful. Both then and now, to Maddie's surprise, no wedding band or engagement ring graced the third finger of Furey's left hand. Perhaps they had divorce in common as well. She wondered if Furey had a child or children.

To Furey's left, an empty chair, then a priest, Father Bartell Darcy, Maddie assumed. The priest sat with his hands resting on a scuffed leather satchel fat with files. He was athletic, sturdily built, with the ruddy skin of someone who had just stepped off the football or rugby pitch. His hands were rough and calloused, the hands of someone who worked outside, a farmer or construction worker or fisherman. Sitting beside the priest was Maddie's aunt, Katie Devlin, and her cousin, Bumper's mother, Trish Sullivan.

"Who invited that goddamn Sassenach?" Katie Devlin's words exploded from her mouth like the swears of an Irish hurler who has been fouled. Hot weather fashions did not favor her. Her pendulous breasts spraddled her chest as invitingly as plastic bags stuffed with used clothing for a church rummage sale.

"I did," Furey said. "She is named in the will."

"Let's go, Trish, before she piles another dozen stones on Seamus's grave." Katie tried to stand, but the legs of her chair had interlocked with those of Trish's and she could not push back from the table.

"The terms of the will require all the beneficiaries to be present when it is read," Furey said. "If not, everyone forfeits their inheritances."

Father Bartell, sitting opposite Trish, raised his hand in a sign of benediction. "May God turn the hearts of those who don't love us," he said to Katie. "I am Father Bartell," he said to Maddie. "Please, sit." He gestured at the empty chair between Attorney Furey and himself.

"I'm Maddie Devlin."

"She'll plant horns on your head," Katie warned Father Bartell, "and sow worms in your innards."

"We'll have none of those old country curses in my office," Michelle Furey said.

Father Bartell patted the crown of his head. "Slow-growing horns."

"Don't play the fool, Father," Katie said.

Father Bartell undid the straps of his satchel. "I administered Last Rites to Father Gabriel Finn and heard his last confession. When Father Gabriel was young and fresh from the seminary he heard the last confession of your uncle, Clancy. On his death-bed Father Gabriel violated the Seal of the Confessional. Clancy had confessed to him Michael was innocent of Seamus's death and that he had sworn a false oath against his brother because of an inheritance he did not receive. He made Father Gabriel promise to get the *Irish Times* to print a correction. Being fresh from the seminary, Father Gabriel didn't think he should violate the Seal of the Confessional. As he aged, his promise to Clancy ate at him. On his own death-bed, he gave me these." Father Bartell spread on the table photocopies of the original article from the 1916 *Irish Times* branding Michael Devlin a traitor, and Father Gabriel's letter to the editor recounting Clancy's confession. "I promised Father Gabriel I'd deliver his letter. The *Times* agreed to print a retraction."

Father Bartell placed a thick document on the table. A blue ribbon extended beyond the bottom of the last page. "Clancy confessed a second sin to Father Gabriel, carnal knowledge of a married woman. Maud O'Donnell. I tracked her down in a nursing home. She remembers it like it was yesterday. She was the one who made Clancy go to Father Gabriel. This is her affidavit." He tapped the cover page with his finger.

Maddie held the document by its edge as if it were a holy text made fragile by age. She read Maud O'Donnell's affidavit, then read it again. She brushed her fingertips against the raised lettering of the notary public's seal. The gold leaf on which the seal had been impressed looked authoritative, magisterial. No rational person could deny the truth of an affidavit with such a seal. She passed it to Trish. Katie attempted to intercept it, but Trish pushed her aunt's hand aside. Trish's lips moved as she read. When the time's right,

Maddie decided, she would insist her grand da be disinterred and reinterred beside his brother Seamus. She would insist he be honored with the celebration of a proper funeral Mass. She would invite Trish to stand beside her at the graves of their grand das, Devlins both, one family under God. And Katie, too, but she doubted Katie would rewrite the past even if the rewrite was a true war story.

"That is the inheritance Father Gabriel left each of you," Father Bartell said.

"I disclaim," Katie said. "That's the right word, isn't it, when you refuse an inheritance?"

Michelle Furey opened her mouth to speak, but Father Bartell silenced her with a wave of his hand. "Is *ira* a cardinal or venial sin, Ms. Devlin?"

Katie flashed a smile that showed she, too, once shared the beauty of the Devlin women. She loved showing off, especially in front of men of the cloth. To her, both Father Curry and Boston's cardinal were ignorant men who recited cant from memory. Jesus had told her so. Over her Princess phone.

"Some *ira* is considered to have value. The desire for revenge is ethical if it is reasonable and proportional, such as *ira* caused by a gross injustice against an innocent person. It becomes sinful when it exceeds reasonable limits, such as exacting vengeance on one who does not deserve it or from an improper motive. In that case, prudence and justice, cardinal virtues, demand the desire for revenge be renounced."

"You know your doctrine," Father Bartell said.

"I know where this is going." Katie glared at Father Bartell, then pointed at Maddie. "Behold the devil's maidservant, Babylon the Great, the Mother of Harlots and Abominations of the Earth, here to cleave your tongue to the devil's. Trish. Come along, dear."

"No, Aunt Katie," Trish said. "For Father Gabriel to do what he did, for him to violate the Seal of the Confessional, tells me what he says is true, that Uncle Clancy lied, that Uncle Michael did not kill my grand da. It's over, Aunt Katie. It never should have been, but it was, and now it's over."

"You cooked this up, Maddie." Katie spoke through clenched teeth. "You and your doxie lawyer tricks. Don't be such an eejit, Trish. Don't fall for the devil's fast talking guile. He's blinding you so you'll forgive Maddie getting the Jew off scot free for murdering your son."

"It is your tongue that cleaves to the devil's, Aunt Katie," Trish said. "I grew up on hatred, yours and my da's, but I won't grow old on it and I won't die with it."

"May the devil give you an Aussie kiss, Maddie!" Katie bulled her way out of the conference room, elbowing the back of Maddie's head. Maddie did not remonstrate with her.

"I have a plane to catch," Father Bartell said. "The documents are yours. If you have any questions, Attorney Furey knows how to contact me."

"I apologize for my aunt," Trish said.

"Old hatreds die hard," Father Bartell said. "Pray God will heal her."

Michelle Furey escorted him to the door. When she returned, Trish asked, "Is there somewhere Maddie and I can talk?"

"You can use this room. I have a will and trust to finish drafting."

Maddie and Trish sat opposite each other at the small round table, the documents between them. Heat crowded the room, shrinking it, slowing the second hand that marked time on the wall clock so that it took two minutes, three, maybe four, to make a complete circuit. "It's awkward," Trish said at last.

Maddie's inner voice, silenced by this unimaginable new information, remained mute. Outside, the wail of a police siren grew louder, peaked, then faded into silence. Horns sounded as traffic returned to its normal pattern. A pigeon lit on the window sill. Maddie knocked on the glass to scare it away, then said, "Let's not ignore the elephant on the table, Trish. Me defending Avram Levy."

"Is Aunt Katie right?"

"I'm not a doxie lawyer."

"So why are you defending him? Do you, did you, hate me that much?"

"Not you. Maybe. I don't know."

"Why, Maddie? Why?"

Maddie's inner voice stirred. "My boss forced me to cover the arraignment. Since then it's like . . . I don't know, like I'm in a trance. Hypnotized. It's like an out of body thing. I'm floating up there watching myself like I'm dead." She shushed her inner voice. "I don't know why, Trish. I really don't."

"I need to know."

"If I knew, I'd tell you, no matter how painful."

"For you or for me?"

The self-control that enabled Maddie to hide her reaction in court when the judge ruled against her fled like a coward from the battlefield. Her head slumped. Her shoulders sagged. Her hands seized up into fists. Her mind abandoned her vocal chords.

Trish hoisted her purse onto the table and removed a spiral notebook. "This is Charles's. He recorded every chess game in it." She squeezed it to her breast as if it were her son, then slid it across the table to Maddie. "Go to his last match. It's a complete game. The opponent's name left blank. Who-ever recorded those final moves, maybe he killed Charles."

"Where did you get this? Charlie take it from the crime scene?" Maddie studied the chess notations. "These are just letters and numbers, more like printing than writing. Can you identify them as Bumper's handwriting?"

"Except for the last few notations. Those aren't his." Trish covered Maddie's hand with hers. "If the Jew didn't do it, Charles's killer is still out there."

"He has a name, Trish."

"I don't want an innocent man convicted and I don't want a guilty man to get away with it."

"Can I take this? I've worked with handwriting experts. There are two or three I want to show it to."

"They won't destroy it, will they?"

"I'll make sure they don't."

Trish nodded.

"One problem," Maddie said. "There may not be enough here. Graphologists prefer working with complete sentences, several if possible. Whatever the conclusion, same person, different person, with such a skimpy sample, a few letters and numbers, a good attorney would destroy the expert on cross-exam. Without more I doubt there's enough here to stand up in court"

Trish withdrew into her chair.

"But it's something to go on, something worth investigating." Maddie closed Charles's spiral notebook. "Does Charlie know what you're doing?"

"No."

"Don't tell him. Don't tell anyone. If it's not Levy, the real killer might get spooked and figure a way to cover his tracks." Maddie made room for the notebook in the zippered central compartment of her purse. "It never goes away, Trish. I still cry myself to sleep on her birthday. I can't tell you how many times I thought about killing myself so I could be with her. It got worse after my ma and da died. More people to join in the next life, fewer to hurt in this one."

"I'm not ready for huggy-kissy. I don't know if I ever will be."

"We're the only ones left, Trish."

"Either way it dies with us."

Maddie wanted to say something, but she bit her tongue. For her, it had to end now, today, in this room, not thirty or forty or fifty years in the future when both she and Trish lay moldering in the grave.

Maddie struggled to compose herself. Was this another step toward her overcoming her impacted rage? The feud, the curse, jail running in her blood, had been part of her life since birth and now, suddenly, at least for her, it was no longer. She felt as if someone had sat her down and said her parents were not her parents but caretakers who had brought her up because her birth mother had abandoned her on the steps of a church. She felt adrift, as if the law of gravity no longer applied. Maddie wished Trish felt the same way. Maybe it was the shock of Bumper's death. Or, the sudden revelation. Or, both.

"I have to go," Trish said. "Aunt Katie'll start gossiping and Charlie'll ask questions if I'm gone too long."

"We should leave separately," Maddie said. "I don't want people seeing us together. You go first. I'll stay and talk to Furey so she won't say anything."

Alone with Maud O'Donnell's affidavit and Father Bartell's photocopies, Maddie wiped a tear from her eye. She felt no joy, no happiness, just an overwhelming sadness, for herself, for Trish, for the heritage of hatred that tore asunder generations of the Devlin family; but more for the soul of Father Gabriel, for the agony the old priest suffered as he debated with himself whether to violate the Seal of the Confessional, for the emotional price he paid for his betrayal. For the rest of her life, she vowed, she would pray for Father Gabriel, pray that he find peace, pray that he ascend into Paradise.

Maddie slapped her cheeks as if she were trying to sober herself up enough to drive home after a long night of drinking. She had a crime to solve, a case to win, a cousin she hoped would someday come to love her, to "huggy-kissy." But, what-if the final chess notations were in Levy's handwriting? The spiral notebook would be a damning piece of circumstantial evidence. Charlie's removing it from the crime scene would be an overruled objection overwhelmed by the probative value of the evidence.

Maddie's mind raced like the engine of a car with its throttle stuck open. At this early stage of the case, too little was known with certainty to form conclusions. Lack of certainty did not preclude speculation, did not prevent the parade of "what-ifs". That parade had always been one of her greatest strengths, one of her greatest weaknesses. On the one hand, it opened her mind to possibilities other attorneys overlooked; on the other hand, a surfeit of possibilities often distracted the mind from the truth.

According to the autopsy, Bumper died between ten and one. Capablanca closed at nine. Levy would have to account for four hours. What-if he didn't have an alibi? If he didn't and if the final chess notations were in his handwriting, what then? She only needed one juror for a hung jury, but what Boston jury would give her that? She wouldn't have the leverage to negotiate a decent plea bargain. Her gut was not yet persuaded of Levy's guilt. At least not beyond a reasonable doubt. She wished it were. Reconciling with Trish meant a lot to her. Maybe more than her fiduciary duty to Levy.

Maddie busied herself making photocopies of the last page of Bumper's spiral notebook on the copy machine beside the secretary's work-station. As the machine ejected the last copy into the tray, one of the closed doors opened and Michelle Furey stepped into the waiting area.

"Helping yourself, are you?"

"Way too long." Maddie repeated Furey's greeting. "*Mea culpa*. We're so short-staffed, I don't even have time to blow my nose." From her wallet, Maddie withdrew $5.00.

"I'm not that much of a piker," Furey said.

"This isn't for the copies. It's a retainer. To make me your client."

"I didn't realize my value had fallen so low, but then it's five bucks more than I got for the Elizabeth Fund."

"I want everything that happened this morning subject to attorney-client privilege. I need something more than your word you won't tell anyone."

"My word isn't good enough?"

"Nothing personal. Just business."

"I suppose you want an engagement agreement."

"Belt and suspenders."

"Why are you shitting all over me?" Furey's voice quaked with rage.

"Wrong place, wrong time."

"Take your fucking fiver and get out of my office."

Maddie stood transfixed as if a judge had just held her in contempt and sentenced her to thirty days for nothing more than zealous advocacy on behalf of a client.

Furey reached for the phone. "You going to make me call the cops?"

"Christ, can't we start over?"

"What's to start?"

"Can't we try and be friends? There aren't many woman attorneys and even fewer Irish woman attorneys and maybe our practice areas are poles apart, but that doesn't mean we don't put up with the same shit from our so-called brothers at the bar and couldn't use some moral support from time to time."

"I don't take shit from so-called sisters either, especially sisters who avoid me after I donate my services to them."

Maddie sensed her impacted rage struggling to free itself. Change the subject, she told herself. "How about dinner tonight? My treat." She hesitated. "Or tomorrow, if you have plans tonight."

"Is that your idea of an apology?"

Furey's put-down energized Maddie's impacted rage the way a bolt of lightning had the Frankenstein monster in the movie. In her mind's eye, she saw an ogre pulling apart the bars of its cage to create an opening large enough for it to escape. She saw it smashing the photocopy machine, trashing Furey's office, advancing on Furey, fists clenched. She raced through her catalog of coping mechanisms, rejecting one after another, until, at last, she closed her eyes and visualized herself lying on a beach at sunset, the sun melting into the ocean leaving behind a tail of red on the surface of the water. Seagulls drifting on air currents sang to each other. Waves lapping the shore provided a gentle backbeat. As the red tail of the sun approached closer and closer to the beach, the ogre, exhausted by its efforts, passed out on the floor of its cage.

"Maddie. Are you okay?"

Maddie opened her eyes. "I didn't mean to be so crass."

"Must be your inner trial attorney."

"Life's one fight after another, in court and out."

"Welcome to the circus. Look . . . Why not come over my place instead? I was planning to bake some of my famous Irish soda bread. The recipe's been in my family since the time of the sagas."

"I've been known to burn toast."

"I'll lock the toaster in the closet." Furey scribbled her home address on a piece of paper. "Eight o'clock. Save some appetite. I like to nibble while I bake."

-3-

Visiting the morgue to view the remains of victims allegedly murdered by her clients was a routine part of Maddie's job. Corpses before they were prettified by funeral directors no longer nauseated her. She intellectualized them as road-kill on the highway of life. But Bumper Sullivan's chalky pallor, his torso defaced by a web of autopsy scars, his boyish size, boomeranged her back to Elizabeth's autopsy and the recurring horror of what she imagined Elizabeth's tiny body had looked like when the medical examiner had finished. As the diener rolled Bumper into the ice box, the aura of his whiteness wrapped itself around Maddie like a shroud.

At police headquarters, she rode the elevator down to the property room in the second sub-basement to inspect Levy's personal effects. Acquittals and convictions were often measured from the odds and ends retrieved from the defendant's pockets at the time of his arrest, inventoried and labeled by the property clerk, sent to the lab for analysis, and finally delivered to the district attorney or defense counsel for use at trial.

"Levy's stuff," she said to Angelo Capitao, the property clerk.

Capitao perched on his stool like an ape sunning himself on a rock. A cheap cigar, lit in spite of a smoking ban, unraveled in his mouth, staining his chin a diarrheal brown. "You wanna see the kike's shit, ask the wop." His cigar glowed with each word.

"I thought you were the wop."

The wop. The don of the Boston police department. Dante Ugolino. Commissioner Stereo. One of Maddie's black defendants told her the brothers called him Commissioner Stereo, as in stereotype. After Charlie's first election as mayor, he appointed Ugolino commissioner of police as a reward for delivering the North End vote. Heavy at the time, Ugolino had doubled in weight since his appointment and now looked like he wore a bullet proof vest under his skin. In order to appoint him to a second term, Charlie had to persuade the city council to adopt an ordinance exempting the commissioner from the department's physical fitness standards.

"Judas is here," Therese Sroka, Ugolino's secretary, informed him as Maddie signed the visitors' log. Younger than Maddie, Therese dressed like the elderly women who sat outside the store-fronts on Prince Street in Boston's North End observing life pass by.

Ugolino's door popped open.

"Who's Professor Husam al din al-Saffah?" Maddie asked as she settled into a captain's chair adorned with the seal of the City of Boston Department of Police. "His name's above mine in the log."

Ugolino blew his nose. "I had lunch with the governor last week, something we do regular. He provides the lobster, I provide the gossip. We got to talking about the Superior Court vacancy, the one here in Suffolk, and he asks me what I think of a legal aid attorney."

"The SJC vacancy is more tempting," Maddie said. An Associate Justice of the Massachusetts Supreme Judicial Court was on the verge of reaching mandatory retirement age.

"Either way, I tell him the idea sucks 'cause they're all too soft on crime; but you know the governor once he sets his mind and the concrete cures."

"Professor Husam al din al-Saffah. Tell me about him."

"Professor who?"

"The name above mine in the visitors' log."

Ugolino eyed her. He knew enough about criminal trial procedure to realize that the prosecution would be required to disclose Professor al-Saffah's identity to the defense as part of pre-trial discovery if al-Saffah were to testify. If it were anyone but Devlin he would bow to the inevitable, but he'd rather make her work for the information. Let her file her discovery motions. Let her whine to the judge if the DA was not forthcoming. He shifted his bulk from the left arm of his chair to the right, shifting his thoughts from one side of his brain to the other. The chair groaned under the torture of his weight.

"A concerned citizen."

"A concerned citizen?"

"A mullah," Ugolino wheezed. "The Imam from the Disciples of Abraham Mosque. A professor of Islamic studies at UMass-Boston who specializes in comparative religions. He offered himself as an expert witness to provide a religious context for Bumper Sullivan's murder."

"Religious context?"

"Motivation. One of the elements of the crime, as I'm sure you know. Relevant on the issue of bail as well. I'm not telling you anything you won't find out when you get the DA's witness list."

"So why do you want a change of venue?"

Ugolino leaned forward and enveloped Maddie in the body odor obese people have even when they are fresh from the shower. "Jesus fucking Christ, Maddie. Kick a sleeping dog and you'll get rabies."

"Not me. I'm immune. Where's Levy's shit?"

Ugolino pointed to a Golden Grapefruit box adorned with a smiling sun that promised nature's sweet goodness. Flesh hung down from his arm like a pouch weighted with heavy water. "Therese will show you to an empty office."

The only thing with rabies was the skull cap on the library floor. But, how to find the rabid dog that left it there?

Many of the things confiscated from Levy were irrelevant to his defense: a paperback edition of *The Holy Scriptures*; a worn copy of Martin Buber's *I and Thou*; a new copy of a novel unknown to her, *A Canticle for Leibowitz*; a bus schedule for the New York-Boston route. The rest were problematic: an Emergency Medical Technician certificate issued by the American Red Cross suggested he knew how to administer blood transfusions; a notebook, in Levy's handwriting she assumed, with annotations of six chess games between him and Bumper Sullivan, none of which were played the night of the murder, indicated he had a relationship with the victim; but a pocket calendar with the entry "chess?" penciled in for the Thursday evening of the murder suggested they may or may not have played chess that night.

Classic circumstantial evidence, she thought, made less circumstantial by the presence of the little cap on the library floor. Whatever Levy's explanation, it would fall on deaf ears, ears deafened by the prosecution's harping on that little cap the way nuns harped on original sin in parochial school. She had tried cases where juries voted murder convictions on weaker circumstantial evidence, verdicts affirmed on appeal, and she knew in a case like Levy's no juror would give a passing thought to reasonable doubt. As long as the prosecution had more challenges than there were Jews in the jury pool, Levy was signed, sealed, and delivered. Unless he was innocent and–a very big and–she pulled a Perry Mason and produced the real killer.

Yet, Ugolino's demeanor, the way he parried her question about the change of venue, flew off the handle rather than answer it, when considered in the context of his leak to the press, aroused her skepticism. And, according to Harriman, he had halted the investigation. He had to be afraid she'd find evidence implicating someone else. He must be protecting someone. Himself? Another member of Capablana? Get a grip, she cautioned herself. Don't let the heat fry your brain. The evidence still pointed to Levy. She had nothing to substantiate her change of venue theory, nothing but a feeling in her gut and the spiral notebook Trish had given her with notations of a chess match. No, she was not persuaded Levy was guilty beyond a reasonable doubt; nor, however, was she persuaded of his innocence.

The smiling sun on the grapefruit box mocked her as harshly as the real sun mocked the city of Boston.

-4-

Maddie's confusion over her motivation for defending Levy, her hemming and hawing in response to Trish's why, intensified nature's demonic heat as she walked down Cambridge

Street to the Charles Street Jail to interview Levy, her first up-close contact with her client. Motivation had never been an issue for her before. The cases came in. Frohling assigned them. The hardest always to her. She did what she had to do. Trial, plea bargain, whatever, then moved on to the next case. Eight years of moving on to the next case. Nameless faces and face-less names. Until now. For once, for the first time, she needed certainty. Clarity.

At the jail a guard, bone thin and black with a ring of keys so heavy weighing down his right hip he listed to the right, escorted her to a tiny room where a matron in her early sixties, white of hair and pleasant of face, waited. Age defying, the matron's skin was unlined and sagged only slightly beneath her jaw, beneath her eyes. Despite her masculine uniform—police style jacket, matching skirt, dark blue shirt and tie, low heels—she looked like everyone's favorite grandmother. Maddie had not known either of her grand mas. The Irish of that generation died young, if not from disease or hunger, then from British bullets.

"I have to search you."

"I'm an attorney. I have a bar card."

"I know who you are."

In the years Maddie had visited clients at the Charles Street Jail, she had never been searched; but she gave the matron her purse and opened her briefcase. The matron leafed through the files, more slowly than Maddie thought appropriate, then patted her down, front and back, head to toe, under her skirt to check for weapons or drugs. The matron nodded and the guard who had refused Maddie's request to look away during the search walked Maddie to a bare room furnished with a small wooden table outlined by cigarette burns and two straight-back slatted chairs lacking arms or cushions. Nicotine discolored the ceiling and walls, an institutional beige yellowed from years of cigarette smoke. The stale, brackish air made her eyes sting. Balls of dust hung from the holes in the grating that secured the only air duct. Someone had carved a skull into the corner of the table and she wondered whether it had been an attorney or a prisoner.

With a jangle of his keys, the guard shoved Levy into the room, then slammed and locked the door.

Levy slumped into the vacant chair and sat on his hands. He wore a navy-blue skull cap identical to the one found near Bumper's bloodless body. Fuzzy sideburns extended below his ear lobes to the middle of his broad, pointless chin, accentuating his spherical face. A lifetime of eating traditional kosher food girdled his waist and hung over the top of his pants. Sitting, his entire body seemed conquered by a slouch as if his backbone weren't strong enough to hold his weight erect. Maddie ignored her first impression, something C. J. Ant had taught her the how and why of doing.

"Remember me?" Maddie asked. "I need to ask you some questions."

"Today is the Sabbath. The holiest day of holy days. To answer questions would be a desecration."

"How can talking be a sin?"

"Why are your arms and legs exposed? Why aren't you wearing a wig?"

"How did your skull cap end up on the floor of the library at Capablanca?"

"You are *traif*. If you were Jewish you would understand."

"I'm not your rabbi," Maddie said. "I'm not your spiritual counselor. I'm your lawyer. What I need to understand is the law, the secular law, the criminal law of Massachusetts. Jewish law is as relevant here as the rules of baseball."

"What you need to understand," Levy said, "you will never understand. Talking today is a sin. It can wait until tomorrow."

Levy sat quietly, his lips moving, concentrating on his lap as if he were afraid to make eye contact with her. Maybe he was, Maddie thought, or maybe he considered her so contemptible that she was not worthy of eye contact. She counted to herself, one-Mississippi, two-Mississippis, three-Mississippis, how many Mississippis before he looked up. She studied his face. He did not flash the desperation of someone falsely accused. He seemed indifferent as if he believed his fate was predestined. Murderers did not act this way. Most crowed their innocence; some boasted their guilt; a few pissed their pants. Would his indifference support an insanity defense? Not in her experience.

After the twentieth Mississippi, she asked, "How did your skull cap end up on the floor of the library at Capablanca?"

"It's a *yarmulke*. I wear it as a sign of my respect to Hashem."

"Hashem?"

"He whose name may not be spoken."

"God?"

"*Yod, Heh, Vav, Heh*. The tetragrammaton. Too sacred to be spoken." Levy pushed his yarmulke around his head until hair fell over his eyes. "My father of blessed memory gave me twelve for my bar mitzvah. I told you that before. Don't you pay attention?"

"No, you didn't," Maddie said. "Not me. Who have you been talking to? Someone from the DA's office? What else did you say? Were your statements voluntary? Was an attorney present?"

Levy ignored her. "I didn't know one was missing until I was arrested."

"Answer my questions, damn it. Your case may turn on whether you waived your Fifth Amendment rights."

"I didn't know one was missing until I was arrested."

"The immaculate disappearance. Is that what you're saying? Can't build a defense on that."

Levy's statement troubled her both because of what he said and how he said it. It was simple, declarative, not accusatory the way the guilty who feigned innocence talked. On the other hand, the tone of his voice—flat as if he were reading names from the phone book, his body language, his demeanor—reminded her of a study of fanaticism she had read in college which posited that fanatics who murdered in furtherance of their worldview believed so strongly they had not committed a crime they exhibited no signs of guilt when they lied. Truth serums and lie detectors were useless. Cross-examination could not break them down. She had never defended a fanatic. She didn't know anyone who had. Yet, in her meeting with Rabbi ben Reuben and Moskovitzky, they had not hinted Levy had a dark side. Had wishful thinking blinded them to reality?

"I want you to copy something for me." Maddie withdrew from her file one of the photocopies of the last page of Bumper's spiral notebook she had made in Michelle Furey's office. She studied Levy's face for a change of expression, a hint, a clue, as to whether it was his handwriting or not, but his eyes remained as blank, as dead as Bumper Sullivan's had been before the diener lowered Bumper's eyelids.

"It is forbidden to write on the Sabbath."

"Could you at least tell me if it's your handwriting?"

Levy closed his eyes. His lips moved faster. Piety or fanaticism, Maddie wished she knew what his refusal meant. Clients who refuse to cooperate were a lawyer's worst nightmare; but Levy was unlike any uncooperative client she had ever represented. She hoped she hadn't thrown away that study of fanaticism when she weeded out her college course books, or, at least, kept her course notes. She would settle for finding the syllabus with the reading list. Thank God for the Boston Public Library.

She waited, doodling in the margin of her yellow legal pad, cartoons without captions, people standing before a judge, a cop chasing a robber, a politician with arms flailing addressing a rally. She had met Jews at bar association functions, several in law school, a few at college. Loser Larry Gingold, her colleague at SCLS, was the only Jew she had extended contact with. She didn't know him any better than any other office buddy, but she knew him well enough to hope he was not an exemplar of his people. Levy was not like those Jews. He reminded her of the boys at Holy Name who graduated to the seminary rather than college or the armed forces or a job because they were afraid of life. She could not stomach those kids; no one could but the priests who labored so hard to scare them into the priesthood.

"The handwriting, will you at least look at it?"

"They call me Christ killer," Levy said, his eyes still closed. "The guards threaten to throw me in with the other prisoners."

"I'll draft an affidavit."

He opened his eyes. "I cannot swear an oath."

"It's a civil oath, swearing to tell the truth under the pains and penalties of perjury."

"I will affirm, but I will not swear an oath."

Another refusal. More doubts of his innocence. "Tell me about the yarmulke."

"They won't serve me kosher food. Rabbi ben Reuben brings me one meal a day."

"Charles Sullivan died because someone drained the blood from his body. At the crime scene, the police found syringes and plastic tubing, both wiped clean of fingerprints, and your yarmulke under a nearby chair. A possible chess match with the victim for the night of the murder was on your pocket calendar. Now tell me about the yarmulke. How did it get there?"

Sprinkle in one or two expletives, fucking pocket calendar, fucking yarmulke, Maddie's impacted rage urged. Scream them as loud as you can. She lowered her hands below his line of sight and clenched her fists, then opened her hands so she could grip the legs of the chair. Berating clients rarely worked and she knew that berating this client would only cause him to retreat deeper into his shell. She needed him outside his shell, at least with her. At least with her.

Levy said something, in Hebrew she assumed. The tone of his voice startled her, the voice of a beggar, not one seeking alms, but one beseeching God. "Am I accused of the blood libel?" He paled as if the souls of every Jew who had faced that accusation poured into him from across the centuries. "Pray for me."

Clients had gone holy on her before, usually immediately after screeching their innocence. Going holy made them appear sincere and sincerity bred credibility. Juries would rather convict an innocent atheist than a guilty believer in God. Defendants with street smarts rehearsed going holy. For someone going holy, Levy seemed too in awe of the accusation. Was he suppressing his fanaticism? Was his piety an act? His withdrawn personality an act? Only a fanatic whose eyes were gouged out by true belief would commit a blood libel. Levy appeared to lack the fire. Unless he believed he was doing God's will. Did he drain Bumper's blood because he believed he was doing God's will? She wished she knew. Was that his handwriting in Bumper's notebook? She wished she knew. Which Levy was the real Levy, the pious rabbinical student or the fanatic, or was he both? She wished she know. What was the answer to Trish's why? She wished she knew. Maddie crammed the file into her briefcase and rapped twice on the door to summon the guard.

On the street, the heat assailed her.

-5-

Maddie sat alone in a back-corner pew of St. Elizabeth of Portugal Catholic Church. She had driven to New Bedford, almost two hours, far enough away, she hoped, that she would not be recognized. The few parishioners who took note of her reacted because she was a stranger, not because she was Maddie Devlin. She felt like a stranger, not in the sense of being a foreigner, but in the sense of being estranged from herself, from her life.

Maddie had not planned to go to Saturday Mass. She had been sleeping so poorly that not having to wake up early on Sunday morning held little attraction, but Levy had left the taste of garlic in her mouth and she hoped the ritual of the Mass would cleanse her. She believed in the comfort ritual provided, not in its religious symbolism. Ritual she hoped, would provide this cleansing.

Anyone who felt aggrieved by Mayor Charlie or persecuted by society could have murdered Charles, but only an insane madman or a fanatic to advance a political or religious cause would have drained his blood. If Levy were that madman or fanatic, she doubted an insanity defense would succeed. He clearly knew the difference between right and wrong. Worse, the preparation for his choice of the wrong proved it was clearly premeditated. For that reason, the irresistible impulse variation of the insanity defense was inapposite because of the methodical nature of the crime. While he might be insane in a clinical sense, he seemed to fall outside the legal definition of insanity.

Levy qualified for a psychiatric workup, but she doubted he could afford to pay for one. Would the rabbi or Mosko-vitzky pay? If they did, she would not have to disclose any adverse conclusions. If they did not and she persuaded the court to order the Commonwealth to pay, she risked the court appointing a neutral whose report would be available to both sides. She risked the neutral concluding that the crime fit the accused and the accused fit the crime. And if the neutral con-cluded otherwise, she doubted it would matter. The opinions of a thousand psychiatrists would not trump the physical evi-dence. The most rational and dispassionate of juries would be warranted in dismissing the blathering of a shrink as so much mumbo-jumbo and convicting Levy based on the skull cap and the inferences drawn from his personal effects. The crim-inal defendant-friendly justices on the Massachusetts Supreme Judicial Court would have no choice but to affirm. Only pros-ecutorial error would save Levy and a good defense attorney never went to trial on the wing and prayer of prosecutorial error.

Maddie rose and joined the line awaiting Communion. Passing through on my way down the Cape, she would say if the priest remarked that he hadn't seen her before. In all her years representing defendants in criminal cases, she had never asked whether they had done it. Experienced attorneys never did that. Only mob or gang attorneys with their outhouse mo-rality and bulging bank accounts were completely indifferent to the foreknowledge of their client's guilt. Her temptation to ask Levy if he murdered Bumper Sullivan was not a sin; that was black letter Catholic dogma. No, her ambivalence on whether he answered yes or no, her wisp of a wish he would confess his guilt to her, those were the sins, sins of the heart.

So, why am I still here? she asked herself as the priest placed the Host on her tongue. She felt overwhelmed by the parade of "what-ifs" which forced her to focus on possibilities that should be overlooked while distracting her from the facts. But for this parade, she would be convinced of his guilt beyond a reasonable doubt. She had handled cases where she thought her clients innocent even though the facts were stacked against them. In those cases, her skepticism was rational. In this case, it was an irrational rationalization. Either I'm insane, she concluded, or my subconscious is still poisoned by hatred of Trish and lust for revenge. I wish, Maddie thought, it was nothing more than this infernal heat.

The Mass concluded, Maddie made the sign of the cross, then stepped out into that heat.

-6-

Maddie made time for a light supper and a shower before going to Michelle Furey's. As the hot water stung her face and bounced off her shoulders, she struggled to remember whether there had been a similar invitation years earlier when the Elizabeth Fund was incorporated. If there were, it had been hidden inside a hint, a hint she had been too afraid to recognize. She did remember visualizing what it would be like to be in private practice with Furey. Then, as now, she knew little of wills or trusts or probate, only what she had learned in law school. In law offices with two or three or four attorneys, it was common for attorneys to specialize in different areas of the law. It created synergy. In a law office of two, it would have been a different kind of synergy.

Tonight would be a test to see if they could get along on a person-to-person level, a necessity in a two person law firm. If they did, she would broach the subject of practicing together on a second or third date. She laughed at her use of that word, "date," but it was appropriate. When attorneys considered whether to form a partnership, it was like a courtship. Maddie wanted to be courted.

She dried herself and dressed. Wanting to play the polite guest, she stopped at a package store for a six pack of Guinness—what else to drink with Irish soda bread?—and rang Furey's doorbell within minutes of the appointed time.

"Welcome," Furey said. Her smile radiated a warm welcome even in the unseasonable heat.

Furey lived within walking distance of Cleveland Circle in the garret of what once had been a grand mansion gut-renovated and subdivided into condominiums. Her kitchen, the maid's room when a Gilded Age family lived in the mansion, was outfitted with granite countertops, appliances with doors of brushed silver, and a window that looked out on a carriage barn that once housed several horses and carriages but which had also been converted to condominiums. Furey's circular living room faced down Beacon Street toward Fenway Park. It had four floor-to-ceiling windows and one solid wall on which hung a framed print of Francis Bacon's 'Study after Velazquez's Portrait of Pope Innocent X' or "The Screaming Pope." "It talks to me," Furey said in reply to Maddie's gasp.

"What does it say?"

"That even the Holy Father doesn't always believe."

In the kitchen, Maddie opened the first two bottles of Guinness. The granite, cool to her touch, gleamed as if it had been polished. Maddie wondered if drafting wills and trusts, probating estates, was so lucrative or whether Furey enjoyed the good fortune of a noble birth or generous inheritance. Maddie doubted that. What Irish immigrant not named Kennedy did?

"Shall we?" Furey said as she measured four cups of flour into a mixing bowl, added two tablespoons of sugar, one teaspoon of salt, and a teaspoon of baking soda. "Care to whisk?" she asked. While Maddie whisked, Furey measured four tablespoons of butter. "People say use an electric mixer, but muscle power provides the secret ingredient."

"You mean the sweat?"

With a damp cloth Furey wiped sweat from Maddie's forehead, cheeks, and neck.

"Feels good."

Furey sipped her Guinness as if it were champagne. "Perfect." She led Maddie to the sink where they washed their hands, sharing the stream of water, the soap, the hand towel. "Now, we work in the butter by hand, tablespoon by tablespoon, until it resembles a coarse meal." Beneath the surface, their fingers rubbed against each other, then became tangled. They both laughed as their fingers slipped free. "Now the raisins," Furey said. "One cup. It took me years of trial and error to decide one cup was the correct proportion for four cups of flour."

"I thought you said this recipe was in your family since the time of the sagas."

"A girl's allowed a bit of exaggeration. Another Guinness?"

"What about the nibbles you said you ate while you bake?"

"We're in the mixing phase. Baking comes later."

Furey washed her hands again, then cracked a large egg into a small bowl and stirred in fourteen ounces of buttermilk. After several stirs, the ingredients coalesced into a liquid of uniform color. Slowly she poured this liquid into the flour mixture.

With a wooden spoon–once part of her grandmom's trousseau, Furey explained–she mixed the liquid into dough until it was stiff, then excavated a well in the center of the mixing bowl. "When I was a young lass helping my grandmom, digging out the opening was my favorite part. I loved dipping my fingers deep into the mixing bowl, scooping out the batter, licking it off my fingers. Want a taste?"

Gently, Maddie grasped Furey's wrist and guided Furey's hand toward her mouth, closing her lips around Furey's fingers one by one, little finger, index finger, the other fingers, filling her mouth with the batter. Slowly, she withdrew Furey's fingers. "Yum."

"If you think it's yummy now, wait 'til it's baked. Want another taste?" Her eyes sparkled like droplets of water reflecting the sun at its zenith. She scooped up a dollop of batter on her finger and offered it to Maddie.

Before Maddie could indulge, the phone rang. Furey depressed the speakerphone button.

"Attorney Furey? Maud O'Donnell calling from Dublin, like you asked."

"Thanks," Furey said. "I'm with Maddie Devlin. We're baking Irish soda bread."

"Mary Ann? Michael's granddaughter?"

Maddie remained silent.

"I've wanted to make this call for a long time," O'Donnell said.

"You could have picked up the phone." Maddie bit her tongue. Why did every conversation turn into a cross-examination?

"They called me Clancy's whore. Who'd ever believe a whore?" Maud's voice sounded old, cracked as if parched by time, as she told the story of a young and foolish school girl who succumbed to the blarney of a married man who filled her head with promises about the life they'd live when he divorced and inherited his grand da Patrick's homestead. Divorced in a nation where divorce was against the law. Her voice fluctuated from whispers barely audible to shouts strong and full throated, easily heard.

"Patrick left the homestead to my grand da Michael," Maddie said.

In the background a bell tolled. "Fifteen minutes to early Mass," Maud said.

Furey dusted her hands with flour and gently kneaded the dough just enough to shape it into a sphere.

Maud's voice trembled as she described how Clancy never spoke to Michael again, how overnight, Clancy became a different man, bitter, angry, withdrawn, living for his next drink and nothing more.

Furey patted down the dough, smoothed out its surface.

Maud cleared her throat. "One morning he showed up with a bottle of vintage Bushmills. Bushmills was distilled in the north and, well, people on the Republic side of the Troubles didn't drink Bushmills. I asked where he got it. He refused to say. We argued. He tried to force himself on me. I cracked him one with a skillet. I didn't think much of it at the time, but after the ambush, the execution, I realized what Clancy had done."

Furey greased a baking sheet and set the ball in its center, then molded it into a rounded loaf. With a serrated knife, she scored the top of the loaf, an inch or two deep in the shape of an X so the heat would have a direct path to the center while it baked.

Another bell rang. "Five minutes to Mass," Maud said. "I have to go."

"Will you repeat this to my cousin Trish, Beatrice Devlin Sullivan, Seamus's granddaughter?" Maddie asked. "And her aunt, Katie Devlin? They need to hear this from you, especially Katie."

Furey put the soda bread in the oven. Forty-five minutes to bake. Best served hot from the oven.

"With God's blessing." Maud hung up without saying good-by.

Maddie's eyes welled with tears. Furey dampened a cloth in cold water and dabbed Maddie's eyes, patted her forehead, wiped her cheeks and neck. Maddie tried to thank Furey for the phone call, but her sobs trapped her words so she hugged Furey and wet Furey's hair with her tears and felt such a need for a catharsis that she kissed Furey full on the mouth, something she had never done with another woman, something she had not done with a man for longer than she could remember, and Furey led her by the hand into the living room where on the floor aglow with the ambient lighting of Brookline and under the watchful eyes of The Screaming Pope, they made love and Maddie felt a satisfaction she had never felt with another person, man or woman, a satisfaction she never felt with Richard Gloucester who, once upon a time, she truly loved. Together, they savored the Irish soda bread and finished the Guinness, then made love again. Hours later, Sunday morning's sun rose on them asleep in each other's arms, crumbs from the soda bread clinging to their sweat-dampened skin.

Chapter 3

Sunday, April 12, 1981

-1-

In the early morning heat of the Sunday of Charles F. Sullivan, III's funeral, shortly after first light but before the sun breached the horizon, the reddening dawn sky foretold another day just like the day before and the day before that and the days before that, so many days that Boston could no more remember its last snowfall than it could what life was like before Charles's murder.

Mabi, the token African-American member of the Capablanca Chess Club, sat naked in bed, listening to his own heavy breathing. He unfolded a frayed, creased poster of a black basketball star now many years retired, many years forgotten by white sports fans except the few obsessed with professional basketball. It was the only relic he had taken with him when he moved out of his parents' home, that and a lingering desire to learn the meaning of Wallaca and vivid memories of his brother Jim Ed.

His soul burned hotter than the weather. He dozed on and off, his sleep made fitful by his dreaming of a little boy named Leroy Wallaca who shared a bedroom with his brother and a basketball poster tacked to the ceiling. He dreamt the leprechaun floated down from the ceiling like a snowflake and settled on the pillow beside Leroy's head. It whispered into the ear of the sleeping Leroy that he was descended from generations of leprechauns going back thousands of years to the beginning of time. Leroy awakened and asked the leprechaun how a little black boy could be descended from generations of white leprechauns. "Bad luck for life not to believe in me," the leprechaun said and before Leroy replied, it vanished. Leroy stood on the bed and tried to scrape the leprechaun off the poster. In his dream, Mabi shouted to Leroy, but Leroy ignored him, begging the leprechaun to come back. No politicians. No campaign contributors. No tuft hunters, brown-nosers, or favor seekers. To allow the public to bear witness, Boston's public television station would televise the Mass without commentators or comment. Reporters would be barred from the church and cemetery, but to appease them and to satisfy the public's curiosity, its need to know how Boston's first family was coping, Charlie insisted on holding a news conference later that day. Trish's complaint it would turn the funeral into a campaign rally went unheeded. From church to cemetery, the cortege would pass through the wards Charlie carried in his last election.

After finalizing the funeral arrangements, Charlie and Trish had attended Saturday night Mass. Trish had sat silent through the Introductory Rites, not responding with the rest of the congregation. The Liturgy of the Word was a mere buzz in her ears, as annoying as a mosquito. Father Curry's homily, speaking of death, forgiveness, resurrection, and eternal life, was like a pagan's spear puncturing the heart of her grief. What good was Father Curry? What did he know of the death of a child? She needed to talk to someone who had been through it, someone who had lost a child. She thought of what Maddie had said in Michelle Furey's office, how the hurt never went away, how she still cried on Elizabeth's birthday, how she thought about committing suicide. Maddie was the one to talk to, but Katie would crucify her and Charlie would do worse. But what could be worse? Charles was dead and death was eternal. Those thoughts kept Trish company through the night, accompanied her to the funeral Mass, and, as she rode in the cortege, to the cemetery.

Later that Sunday morning, Mabi and Spider, Mabi's warlord, waited for Virgil, the janitor at the Capablanca Chess Club, outside the African Meeting House where Virgil was the custodian, a second job, more a labor of love than anything else as the pay was minimum wage when there was money enough to pay him. "If that old man don't hurry," Spider said, honking the horn, "Bumper's box be dirt covered 'fore we get there."

Virgil hobbled forward and leaned against the door frame. The wood was dry and cracked with age like the earth after a severe drought. He hooked his cane over his forearm. "Welcome to Nigger Hill."

"I heard of Nigger Heaven," Mabi said, "and Nigger Hell, but never Nigger Hill."

"It's where you're at." Virgil rested his hand on the brick. It needed pointing. Time and the weather had gouged out chips.

"I thought this place Beacon Hill," Mabi said.

"Bet you never heard of Cato Gardner neither. He came from Africa and raised the money needed to build this church. See his plaque up top the door."

"Ain't much of a church," Mabi said.

Virgil closed and locked the front door. "The oldest black church in the U.S. of A. Built in 1806. Blacks they built it 'cause they had to sit in the balconies of white churches. That's called segregation."

"Them balconies closer to heaven, further from hell," Mabi said. "Still, they get what they deserving praying to white bread Jesus. Be no segregation if they prayed to Allah."

Virgil limped to the car. "Welcome to Nigger Hill," he said to Spider.

Spider laughed. "If there be a nigga on this hill, I s'pose white folks calling it nigga hill."

Virgil asked, "Would they be calling it fool's hill if there be a fool on this hill?"

"Depends if that nigga be a fool," Spider said.

"Or that fool be a nigga," Virgil replied.

The air conditioner of the limousine transporting Charlie, Trish, and Katie Devlin to Bumper's funeral labored to cool the limousine's interior. Sweat accumulated at the base of the driver's neck, stained the collar of his shirt, an odd pattern, an upside- down mountain range. George Harriman, riding shotgun in place of the head of Charlie's security detail, guzzled bottled water, rubbing the bottle across his forehead, up and down his cheeks. The limousine's tinted windows darkened the sun, but did little to repel the heat that built up inside the passenger compartment street by street as the cortege passed through Boston's neighborhoods. Grief doubled the ambient temperature. Burrowed into the corner of the limousine's back-seat, Trish in the opposite corner, Katie Devlin between them, Charlie rested against the window. The glass warmed the side of his head. He ignored the passing neighborhoods. He ignored the people lining the sidewalks thrusting signs of sympathy above their heads. Ward heelers had brought out the loyalists, the lackeys who depended on him for their daily bread, their evening beer and chaser. Their expressions of mourning were as sincere as his at the wake or funeral of a constituent's cousin where he curried favor with his people, collecting votes by the show of his face, the slap of his hand on a back, the murmur of 'my condolences for your loss.' How many candles had he lit to help ferry unknown souls to Heaven? How many of those unknown souls had arrived there? On the sixth day, God created Southie.

A pothole jolted the limousine. Water cascaded out of Harriman's bottle wetting the front of his shirt. Charlie tapped a warning on the glass partition. Someone would sacrifice their job to that pothole. He was in a new place, Charlie was, an undiscovered place, a place as alien as the worlds in the monster movies Bumper once devoured on Saturday afternoons. Now, the monsters of this world had devoured Bumper. No. Not the monsters of this world. Him. Charlie Sullivan. He alone. He was the monster of this world. He had devoured his son. The Irish had a way of doing that, devouring their own. The sow always ate its young. Had he made it to the library sooner, Bumper would be alive. How many minutes sooner? Five? Ten? A tick or two?

The cortege slowed for traffic. No sirens, Charlie had told the police escort. No running red lights or stop signs. No speeding. No signs of privilege to desecrate his son's funeral. Voices muffled by the closed windows mouthed words of sympathy. He wished he could stop, accept their embrace, but how could he? A tick or two. Were the Bruins highlights that important? They could have waited. For the highlights, there was all the time in the world; for Bumper, a tick or two.

He had relived that night many times over, the night of Bumper's murder, an endless video loop with God's finger eternally welded to the replay button. For the rest of his life he would relive that night. On his death-bed, it would accompany him down the dark corridor toward the light, accompany him through the gates of hell, accompany him as he stood before God awaiting judgment. The night of Bumper's murder. He closed his eyes. No longer in the back seat of the limousine, no longer escorting his son's body from church to cemetery for eternal internment, no longer in this world.

Damp and clammy from the steam heat of Boston Garden, Charlie draped himself in front of the window air conditioner while he watched the television highlights of that night's hockey game between the Boston Bruins and Montreal Canadiens. The players had skated at half speed on ice the consistency of the syrupy slush sold at Revere Beach in summer. Fog had obscured the game's one goal and he hoped the television replay would give him a clear view.

Hockey was his one respite from the pressures of being mayor of a city riven by court-ordered school busing, the pressures of his campaign for elevation to the United States Senate, the pressures of being a father and husband, the pressures of his wife's opposition to moving the family to Washington if he won, the pressures of fearing for his soul and the soul of his wife and son.

With Bumper's death, would he, could he, ever watch another hockey game? Ever lace up his skates to play in an amateur league? If Bumper had died at the hand of a hit and run driver, died from being mugged on the T . . . but hockey.

Slouching against the bedroom door, Trish squinted to read the tiny numbers on her watch. She felt floppy as if the heat had incinerated her bones.

"Charles should be home by now," she said. Exercising a mother's prerogative, she referred to her son, Charles F. Sullivan, III, as Charles rather than Bumper. "Call the cab company."

Charlie pulled a tissue from a box and spit a wad of phlegm into the palm of his hand. "He must have locked himself in the library." A chess prodigy, Bumper had full membership privileges at the Capablanca Chess Club, on paper a municipal recreational facility but in reality a club whose membership decisions were subject to the mayor's whims and caprices.

"It's a school night, Charlie."

"After this replay."

"That's another stone on our grave." *Trish retreated into the bedroom.*

Charlie squatted in front of the TV as the announcer recapped the Bruins loss to the Canadiens. On the replay of the game's only goal fog absorbed the puck and he settled for the announcer's description, Savard hip checking Bourque off the puck, the pass to Lafleur who skated through center ice with Cournoyer on his right wing, the deke bringing Cheesie out of the net, faking the pass to the wing, then scoring in the upper left corner, the one hole in hockey argot. Charlie doubted the goal judge saw the play any better than he did, but things like that happened when the Bruins played the Canadiens.

The hip check, the pass, the center ice skate, the deke—which of these cost Bumper his life? Charlie tapped on the barrier between the limousine's back seat and front and gestured for Harriman to pass back a bottle of water. Trish ignored his asking whether she wanted one. As did Katie.

"The cab company, Charlie." *From the bedroom, Trish's voice sounded wee and small. A cab company dependent on the Boston Licensing Commission for hackney licenses chauffeured Bumper to and from Capablanca.*

Charlie poured two glasses of iced tea and carried them to the bedroom. Trish paused from her nightly reading of the Bible and marked her place with a red leather bookmark bearing the likeness of her favorite saint, St. Charles of Sezze. Each year, she celebrated his feast day, January 5th, by serving lamb out of respect for his humble origins. Charles of Sezze was an illiterate shepherd who risked his life to aid those stricken in the plague of 1656. To her, he was a true hero of the Church, not one of those born and bred into the papacy like the Medici popes and cardinals.

"The cab company." She rubbed the glass across her forehead.

"Let him be. It's the one place he's really happy."

"He won't have that in Washington."

"He'll have more. He's outgrown Capablanca."

Chains of causation, Charlie thought, as he sipped his water. Both life and chess were chains of causation, random events tied together in ways unforeseen. Was the cause of death the first link in the chain or the last? Was checkmate ordained on the game's opening move?

Bumper's grandfather on the Sullivan side, Charles F. Sullivan, Sr., had taught him chess while Bumper recuperated from an appendectomy. Charlie the First, as he was known, played for whiskey with beer chasers in bars throughout Boston, losing only after the rewards of winning had so dulled his brain and dimmed his senses he could no longer tell the castles from the knights, the bishops from the pawns, the king from the queen, white from black. By the time Bumper had healed and his stitches had been removed, he dominated the man who called himself Charlie the First. For his birthday, Mayor Charlie arranged formal lessons with Pete Kelly, Boston's only grandmaster and Capablanca's president, and for Christmas, a Club membership.

Bumper savored the novelty of being treated like an adult more than popcorn at the movies or chocolate syrup in his milk. When he sat king of the hill at the chessboard, childhood's dark side—bogeymen under the bed, nightmares of dying while asleep, priests vomiting visions of hell while their hands fumbled with the belt buckles and zippers of acolytes and altar boys, bullies pissing on naked feet—dissolved in the checkmates he inflicted on the Club's members. At Capablanca, he had no bedtime. Preparing

THE FIRE THIS TIME

for a tournament, he had no homework. If he won, his reward was tickets to the Bruins or, in summer, the Red Sox.

In the limousine, Charlie gulped his water. In his memory, in his bedroom, he gulped his tea and changed the subject to buy Bumper a few more minutes at Capablanca. A few more minutes. Another tick; another tock.

"The governor called," he had said to Trish. "He wants to name a Jew to the Superior Court. His poll numbers are slipping and he needs their money. He asked for a recommendation. If I give the governor a real money bag, I'll score his endorsement for the Senate primary which is worth something even if it isn't worth as much as he thinks."

"We'll stay in Boston, thank you."

Charlie's mouth drooped with exasperation. "Mayors are a dime a dozen, hon, but there are only one hundred United States senators."

"What kind of father would take Charles away from the one place he's happy?"

"One who would take his son to a place where he would be happier." Charlie scooped the car keys off the dresser, winked Trish a kiss, and stepped into the inferno.

Happier? Are there chess boards in heaven? If it wasn't the hockey highlights that killed Bumper, was it his lack of urgency on the drive to Capablanca, dawdling as he planned strategy for his Senate campaign in his mind?

Driving to Capablanca, Charlie reviewed in his mind for the hundredth time the results of the polls he had commissioned to help him plot his campaign strategy. Running state-wide was not the same as running in the city of Boston. His organization lacked presence beyond the city limits, lacked the ability to get out the vote in the wards or precincts favorable to him outside Boston, or suppress the vote in those that weren't. The dynamics of the election also differed. State-wide he would need the black vote. In his mayoral campaigns he was able to pacify black voters with lip service because their vote was irrelevant to the outcome. Statewide he would have to lure them to his side. And he would need Jewish money to fund his campaign, something also less critical in Boston. All without alienating his natural constituency of angry white voters. It would be tricky, but he was confident he could pull it off. Reagan had.

Charlie capped the empty water bottle and tossed it on the floor of the limousine. Drops had dribbled on his dress shirt. He patted them with his handkerchief. He glanced at Trish, wishing he could read her mind. He didn't have to. Her face told him what she was thinking. It's your fault, her face said. And her face was right.

Charlie parked between the stone lions that guarded the front entrance of Capablanca. He dragged himself up the granite steps. His breath rattled in his lungs, the sound reminding him of his mother's death rattle. He coughed up a wad of phlegm; then, another. He leaned against the front door to catch his breath. His lungs ached. His chest felt like it was constricted by an ever tightening straitjacket. Slowly, he crossed the foyer to the circular staircase leading to the Club's second floor. Gripping the banister, he pulled himself up the stairs, pausing to pant on every other step. With each pant, he considered what punishments to inflict on Bumper. Take away his bicycle. No television for a few days. Extra chores like sweeping the winter's grit out of the garage, or raking the dead leaves from beneath the shrubs. Nothing too harsh, but harsh enough so Bumper understood he should never, never, never pull stunts that worried or frightened his mother. That, Charlie would explain with a wink and a smile and a playful slap against the side of the head, was a spanking offense. He coughed up more phlegm, grinding it into the carpet with the tip of his shoe, then struggled to open the library door with his shoulder. If this was a preview of old age, he hoped to die young.

A small reading lamp on the fireplace mantel glowed yellow. It illuminated the library and imbued the mahogany paneling with a rich, peaceful luster which was what Charlie imagined the paneling in a Senate office to have. He wished the mayor's office had that look. He despised the poured concrete of Boston's City Hall. Cement had the charm of a grave liner, and Charlie felt himself stepping into the grave each time he entered the building. He longed for Washington's hallways of marble.

In front of the fireplace, Bumper sprawled on a high backed red leather couch. One hand, fist clenched, flopped across his face, the other hung down by his side, fingers dangling above the thick nap of the carpet. His feet rested on the arm of the couch. His sneakers were unlaced in the school-yard style. Less than a week old, they were already scuffed from pick-up basketball games and Little League tryouts. Bumper wanted to pitch—it was the part of baseball closest to chess—and over the winter Charlie hounded the Red Sox for their pitching coach to teach Bumper to throw a curve. At his age, the coach advised against it, his bones being too fragile to handle the torque.

"Bumper!" Charlie's voice was soupy, phlegmy.

Charlie shook his son. No response. He kneeled beside the couch and searched Bumper's wrist for a pulse. Nothing. He put his ear to Bumper's chest. He thought he heard a heartbeat. He covered his other ear with the flat of his palm. It was his, not Bumper's, the heartbeat. He pinched Bumper's nose shut, squeezed open his mouth, and blew as hard as he could. Bumper's chest did not rise. With his fist, he pounded Bumper's chest. Still, no heartbeat. Charlie pried open one of Bumper's eyelids. The pupil, dilated, yawned open.

Bumper was dead. His son was dead. Nine years old. Dead.

He took a deep breath, then lay his head on Bumper's chest, cursing the God that punishes the son for the sins of the father. Tears occluded his eyes.

Charlie took another deep breath, then wiped the tears from his eyes with the tips of his fingers. He grasped Bumper and lifted him off the couch and hugged him and rocked him back and forth as he had when Bumper had colic and had to be comforted and cooed to sleep and he tried to sing him a lullaby; but the words jumbled up in his head and all he could remember was "Down came the cradle, baby and all" which he sang over and over until his voice dissolved into a cough and tears flowed from his eyes like the phlegm clogging his throat. He lowered Bumper on the couch and pried open his clenched fist and smoothed his shirt and straightened his legs and crossed his arms over his chest and made the sign of the cross and tried to recite the Act of Contrition, but could not remember what came after '. . . I detest all my sins' even though he had started reciting it before he could pronounce all the words correctly. He attempted the Twenty-third Psalm, but his mind went blank after "the valley of the shadow of death".

What would he say to Trish? His words were a politician's words, words for constituents at wakes and funerals, words of public condolence written by speechwriters; but for his wife, what words did he have?

Out of the corner of his eye he noticed a skull cap beneath one of the chairs of the chess table closest to the couch. It was inside out. He crawled over to it. Stitched inside the lining was a name, Avram Levy. He shook his head to dislodge, to expel, the cancerous thought that he should take the skull cap, find this Avram Levy, exact revenge; but he knew better. He knew enough not to disturb evidence at a crime scene. He left the skull cap untouched, the crime scene uncorrupted.

He looked around. Under the couch, a spiral notebook, Bumper's spiral notebook in which he recorded all his chess matches, move by move, in standard chess notation. It was open to the most recent match, the one he had apparently played that evening. Date:

April 9, 1981. Opponent: A blank. An empty space. Location: Capablanca Chess Club. Played: Black. It made no sense. Bumper never omitted the name of his opponent. Unless it had been erased. By the murderer. By Levy. Charlie held the page up to the lamp on the mantel. In the yellow light, it glowed like an illuminated manuscript. No erasure; the space was blank. Why? Was Bumper ashamed to play Levy? Was he afraid Levy would checkmate him and he didn't want to record losing a match to a Jew? Or, in the rush of the moment, had he skipped over the name of his opponent, a typical goof for a nine-year-old?

Charlie didn't understand chess notation, but he knew the white moves were on the left, the black on the right, and that "checkmate" entered beside a move meant that player had won. Entered as white's last move: checkmate. Whose writing? Not the same as the earlier moves. Not childish enough to be Bumper's. No matter. Bumper had lost his last match. To a Jew. And now he was dead. Charlie closed Bumper's spiral notebook. This is not evidence, he thought. It's a relic, something to be venerated as if it were the finger bone of a saint, a sliver of wood from the Cross, something tangible to remember his son by, something for him and Trish to cherish, to cry over, to lament the future that never would be. He tucked it into the waistband of his pants in the small of his back.

Once again, Charlie's eyes burned with tears. His lungs ached. He kissed Bumper on the forehead, then stumbled out of the library in search of a phone. He had to call Detective George Harriman of the Boston Police Department. Maybe Harriman had words.

Another pothole, another jolt. Charlie opened his eyes. The heat inside the limousine had intensified. The stink of grief seared the air. It emanated from his pores. It coated the inside of his mouth. Scarred his lungs. Dried the tears in his eyes. Baked love out of his heart. The cortege slowed as it approached the cemetery. In his mind's eye he dumped a bucket of ice water on himself, slapped himself across the face, once, twice, a third time, desperate to shock himself awake. He faced a challenge, one he had never faced before, perhaps one of the most important of his political career, sharing his grief with the people of Massachusetts without whimpering, without wailing. Whimpering and wailing was for women. Not for the mayor of the city of Boston. Not for the next United States Senator from the Commonwealth of Massachusetts. He would go forward with the news conference. Today. Not tomorrow. Not next week. Today. Doing so, he would stare down Bumper's empty grave, dare it to swallow him, mock it when it didn't. He closed his eyes as the cortege passed through the cemetery gates.

Between Trish and Charlie in the back seat of the limousine, Katie Devlin's mouth moved in silent prayer. She crossed herself, then sighed. Was she praying for Bumper's soul, Charlie wondered, or for God to strike me down? God already had. By letting him live.

The telephone rang and rang and rang until Katie Devlin realized it was the real telephone, the ancient black bulky phone which crowded her night table beside her pill bottles and Holy Bible, and not the petite pink Princess phone secure in her night table drawer through which Jesus spoke to her, she to Jesus. Katherine Meaghan Devlin, born in and of the old country, spinster sister of Trish's da, Trish's favorite aunt, tolerated one informality in her life. She allowed people, friends and family, even strangers, to call her Katie, and, only then, because Jesus had done so in their first conversation. Too sleepy to answer the phone, too hot, too tired, she let it ring; but like the devil who created a new temptation with every click of the clock, the ringing persisted. Sliding her sleeping mask on to her forehead, she answered.

"We're on our way over," George Harriman said, "Charlie and me to pick you up. Be there in about ten minutes."

"Why? What's wrong?" Katie bunched her nightgown in front of breasts, pendulous with age and calories. Once she had enjoyed the rakish beauty inbred in the Devlin women, her hair redder than the setting sun, but age had whitened her hair, thickened her body, and curved her upper spine so she walked with her head angled forward, her shoulders hunched.

"It's Bumper."

Katie twisted the nightgown, noosing its collar around her throat.

"He's dead, Katie. Murdered. His blood drained. Every last drop."

"Passover. The Jews are baking their matzoh." She crossed herself and prayed for her Princess phone to ring.

"Charlie wants you there when he tells Trish."

Inside the limousine, time crawled and the limousine crawled with it. It was an endurance race Charlie ran, a race he wanted to end; but it never would. After the funeral, the press conference. The Senate race. The election. Maybe six years in Washington. Twelve. Eighteen. Maybe none. A race with no finish line. A race death would not end if the Catholic doctrine of the soul's journey were true. All the money in the world would not buy the indulgences he needed to escape his fate. Bumper was dead and would always be dead. And he would be famous in Hell as the father who put hockey highlights ahead of his son.

Thirty minutes later, Harriman parked across the street from the Sullivans' house. The car was standard issue for police detectives, black, chromeless, oversized exterior mirrors, heavy duty engine, unmarked but easily recognized. It blended into the shadows of the trees that canopied the street. Moths danced on the heat waves that distorted the street lights. Silent but for Charlie's wheezing, they watched Trish pace back and forth in front of the picture window with the regularity of a metronome.

In her mind's eye, Katie saw her ma pacing the same way as her ma awaited word on whether Katie's da had survived the ambush. She heard once again the voice of the priest when he came to tell them the Brits had killed her da and, later, that her uncle had been executed and, later still, the tone in which he spoke when her ma passed away in her sleep, her death mask bearing the scars of her life. Those memories had stowed away with Katie and her brother, frightened teenagers smuggled out of Dublin, consigned to steerage on the ship to New York, and to third class on the train from New York to Boston. Now, years later, watching Trish, her brother's daughter, pace back and forth, those memories were as real as loose dirt beside a freshly opened grave. Harriman helped her out of the car.

"I've buried as many people as I can in one life," Katie said.

He nudged her toward the house. "Trish needs you."

Trish flung open the front door. "Charlie! Aunt Katie! Where's Charles? Which hospital? Take me to him."

Katie wrapped Trish in her arms and whispered in Trish's ear, "He's dead."

"Dead?" Over Katie's shoulder she saw George Harriman on the sidewalk at the foot of the stoop, his head bowed. She pushed Katie aside and rushed down the steps. "How, George?"

Harriman bit his lip. "Murdered, Trish. Murdered."

Trish shrieked and collapsed against him, almost toppling him. Harriman grabbed the wrought iron railing to steady himself, then wrapped his arm around Trish's shoulders and helped her up the steps, into the living room, to the couch. Trish gripped Harriman's arm. He peeled open her fingers and lowered her on to the couch.

Through the night, Trish shuddered in Katie's arms like an infant fighting a high fever. Charlie paced from kitchen to living room to bedroom and back, avoiding Bumper's room. Harriman

worked the phone, coordinating Bumper's autopsy, the exam-
ination of the crime scene by forensics, the arrangements with
the funeral home, the press bulletin. A police detail guarded the
street, keeping reporters at bay. At first light, Trish finally dozed off.
Slowly, her sleep deepened, became less fitful. Her facial muscles
relaxed. She breathed in little gasps as if she were dreaming she
was crying.

Harriman kneeled beside Katie and squeezed her hand. "You
holding up?"

"Do you think it's the Jews?"

"Get some sleep, Katie. It's going to be a long day."

Charlie reached across Katie's lap and fumbled for Trish's
hand. Her fingers lay limp and lifeless on her leg. He covered
her fingers with his, gently squeezed them. Trish did not respond. Katie shifted in her seat, separating his hand from Trish's. He withdrew his hand, folded it into his lap. The cortege
arrived at the open grave. The driver hastened to open the back
door of the limousine. It had been two long days, two long
nights. Now, another long day, another of the death march of
never ending long days. Now and forever. He stepped into the
heat. He would not wilt.

At the cemetery aides from Moynihan's Funeral Home
held umbrellas to shield the mourners from the sun. The membership of Capablanca formed an honor guard through which
Charlie and Trish and Aunt Katie passed to reach the grave.
Trish wore neither veil nor makeup. Grief twisted her features
into those of a gargoyle on a Gothic cathedral. Throughout the
graveside service, Trish's expression did not change: not when
the cardinal sprinkled holy water on the coffin; not when cemetery workers lowered it into the grave; not when the rich black
loam, shovel by shovel, cascaded off the coffin's slippery shine;
not when stones bounced off its polished wood, sounding like

shots from a child's cap gun; not when the members of Capablanca lined up to offer condolences, Mabi, Capablanca's only African-American member, at line's end.

"I'm Mabi," he said when Trish reached him.

"Did you know Charles well, Mr. Mabi?" Trish asked. He dressed like a young associate at one of Boston's Brahmin law firms, tailored suit, white shirt, regimental striped tie.

"Just Mabi. We chess played, ma'am. Charles always won."

Trish's lips quivered.

"This cemetery sure be looking nice," Mabi said. "My brother he's buried in a city cemetery. Weeds so bad we bring scissors when we visit. The old potter's field. White folk call it Nigger Heaven."

Trish touched his upper arm. "How can people be so full of hate they hate the dead?"

-2-

Maddie Devlin connected a borrowed video cassette recorder to her television to videotape Charlie Sullivan's press conference. Michelle Furey had insisted Maddie watch it at her place–I have a VCR, she pointed out–but Maddie needed to concentrate and to concentrate she had to be alone, not distracted by the strange attraction she felt for Furey. Sudden, unforeseen, it had welled up from deep within her like the lava of a long dormant volcano. Church dogma–that sex with persons of the same gender violated both divine and natural law–had been drummed into her from early childhood. It was little consolation that homosexual desires without consummation were not considered sinful. She had leapfrogged the desire stage. If it were a sin, why did she feel so fulfilled? So at peace? Focus, focus, she chastised herself.

One of Mayor Charlie's endearing qualities was that he strayed off-script whenever his mouth started moving. So harebrained was he that a talk radio host once labeled him the Happy Harebrain. In the social halls of Boston's Irish and Italian neighborhoods, people laughed with, not at, Charlie's harebrain; but the United States Court of Appeals for the First Circuit cited it as a reason for affirming one of the nation's toughest school busing orders designed to integrate Boston's racially segregated schools. They learn better when they're schooled with their own, Charlie had testified in the busing trial before United States District Court Judge W. Arthur Garrity, Jr. who was so outraged at that testimony he devoted several pages in his initial court opinions and several more in subsequent opinions attacking and refuting it. Charlie wore those court opinions as badges of honor on the campaign trail, his defiance blinding the voters of Boston to his complicity in the court orders that roiled the city.

Charlie's harebrain vexed Maddie. Maddie knew Charlie understood the problems that would arise both for the prosecution and for his Senate campaign if he pronounced Levy guilty beyond a reasonable doubt and urged, better begged, a jury to convict. It would not surprise her if he spoke of blood libel. Reason did not always control Charlie's actions. At times, he spoke and acted with the underdeveloped brain of an adolescent. If he did now, maybe she could use it to Levy's advantage in court; but it would also guarantee the change in venue Ugolino had schemed to obtain. Maddie tested the video cassette recorder, pulled a chair up to the television, and unfolded a tray table for her pot of tea. When Charlie stepped up to the podium, she pushed the record button.

The camera zoomed in on the mayor's face, on his nose, the nose that caused his detractors—especially the righteous liberals who lived in the ritzy suburbs beyond Boston's city limits—to mock him as Boston's Jimmy Durante, twice the nose, half the sense of humor. The tight focus made his nose look like a top-down view of a mountain after an avalanche, the nose of a boxer who had been knocked out in the first round of every bout he had fought.

It wasn't boxing that gave Charlie his nose; it was hockey. Twice Charlie had broken his nose playing hockey, once in high school, once in college. Shaped like a blob of oatmeal fallen off the spoon, his nose would embarrass most men. Not in Boston. Not in Southie. People still stopped him on the street to thank him for his exploits on the ice, to ask him to sign autographs for their children. His nose was his calling card. In Southie's bars and taverns, people bought him drinks because of the cross-check he made that freed Pierzynski to score the winning goal for Holy Name High School in the Massachusetts Super 8 state championship game, Holy Name's one and only trip to the Super 8 Hockey Tournament. Neighborhood recognition became citywide when he earned a hockey scholarship to Boston College and saved a NCAA championship by diving into the goal crease over the body of the injured goalie as time wound down, deflecting a slap shot with his eye socket and cheekbone. Hockey fans had elected him to the City Council, and, a few years later, with Boston euphoric over Bobby Orr and the Big Bad Bruins' first Stanley Cup in decades, they had elected him mayor. Term after term they had re-elected him, the opposition weakening with each election.

Charlie's political machine was reminiscent of Chicago of the Daley era or New York of Boss Tweed's time. With his appointees controlling the Boston Redevelopment Authority and the Boston Zoning Board of Appeals, Charlie personally issued the zoning and building permits for the office towers and hotels that revitalized Boston to developers who awarded the work to the right contractors, who hired people out of the right union halls. If a restaurant needed a liquor license, Charlie's henchmen on the Boston Liquor Licensing Board approved it if the right wholesaler vouched for the restaurateur, the right distributors provided the produce, the beef, the fish. He distributed real estate tax abatements as if they were papal indulgences, proportionate to the applicant's contributions to his campaigns. When video games resurrected the penny arcade, he rammed a regulatory scheme through the Boston City Council mandating a municipal permit for each machine; not each arcade, each machine. To protect the youth of the city, he explained at the press conference when he signed the ordinance. He, of course, controlled the permits. People beholden to him could mobilize more campaign workers, raise more money, than any candidate other than those named Kennedy.

"Mr. Mayor." James Goddard, a wire service reporter and senior City Hall correspondent, always asked the first question. "On behalf of the press corps, please accept our condolences. How is Mrs. Sullivan?"

"Thanks, Jim. It's been difficult. She's doing as well as can be expected."

"Mr. Mayor." Franklin Crocker of the *Boston Globe* stood.

Charlie's facial muscles tightened as the camera panned from him to Crocker who was referred to as "Crocker Shit" by Charlie's inner circle. The *Globe* had supported Charlie in his first run for mayor, then abandoned him when he ran for reelection because it perceived his opinions on school busing and the distribution of low income housing throughout the city to be too similar to such ardent segregationists as Ross Barnet, George Wallace, or Lester Maddox. When Charlie announced his candidacy for the U.S. Senate, the *Globe* editorialized a plea he not run, arguing he would divide the Democratic Party and prevent the election of a senator in the tradition of John Fitzgerald Kennedy and the current senior senator from Massachusetts, Edward Moore Kennedy. Some tradition, Charlie joked to his aides. One hunted pussy 'round the clock; the other drove it off bridges.

"Any new developments on the investigation?" Crocker asked.

"No."

Charlie's composure came through on television because he knew how to use the small screen to his advantage. He alternated eye contact with the camera as if it were a constituent sitting across from him in his office and eye contact with the reporter asking the question. He modulated his voice so it did not sound pre-recorded. He held his hands and head steady. When he paused to blow his nose, he made it look as if he were struggling to overcome a deviated septum his parents could not afford to have surgically repaired.

"Chief Ugolino," Charlie continued, "has assigned the investigation to Detective Angelo Procaccino, a thirty-year veteran of the police department well-respected for the thoroughness of his investigations. Detective Procaccino has linked the skull cap to Avram Levy who, as you know, is in custody. Several more like it were found in his apartment."

Angelo the Sweeper, Maddie thought. She called him that because Ugolino, according to gossip among the defense bar, assigned him to cases where the chief wanted inconvenient

THE FIRE THIS TIME

facts swept under the rug. Maddie had encountered him in defending a busboy in the Flying Dragon arson case in which the building housing Chinatown's Flying Dragon restaurant had been gutted by fire. The prosecution theory was that the busboy was acting on behalf of one of the Chinese triads, China's version of the mafia. Maddie's defense theory was that the owner of the building, a parochial school classmate of Ugolino's, had torched it for the insurance. Maddie could not break Procaccino on cross-examination. Years later, the owner of the building confessed to the arson on his death bed. By that time, Maddie's client had died in prison, silenced by a guard on the triad's payroll.

Procaccino added several new layers of mystery to Levy's case. What facts did Ugolino want swept under the rug? Who was he protecting? Why? No wonder, Maddie thought, he wanted a change of venue. No wonder he wanted to lay off on the defense the work the police should be doing. Once again, her temptation to ask Levy if he murdered Bumper Sullivan, her wisp of a wish he would confess, agitated her.

"Say, Mr. Mayor." Tony Cochoni of the *East Boston Patriot* waved.

Maddie read Charlie's mind through his smile. Cochoni was Charlie's pet reporter. For him, "off the record" meant off the record. Now and again Charlie had a few beers with him without worrying every word would appear on the next day's front page. Trish appreciated he didn't feel obliged to interview her every time they met. Charlie rewarded Cochoni's discretion by leaking him enough scoops to make the *Globe* and the *Herald-American* jealous. "Rumor has it that Capablanca's only black member played chess with Bumper that night."

"His name is Mabi and that rumor is true."

"Was he in conspiracy with Levy?"

"No. He left Capablanca when it closed and has an alibi for the rest of the evening."

"Have you questioned him?" Crocker shouted.

"I haven't questioned anyone," Charlie said.

"The police, I mean."

"The police have undertaken a thorough investigation and are confident in the accuracy of the outcome of that investigation, as is the district attorney." Charlie stared straight into the camera and Maddie felt he was in her living room challenging her to make something of the fact that the police investigation had started and stopped with Levy's skull cap and that, arguably, he had just pronounced Levy guilty. Charlie's harebrain was as cold and calculating as Ugolino. Angelo the Sweeper changed the game within the game. Her instincts told her more, much more, was going on than trying to force a change of venue.

"Is it true Mabi attended the funeral?" Cochoni asked.

"Everyone from Capablanca did."

Charlie pointed at Makim Obawa from the *Roxbury News*, a black weekly.

Obawa rose as if standing would elevate his question to a level of importance it would lack if asked while seated. "We in the black community know Mabi as the leader of the Trojans. Some believe the Trojans control the trade in the drugs poisoning our streets. Why would someone like him join Capablanca?"

Charlie paused to add import to his response, then repeated the question, a strategy Maddie had woodshedded her witnesses to use to buy time. "Why would someone like him join Capablanca, you ask. Perhaps, you should ask him. On a more serious note, Mr. Obawa, as you know Capablanca is a municipal facility. As such it is open to all city residents without regard to race, religion, or national origin. To refuse admission to a city resident for one of those reasons is a violation of federal law. Are you advocating the city deny membership to Mr. Mabi because of his race?"

Maddie sensed the press conference was becoming an ordeal for Charlie. Rapid eye blinking was the first sign his harebrain was struggling to free itself.

Crocker pointed his pencil at the mayor. "I understand Levy's bail hearing is Friday. How would you rule on his application for bail?"

"How would I rule? I would give the safety of the community due consideration. A person accused of murdering a young child in such a horrific way should not be released before trial."

"So you're advocating preventive detention," Crocker said.

"Preventive detention is a buzz word fuzzy-thinking liberals like the *Globe* use to deceive the public. What I advocate is common sense. Every parent, black or white, Christian or Jew, rich or poor, will sleep better knowing someone accused of such a heinous murder is not free to prey upon other innocent children. The numbers don't lie. Countless crimes are committed by people free on bail. Protecting the community is one of the reasons bail may be imposed. I wish your editors would climb down off their polo ponies and wake up to real life."

Polo ponies, Maddie thought. He's on the verge of losing it. Maddie sipped her tea. It had cooled to the point of being bitter. Not losing it, she realized. Hitting a home run. Charlie's core voters would certainly agree the *Globe* was an elitist paper pandering to readers insulated and isolated from the real world by their bank balances. Polo ponies was the perfect symbol, concise, quotable, the image of the filthy rich. It would resonate with voters happy to afford a dog for the kids, not a pure bred, a mutt. It would play well outside the city among voters who didn't read the *Globe*. It would align him with the majority who lived paycheck to paycheck. In her mind's eye, Maddie saluted him.

"Hey! Give someone else a break," Cochoni shouted. "Are you saying judges are too soft on criminals?"

In Charlie's first campaign, criminals were portrayed as victims of societal conditions beyond their control. In his most recent, they were stereotyped as predatory deviants who victimized the innocent and law-abiding. Maddie's years in legal aid had taught her Charlie was right about seventy-five percent of the time.

"If every judge spent time riding in a patrol car or, even better, walking a beat, they'd show more common sense in their application of the bail statute."

The harebrain was peeking out, fighting to liberate itself from the calm, rational man temporarily controlling it. Maddie knew this demeanor, if Charlie maintained it on the witness stand, would overwhelm the jury. If the evidence were there, no feeling person would vote to acquit the man accused of murdering his son. Yet, to her and her alone, Ugolino's machinations whispered Levy's innocence, whispered that the police knew something that pinpricked a hole in what seemed like an airtight case. Emotion would patch that hole unless she figured out some way to neutralize it. Or, found the real killer, if it weren't Levy. To ask or not to ask, that is the question.

SCLS couldn't afford to hire a private investigator, at least one capable of finding anything not beneath a flashing neon sign screaming "Look Here!" In all her years as a public defender, she had never persuaded the court to order the Commonwealth to pay for a private investigator for an indigent defendant even though the U.S. Constitution and the

Massachusetts Declaration of Rights arguably mandated it. Maddie Devlin, P.I., a wonderful title for a television series. She'd insist on a jazz score like the old *Peter Gunn* show her da watched religiously.

"Do you think Levy can get a fair trial in Boston?" Maise Davis, a television anchor, asked. Maise anchored the 6:00 and 11:00 news on the least-watched of Boston's three network television stations. Unlike most anchors, she wanted to be a field reporter, but the salary and perks of being an anchor in a market as big as Boston's were too good to trade down for being a reporter for a local station in a smaller market. Her overtures to the networks and to local stations in New York and Los Angeles had been ignored.

Charlie stepped back from the microphone so he would have to raise his voice, an old trial attorney trick Maddie recognized from her own repertoire. "As the *Christian Science Monitor* editorialized, Boston does not need another Sacco and Vanzetti. And, I would like to add, Boston does not need its own Dreyfus either."

Not the *Monitor*; the *Globe*. A slip of the tongue so minor it would not undermine Charlie's credibility as a witness at Levy's trial. Two teaspoons of sugar did not sweeten the bitterness of her tea. She spit the mouthful back into her cup.

"Mr. Mayor." The camera focused on Aaron Finegold, a reporter from *The Daily Herald*, a Jewish newspaper that circulated throughout New England. "I appreciate your sentiments, but I must remind you that on Friday leaders of the Jewish community requested police protection at synagogues during Sabbath services and you refused. Yesterday morning, a bar mitzvah in West Roxbury was disrupted when vandals threw smoke bombs through the synagogue windows. By refusing to act, is not the city condoning if not promoting anti-Semitism?"

"No one is more opposed to anti-Semitism than me, Aaron, but I can't assign police units to every synagogue. The rest of the city would go unprotected. The people of Boston are good people. Anti-Semitism is the illness of the lunatic fringe. A few smoke bombs do not a holocaust make."

The harebrain was wrestling its way to freedom. The hot television lights reflected off the sweat accumulating on Charlie's brow. He blew his nose to clear his nasal passages.

Crocker waved his hand like a first-grade boy desperate to go to the bathroom. "Do you think it proper for an elected official to permit his position on an issue of public debate to be influenced by a personal tragedy?"

The mayor's press secretary intervened. "It's been a long day."

Charlie nudged her aside. "Public debate? What public debate? It's not a matter of public debate that Boston should be safe for my son, for yours, for everyone's."

"Is Boston safe for Jewish sons?" Finegold asked.

"The arrest and prosecution of Avram Levy are not anti-Semitic acts, but rather proof justice is blind in America. Crime victims also have rights and the most important is having the person who committed the crime apprehended, brought to trial, convicted with due process, and sentenced to time to be served rather than suspended. As long as I am mayor of the city of Boston, due process will not be a shield behind which people who murder out of hatred can hide from justice. This defendant will be judged in accordance with the American system of justice, which guarantees him a fair trial before a jury of his peers and representation by competent counsel at the expense of the Commonwealth if he can't afford to pay."

Charlie paused, his mouth open as if he were debating with himself to say something else, then pointed to a woman sitting at the end of the front row. "You've been very quiet this afternoon," he said to Anne McGann, editor of the woman's page of *The Lighthouse*, the weekly newspaper published by the Archdiocese of Boston. "Do you have a question?"

"I was just thinking you and Charles must have been very close."

"Me and Bumper would go to Bruins games together, Fenway Park, watch road games on television. Movies, bowling, pizza, the kind of things you do with a kid his age."

"Did you and he ever play chess?" McGann asked.

"He'd have none of me." Charlie smiled. "I wasn't good enough."

"Did he enjoy campaigning?"

"He was a natural. Do you remember the time he stumped the Democratic Solidarity Dinner with a riddle? What did the deep sea diver have for lunch?" He paused. "Peanut butter and jellyfish sandwiches."

Everyone laughed, Charlie the loudest, until his laughter disintegrated into sobs. Tears streaked his cheeks as he struggled to rein in his emotions. Failing, he stepped back from the microphone, then hurried from the podium, from the room. His press secretary announced the press conference was over.

Maddie rewound the tape and watched it again. She couldn't get out of her mind the thought that Charlie and Ugolino knew of a weakness in the prosecution's case that might lead a thinking juror–and she only needed one–to have reasonable doubts. Perhaps Bumper's opponent across the chess board that night, Mabi, was that weakness. Perhaps Mabi was the intended beneficiary of Angelo the Sweeper's skullduggery. Had his alibi been corroborated? Charlie certainly tried to create the impression it had. But, Mabi's name had not appeared in the *Globe*? Or, the *Herald-American*. It wouldn't be beyond Charlie to plant that question with his pet reporter. Charlie hadn't flinched when Mabi's name came up. He had acknowledged the truth of the rumor the way a proud parent acknowledged a son or daughter who won a prize at the school spelling bee or science fair. Was Charlie's confidence a bluff? Or, a tell?

She admired the way Charlie was playing politics, Boston's favorite blood sport. Levy's trial would be the engine that drove Charlie's Senate campaign and nothing would be allowed to make that engine sputter. Free press coverage of Levy's trial, Charlie's and Trish's grief, would be more effective, more valuable, than millions of dollars of campaign ads extolling Charlie's positions on the issues. Any Democrat who opposed him in the primary would be condemned as heartless, or worse. The name of the hapless Republican opposing him would rarely, if ever, be mentioned. Bumper's absence from the campaign trail would speak more eloquently than any words his speechwriters could write. There was something callous and coldhearted, something odious and repellent, about Charlie riding his son's murder to the United States Senate; but Bumper was dead and nothing Charlie did on or off the campaign trail would resurrect him.

Maddie cursed the "what-ifs" parading through her mind like the marching bands on Southie's West Broadway, then East Broadway, during Boston's St. Patrick's Day Parade. At the heart of each band like an oversized bass drum on wheels was the biggest "what-if" of all, Michelle Furey. She wished she were on Furey's bed, the beady eyes of "The Screaming Pope" ogling her naked body. She wished Furey's tongue was gently lapping her labia, then burrowing into her vulva, deeper, deeper, until it found her clitoris, attacking her clit, pounding against it, as if she, Furey, wanted to dislodge it. The orgasm washed over her like the chill of plunging into the ocean at Carson Beach in early spring before the new season had warmed the water. Too quickly, the last marching band exited her mind and only the echo of the bass drum remained, fading step-by-step as it moved away from her.

Maddie clicked off the television and dumped the cold tea in the sink, running the water so it wouldn't leave a stain.

Outside, there was no relief from the heat.

-3-

The television pundits were still analyzing Charlie's performance at his news conference when a group calling itself Bumper's Brigade claimed responsibility for the wave of anti-Semitism plaguing the Greater Boston area since Bumper's murder. "We disrupted yesterday's bar mitzvah at Temple Beth Sholom in Jewtown Sharon," they proclaimed in letters to Boston's newspapers and television stations. The letters were printed or broadcast uncensored. "We broke the windows in kike stores in Hymieville Brookline. We spray painted the interior of the kosher deli on Beacon Street. We cut the sidelocks off Jews walking to Saturday morning services in Rich Jew Newton. We are not the lunatic fringe. We are the mainstream and we have only just begun."

The prisoners in Levy's cellblock tallied the incidents as if they were scoring a prize fight: Christ Lovers eight, Christ Killers zero. Outside the Charles Street Jail, a mob paraded with signs demanding Justice! Southie's teenagers marched along the route of the St. Patrick's Day parade carrying a gallows with Levy's effigy hanging from it. An occasional priest begged for tolerance, but Boston's Catholics interpreted the cardinal's silence as an endorsement of the Brigade. Ugolino bitched about the strain on the limited resources of the police department, but refused to cancel vacations or personal leave or request the governor to call out the National Guard or the president to deploy the army. Mayor Charlie issued a statement urging "the good people of Boston to reject lynch mob mentality and repudiate violence." In Boston's subways and on its busses, in the elevators of its office buildings, in its bars and beer joints, its shopping malls and supermarkets, its movie theaters, on its sidewalks, on Boston Common, in the Public Garden, at Fenway Park, at Boston Garden, people eyed each other, wondering who belonged to Bumper's Brigade, how to join. The Brigade claimed responsibility for so many anti-Semitic acts the *Boston Globe* likened it to the rats that had spread the plague throughout medieval Europe.

With each new desecration, Boston's Jewish community distanced itself further from Levy, disowning him the way status-seeking parents disown wayward children. The majority of Jews avoided social and business contacts with Gentiles so they would not have to apologize for Levy. The more militant agitated for the formation of a counter-terrorist group, a *Haganah*, to enforce the biblical dictum of an eye for an eye. One or two, such as Rabbi ben Reuben and Jacob Moskovitzky, begged the Jewish community to support Levy, but their pleas were ignored. Sacrifice the one to save the many was the consensus.

-4-

That evening, Trish Sullivan set Charlie's traditional Sunday night dinner before him, pan-fried shoulder lamb chops, a baked potato, and baby carrots. Charlie rotated his dinner menu day by day the way a diner rotated its blue plate specials. He never ate green or leafy or chicken or fish except when forced to at political fundraisers.

"None for you?" He sliced open the mottled brown potato, squeezed out a crown of white, and centered two squares of butter on it. Yellow rivulets trickled between the hot crevices and Charlie mixed his carrots in the butter pooling beside the potato. "You should eat."

"The horrible things they're doing in Charles's name. Make them stop."

"I released a statement. What more can I do?"

"They're stealing Charles from us. He deserves a better legacy than hatred. It's what people will think of when they hear his name. Is that what you want for him?"

"It'll die out." Charlie sliced the fat off his chop and dipped it in the butter.

"I wish you never found that little hat. I wish you'd thrown it down the sewer. I wish they never arrested the Jew. Charles would be able to rest in peace."

"You'll feel better when the heat breaks."

"Make it stop. If you don't, I'll tell people you're behind this Bumper's Brigade. I'll tell them it's a dirty trick to win an election."

Charlie stopped chewing. "Christ, Trish. It's beyond my control."

"You let this go on, you're no better than the Orangemen of Belfast."

Charlie shoved aside his dinner. He no longer had any appetite. If he ever had one. Maybe it was just a reflex. Eating. Trish's preparing it certainly was. A reflex. A distraction. A failure.

How to calm her down. No. Wrong question. How to help her deal with her pain. Bumper's Brigade was beyond his control. It was true, but he shouldn't have said that. He shouldn't have. He reached for the phone.

"George," Charlie said before Harriman could say hello. Charlie's voice was hoarse, as if his throat were raw and red from a day of crying. "Trish and I . . . we . . . need to know how Bumper spent his last hours. Could you talk to whoever was at Capablanca that night, anyone who might have seen or talked to Bumper?"

"I'm sure Ugolino's on it."

"I want you on it."

"I doubt I'll learn anything of value beyond what the chief's turned up."

"For me and Trish."

"Chief don't like it when people go behind his back. He'll have me pounding a beat in Roxbury."

"I'll need a head of security in Washington."

Harriman decided to take the Joe Friday approach from *Dragnet*, his favorite television cop show. He'd start with Charlie's boys, members of Capablanca who were either part of Charlie's inner circle or owed him for favors past. They'd be sympathetic, prone to exaggeration. He'd record and transcribe the interviews, neither comment nor editorialize. Just the facts, ma'am. Let Charlie make of them what he would.

Harriman would interview Patrick Reilly first. Reilly had been appointed clerk-magistrate of the Boston Municipal Court because the governor owed Mayor Charlie a favor. Egged on by his dad, Bumper always called Reilly "Spud" because his gut hung over his belt like a bag of potatoes falling off a counter.

Next, he'd interview Robert O'Malley, chief enforcement officer of Boston's Department of Inspectional Services who had played hockey with Charlie on the Holy Family High School Super 8 championship team and against him in college, O'Malley's Boston University squad losing to Charlie's Boston College team in the NCAA championship game.

Brendan Nolan, Bobby Doyle, Sheila Diggle, others.

And, Pete Kelly, an at-large member of the Boston City Council and Capablanca Club champion. Kelly had first played chess with Bumper three years ago, taught him strategy Charlie the First could never have conceived, coached him between tournament games, and never shushed him when he shouted after a good move. Bumper sucked up the respect of these men, though he could live without the Reillys, the O'Malleys, the Nolans, but not Kelly. He fed on Kelly's respect the way Charlie fed on the love of the voters.

After completing his interviews of Reilly, O'Malley, Nolan, Kelly, and others at Capablanca on the night of Bumper's murder, George Harriman prepared two documents, one a sanitized set of transcripts for Trish in whose eyes Charles was as uncorrupted as the baby Jesus, the other an uncensored set for Charlie. He figured Charlie knew about Bumper's attitude toward blacks, probably approved of it since it mirrored Charlie's as well as that of Charlie's dad, Charlie the First. The interview tapes and his notes he'd stick in the bottom of a desk drawer in the unlikely event they would be needed someday.

If Trish read the censored version of the transcripts, she would learn that Bumper and Mabi had played chess the night of Bumper's murder; that Bumper recorded the moves in his notebook; that Reilly, Kelly, Nolan, O'Malley, and several other members witnessed the match; that at closing time, Bumper and Mabi agreed to finish the match on another day; that when the Club closed Mabi and the other members left while Bumper, Virgil, the African-American janitor, and Brian Cairns, the Club manager, remained. Mabi corroborated this narrative, at least the parts concerning him. Virgil stated he left after cleaning up the game room, stopping by the African Meeting House on Beacon Hill, the first black church in Boston where he also was the custodian, to vacuum the sanctuary. Cairns confirmed the time of Virgil's departure and further stated Bumper was in the library when he locked up and left at approximately 9:30.

If Charlie read the unexpurgated version of the transcripts, he would learn about the interaction between Bumper and Mabi across the chessboard. Bumper had teased Mabi, saying he had seen Mabi before but wasn't sure where, maybe in one of the dioramas in the Museum of Science, a cave man with a club, or as one of the natives in the original *King Kong*, or as Kong himself. Bumper hadn't stopped there. He boasted to Mabi he didn't understand why his dad gave so many blacks city jobs or was nice to them at election time; but he figured what was right for his dad and his granddad was right for him. Hatred, like chess, made Bumper feel powerful, superior, and he knew at the age of nine he would always hate, that it was as natural for him as praying the Rosary.

Bumper didn't limit his racism to Mabi, but extended it to Virgil, the Club janitor. Every member knew he demanded Virgil be fired the first time he stayed past closing. Virgil had found him in the library surrounded by books, plumbing the secrets of past international grandmasters, and told him the Club was closed and he best be getting along. I'll get you fired faster than you can suck down a watermelon, Bumper threatened. Harriman explained the emptiness of Bumper's threat in his report. Funded through Boston's recreation department, Capablanca was a municipal facility like the skating rinks and swimming pools, parks and tennis courts, the Franklin Park zoo. The Club's employees, as decreed by the Massachusetts Supreme Judicial Court, were protected by civil service laws that clearly defined the reasons people could be fired or disciplined and which granted the employee right of an appeal, first in a hearing before the civil service commission, then a hearing in court. And in the case of war veterans like Virgil, a member of the 92nd Infantry Division in World War II, dubbed the Buffalo Division because it was descended from the Buffalo Soldiers of the 10th Cavalry Regiment, the added protection of the Veteran's Preference Act which gave veterans a preference for being hired for certain municipal positions.

Charlie was advised at the time by the city's law department that the best he could do was to order Brian Cairns to reprimand Virgil for insubordination—in a dignified manner so as not to provoke a Federal civil rights suit—and place a disciplinary warning in his personnel file. With a paper trail of warnings, the city solicitor concluded, in a year or so Virgil can be put out on the curb with the week's trash.

Bumper's harassment of Virgil did not stop there according to the interview transcripts which included an account of Bumper's behavior when demanding Virgil fetch sodas for him and all the spectators.

Two things intrigued Harriman when he reviewed the transcripts. First was the way Mabi ignored the insults to himself and Virgil, concentrated on his chess moves, and agreed to resume play at a later date. He puzzled at Mabi's self-control, his restraint, in the face of Bumper's conduct. It was as if Mabi was following a script, implementing a well-conceived plan, a game of chess off the board. Second was that none of the people he interviewed stated that Levy was present that night. No one placed him at the scene of the crime, a loophole in the case on which Maddie Devlin could construct a defense. One juror was all she needed.

Harriman debated with himself whether to tell Maddie. Guilt or innocence, truth or justice, in the context of this case he cared little. His concern, his only concern, was Maddie. What were the consequence to her if she won, if she lost? He owed it to Brian to do best by his daughter, to protect her, if necessary from herself. Maddie was relentless, as relentless as her da had been on Guadalcanal. When she set her mind to something, she was unyielding. Obstinacy polluted her perseverance. She lived and breathed the old Irish proverb that the road to heaven was well sign-posted, but badly lit at night. Telling her would illuminated the signposts. Brian would want him to.

"Angelo got their first," Ugolino said when Harriman pointed this out to him. "He says it's an old Jew trick–create a distraction to send us on a wild goose chase by making someone else look guilty. Evidence of the brilliance of the Jew's plan. We got our man. We've had him since the night of the murder. *Res ipsa loquitor* or whatever the fuck attorneys say when the case is open and shut."

Not all attorneys, Harriman wanted to reply, but didn't so he wouldn't have to endure one of Ugolino's infamous rants.

Chapter 4

Monday, April 13, 1981

-1-

The Monday morning sun that cast Maddie Devlin's shadow across City Hall Plaza as she walked toward the New Courthouse which housed the Social Law Library harbored no April showers. Glare reflected off the bricks, burning into her eyes, burrowing into her brain. Her head ached. Bumper's Brigade frightened her. How soon before it turned its wrath on her? She had suffered such opprobrium before, the Black Panthers picketing outside the legal aid office building, outside her apartment building, outside the courthouse; but picketing was shouting, signs waving, fists clenched in the air, so peaceful compared to the violence of Bumper's Brigade.

The Vancini case. Tony Vancini, an anti-busing militant, had been accused of sabotaging the brakes on a school bus carrying black children from Roxbury to the North End. It crashed into a Jersey barrier. One fatality. Several serious injuries. Refusing to be intimidated, Maddie had persevered, persuading the jury, eight Caucasians, one African-American, two Asians, a Hispanic, that the evidence was insufficient to find Vancini guilty beyond a reasonable doubt. She had used an alibi defense. Vancini was at the home of Louise Day Hicks who had leveraged her opposition to forced busing into a seat on the Boston School Committee plotting legal strategy with other militants. Six witnesses including Hicks corroborated his testimony. A defensible verdict, well within the legal definition of "beyond a reasonable doubt"; but Boston's black community which thought the alibi a lie and the testimony perjury didn't see it that way. The jury had passed judgment and it was not for Maddie to second guess them publicly. Privately, she had her doubts. Technically, she fell within the black letter legal definition of co-conspirator, she and the Suffolk County DA who had assigned the trial to an attorney so freshly minted the ink on the certificate manifesting his admission to the bar had yet to dry. Once again, Birmingham north. Now, many trials later, she didn't want to think about how Bumper's Brigade would react to Levy's acquittal. She didn't want to be its co-conspirator.

Maddie paused to sit on the wall of the waterless fountain beside the Kennedy Federal Building, the JFK Building in local slang, dangling her feet where water once bubbled. The water spigots, black like dead branches in the aftermath of a forest fire, reached skyward, praying for rain. A dead pigeon, heat swollen, lay beside one of the drains. She saw herself as that pigeon, left to rot in the ungodly heat. She could rationalize risking all on a winnable case, but an unwinnable case? Martyrdom had a perverse appeal to her, but not the type of martyrdom Levy would confer.

She had had unwinnable cases in the past. Too many to count. Those she plea bargained, negotiating a disposition more lenient than the sentence that would be imposed after a guilty verdict. Trials were like sand in the gears of the criminal justice system; plea bargains the lubricant that flushed the sand from the gears. The more burdensome a trial was on the prosecution or court calendars, the greater the motivation to dispose of a case as quickly as possible, a motivation which often resulted in more lenient dispositions. The reverse was also true, a guilty verdict after a lengthy trial often resulted in a sentence much harsher than what could have been plea bargained. The majority of judges understood this and played the game, especially since a judge's performance was evaluated based on the number of cases closed, not the quality of justice dispensed.

Most plea bargains Maddie entered in the win column. Most of her clients were better off than if they had gone to trial. But not all. She also plea bargained the hopeless cases, the guaranteed convictions, the cases where the prosecution's evidence was air tight. Those she entered in the loss column because they did little or nothing for her client other than avoiding the spectacle of a trial. Plea-bargaining Levy would be such a loss, maybe not in the eyes of the other lawyers in the office, but in her eyes. Unless Levy did it. That would place her on the doorstep of the moral outhouse occupied by mob and gang lawyers, one foot over the threshold. Bumper's Brigade would win whether Levy did it or not. She felt she was standing in front of a firing squad like her grand da, her innocence or guilt irrelevant to her execution. She gathered her strength and continued to the Social Law Library.

What did Ugolino know that she didn't? Why is Angelo the Sweeper leading the investigation? Everything about Bumper's death, its timing, its crime scene, its method, reeked of intricate design, everything except the skull cap embroidered with

Levy's name. The neatness of the Capablanca library—every book in its proper place, the chess men resting in their ranks while awaiting their next players, the chairs nesting against their tables unmoved since the last checkmate—created a sense of order within the library which made the skull cap, like Bumper's body, too adventitious a circumstance. Without it, there would be no defendant, no indictment, no trial. It was the strongest element and weakest link in the prosecution's case. Attack it directly, create doubt in the minds of the jury, in the mind of one juror, regarding its presence on the library floor, transform it from the confession of a murderer to the symbol of an innocent man being framed and an acquittal or at least a hung jury was possible. More than possible if she could pull a Perry Mason and finger the real killer. If there were a real killer other than Levy.

Harriman had told her no one placed Levy at the crime scene, at least not prior to the Club's closing. Ugolino, Harriman also said, knows this. Bumper's chess game with Mabi had adjourned, but Mabi had an alibi. Levy didn't. Neither did Levy have any reason to return to Capablanca after it closed other than to kill Bumper. The prosecution would crow this point repeatedly. Whatever logic she had on her side would be as effective as a pea shooter against the howitzer of emotion the prosecution had in its arsenal.

One juror out of twelve. In Boston, a possibility, more remote than she was willing to admit to herself; west of Worcester, unlikely as long as the trial did not end up in Hampshire County where a faculty member of Smith College or Mt. Holyoke College or Amherst College or the University of Massachusetts might sneak onto the jury. This must be why Ugolino wanted a change of venue. But he wouldn't assign the investigation to Angelo the Sweeper if it were this simple. She had to do better.

The uncertainty of her motivation for defending Levy unsettled her. Her motivation was like an arc of electric current jumping between two electrodes, one being her desire to reconcile with Trish to end the blood feud between her side of the family and Trish's, the other her need to avenge two generations of wrongs, reconciliation be damned. Her uncertainty trapped her between competing fiduciary duties. One to Levy as his attorney. A second to Trish as her cousin. A third to her grand da Michael. A fourth to herself. Frohling had sprung the trap, refusing her request to recuse her.

"You're the best we've got," he had said. "If you really want out, you know where the door is."

It was the unknown on the other side of the door that frightened her. For all her bravado in the courtroom, SCLS in many ways was like a protective cocoon outside of which she feared she would not function as effectively. If only Michelle Furey would welcome her, Maddie, into her law office as she had her bedroom, but an enduring law partnership needed a stronger foundation than passionate sex.

Suppressing these thoughts, Maddie signed into the Social Law Library, one floor below the courtrooms and chambers of the Massachusetts Supreme Judicial Court. Trial attorneys deep in their cups joked about the Freudian symbolism of this arrangement. To Maddie, it was more mythological. Like Greek gods, the SJC judges reigned in their pantheon while attorneys mined the law books beneath their feet in search of sacrifices that would buy their votes. Or, oracles to explain them. Maddie needed more than an altar of sacrifices or a Delphic virgin. She had to do better.

Michelle Furey had volunteered to help with the legal research, but Maddie had demurred. "I read my own cases," Maddie had explained, "refusing help even from attorneys with criminal defense experience. Cases have nuances which are lost when court opinions are reduced to summaries, opening paragraphs recitation of the facts, then the question or questions of law before the court, the holding or holdings, important dicta if any, a reprise of the court's reasoning. Law students, at least the bright ones, produced creditable case summaries, but the real import of a case, its relevance, its usefulness, lay in its nuances which often are often found only in the silences between the lines. Legal research for Levy's case will be a hunt for nuance."

The words had spewed out of her to hide the other reason, the real reason, she had refused Furey's help. Her feelings for Furey scared her. For them to be able to work together, whether on the Levy case or in the same legal practice, she had to overcome her fear that in Furey's mind their relationship was built on lust. Either that or neuter her feelings as if she were a cat that had to be spayed. She hoped when the Levy case was over, she'd have time to sort this out, if there was still something to sort out.

Now, she distracted herself by concentrating on the legal research she needed to do. Religion and murder did not intersect very often in American law, certainly not as frequently as murder and money, murder and sex, murder and race, murder and revenge, murder and thrill killing; but, maybe, somewhere there were cases, a case, one case, in which a killer acting under the spell of intense religious fervor, a zealot perhaps, was acquitted, whether on the ground of insanity or the Establishment or Free Exercise clauses of the First Amendment. California, where ritual slayings and satanic cults were as common as stalled freeway traffic, might provide precedents. The Salem witch trials, some of whose original records were still extant, merited investigation. That cult in Florida that chopped off the heads of roosters . . . she wished she remembered its name. She had to do better.

She slogged through her research, the dust from books unopened for decades accumulating on her fingers, smudging her blouse and skirt, streaking her cheeks and forehead, clogging her pores, causing her to cough and clear her throat every few minutes. She winced at the paper cuts appearing at the tips of her fingers. Stacks of books imprisoned her in a bunker of words. The sameness of the cases, barren of useful legal precedent relevant to Levy's case, caused her to question the quality of her research. Had she missed a case? Had she misread them? Overlooked a subtlety which would distinguish the precedents arrayed against her? Or, was it the insanity of her quest? She had to do better.

Several hours later, Maddie walked along Tremont Street following the red line in the sidewalk that guided tourists along the Freedom Trail. She paused at the Old Granary Burying Ground, the last resting place of John Hancock and Samuel Adams. Each headstone, as colonial custom dictated, had a death's head carved into it, albeit so benign in appearance it bid welcome to the grave the way an innkeeper bade welcome to a traveler after a long, hard journey. She did not understand the quirk of fate that caused some to be buried in the Old Granary, where the letters on the stones were still crisp and clean and easily read after two hundred years, and others of equal importance to be buried a few hundred yards away in King's Chapel, where the same two centuries of weather polished the lives of the dead into a smooth anonymity. She wondered if the same quirk of fate operated in Traitor's Hell, the cemetery where her grand da Michael was buried. What of the graves of her namesakes, Mary and Ann Devlin? She hoped the weather had not consigned them to the ages, anonymous in death but for a jail register on display for tourists. As for her grave, she did not know whether she wanted its market to exist in 2181, its lettering legible. She prayed Elizabeth's with its bas relief of a baby lamb would.

Maddie's da had drummed the Devlin family history into her since she was old enough to read and since then she had lived within that history the way the faithful live within a belief in God. The thought of Elizabeth's grave, of her grave in one hundred years, cast her back to another Devlin grave. Another Ann. Revered was this Ann Devlin in the memories of the people of Aughrim, wherever they may be, because Ireland did not shun its birth mothers, just its fathers, like her grand da Michael. The eighteenth of September, 1851. Glasnevin Cemetery. On the Finglas Road. O'Connell Circle. The Cross of Ardboe. Ardboe. For centuries, the historic home of the Devlins. On the western shores of Lough Neagh. The Tyrone shore. "Crux Mea Stella" – The Cross is My Star. The Devlin motto from the coat of arms granted to one of the original O'Doibhilins in the twelfth century Anno Domini. The O'Doibhilins, now the Devlins. Maybe, Maddie thought, if she changed her name to O'Doibhilin, no, to Smith or Jones, her luck would change. A piece of paper filed in the probate court and she would be a new person, a person liberated from her family history. She had to do better.

She cursed the heat.

-2-

Maddie skipped lunch. Once again, the heat had melted her appetite. According to a story in that morning's *Herald-American*, the food carts and restaurants where Boston's office workers usually lunched had suffered significant reductions in business during the heat wave. No one had the energy to eat.

At the Charles Street Jail, a matron, Irene Blodgett, passed her through security with a scowl, a pat-down and a thorough search of her purse, and briefcase.

"Shave for court," Maddie told Levy whose beard was untrimmed and scruffy, an ascot of horsehair.

"If you were Jewish you would know my beard is a sign of respect for Hashem."

"Where do you live?" she asked.

"You should know that already."

"I ask the questions. You answer them. Those are the rules of the game even when I know the answers to the questions I'm asking." She started to add she wanted to observe his demeanor, his body language, as he answered her questions to gauge how he would behave on the witness stand; but decided that doing so might cause him to modify his behavior. She needed Levy in his natural state, whatever that might be.

"I want a Jewish attorney."

Levy's refusal to cooperate made her feel like an interrogator trying to squeeze information out of a member of the resistance. She wished torture were an option. "I asked where do you live?"

"*Traif.*"

"Meaning."

"Vile. Polluted. Not fit to be looked upon by the eyes of Hashem."

"I've had worse Irish curses thrown at me."

Levy pulled at his beard the way someone who never had grown a beard before does. "Not an Irish curse. Not a Jewish curse. Not any curse."

"I'm glad we cleared that up." She raised the decibel level of her voice to that of a thunderclap so close it hurt the ears. "Now, where the fuck do you live?"

Levy recoiled like a young child fearful for his life. His face contorted. He inhaled sharply, then jettisoned his silence like a child afraid of the storm. "Chelsea," he stammered. "Near the Orange Street *shul.*"

"*Shul?*"

"Synagogue."

Maddie scribbled notes on her legal pad, placing his replies in quotation marks. She usually taped her client interviews, but she worried Levy would play to the microphone rather than act naturally. "Since when?"

"Last September."

"Mother?"

"Of blessed memory."

"Father?"

"The same."

"Why did you move to Boston?"

"To study with Rabbi ben Reuben."

"Work?"

"A janitor in a funeral home." He picked at the skin around his fingernails.

She showed him the photocopy of the last page of Bumper's spiral notebook again. "Your handwriting?" She pointed to the notations of the last several moves.

"No."

"Positive?"

Levy muttered something under his breath in a language Maddie assumed was Hebrew. The tone of his voice, the dismissive look on his face, suggested to her it was an epithet. She interpreted his demeanor as a yes.

"Any priors?"

"What are priors?"

"Ever been in trouble before?"

"Always."

"Ever been accused of a crime? Ever been convicted?"

"Will I be released for *seder*?"

"No."

"I did not murder that child. If I am convicted, it will be for a greater purpose."

"Which is?"

"It is not for me to question Hashem."

"You talk like God decreed your arrest, trial, conviction, and sentence."

Levy sat in silence, his ears sewn shut against her words, in Maddie's mind the posture of a cause-driven fanatic. Asked and answered, she thought, the objection she raised when opposing counsel persisted in repeated his question in multiple disguises.

More notes, more quotation marks. Little new information, but she had learned what she needed to know, the answer to the question every trial attorney, both criminal and civil, grapples with: whether to have the client testify. Put Levy on the stand and his subservience to a higher power will convict him regardless of what evidence there may be of his innocence, regardless of how much doubt she could create about how his skull cap ended up on the library floor. To the jury, he would be a true believer, right or wrong determined by whether his act advanced his belief, a fanatic in the root meaning of the word. The witness stand would be his pulpit. Most fanatics were also martyrs and martyrs craved punishment for their beliefs the way addicts craved their next fix, the way penitents suffering the scourge of the plague craved flagellation.

She would never gain his acquittal if he testified. Nor a mistrial. Nor reversible error. The jury would convict him faster than the IRB condemned her grand da. And, perhaps, just as wrongly, though she was skeptical.

A plea bargain was her only viable strategy. Convince the prosecution she had a winnable case, harp on the fact no one placed him at the crime scene, and negotiate the lightest sentence she could; but, first, she would have to persuade Moskovitzky and Rabbi ben Reuben to endorse her approach, something that might prove more difficult than finessing the DA. And, she would have to resolve her outhouse dilemma.

Levy wrapped the sidelocks beside his left ear around one of his fingers. "You think I did it."

She flinched, then struggled to regain her composure. Levy did not react.

A statement, not a question. No hint of accusation in his voice. Nor anger. No sign of the frustration so common when the client realized that she knew he was guilty. Levy's profile, well-educated, well-read, religious, Jewish, meek yet superior, did not fit the profile of a murderer; but this profile made him a logical suspect for this unique murder. His own conduct reinforced this logic. So what-if the skull cap seemed out of place at the murder scene. Every murder had its own internal logic and Levy's fanaticism, his subservience to God, to his fate, whether real or feigned, was the logic of this one, a logic powerful enough to overcome his absence from Capablanca the night of Bumper's murder. She gathered her papers.

"I have to prepare for Friday's bail hearing."

The solid steel door slammed shut behind her. The rail-thin guard with the key-jangling hip escorted her down a corridor to a sliding door of steel bars controlled by an electric switch in a distant room. The jangle of the keys, the steel bars, the remote-control door, all dissolved the reasonableness of her doubt in an acid bath of emotion.

-3-

Carmelita Delgado, the receptionist at Suffolk County Legal Services, waved a pink message slip. "Jeffrey Mosca expects you at seven."

"Let him expect all he wants," Maddie said.

"He said it's urgent."

"What isn't?"

"Don't take it out on the messenger."

"Give me better messages."

The Mosca firm, like most of the big Boston law firms, donated the labor of new associates and summer interns to Suffolk County Legal Services and other legal aid organizations to do grunt work, legal research, draft memos to be wrestled into briefs, handle arraignments. She had met Mosca at the fundraisers those firms took turns hosting. He practiced law on Oriental rugs while she huddled with her clients in the corners of dimly lit courthouse corridors or sat on wooden benches beneath which cigarette butts, coffee containers, cellophane wrappers, wads of gum, collected like ancient artifacts that would define this civilization to future archeologists. Mosca negotiated multi-million-dollar transactions while she plea bargained multi-year prison terms. He closed deals over cognac at private clubs with views of Boston harbor while she closed deals over cold, bitter coffee purchased at the concession run by the Massachusetts Commission for the Blind. She doubted he had ever been inside a courtroom while she lived inside courtrooms so crowded defendants and their victims often shared the same hallway, the same benches, while they waited for their cases to be called. She had broken up more than one fight in those hallways. His office coat closet was probably larger than her office cubicle, sixty-four square feet of space encircled by portable metal partitions.

She phoned from the conference room because it had floor-to-ceiling walls.

"Mosca, Baruch, and Cohn."

The receptionist spoke with a clipped British accent. Her nasal pronunciation denuded the names of ethnic identity, making them sound as Yankee as Ropes & Gray or Choate, Hall & Stewart. When one of Boston's oldest Yankee law firms imported its receptionist from England, the Mosca firm did likewise as if the accent of the person who answered the phone bespoke the quality of law the firm practiced or the ranking of its lawyers in Boston's social hierarchy. Maddie understood how money and privilege enabled these firms to obtain green cards when the immigration service routinely deported her clients whose accents were Hispanic or whose names ended in vowels or whose skin was the wrong shade. She resented that she and her clients were not created equal.

Mosca's secretary came on the line. "Attorney Mosca will meet with you at seven this evening. He does not brook tardiness."

"What about no-shows?" She hung up before the secretary could reply.

After finishing the first draft of the brief for Levy's bail hearing, Maddie freshened up in the SCLS ladies' room, then wandered around downtown Boston. The early evening air retained the day's heat. Sunset would not bring the steep drop in temperatures that normally accompanied April hot spells. Downtown Crossing smelled like a fast-food restaurant, the stink from each grease palace more nauseating than the last. Her appetite had not returned so she bought a coffee and donut for supper, a plain old-fashioned so she could dunk it. Her curiosity about Mosca's call dissolved her defiance as quickly as her coffee dissolved the donut. Shortly before seven, she signed in with the lobby security guard at the Massachusetts Bay National Bank Building where the Mosca firm had its offices on the top thirteen floors. Marble, marble everywhere, she thought, but not a Michelangelo to be found. Someday, if she had the money, she would replace her grand da Michael's stone with a marble mausoleum, one visible from outside the walls of Traitor's Hell, a memorial to her grand da, a monument to Clancy's venal treachery.

At the sixty-fifth floor, a receptionist eyed her up and down with disdain, as if Maddie had come to clean the bathrooms and lacked only a mop and bucket. Maddie straightened her posture until she stood as erect as the parochial school student she once was. She knew she looked like an overripe lettuce leaf, wilted and withered. She could smell herself. She didn't care. "You will," Maddie said, "escort me to Attorney Mosca's office." With lifted head and military bearing, the receptionist led the way through the labyrinth of the law firm. Maddie marveled at the way the receptionist's body language told Maddie to go fuck herself.

Maddie accepted Mosca's handshake. It was decisive, as if he were trying to demonstrate he considered women to be the equal of men. Yet, his eyes concentrated on her breasts. Let him lust. It would add color to his cheeks, which had the fluorescent pallor of a man who lived indoors. The soft light of his desk lamp added a hint of jaundice and reflected a shine off his gold glen plaid suit, custom tailored to disguise his bulk. No woman would include him in her erotic dreams.

Mosca's office, Maddie estimated, would hold ten legal aid cubicles while his desk would not fit in hers. The fabric on the chairs, couch, and curtains matched the accent wall-paper behind the desk: stripes of varying widths in six shades of brown. The view looked north and she wondered if he could see New Hampshire on a clear day. Miniature trees flanked the couch where he gestured for her to sit. Living, not plastic. Their leaves smelled of furniture polish.

Mosca leaned against the edge of his desk, the coffee table between them. "We're opening a Washington office and need an experienced trial attorney to fill out the staff. We expect a lot of white-collar defense work."

"We don't get many white collars at legal aid."

"You'll start at $75,000 a year, which gives you credit in our salary structure for four years' prior experience."

"I have eight."

"If things work out, we'll raise you to the level of an eighth-year associate on your first anniversary."

"That leaves me a year behind."

"You'll have a three-year contract with generous relocation expenses. You'll start Monday and have a month's orientation here before moving to Washington."

"I have a bail hearing Friday."

"Monday is after Friday."

"The court won't let me withdraw unless my replacement files an appearance."

"I've secured one. Howard Kaplan."

"Never heard of him."

Mosca tapped a sterling silver letter opener against his palm. Its reflection danced on the ceiling above Maddie's head. "He's well qualified."

"A hundred fifty thousand and a full partnership after two years. Without capital contribution."

"This is not a negotiation."

"At least we see eye to eye on one thing."

"A hundred fifty thousand and consideration after five. You'll write your own letter of recommendation if we ask you to leave."

"What if he's innocent?"

"Don't play defense attorney with me."

"I don't play defense attorney. I am a defense attorney."

"I want your answer in the morning."

"It's always morning somewhere in the world."

The receptionist walked Maddie to the elevators with heightened disdain. The way Mosca refused to rise to the bait of her smart-ass answers, his doubling her starting salary after minimal provocation, told her this was a more desperate bribe than the Superior Court judgeship Ugolino had offered. The rabbi and Moskovitzky had been right. About Mosca. About Boston's Jewish community. About what was really at stake in Levy's defense. Where were the Jews, she wondered, who taught the Irish how to fight?

The elevator's descent roiled her sense of balance. She supported herself against the back wall. Irish history, her family history, was replete with traitors. Anonymous men who informed on her namesakes. Others buried in time. Clancy, who sold his honor for a bottle of Bushmills. What of Jewish history? What of Jeffrey Mosca? What was the moral difference between a bottle of Bushmills and a new life in a new city with a new career and, in a few years, more money in the bank than her da earned in his lifetime?

She gripped the railing that circled the interior of the elevator. Mosca's logic was straightforward. Jews needed Levy to be convicted and receive a long prison sentence. In the public's eyes, he was guilty. That was the only reality the public would accept. The public's perception of how criminal law worked was that the guilty went free on technicalities, not because they were innocent. If this happened, the public would only see that a Jew got away with the horrific murder of a Catholic boy. Jews everywhere would suffer. To quell this anti-Semitism, he must be represented by Jewish counsel, convicted at a trial everyone thought fair, and severely punished. Only then would Levy be dismissed as a freak, an aberration, a lunatic. Only then would the alliance between Christians and Jews in Boston, so profitable to both, be rebuilt. Everyone would win but Levy.

She struggled to dodge the stampede of her thoughts, all as irrational, as aberrational, as the heat wave. Levy would be Kaplan's problem. She would be able to look the rabbi and Moskovitzky in the eye. She would be a new person with a new life without having to change her name from Devlin to O'Doibhilin. Or, to Smith or Jones.

But, what of Trish? Would she accept Levy's conviction as the final word? Or, would she believe his murderer still roamed Boston's angry streets? She was a jury of one and for Maddie the only juror who mattered. Maddie vacillated; now convinced Trish would see it her way, now convinced Trish wouldn't. Had she done better?

As Maddie exited the air-conditioned office tower, it was like stepping into an oven so unlike the April of Elizabeth's death. That April had been cold, wintry, snowy, so much snow the Red Sox cancelled their home opener and the rest of the first home stand. The buds which had blossomed and bloomed during a late March warm spell had withered and died. Over time, Maddie deluded herself into believing that in a season-able April her daughter would not have died. She blamed God for the ill-seasoned weather and stopped believing in Him the moment she saw Elizabeth's tiny corpse swaddled in white in the bassinette in the hospital morgue. As the Aprils passed, her attitude softened, not because she once again believed in God for she never would, but because she needed the familiarity of the rites and rituals of the Church to fill the void. She resumed attending Mass, taking communion, confessing by rote, her personal variation of Pascal's wager.

Were she alive, Elizabeth would be stepping into the world of a teenage girl now, a world of puppy love, music, cos-metics, clothes, movie stars, a world of experimenting, going to dances in the junior high school gym, stealing kisses in the stairwells, a world of movie dates and hanging around shop-ping malls, a world of fighting with her mother because that's what girls that age did, that's what Maddie had done. Would her daughter's first date have been as awkward as hers? Or as embarrassing? Hers, Maddie's, first kiss, Duncan Siward, teeth tightly clenched, lips tightly closed, the pain of braces grinding against the soft, pulpous inside of her mouth. Her second kiss, also Duncan Siward, puckering like a fish darting after flakes of food at feeding time, soft and gentle as she always dreamed it would be. But the dream ended and years later she could not help but think that if the dream had continued her daughter would have been named Patricia or Rose or Maud or some other good Irish name rather than after two English queens. And that she would be alive today. And Michelle Furey would be nothing but another probate attorney.

Chapter 5

Tuesday, April 14, 1981

Maddie sat on the toilet trying to squeeze out whatever was constipating her. She had assumed she would be awake all night, but had slept a deep, dreamless, death-like sleep as if she did not have a care in the world. No visions of Elizabeth. None of Traitor's Hell, nor Kilmainham. No visions of Master Devlin, nor Grand da Michael. No visions of her namesakes, Mary and Ann. Her subconscious had made her decision. After flushing an empty toilet, she telephoned her acceptance to Mosca, whose feigned enthusiasm could not mask his condescension. Fuck him! Fuck Boston! She would insist on a written contract, one on her terms, the money guaranteed for the full term of the contract regardless of when she left or under what circumstances, the letter of recommendation subject to her approval, and St. Patrick's Day off as a paid holiday. Being Irish, she was always on alert for the double cross.

Before going to her office, she visited Rabbi ben Reuben to advise him she intended to resign the case after the bail hearing. The rabbi sat quietly at his desk, his white hair a halo against the black bindings of the books on the shelves behind him.

"Jacob's grandson has found a Jewish lawyer to replace me. Howard Kaplan. Levy fights me. Says I'm unclean. *Traif,* he calls me. Says he wants a Jewish attorney. It's like a broken record. He wants a Jewish attorney. I wouldn't dare risk putting him on the witness stand. Maybe, he'd be a better witness for Kaplan. Jacob can tell you how essential cooperation is."

"As is," the rabbi said, "the lawyer's belief in her client's innocence."

"Not as much as knowledge of her client's guilt."

"Avram told me when I delivered his dinner last night." The rabbi clasped and unclasped his hands, sliding his fingers back and forth through the valleys between his knuckles. "Doubt is a natural human condition. Jacob and I would be lying if we denied having a scintilla of doubt about Avram's innocence. Yet, we do not abandon him."

For decades, the pain in the rabbi's hands had deadened his emotions, his feelings. Now, that pain gave them life. The last five days had awakened him from the fog of complacency created by living in the United States. It was a thin veneer, he now realized, thin and easily pierced, that shielded Jews in America from the landslide of hatred that had buried them alive in Europe and Russia. He wished he had saved his yellow star from the old country. In Boston, he would wear it as an act of defiance, of rebellion, of assertion of his identity. If the *goy* have Bumper's Brigade, let the Jews have the Yellow Stars.

"Who is this Howard Kaplan?" the rabbi asked. "A *schmuck*. A check casher. Jacob's grandson is convinced you will win. He fears Jews will pay for Avram's acquittal. In reality they, we, will pay for his conviction." The rabbi paused, gathering his thoughts. "Let me share a story with you from the *Talmudic* commentaries."

Maddie shifted in her chair, suddenly very conscious of the way the wire supports of her bra cups chafed against her skin. In parochial school, she had squirmed whenever the nuns told Bible stories as a way of drilling one religious lesson or another into her. More than once the smack of a ruler against her open palm had stilled her. The plot never changed. Sin. Punishment. Redemption, sometimes. Repetition had dulled the impact of those Bible stories, her familiarity with them breeding her contempt for them. She cloaked her face with a mask of attentiveness. She had been compelled to listen then; she was compelled to listen now.

"Hundreds of years ago in central Europe," the rabbi began, "a learned man named Solomon traveled from village to village answering questions that stumped local rabbis. A man of simple tastes, he refused all payment for his wisdom except the necessities of life, plain food for nourishment, sturdy clothes for warmth, and dry straw for bedding. He wore a simple gabardine coat and a black fur hat, gifts from a tailor for whom he had solved a difficult problem. Mendel, the lazy son of a local rabbi who sought to become known as a sage so he could accept the gold Solomon refused, stole Solomon's hat and coat and rushed to a village at the far end of the province where he posed as Solomon and received great riches for dispensing platitudes to the unsuspecting."

Maddie rotated her shoulders. She wished she could unclasp her bra. The fact she had not heard this story before did not ease her discomfort.

"The duke who ruled this province was a virulent anti-Semite much like those who have risen up against Avram. When word of a new wise man reached him, he contrived a test. Jew, the duke said to Mendel who posed as the wise man. Give me your fur hat. The duke dropped two pieces of folded paper into it, saying one was blank, the other had the word 'Jew' written on it. Pick the blank paper, the duke challenged Mendel, and I shall reward you with your life. Pick the other and your life shall be forfeit to me."

Maddie interrupted. "There is an Irish variation of this story. It was not a duke, but a British royal. It was not a Jew, but an Irish priest."

Rabbi ben Reuben frowned. "Dressed as a beggar, Solomon saw through the duke's subterfuge but dared not intervene. Mendel, unwilling to risk his life, called forward the beggar, not recognizing him as Solomon. Your test is too easy, Mendel said to the duke. This poor wretch shall draw for me. If the beggar drew the blank, Mendel would claim it for his own. If not, Mendel would quickly draw the remaining piece. Mendel didn't believe the duke would slay a wise man when he could slay a beggar."

"In the Irish version," Maddie said, "the priest realized neither piece was blank and took one from the hat and swallowed it. The remaining piece, he said to the royal, is written upon."

"As did Solomon," the rabbi said. "The duke pinned a yellow star over Mendel's heart and remanded him to the custody of his archers. Solomon he rewarded with Mendel's fur hat." The rabbi removed his half-glasses and wiped the corners of his eyes with a tissue. The light from his lamp reflected off the moisture in his eyes, turning them into miniature spotlights likes the ones that ornamented the walls that encircled the Charles Street jail. "What was the moral of your story, Ms. Devlin?"

Maddie hesitated. It had been a bedtime story her da told her when she was a little girl. If it had a moral, he never said.

He just told it and she listened and he kissed her on the forehead and wished her pleasant dreams. Morals were for fairy tales like *The Three Little Pigs*.

"The kabbalist," the rabbi said, "teaches Hashem ordained for the Jewish people to survive as many traitors as there are stars in the firmament before the Messiah will come." The rabbi paused. "Your resignation will send a message that Avram is guilty and incite Bumper's Brigade to greater violence. The Solomons will survive. The Mendels will die by their own tricks. Which are you?" The rabbi rose. "Excuse me. It is time for services."

Outside, the temperature had risen two degrees since sunset and Bumper's Brigade claimed responsibility for pelting diners at a kosher restaurant with dead pigeons.

Chapter 6

Wednesday, April 15, 1981

The oppressive crematory heat was Commissioner Dante Ugolino's most effective weapon for maintaining law and order. The weather consumed people, incinerating their life force, even those in Bumper's Brigade. For the first time since Bumper Sullivan's death, John Chancellor, Dan Rather, and Frank Reynolds did not originate the national television network news from Boston. *The New York Times* which had doubled the size of its Boston bureau reduced it to normal staffing levels. Both wire services scaled back. The *Washington Post* recalled its reporters but for a stringer a few years out of journalism school.

Avram Levy still dominated the local television news, radio newscasts, and front pages of both Boston newspapers which seemed to be competing for a Pulitzer Prize for salaciousness. The *Globe* ran a feature article about a college professor who sued the school where he taught for violating his First Amendment rights, freedom of speech, freedom of religion, by denying him tenure because he argued that vampirism among Jews was genetic, much like hooked noses and avarice.

The *Herald-American* countered with an opinion poll it commissioned: Ninety-one per cent of the mothers of school age children who were Catholic felt Massachusetts should reinstate the death penalty for crimes like Levy's and that he should be executed if convicted, as did seventy-four per cent of all mothers with young children. The pollster did not disclose whether Jewish mothers were included in its sample.

Not necessary, Ugolino told Rabbi ben Reuben when the rabbi asked for an increased police presence at synagogues and temples during the period commencing with Levy's bail hearing on Friday morning and ending with Passover's second *seder* Sunday evening.

Weather reports predicted the heat would continue unabated.

Chapter 7

Friday, April 17, 1981

-1-

Judge Simon Gomita banged his gavel to quiet the courtroom so that Avram Levy's bail hearing could begin. Appointed to the bench in 1967, Gomita heard only criminal matters and had earned the respect of both defense counsel and prosecutors. He knew the law, let attorneys try their own cases, and didn't reject legal arguments because of their novelty. The chief justice of the Superior Court routinely assigned the most sensitive cases to him because he was thorough, discreet, and rarely reversed on appeal. Exempted from military service because of a medical deferment, he had the physical stature of a man who could still fit into the uniform he never wore and an intellectual curiosity about military tactics and strategy ranging from *The Battle of Algiers* to Sun Tzu's *The Art of War* to Homer's *Iliad* to the latest theories of mutual assured destruction. *Dr. Strangelove* was his favorite movie.

The courtroom's air conditioning did not temper the emotions of the mob that competed for the few seats reserved for the public. People crawled over each other like rats swarming through the tunnels of Boston's archaic subway system. An elbow to the sides here, a kick to the ankle there, and another body shoehorned itself in, adding to the sweat and stink of the overcrowded room. Talk of a public lynching suppurated the air, one noose for Levy, a second for Maddie Devlin. The more militant argued for the guillotine or the rack or both.

Boston's Tactical Police Force, in riot gear including masks in case they had to deploy tear gas, patrolled the courtroom and adjacent corridors. The Massachusetts State Police had responsibility for the rest of the building. Observers from the U.S. Department of Justice monitored the hearing, equating Boston with Birmingham or Jackson and Massachusetts with Alabama or Mississippi in the early 1960s, another of the aftermaths of court-ordered busing. Although Massachusetts had abolished the death penalty, one of the many concerns of the Department of Justice was that someone would take the law into his own hands and that neither Boston nor the Commonwealth would exert itself to prevent vigilante justice. Mayor Charlie did not understand how federal monitors could prevent an assassination, but he understood his constituency and knew that if secession were put to a vote, it would easily carry the city. His private polls showed him a lock to be Massachusetts's next United States Senator.

A spectator scrawny to the point of emaciation with long stringy hair tipped with beads and wearing a Free Bobby Sands tee shirt mouthed an obscenity and gave Maddie the finger. Bobby Sands. She had lost count of the number of days into his hunger strike. From Robert Emmet to Bobby Sands to me, she thought, the line seemed more direct than ever. Before the spectator could lower his hand, Gomita slammed down his gavel and ordered him jailed for contempt of court, remanding him to custody pending a hearing scheduled for Wednesday, May 13th, which, Gomita said with a loud, clear voice and fear-inducing snarl, was the earliest opening on his calendar.

About one hour into Levy's bail hearing, Assistant District Attorney Don Miguel Bonturo called Professor Husam al din al-Saffah as his next witness. Maddie had anticipated this, prepared for it, but not for al-Saffah's guise. A dark, gaunt figure, cloaked in black, mounted the witness stand. The glow of the whites of his eyes exaggerated the coal pits of his pupils. A jagged scar split his cheek like a lightning bolt in the night sky or a firebreak in a forest. He reminded Maddie of the devil in "Night on Bald Mountain" and the weeks of nightmares she had after seeing *Fantasia.*

"I object, Your Honor," she said before al-Saffah settled into the chair on the witness stand. "Relevancy."

Gomita harrumphed, one of the warnings he gave counsel when his patience was beginning to fray. "Mr. Bonturo."

"The witness is a professor of Semitic studies who is an expert in comparative religions." Bonturo's head squatted on his shoulders as if his neck had been surgically excised. His face was pie-shaped, flat, two dimensional, his nose and the grotto between his lower lip and the point of his chin the only features with a third dimension. People called him "Fireplug" and joked about dogs mistaking him for a hydrant. Others spread rumors he worked his way through law school as a tackling dummy for the New England Patriots. Those with pretensions said he looked like an early Picasso cubist portrait. Bonturo did not realize he was being insulted. To him, being ragged was an expression of camaraderie and a sign of his acceptance into the fraternity of attorneys. "He will testify," Bonturo continued, "about the peculiar historical and religious aspects of this crime."

"This is a bail hearing," Maddie said. "Not a trial."

"Let me review the bail statute," Gomita said, bending over a statute book taken from the shelf behind him.

The hearing lapsed into a state of suspended animation. Maddie counted down from one hundred. Bonturo doodled. Reporters made notes. Television sketch artists worked on background scenes. Al-Saffah bowed his head, folded his hands. The police scanned the room, alert for sudden or suspicious movements. Court officers armed with handguns flanked Levy, ready to subdue or restrain him, or, if necessary, defend or protect him. Within limits. They had decided among themselves no one would take a bullet for the Jew. Catch the assassin? If they could. Submit him to the criminal justice system? If they caught him. Intercept his bullet? No. Never. Levy shifted his weight. His chains clanged. The court officers jumped. Bonturo sniggered. One of the Justice Department observers whispered into a micro recorder. Maddie's countdown reached thirty-three. Gomita returned the statute book to its shelf.

"Ms. Devlin," the judge said. "Could you foresee any circumstances under which Mr. Levy would jump bail before trial?"

Maddie adjusted the goose-neck of the microphone on the lectern reserved for defense counsel. The only sound in the courtroom was the soft tapping of the court stenographer's machine. Maddie wished someone would cough or sneeze. Her answer, she knew from previous appearances before Judge Gomita, would lead to another question and every answer thereafter to another until her final answer was the same as Gomita's conclusion. She measured her words with care knowing the choice of an imprecise word would weaken her argument or, worse, cause it to be misinterpreted or misunderstood. Simple language, she decided, would be best. "If

Massachusetts had not abolished the death penalty and if the evidence against Mr. Levy were air tight, he would have nothing to lose by jumping bail; but the death penalty has been abolished and the evidence is not air-tight."

Titters cascaded throughout the courtroom until Gomita gaveled them to silence. "He is charged with a crime punishable by mandatory life imprisonment. Why would that not be incentive to jump bail?"

"The law does not deal in hypotheticals, Your Honor. Especially the criminal law. Anything is possible, but very little is beyond a reasonable doubt."

"Is that the evidentiary standard at a bail hearing?"

"Mere possibility is not the standard."

"Neither is 'beyond a reasonable doubt.' I am required to admit a defendant to bail unless I determine, in the exercise of my discretion, releasing him will not reasonably assure his appearance at trial. In order to make that finding, I must determine whether Mr. Levy's perception of the likelihood of conviction and subsequent sentencing is such that he will flee. Why isn't the testimony of this witness relevant to that inquiry?"

"Because until this witness testifies, Mr. Levy will not know what his testimony will be. The testimony itself may change Mr. Levy's perceptions. If he is not likely to flee now, he cannot be held without bail because you admit testimony in his presence at this hearing which manufactures the likelihood of flight. It's a form of entrapment which is contrary to law both for the police and for judges."

"I could sequester him," Gomita said.

Maddie wished Gomita would. It would violate Levy's constitutional right to confront the witness against him. Gomita, unfortunately, was too astute to make such a fundamental mistake.

Gomita continued, "Mr. Levy may not know what this witness's testimony will be, but he may know from other sources the information the witness will provide."

"In that case, it should be excluded as being so inflammatory as to be prejudicial."

"Are you suggesting I will be swayed by inflammatory evidence?"

"You are not the only audience. This witness's testimony may be inaccurately reported by the press and misunderstood by the public. They may become even more enraged, which will incite further action by Bumper's Brigade and make it impossible to select an impartial jury for trial."

"Are you prepared to waive your request for bail?"

"Are you prepared to close this hearing to the public?"

"No." Gomita's voice froze the humidity in the courtroom.

Maddie glanced around. She did not see Moskovitzky or Rabbi ben Reuben. Hornstein smirked. C. J. Ant nodded approval. Michelle Furey smiled. Levy had the expression of someone listening to a speech in a foreign language. If bail were denied by the court rather than waived by defense counsel, Maddie would be beyond reproach. Yes, it was form over substance. Yes, it was faking the good fight. That would be her strategy, to appear beyond reproach, to be beyond reproach. "No, Judge. The defendant will not waive his request reasonable bail be set."

"I am inclined to let this witness testify provided Mr. Bonturo can qualify him as an expert in comparative religion."

"Please note my objection for the record."

The rules of trial were so courtly. No matter what Maddie thought of a judge or his ruling, she registered her opinion by asking the judge to note her objection for the record. This simple phrase could mask contempt, disgust, dismay, disbelief, and on rare occasions, merely dissatisfaction. Experienced trial counsel mastered the skill of mouthing this simple phrase in a monotone which never varied, which never revealed their true reaction unless they intended it to. She was better at this than Bonturo, who announced his objections like a batter arguing a called third strike with a blind umpire. Like those batters, he had been thrown out of the game more than once, held in contempt, fined, threatened with imprisonment. Maddie hoped she could bait him into erupting without Gomita realizing what she was doing.

"We'll take the morning recess now," Gomita announced, "and reconvene in fifteen minutes."

The court officers flanking Levy closed ranks around him, keeping everyone away save for Maddie who tried to explain why she did not waive bail. The more she talked, the blanker his expression became until she excused herself to use the ladies' room. Security accompanied her. As the recess dragged on, those who had rushed to buy coffee or use the bathrooms drifted back. Reporters lined up at the pay phones to transmit preliminary stories to their copy editors. Television news personalities primped and preened in preparation for taping background filler to use on the evening news. Attorneys joked about the judge being on the phone with his stockbroker or his bookie or arranging an afternoon tee time or an illicit liaison at the Parker House. Maddie refused all requests for interviews. By the time the recess reached thirty minutes, Rabbi ben Reuben and Moskovitzky had arrived.

"Predictable," Maddie said in response to the rabbi's question. "Charlie Sullivan described the appearance of the library when he found Bumper's body and identified the skull cap he found under the chair. Forensics described the tests it did on the hair found in the seam and on one of Levy's hairs and concluded both came from the same head. The coroner gave his report on the cause and time of death. Bonturo called Professor Husam al din al-Saffah as an expert on comparative religions and Gomita overruled my objection. The court's been in recess since then."

Moskovitzky handed Maddie a thick file. She had time only to scan the first few pages before the hearing resumed.

In response to Bonturo's well-planned and well-phrased questions, a selective biography of al-Saffah was entered in the court record: degrees from universities in Cairo and Beirut; teaching appointments to the Arab-American school in Saudi Arabia and Leeds, one of the lesser British universities; publication of numerous books and articles comparing the Semitic religions and explicating the influence of Christianity on their development—the normal indicia of a professor asked to testify in court as an expert concerning his academic specialty. Al-Saffah answered each question with precision and conviction as if he were trying to convince the court and the media he belonged on the faculty of Harvard rather than that of a secondary commuter campus of a state university. Bonturo had woodshedded him well.

"Do you wish to cross-examine on qualifications?" Gomita asked when Bonturo finished.

Maddie positioned herself at the lectern. "How, when, did you get your facial scar?"

"Objection!" Bonturo's face reddened.

"It's a foundation question, your Honor."

"You may have it *de bene*."

Al-Saffah caressed the scar with the nubs of his missing fingers. "I do not remember not having this scar."

"Does June, 1937, refresh your recollection?"

"I received my degree from Beirut that year."

"May I approach, Your Honor?" Gomita nodded and Maddie walked slowly to the witness stand, leaned against the railing next to al-Saffah's chair, and looked directly into his eyes. Images of *Fantasia* flashed through her mind. Willing herself not to break eye contact, she removed a page from Moskovitzky's file and held it so the blank side faced al-Saffah, then paused as if she were reading it. "Is it not true, Professor, you suffered your facial scar and lost your fingers in a terrorist raid on a Jewish stone quarry in Haifa in June, 1937?" She lay the sheet of paper face down on the railing.

"Objection!" Bonturo shouted, half-rising from his chair.

"Bias, Your Honor. The defendant is Jewish and the precise accusation against him, a blood libel, is made only against Jews. This witness has a history of anti-Semitic terrorist activities. This history is essential to your consideration of his credibility."

"You may have the question."

"I am a professor of Semitic studies. I have spent my life studying comparative religions, the ways in which people record and interpret God's revelations."

"Perhaps the British Parliament debates of July, 1937 concerning the Peel Commission Report will refresh your recollection. Are you the same Husam al din al-Saffah who is mentioned so prominently?"

"Zionist lies."

Maddie withdrew the sheet of paper and returned to the counsel table. She picked up a report prepared by the rabbi comparing and contrasting Judaism and Islam, then paused until she sensed Gomita's anticipation was edging toward impatience. Impatience tended to defeat the yawns of boring testimony and focus the attention of judges. It was analogous, C. J. Ant had once explained, to a partially clothed woman being sexier, more alluring, than a naked one. When she had hooked

Gomita, she asked her next question. "Islam and Judaism are both Semitic religions, are they not?"

"Yes," al-Saffah replied.

"Abraham is a patriarch of both religions?"

"Yes."

"Both religions share many common beliefs?"

"Yes."

"But their development diverged?"

"Yes. Allah sent his messenger Muhammad to purify the corruption of Abraham's religion caused by Jews and Christians."

"And your mission in life is to speed up the purification process, is it not? No further questions." She looked directly at him. I'm digging up your past, her eyes said, and this morning I've put the first skeletons on display.

"The witness qualifies as an expert," Judge Gomita ruled. "As defense counsel so ably reminded me, the issue of bias goes to his credibility and the weight to be given his testimony, not its admissibility. Proceed, Mr. Bonturo. You may have your objection, Ms. Devlin."

Maddie glanced at Rabbi ben Reuben and Moskovitzky. The night before in the rabbi's study they had educated her on the history of the blood libel accusation to prepare her to cross-examine al-Saffah, reviewing with her the litany of false accusations that Jews murdered young Christian boys for their blood to bake Passover *matzoh*: Norwich, England in 1144; Blois, France in 1171; southwestern Germany between 1336 and 1338; Poland in the thirteenth and fourteenth centuries and again in the first half of the eighteenth; Russia in the nineteenth and twentieth centuries; the Damascus affair of 1840; the Beiliss trial in Russia in 1913; and the Massena, New York incident in 1928.

"Five popes," the rabbi had explained, "denounced blood libel accusations as false: Innocent IV, Gregory X, Martin V, Paul III, and Clement XIV. Confiscation of Jewish property and the aggrandizement of the local church and clerics inevitably followed blood libel accusations, both of which suffered from extreme poverty before the accusation and enjoyed comfortable wealth after."

"The cases," Moskovitzky had said, resting his elbows on the rabbi's desk, "are nothing more than contrivances engineered by recognized anti-Semites to legitimize looting."

"Not one allegation of blood libel," the rabbi had added, "has been proven in the nine hundred years the accusation has been utilized to justify violence against Jews and forfeiture of their property."

"So what?" Maddie had replied. "The falsity of a blood libel accusation in Norwich, England in 1144 does not establish Levy's innocence in Boston, Massachusetts, in 1981."

Now, Bonturo asked his next question, raising his voice for the benefit of the judge, the police, the reporters, the spectators. "Professor al-Saffah. Please explain the historical and religious significance of the blood libel accusation, and its relevance to the murder charge against Avram Levy."

Al-Saffah took a deep breath. He, too, Maddie thought, knows how to bait his audience. "I've made a careful and complete study of the historical record. Most commonly, this accusation is made when a Christian child disappears and cannot be found. A suspect is apprehended, always Jewish, and his property is confiscated. Then, as if by miracle, the child reappears and provides the evidence necessary to convict the accused. Symbolically, it is a reenactment of the crucifixion and resurrection. From a practical viewpoint, it is a mechanism to transfer and redistribute wealth and property."

"In your expert opinion," Bonturo asked, "is this explanation correct?"

"No. It is a false explanation fabricated by the Jews themselves to make them appear persecuted and to mask the real reason for their ritual murders."

"Please explain."

"The purpose of this false explanation is to mislead people into believing the crime did not occur."

Gomita wrote furiously in his notebook. Maddie habitually watched judges to gauge their reaction to testimony. When a judge's attention wavered, she changed her line of questioning or, sometimes, called a different witness. If the testimony were essential to her case, she moved around the courtroom until she was in the judge's line of sight. Gomita's undisguised interest in al-Saffah's testimony worried her. It was a gauge of its persuasiveness. Judges did not daydream through testimony likely to influence their decisions. Bonturo paused to let Gomita finish taking notes.

"Are you saying Jews do engage in ritual murder but offer a false explanation as proof they do not?"

"Objection," Maddie said. "Leading the witness."

"This is a bench hearing, Ms. Devlin. You may have the question, Mr. Bonturo."

"Precisely," al-Saffah said. "By convincing everyone the historical explanation is false the Jews mislead them into believing the ritual murder did not occur."

Gomita stopped taking notes. Another bad sign. He was not losing interest. On the contrary, his interest was so heightened he did not want to distract himself with note taking. He had the court stenographer's transcript to fall back on.

Bonturo paused, as if he were an actor playing an attorney in the movies or on television. "Based on your study of the historical record, in your expert opinion what is the correct historical explanation for the occurrence of blood libel murders?"

Gomita leaned toward the witness. Maddie did likewise.

"The truth has been hinted at by those who observe that these crimes always occur near Passover. Not because Jews use Christian blood to make *matzoh*. They don't. The truth goes back much further than 1144. It goes back to the significance of Passover for Jews. Blood and death are central elements of the Passover story."

Al-Saffah's testimony wove a spell over the courtroom. The reporters at the press table, the sketch artists, the spectators, the police, the court officers, the monitors from the Department of Justice, the rabbi, Moskovitzky, Maddie, Levy, Bonturo, Gomita, everyone listened with the intensity of acolytes awaiting a divine revelation. The court stenographer, a veteran of many trials, recorded every word. Her smile hinted at her dreams about the things she would buy with the money she would make selling copies of the transcript, a new car: a Cadillac, first and foremost. All eyed al-Saffah.

"While Egyptians held the Jews in bondage," al-Saffah continued, "the Egyptians hurled their sons into the Nile River."

"Whose sons?" Gomita interrupted.

"The sons of the Jews. This is commemorated at the *seder* by mixing red wine, symbol of the blood of infants, into the *haroses*." Al-Saffah spoke slowly. "When God, as it is set forth in the *Old Testament* fable, visited the ten plagues on Egypt, the tenth plague was the slaughter of the Egyptian first born. Jewish first born were saved because God instructed the Jews to mark the lintels of their doors with the blood of the *Paschal* Lamb so He would pass over their homes. To this day, the first born sons of Jewish families fast and pray the day before Passover to commemorate this.

"The Passover story is retold every year at the *seder*," al-Saffah continued, "and stresses the obligation of every Jew to memorialize the experience of his forefathers on the night they left Egypt by reenacting it. Eating *matzoh* is part of this, but Christian blood is not part of the recipe for *matzoh*. This superficial explanation distracts us from fully comprehending how Passover is celebrated."

"Is it your expert opinion," Bonturo asked, "that Jews have been engaging in the ritual murder known as the blood libel as part of their observance of Passover since the Exodus because of the commandment that they must reenact the experiences of their ancestors on the night of their departure from Egypt?"

"Objection. Leading the witness."

"A bench hearing, Ms. Devlin."

"Preserving my objection for appeal."

"Of a bail hearing? Overruled."

"Yes. By committing blood libels, they are reenacting the slaying of the first born sons of the Egyptians."

"Your witness," Bonturo said to Devlin.

"Will you finish up before lunch?" Gomita asked.

"No, Your Honor."

"We shall recess now so you can proceed without interruption. Court will reconvene at precisely two p.m."

-2-

Four court officers escorted Levy to one of the holding cells in the basement of the New Court House. Built during the Great Depression as a public works project, it was called the New Court House to distinguish it from the Old Court House

190

built several generations earlier. As an example of architecture, it had the character of the political hacks who had profited from its construction. As a building, it had their quality. Like most Massachusetts public construction projects, decay had set in about the time of the ribbon cutting at the dedication ceremony. Now, some fifty years later, the trial bar dubbed the New Court House Jericho as they waited for the clap of thunder or the truck backfire that would cause its walls to come tumbling down.

Narrow and cramped, the basement holding cells lacked furniture except for a bench built into the wall and sandpapered smooth by fifty years of prison denim. A guard positioned a paper plate with a peanut butter and jelly sandwich on the floor outside the bars. With his foot, he lined it up with the opening at the bottom of the door. Starch sharpened the creases in his uniform. His boots, steel tipped, ideal for kicking hapless prisoners, rode up his legs to just below the knees. His tie rested on the bulge of his belly like a bib on a pudgy baby. He looked like an extra in a bad World War II movie.

"Is the Jew hungry?" the guard taunted. He nudged the plate along the floor like a hockey player moving a puck up ice, then kicked it with the instep of his boot. The plate skimmed along the floor before hitting Levy's foot. The sandwich caromed into a mound of dust neatly collected under the bench by a previous detainee. "Enjoy." The guard winked.

Levy rested his arms on his lap. His muscles ached from the weight of the steel bands around his wrists and the chains binding his wrists to his waist and ankles. The chains chafed his skin and he had the urge to scratch. When he was young, he scratched insect stings and bites until his arms bled. Skin stuck to his sleeves when the blood dried. His mother bandaged him with love then, and he wondered if she would love him now. He forced his fingers beneath the wrist band and dug his fingernails into his raw skin. The more he scratched, the more it itched. The more it itched, the greater the pain. The greater the pain, the harder he scratched. His skin split open and blood smeared his arm. His mother would not come and soak away this blood, nor clean and bandage this wound, nor feed him chicken soup, scold him with a smile, comfort him with a hug. He thanked Hashem his mother of blessed memory had not lived to see this day.

-3-

In the conference room at Suffolk County Legal Services, Maddie, Rabbi ben Reuben, and Moskovitzky pondered the logic of al-Saffah's testimony. Maddie spread a lunch of apple slices, honey, cheese, hard rolls and coffee on the conference table. The rabbi nibbled at a piece of bread, collecting the crumbs from the hard crust as if he were saving them for another meal. Moskovitzky dipped an apple wedge in the honey, then set it aside. Usually doing well in court made Maddie hungry, but the heat still sapped her appetite.

"We need a *golem* like in Chelm and Prague," Moskovitzky said

"He's making a leap of faith and disguising it as a logical conclusion," the rabbi said.

"I can't cross-examine a leap of faith," Maddie said.

"Think it through," the rabbi said. "First, he testifies Jews have contrived a false explanation to deceive the public into believing a ritual murder has not occurred; then he says there was a ritual murder and offers the real explanation. How can that be?"

Maddie said, "Saying there was no murder doesn't mean there was no murder. People once said the world was flat. Saying so didn't make it flat."

"Flat, schmat," Moskovitzky said. "She should care, her and my grandson." He picked up a hard roll and tried to tear off a piece, then put it down.

"What would Howard Kaplan do?" Maddie asked. "What would you do?" she said to Moskovitzky.

"Force him to answer the rabbi's question."

"I'm going to waive cross-examination and rest without putting in any defense."

"You're condemning Avram to prison," the rabbi said.

Maddie sipped some coffee to build a pause into the conversation. Silence created anxiety and anticipation. Anxiety and anticipation created good listeners. She needed two good listeners. The deaf were rarely persuaded. She took another sip of coffee. "Suppose I cross-examine al-Saffah or the rabbi testifies and we manage to cast reasonable doubt on his testimony. First, that's not the standard of evidence at a bail hearing. Second, Bonturo still has his suicide argument. Third, al-Saffah would gain the benefit of experiencing cross-examination. Fourth, Bonturo would gain the benefit of hearing the rabbi testify. Fifth, Levy would gain nothing because he won't be bailed no matter what we do. Trial is war. You choose your battlefield, sacrifice a battle when necessary to win the war, and you never expose your flank."

"What I would expect from a lawyer who thinks her client is guilty," Moskovitzky said.

"Wishful thinking has reduced your doubts to a scintilla."

"If you were defending Robert Emmet," Moskovitzky replied, "would you be so cold and clinical?"

"As cold. As clinical."

"I've been an attorney," Moskovitzky said, "almost twice as long as you've been alive and I've learned there are times when moral principles, not the individual client, come first. This is one of those times."

"The public isn't the client," Maddie said. "History isn't the client. The only client who matters is Avram Levy and the only audience that matters is Judge Gomita today, the jury tomorrow. Disclosing defenses at a preliminary hearing prejudices Kaplan's ability to try this case. Find some other way to rebut al-Saffah. Call your own press conference. Hire a PR firm. Co-opt the media. But do not tell me what I should or should not do inside that courtroom."

"Resign now," Moskovitzky said. "I'll take over."

Maddie said, "You'll do more harm than good."

"She may be right, Jacob."

"Age has made you weak," Moskovitzky replied.

"Of body, but not of mind." With his little finger, the rabbi swept the bread crumbs into a tiny pyramid. "You speak of moral principles, Jacob, as if we were Talmudic scholars debating some fine point of scripture. We are not in the *bet sefer*. We are on the battlefield. At war. We are fighting to survive. Our survival is our best and only way to defend moral principles. Is that not the lesson of the Passover story?

"Ms. Devlin. After today's testimony, you must have a strange notion of what a *seder* is. Please join Jacob and me at the first *seder* tomorrow night."

"No. I'm sorry. I couldn't."

"You're not curious?"

Maddie's heartbeat accelerated. She breathed deeply to mask her anxieties. If Levy's name were Emmet, she would not, like an informer, allow herself to be bought off by the promise of a few pieces of silver. If Levy were Emmet, the skull cap would be a plant, al-Saffah's involvement a frame-up. She felt as jumbled as a child trying to understand the difference between a lie and a white lie or a truth and a half-truth. She longed for the simplicity of certainty, the comfort of the absolute, the bright line of black-letter law; but, even more, she longed for some sign she was doing the right thing.

Maddie gathered the refuse from the uneaten lunch–apple slices turning brown, cheese sweating from the heat, lukewarm coffee, the pyramid of crumbs–and stuffed it into a brown paper bag. "We have to get back to court."

Judge Gomita denied Levy bail because, as he explained, he was convinced Levy would flee if released. At Maddie's request and over Bonturo's objection, he agreed to report a question of law to the Single Justice session of the Supreme Judicial Court.

"May I have until next week, your Honor?" Maddie asked.

"Wednesday. Eleven o'clock a.m."

-4-

Michelle Furey walked Maddie to her car which was parked on the roof top level of the Government Center parking garage. Walking down New Sudbury Street, Maddie wanted to hold Furey's hand, but the windows of the District 1 police station on one side of the street, the JFK building on the other, stared down at her, at them, with divine disapproval, reminding her of the eyes of the nuns who terrorized her in parochial school if she were not deemed devout enough. Maddie had enough turmoil in her life and she didn't need the additional aggravation that would come from being seen in public holding hands with a woman. Nor the turmoil of Michelle Furey's refusal to hold her hand. She was fleeing to Washington, she now understood, not only for the money, but to avoid being rejected by Furey. She opened her car doors to allow the heat to escape.

"Tough morning," Furey said.

"'Bout what I expected," Maddie replied. "Brandeis himself wouldn't bail this defendant."

"What now?"

"It's Howard Kaplan's problem."

"Who?"

"Some handpicked Jew attorney taking over the case."

"And you?"

"Washington office of the Mosca firm."

"Just like that?"

"Come to D.C. with me." The words escaped before Maddie knew what she was saying.

"My life's here. My parents. Sister and brother. My practice."

"I've got to get out before Boston eats me alive."

"The sow that eats her own children."

"There's the Washington shuttle," Maddie said. "Trains to New York where we can meet half-way. It's not the end of the world."

"Is this good-bye?" Furey asked.

"If it is, you're saying it, not me." Maddie tossed her briefcase into the front seat of her car. "I can't stay in Boston. It's suffocating me." She reached out to hug Furey, but Furey stepped to the side. "It's not you, Michelle. It's Boston."

"Boston. Boston. How convenient to blame Boston. Go to Washington. I'm sure you'll have your pick of the single women on the Hill. The married ones, too."

"I don't want 'women.' I only want you."

"Then stay."

"I can't."

"You're saying good-bye, not me."

From across the roof of the parking garage, Maddie watched Furey step into the elevator and the elevator doors close behind her. She leaned against the car door to regain her equilibrium. She felt like a piece of molten iron on an anvil being pounded into shape by heat's hammer.

Maddie crawled into the front seat, closed the car doors. A straitjacket of heat imprisoned her. Driving home, Furey's voice accompanied her on every radio station she tuned in, AM or FM, talk or all-news or all-sports or easy listening or oldies or rock or classical. On Suzy's Swap Shop, Furey offered one soul, used, with years of penance ahead of it in exchange for a power lawn mower and two hundred feet of garden hose. On Sports Boston, Furey's voice assured the host that the Celtics, now led by a great white hope, would win the NBA championship. On Cousin Brucie's Top 40 Countdown, Furey's voice dedicated every song to an Irish lassie identified only by her initials, MAD.

Maddie shut off the radio and still Furey's voice accompanied her. She inserted a tape in the tape deck; Furey's voice. She ejected the tape; Furey's voice. It was as inescapable as the tap of the valve lifters in her engine, the screech of her power steering when she turned a corner, the squeal of her brakes when she stopped for traffic, the tea stains in the fabric of the front seat.

May fire and brimstone, Furey's voice said, ne'er fail to fall in showers upon you. May every woe that e'er marred mankind dance upon your dish. May the devil cut off your head and make eternity's work of your heart. May the flames through which your soul wanders be bigger than the Conne-mara Mountains were they on fire. May you die without a priest in a town without a church. It is said, Furey's voice continued, you should never rest your eyes beyond what is your own, whether awake or asleep. Did you dream last night of serpents, dragons, and other water beasts? Or, of great birds who arrive bearing honey and depart with plume bloody? The day will come when your arms are bony and thin, your cheeks withered and weathered, your hair gray and thatched with age; the day will come when you drink whey and water with shriveled hags, not mead and wine with warriors and kings; the day will come when you seek the way to the house of judgment. On that day the Son of God will come and claim payment of your debt.

And unsung will be your bones. And unsung will be your bones.

All this and more Furey's voice proclaimed.

Chapter 8

Erev Pesach, Saturday, April 18, 1981

-1-

It was the morning of *Erev Pesach*, the morning of the first *seder*, the morning when Jews searched their homes for every crumb of bread, every speck of *chametz*, and exchanged their everyday dishes for those of Passover; but not on this particular morning because this particular morning fell on the holiest of holy days, the Sabbath, and such secular tasks, all secular tasks, were forbidden on the Sabbath.

Maddie Devlin who knew nothing of the Sabbath bride and thought nothing of desecrating Avram Levy's Sabbath waited in a small dressing room at the Charles Street Jail while a matron, Gloria Mundy according to her hand-written name tag, searched Maddie's pocket book and briefcase. Mundy was husky and athletic, built like a wrestler in the heavyweight division. Her hands were out of proportion to her body, the hands of a football player grafted on to the arms of an overweight woman.

"Let's get this over with, sweets." Mundy sounded as gleeful as a young boy who delighted in focusing sunlight through a magnifying glass to set fire to the coat of his neighbor's cat. Her fingers moved deliberately through Maddie's hair, lifting it to expose the nape of her neck, rubbing her scalp. A stiletto of sensation flashed down the back of Maddie's legs. Mundy jerked Maddie's head back, exposing the cartilage of her neck, and pried open her mouth with her thumb and forefinger. Both tasted of onion and the greasy oil of a cheap grinder. Mundy's finger swabbed the inside of Maddie's mouth, brushing across the lining of her cheeks and the back of her teeth. Mundy's calluses rubbed against her cheeks.

With each touch, Maddie's impacted rage strained against the boundaries that constrained it. She clenched her fists. One punch, she thought. One fucking punch.

"Arms over your head, sweets."

Mundy slipped off Maddie's blouse and undid her bra. Football hands moved from her spine, across her rib cage, below her armpits and swallowed up her breasts. Maddie pushed away, but Mundy's size overpowered her. Maddie crossed her arms over her breasts, but Mundy grabbed her wrists and rotated her arms until Maddie felt they were being ripped from their sockets.

A kick, Maddie thought. A kick in the crotch. More than once Maddie had defended herself with a well-placed kick, often followed by a straight jab to the nose. Her da had insisted she know how to fight back, paid for her to be taught the basics of self-defense. Still, what worked on the street, what worked in an open-ended alley, would not work in a closed room in the Charles Street jail. Yes, she could overcome Mundy; but what would be the follow-up? A criminal charge for assault and battery on a public employee in the performance of her duties. A felony. A classic she said/she said situation. I was patting her down, Mundy would testify, when she attacked me without provocation. Nothing Maddie could say would persuade a judge or jury otherwise. Win the battle; lose the war. *Fág an Bealach*, Maddie chanted to herself. *Fág an Bealach*.

With one motion, Mundy stripped Maddie's skirt, stockings, and underpants and pushed her down until she squatted like a primitive woman about to give birth. Football fingers snaked through her pubic hair.

Hatred, Maddie now realized, was Mundy's ecstasy, her addiction. To Mundy, Levy was just another fix, me her connection. This must be what first generation Irish endured, Maddie thought, landing in Boston to be greeted by "No Irish" or "Irish Need Not Apply" signs, or what African-Americans feel in parts of Boston today. The cocoon Maddie had been born into, the one she didn't realize sheltered her, had been shredded, ripped away, exposing her in a way she had never been exposed. The abstract was now concrete. The rifles of her grand da's firing squad now aimed at her.

"You're clean, sweets."

Maddie dressed, then ran to the ladies' room, the furthest stall. She hung from the door, limp and liquid as a wet rag. There was no toilet seat, no toilet paper. Graffiti covered the walls and ceiling. Reagan ass fucks. Mayor Charlie blows. Warden Spirelet sucks. Phone numbers. Obscenities. Cartoons of penises and balls, tits and pussies. Maddie felt as if she had night sweats, but her mouth was dry, dead bone dry, so dry she feared her lips would crack if she opened her mouth, her tongue would crack if she moved it. She gagged and dry heaved into the toilet. Phlegm, someone else's, floated on the surface of the water, a piece of scum on a stagnant pond. She poked through her purse for a pocket douche or a napkin, but found only a piece of tissue shredded by her keys. She flattened her palms against the walls of the stall to hold herself up. Dry heaves tore through her.

Hatred had always persecuted somebody else, her namesakes Mary and Ann Devlin in Kilmainham, her grand da in Traitor's Hell, Jews like the rabbi and Moskovitzky, the immigrants of her grand ma's generation. Hatred, pure hatred, had always been abstract, experienced vicariously, but now, hatred in its purest form had raped her, deposited its seed in her womb and she knew if she, crazed by the narcotic of vengeance, succumbed to hatred this one time, she, too, would be addicted, always needing another fix, haunting back alleys for her connection, eagerly, happily, paying whatever the price might be. Yet, there was something comfortable about hatred, the way it liberated the mind, amplified the emotions, ordered the chaos of the world into something manageable, understandable. Black and white. White and black. Pluses and minuses. Minuses and pluses. A binary world.

Maddie straightened her clothes and wiped her cheeks with the back of her palm and took several deep breaths as if she were venting nitrogen from her system, and stumbled out of the toilet stall. A new life awaited. Washington. Money. Maybe, marriage. To a man—her fling with a woman over—a man who would father her child, a child who would be christened with a proper Irish name, a name beginning with E in remembrance of Elizabeth.

Gloria Mundy was a messenger not from God, but the devil, an invitation to succumb to hatred, an invitation she would not RSVP because hatred was not the way to her new life. By the time she reached the attorney's visiting room, she had driven her craving into that deep pit where she had caged Richard Gloucester and Edward Hornstein and the Brits who imprisoned her namesakes and great uncle Clancy and the scum she so resolutely represented. And Michelle Furey? No. Never Furey for Furey had reawakened her capacity to love, to live.

The familiarity of the attorney's visiting room, its stale, brackish air, the wooden table lined with cigarette burns, the air vent clogged with balls of dust which looked like gray cheese curls, comforted and consoled her the way the execution of a convicted murderer comforted and consoled the family of his victim.

Next week, Washington. She felt like a convict in the last hours of a long prison sentence.

-2-

"*Traif.* Must you always desecrate the Sabbath?" Levy asked.

Maddie ignored him.

"Why am I still here? Because you think I'm guilty and deserve to be here?"

"No." Maddie explained the inevitability of the outcome of the bail hearing, why she waived cross-examination, why she withheld the rabbi from the witness stand, speaking rapidly, letting her persona for the previous eight years as an attorney who aggressively defended her clients no matter how reprehensible take control of her thoughts, her actions.

"When do I meet this Howard Kaplan?"

"Kaplan's a dead end. He'll take you to trial. Guaranteed conviction. The jury won't see beyond your skull cap. Murder One is life without parole. Murder Two, life with the possibility of parole, but in your case, chance of parole is the same as your becoming a Jesus freak. You're looking at life, probably in solitary since you wouldn't survive a week in the general population. If the warden owes Charlie Sullivan a favor, he'll put you in the general population and let nature takes its course which it will, the first day or two if it takes that long."

Maddie had intended to bid Levy farewell, to wish him luck with his new attorney, but the encounter with Gloria Mundy had recalibrated her thinking. Abandoning Levy to Howard Kaplan would signal the Gloria Mundy's of the world they had won. She was not prepared to concede victory to them, not so much for Levy's sake but for her own. She swallowed some phlegm which she coughed up into a tissue.

"Your only hope is to let me negotiate a plea bargain, a plea to a lesser included offense, probably manslaughter; maybe negligent homicide if I'm really on my game, in exchange for Bonturo's agreeing to a prearranged disposition, a term certain, something less than life, something that will let you die a free man, and assignment to a correctional institution rather than a state prison, protocols regarding your personal safety, kosher meals, the right to practice your religion, whatever else I can dream up."

The more she talked, the more she felt like an actress trapped in a bad movie condemned to speak words someone else had written for her. She spoke so fast her mouth raced ahead of her brain. She coughed again, this time a dry cough which came from so deep inside her that her lungs exploded against her ribcage.

"The judge has the last word, but judges usually accept plea bargains and agreed upon dispositions. It's the grease that lubricates the justice system."

"Why would you do that if you know I'm guilty?" Levy asked. "According to Rabbi Luria and Rabbi Schachter, the

Talmudic commentaries or *Tosafot* make it clear that the Torah prohibits a lawyer from defending a client who the lawyer knows is guilty because it is forbidden to help the criminal escape the consequences of his act, forbidden to assist someone to avoid his just punishment, and forbidden to fail to eradicate the evil in our midst."

Maddie had never seen Levy so animated. His skill at parsing Jewish law would make him a formidable attorney, but she doubted he would be able to persuade many of the Jewish mob lawyers that they were violating Jewish law by defending their clients. She had never considered this in the context of Catholic law. Someday, perhaps, she would; but not today.

"To think or believe something," Maddie said, "is not the same as knowing it. What if there is doubt, no matter how small? What does your Talmud say then?"

"*Tosafot* and Rabbenu Asher would say that the defense is permitted as long as the doubt is sincere and the client is not known to the attorney to be guilty in fact."

"My doubt may be small, miniscule in fact; but it is sincere as is my belief that you are guilty. I believe. I do not know. Is this sufficient for us to continue?"

Levy looked into her eyes, searching them for the answer to her question. This was more, she realized than the children's game of stare-down. She willed herself not to blink, not to turn away, because she feared doing either would be interpreted to mean her doubt lacked sincerity. After several seconds that seemed to Maddie to be several minutes, Levy smiled, something he had never done before in her presence. He leaned back in his chair. "If my case is so hopeless, why would they agree?"

"They don't know I'm withdrawing and they're afraid of me. I'm the David to their Goliath. The Moses to their

Pharaoh. Howard Kaplan? Samson after his haircut. No one's heard of him. No one fears him. He's God's gift to the prosecution. Me? I'm God's gift to you."

"Hashem hateth haughty eyes, *Proverbs* 6:16 and 17."

"As does my church which considers pride to be a mortal sin; but it's not pride when it's a fact. They're trying to scare me off. I just suffered a body search worse than a rape. A real rape is probably next."

"It is also written in *Proverbs* that Hashem hateth those who speak with a lying tongue." Levy paused. "As much as I fear you would betray Anne Frank, I have no choice but to hide in the attic and pray you do not." He closed his eyes and bowed his head. His lips moved. Rapidly. *Adonoy ro-i, lo echsar. Bin-ot desheh yarbitzayni, al may m'nuchot y'nahalayni* . . . When he finished, he opened his eyes and looked directly at Maddie, then recited in English, *The Lord is my shepherd; I shall not want . . .*

-3-

Hours later, Maddie sought relief in the rainbow bubbles of a hot bath. Three empty bottles of Guinness lined the edge of the tub like altar pieces. She opened and drank a fourth, then a fifth. The Guinness felt heavy in her head, heavy behind her eyes, between her ears. Mid-afternoon. Only alcoholics were into their fifth Guinness so early in the day. She had defended her share of alcoholics, always without sympathy. A liar Levy had called her. Someone who would betray Anne Frank. Not the first time a client had called her a liar, not the first time a client had accused her of betraying them, selling them out, always out of anger, frustration, ignorance of how the justice system worked; but never the way Levy had. In his eyes, she was to him what her great-uncle Clancy had been to her grand da. What was she in her own eyes?

The Guinness clouded her mind and carried her back to the year of her fifteenth birthday, 1961, the year of her ma's death, the year her da dragged her to Dublin for Christmas. The morning they arrived Brian Devlin marched his daughter to Arbour Hill Cemetery, the grave of Seamus, one of Grand da Michael's brothers, then to Kilmainham, Dublin's Tower of London, whose prisoners were either executed or forever forgotten until their bones were swept up and given to dogs to gnaw upon.

"Your namesakes," Brian said, pointing to a page from the 1803 prison register on display in the prison's entryway as if it were a sacred document or illuminated manuscript reposing in a church nave. "Mary Devlin, prisoner 94; Ann Devlin, prisoner 98. Six Devlins. The youngest a boy of nine. Killed because Ann wouldn't betray Robert Emmet."

Maddie gripped her da's hand as they walked through stone corridors cold and damp. In tiny cells with slits for windows, she imagined a small boy sleeping on a pile of straw in one room, dead with a bloody head wound on the cold stone floor of another, a skeleton in rags in a third. She saw his shadow darken the hole in the moss-covered stone wall into which the executioner slid the crossbeam of the gallows. She heard his voice where the prisoners stood while the firing squad lined up, readied, aimed, fired.

"Da." Maddie tugged his sleeve until he stopped. "I want to go home."

"You are home, daughter of mine."

Outside the gates of Kilmainham, they caught the bus for Hollyfield, a riverside slum infested by gangs and rats and a cemetery known as Traitor's Hell, where they dumped traitors and sinners excommunicated by the Church. Grave markers, a few whole, most in fragments, were strewn about the bare ground like bones scattered by grave robbers angered by the poverty of the graves they had opened. There were no footpaths, no sidewalks, no roads for hearses to enter or exit, no shrubs or bushes, no sacraments, no last rites. The markers were unadorned except for names, dates. No crosses. No religious symbols. No sign of heaven. Hell abounded.

Maddie followed her da as he zigzagged between the stones. On a slight rise he stopped at a marker, fissured and listing to the side, as grimy as a gathering storm cloud, as smooth as a sunless Irish sky except for its lettering, "M Devlin". Brian made the sign of the cross. "My da. Your grand da. May God have mercy on his soul."

"Grand da was a traitor?" Maddie asked.

In a quiet voice both sad and defiant Brian told his daughter what he had told George Harriman so many years before on Guadalcanal. "I could never get Seamus's side of the family to see beyond Clancy's lies." Brian put his arm around his daughter.

Maddie struggled to understand. Three brothers. Michael her grand da. Seamus Trish's. Seamus killed in a Brit ambush. Michael executed by the IRB as an informer because of Clancy's lies. Trish's da blamed her da for Seamus's death. Trish blamed her. It made no sense, all this blame.

She wished she were back in Boston, attending basketball games with Duncan Siward or jitterbugging at the Friday night dances at the Y or holding hands at the latest Elvis Presley movie, going out for pizza afterwards, making out on her back porch or, when it was cold, in the back hall among winter coats hanging from pegs in the wall, their feet surrounded by boots, stifling their giggles when they heard someone moving about the kitchen. She didn't want to be in Ireland visiting a jail where Devlins had been imprisoned, tortured, executed, or a cemetery where her grand da lay buried in shame. She didn't want to be named for sisters who sacrificed themselves for Ireland's freedom. She didn't want to be Irish.

Now, many years later, sipping her fifth bottle of Guinness, Maddie once again heard her da's voice, dead these many years, reciting the Devlin family history, hers and Trish's, both direct descendants of Robert Emmet. From Robert Emmet to his son, Robert Michael Arthur Devlin, named Devlin rather than Emmet to hide him from the British, to Michael and Arthur being two Devlin cousins, both veterans of the Rising of 1798 and the Rising of 1803 to the Easter Rising of 1916 which begat first her grand da's betrayal by his brother Clancy and, then, the Republic of Ireland.

All this and more Maddie remembered.

Once again it was November of Maddie's sophomore year in college. During her freshman year, Duncan Siward, her first great love, her only love, had faded away like a one-hit-recording star. Against her better judgment, she allowed friends to drag her to the Harvard-Yale game and to a party at Eliot House where she met Richard Gloucester, a Harvard junior who asked her for a date. Suffolk Downs, he said, because my tuition's due.

She didn't know what to make of this Harvard horse player who majored in English and argued that *Richard III* was Shakespeare's greatest play. Once every two or three months her da went to Suffolk Downs with George Harriman, budgeting $25.00 to cover admission, a hot dog and beer, and half a dozen bets, long shots to place, never to win. On a good day he came home with movie money which he gave her with a smile and a kiss. On a bad day, he laughed about the noses that came up short and vowed next time to bet only on Jew horses.

Her da worked hard for that $25.00, fifteen years at two jobs to save up the down payment for their house, nights the janitor at Holy Name High School, days factory work, operating a punch press to attach rings to loose-leaf binders, eight hour shifts, no paid lunch hour, eight hours surrounded by the steady pounding of a battalion of punch presses, surrounded by air humid with machine oil and heated by motors too hot to touch. Insert the rings. Slide in the binder. Push the button. Snatch back the fingers before the press crushed them, which happened to someone every few months, but never, at least not yet, at a punch press operated by her da. Every night he came home five fingered, smelling of grease that never washed away. He hated the factory, her da, but he was proud he did his work the right way, proud he was reliable, proud he provided for his wife and daughter. Maddie respected his pride and loved him for it and prayed it was genetic and that one day she would be able, like him, to get up every morning and do what she had to do for her children.

Gloucester's carefree attitude, on the other hand, his blind faith that his next dollar was at the finish line of the next race, both repelled and attracted her. Yet, in spite of Gloucester's sun-sprite disposition, there was something ominous lurking within his eyes, set deep in their sockets as if they were sinking into his soul, something ominous in their color, a brown so dark it verged on black. His eyebrows merged at the bridge of his nose like a land bridge between two continents that never should have been joined. But, when they kissed, he closed his eyes–she peeked–and imprisoned her fears and worries behind pearly smooth eyelids of love.

Much to Maddie's surprise, her da liked Gloucester and, after much prodding, accompanied them to the track, betting

Gloucester's touts, small, conservative bets, winning bets, twenty-five dollars becoming seventy-five after subtracting admissions, grandstand instead of track side, a hot dog and premium bottled beer (two) instead of draft (one). Gloucester bet big, both short odds and long (which he wouldn't allow Brian to bet), always to win. And exotic bets. Not just daily doubles and trifectas and quinellas, but wheels and boxes and bets based on mathematical formulas requiring a slide rule to calculate. Hundreds became thousands and at the end of the day Gloucester banked the profits for graduate school, a PhD in medieval literature. His life plan was to teach *Beowulf, Les Chansons de Roland,* and *The Canterbury Tales* in the mornings, play the horses in the afternoon, enjoy evenings at home with wife and children, publish an occasional article or book to maintain his standing in the world of academia. He was the first person Maddie had ever met who had mutated a future based on chance into a future plotted with precision.

Sophomore year cantered into junior year, then senior year, and Maddie grew comfortable with Gloucester, the same comfort she felt walking home after church on Sunday mornings, her arm resting in her da's. When the track closed for the season, they went to museums, the Museum of Fine Arts, the Gardner, the de Cordova, the Fogg, the Busch-Reisinger. And overnights to New York–separate beds, separate rooms– for the ballet, Gloucester's great passion, *Swan Lake, Sleeping Beauty, Jewels,* anything by Balanchine or Robbins, anything by City Ballet, ABT, the Stuttgart, the Royal Danish, the Bolshoi. Modern dance as well. The Ailey. The Joffrey. Martha Graham. Gloucester enthused about the athletic grace of the dancers, comparing it to the beauty of the best thoroughbreds. Not original with me, he confessed. Cribbed it from Homer's *Iliad.*

Can a cribbed life be a life well lived? Maddie wondered at the time. For all his reading, his appreciation of art and ballet, his ability to bring light to the Dark Ages, he was in essence a smile, a joke, a wink, a love pat, a shadow who had never known pain. She could not imagine him comforting her after her ma's death as Duncan Siward had or understanding the dread she felt being named after two sisters who lived out their lives in Kilmainham. He demanded little of her and did not need the emotional commitment Duncan required. He allowed her to encase her feelings in a shell, hide them from herself, bury them in the netherworld. He made life simple. She never had to trust her feelings. Or distrust them. Or act upon them. Or refuse to act. Or voice them. Or swallow them. Or even admit she had them.

After growing up in a family riven by its own internal civil war, a family in which the turmoil of feelings and emotions were handed down generation to generation like hair color, like eye color, the peace of mind she enjoyed with Gloucester, a peace that surpassed all understanding, seduced her before she knew she was being seduced. So, when Gloucester asked her to marry him after hitting a five-figure superfecta, they set a wedding date and she became Mrs. Richard Gloucester; then, nine months after the honeymoon touring Sun Belt race tracks and winning enough to pay cash for a center-entrance colonial in Lexington with Revolutionary-era provenance, the mother of baby Elizabeth.

Once again it was that April afternoon, snow in the air, snow on the ground, a winter which would not relent, Suffolk Downs closed because of the weather. Once again Elizabeth was ten months old. Once again the baby-sitter canceled and Maddie begged Richard to care for Elizabeth so she could go to class, Shakespeare at Harvard Extension School, the day's topic, fathers and daughters in Shakespeare. Once again he said he'd take Elizabeth with him to Bennie's, an illegal off track betting parlor where the next race was always minutes away. The call came half way through the lecture on whether Cordelia, Goneril, and Regan were archetypes or unique characters or whether Ophelia or Juliet existed independent of their suicides or whether Shakespeare's concept of women honored or dishonored his queen, the first Elizabeth. At the hospital, an aide escorted her to the emergency ward where curtains separated Gloucester, under arrest, from the world, where George Harriman waited, his hat drooping between his knees.

"The truth, Uncle George," Maddie said.

"A patch of ice. The car spun out of control. Elizabeth went through the windshield. Ruptured an artery. Bled to death. Vehicular homicide. Speeding. And he failed the field sobriety tests. He walked away, unhurt."

Maddie drove to the accident scene and walked the skid marks, black, narrow, and long, very long, thirty-seven steps, heel to toe. In the front yard of a triple-decker, a honeysuckle bush, its branches broken by Elizabeth's fall, its white winter-defiant petals stained red with Elizabeth's blood. For all its beauty, its branches had not been thick enough to cushion an airborne infant. Summers would come and go; first frosts would wither the flowers. Each spring, each new season, new flowers, white, sweet smelling, would blossom, ignorant of the day an infant lay in its branches bleeding to death. She breathed deeply, inhaling the sweet fragrance into her memory.

The feelings she had imprisoned broke free and rampaged through her psyche like rioting prisoners, destroying everything, everyone, that had oppressed them. What use was beauty? It never spared a life. And how many had died for beauty?

Brian Devlin eulogized his granddaughter with words from Yeats:

> Come away, O human child!
> To the waters and the wild
> With a faery, hand in hand,
> For the world's more full of weeping than you
>   can understand.

"He writes like he lost a child," Maddie said after the service.

"Ireland was his only child," her da replied, "and, yes, he lost her."

At Gloucester's trial for vehicular homicide, Ed Hornstein attacked the credentials and competence of the prosecution's accident reconstruction expert, arguing a two-week course in accident reconstruction at the Massachusetts State Police Academy—with only one day devoted to the physics of moving bodies, the coefficient of friction, torque, and other such subjects—did not qualify anyone to reconstruct an accident from skid marks, the size, depth and location of dents on an automobile, gouge marks in the street and curb, and the other physical evidence found at the accident scene. Without a qualified expert, the science was no better than astrology or mythology, Hornstein argued, and a jury could only speculate how the accident happened and speculation would not sustain a conviction. He also attacked the field sobriety tests administered at the accident scene, demonstrating how sober people had trouble counting back from one hundred or standing on one leg or walking heel to toe in a straight line. He played the sympathy card, remaking Gloucester from a drunk and careless driver to a victim, a father who would live his life blaming himself for his baby daughter's death. The jury acquitted in less than two hours. Later, Hornstein represented Maddie's ex-husband in the divorce.

After the entry of the jury's verdict and Gloucester's discharge, Maddie ducked into one of the wrought iron spiral staircases that turned up in odd corners of the Suffolk County courthouse and spun herself dizzy racing down the steps. At the Park Street MBTA stop, she paused at the top of the staircase. Beneath her, the subway. The third rail. The arch of the entrance, the steps down, lured her. The bench where she once sat mourning the assassination of President Kennedy lured her. The Harvard-Ashmont line then, since 1965 the Red Line, its comings and goings, lured her. How easy it would be. How fast. Peace at last. She descended to the subway platform.

A woman, elderly but erect and able to walk without a cane, appeared on the platform. She wore a veiled hat and white gloves and carried a missal. Her hair, white with age, had hints of its former color, auburn. "To what end?" Her ma's voice? "Gloucester who knows the price of everything and the value of nothing will measure his mourning as a miser measures his pennies. And your da? Only God may inflict such pain and only God may relieve it." The woman paused and balanced herself on Maddie's shoulder to dig a pebble out of her shoe, her touch lighter than a breath of air, then melted into the throng rushing up the stairs out of the Park Street subway station into the open air of Boston Common where she disappeared in the gathering fog.

Before summer's end, Maddie filed for divorce, waiving alimony because she wanted Gloucester out of her life forever, resuming her maiden name. Father Curry guaranteed perdition. A Devlin born, a Devlin I'll die, and as a Devlin I'll face whatever judgment God decrees for me, she replied. In September, she enrolled in law school, not Harvard, which accepted her but would not provide financial aid, but North-eastern where she alternated work semesters with study semesters to pay her own way.

Although she viewed law school as a trade school, except for its pretensions the same as training to become a court stenographer or airline mechanic or truck driver or any other trade or occupation whose schools of higher education advertised on the back of matchbooks, she worked hard to give her da the gift of being proud of his daughter. To dull her own pain, she became addicted to her studies, occluding her mind with cases on property law, securities, corporations, estate planning, criminal law, Constitutional law. She lived on legal precedents to avoid the precedents of her life. The joy her da felt at her achievements at law school—law review, magna cum laude, second in her class—brought her a measure of happiness, a brief respite from her pain.

All this and more Maddie remembered as she hiccoughed little sobs and sank further and further into the bath water, drinking deeply the sweet, black Guinness, hugging herself tightly, trying to squeeze out the bad the way she squeezed out pus from pimples as an adolescent. "You'll scar your face," her ma had warned, but she hadn't.

If it didn't work for my pimples, she now thought, why would it work for my soul? How bloody Irish of me. How fucking bloody Irish.

-4-

Shortly after sunset, Rabbi ben Reuben and Jacob Moskovitzky introduced Maddie to the intricate ritual of the *seder* in the dining room of the rabbi's home, a short walk from the synagogue where he presided. The ancient story of Israel's liberation from Egypt was retold in the prescribed order. The *seder* plate bearing the symbols of Passover, *matzohs*, the unleavened bread Jews ate on the exodus; roasted shank bone, symbol of the Paschal lamb, the sacrifice offered on the altar of the temple in Jerusalem; roasted egg, the second offering brought to the temple in Jerusalem; *moror*, bitter herbs which symbolized the bitterness of slavery; *haroses*, symbol of the mortar used to make bricks for the construction of Egyptian cities; and *karpas*, symbol of the arrival of spring and the gathering of the spring harvest; was explained. *Kiddush* was chanted. The four questions were asked by the youngest male present, the rabbi, and answered. The tale of the four sons was told. They drank four cups of wine which, on top of the Guinness, spun Maddie's head like a speeding merry-go-round. The rabbi opened the door for Elijah. The traditional benediction was offered: The following year grant us to be in Jerusalem.

Initially, Maddie sat politely, listened quietly, but before long she participated in the responsive readings. By the end of the meal, when the rabbi and Moskovitzky searched for the *afikomen*, a piece of *matzoh*, the last food eaten by the participants at the *seder*, which they insisted she hide so that it could be found and redeemed, she had warmed to the ceremony of the evening. They were so animated, momentarily children again, innocent and unburdened.

"Why aren't you with your grandson and his family?" she asked Moskovitzky.

"He does not believe in *seder*. Too old-fashioned. Too Jewish."

"This is nothing like what I expected," she said.

"Neither are you," Moskovitzky replied.

"What do you know of this Howard Kaplan?" the rabbi asked.

Outside, in the distance, a muffled sound like the solitary thump of a bass drum echoed, then faded.

"Nothing," Maddie said. "I've never run across him in court. He's not listed in my *Lawyer's Diary*. He has no entry in *Martindale-Hubbell*. It's like your grandson snapped his fingers and conjured him up out of thin air. But, I do know this. If this case goes to trial, it will be an absolute disaster. It should be plea bargained."

"If Avram pleads guilty," Moskovitzky said, "every Jew pleads guilty with him and will suffer worse than his punishment."

"The skull cap under the chair." She maintained eye contact, alternating from one to the other. "The jury will believe he lost it struggling with Bumper. True, he wasn't at the crime scene while Capablanca was open, but he can't account for his time after it closed, can't corroborate his alibi. Home studying alone, no juror will believe that. I doubt the jury would be out an hour before it convicted him for first-degree murder. Life without parole. It's guaranteed. Why risk that when a plea bargain to a lesser included offense and a sentence short of life is doable?"

"Who will negotiate this plea bargain?" Moskovitzky asked.

"Me. Before I join your grandson's firm. They'll cave because they're afraid of me. My track record. Kaplan's unknown. No one's afraid of him."

"What do you think?" Moskovitzky asked the rabbi.

Before he could reply, Maddie continued, "You want me off the case, withdraw Levy's consent and the judge will do it for you. Until then, I'm counsel of record and what I say goes."

Moskovitzky shook his cane in the air. "If the ancient Jews had your attitude I'd be building pyramids in Egypt and the

Irish would still be subjects of Her Majesty, the Queen. Would you have plea bargained Robert Emmet?"

"What's with you and Robert Emmet? You know one speck of Irish history and you think you know it all. If it pleases the court, I'm directly descended from Robert Emmet, that Robert Emmet, and yes, I would plea bargain him to keep him alive so he could fight another day. Martyrdom is overrated."

"We pray for a *golem*," Moskovitzky said, "and what does Hashem send us?"

"Levy's last, best, and only hope," Maddie replied.

"Who is abandoning her client for the Golden Calf," Moskovitzky said.

"I told you I'll cut the deal before I join your grandson's firm."

"*Golems* do not cut deals," Moskovitzky said.

"Good defense attorneys do."

The rabbi stopped massaging his knuckles and folded his hands in his lap. "A *golem* is created out of clay and brought to life by speaking the unspeakable, the name of the Almighty. In Prague in 1580, Rabbi Yehuda Loew created the Yosel *golem* to protect Jews from the blood libel accusation. At Passover that year, the local butcher exhumed the body of a Christian boy, drained its blood and cut its throat, and wrapped it in the carcass of a pig. He planned to bury it in the rabbi's yard in the dead of night, then dig it up the next morning and accuse the rabbi of blood libel, but the Yosel *golem* caught him in the act. The butcher denied it, but finally confessed. Since then, whenever Jews suffered accusations of blood libel, they sought refuge in the belief the miracle of a *golem* would save them. It is said the Yosel *golem* is to this day buried under old prayer books in the attic of Rabbi Loew's synagogue awaiting the time when he is again needed."

"If you think Kaplan's this *golem*, go with him." Maddie felt feverish from the heat, the wine, the Guinness, Moskovitzky's resistance to her logic. If logic would not persuade him, them, retreat was the soundest strategy. The only strategy. Retreat. And, in the morning, open negotiation with Bonturo. A *fait accompli* would bring them around to her way of thinking. If it didn't, let them force her recusal, abrogate the plea bargain, take the case to trial. She mumbled a thank-you for the dinner and an apology for departing so abruptly and slipped out the front door.

Outside, the neighborhood sweltered and the dreams of her new life wilted in the heat like a cheap plastic crucifix in a multi-alarm fire. Washington would be lonely without Michelle Furey. No woman could replace her. No man either. Not even Duncan Siward. But, if she stayed, Boston would devour her. Alive. Something no one, not even Michelle Furey, could protect her against. A hot wind slapped her face. The night sky glowed red and yellow like a sky besieged by a raging forest fire. Plumes of black smoke illuminated by the glow reached one-third of the way to heaven's peak. Sirens blared. She rushed inside to alert the rabbi and Moskovitzky.

"The *shul*," the rabbi said.

As they approached the synagogue, the red and blue lights of police cruisers swept across lichen covered tenement walls. Ululations filled the air with a chorus of laments. They rounded the corner and the synagogue came into view. Moskovitzky pitched forward. Maddie caught him and put her arm around his back and slipped her hand under his arm to hold him up. The rabbi supported himself on her other arm.

"Watch out for the broken glass," she said

Moskovitzky shuddered. "*Kristallnacht.*"

The rabbi prayed, nonsense syllables to Maddie, *Kaddish*, to those who understood Hebrew, then started babbling. "Time was on hot nights like this in Chelsea all the windows would be open and the whirring and clicking of sewing machines, like crickets in the field, was everywhere. Sewing machines. Rented to immigrants doing piecework for the mills. If you complained, a more recent arrival took your place. Work hard. Save. Penny by penny. If the baby didn't catch the grippe, buy a sewing machine. Control your own destiny. A generation for whom sleep was a luxury stolen in front of sewing machines so its sons and daughters could go to college. That wooden sign?" It hung almost within their reach, its Hebrew letters barely legible. "The *mikvah*. People once lined the street to get in. Closed. The shops. A man didn't work a lifetime so his son could become a shopkeeper in Chelsea or his daughter marry one. No, they worked a lifetime so when they died their sons and daughters would drive in from Newton or Brookline or Sharon to post the Closed sign. Another peddler had made his last sale."

On the curb, Shlomo the bookseller sat among the charred pages of Bibles and prayer books and *Sefer Torah* and Talmudic commentaries, the writings of Maimonides, the writings of Buber. "Ruined. Everything." His frail voice sounded like a sickly young boy's. He receded into the ashes of his store.

They continued their pilgrimage, the weight of Moskovitzky on one side, the rabbi on the other.

"Rabbi!" Yosef, the butcher, cried.

They stepped over pieces of glass painted with fragments of the Hebrew letters for "kosher". Shards jutted out of the window frame like the teeth of a piranha.

"Did they steal much?" Maddie asked.

"Would they have stolen everything," Yosef said.

"God of Job!" The rabbi gagged.

A disemboweled carcass of a pig, its side torn open, sprawled on the floor in front of the main display case. Swarms of flies blanketed it. Scores of cats, every stray in Chelsea, fought for position. The fittest clawed at the pig's carcass and slurped its body fluids. Rats bigger than small cats gorged on the pig's eyes and ears and tongue, scarring its face and head with gouges made by their sharp, pointed teeth. Swine blood stained the pale yellow poultry a deep red and pork fat desecrated the kosher beef. The floor shone like a sea wall covered with fresh guano.

Maddie doubled over and vomited her *seder* meal, but the cats and rats continued feeding. Only the flies, buzzing their approval, assayed her puke. Eleazer the grocer gave her a bottle of soda water. "The old country has come to the new," he said.

"The synagogue." The rabbi's voice cracked.

Its exterior was untouched. The cornerstone, granite, proclaiming "1890," was as resolute as the day it was dedicated. The stained-glass windows, which portrayed scenes from the Holy Scriptures in triptychs of many hues, unbroken, caught the fire's light and hurled it back like thunderbolts. It made no sense to Maddie that this fragile glass survived the maelstrom on the streets, unless it had been intentionally spared. By whom? The hand of God? Or, the hands of people with the sickest of the sick sense of humor?

With Maddie's hand in the small of his back, the rabbi seized a railing and pulled himself up the shallow front steps of the synagogue. Moskovitzky followed. The lock had been gouged out of the wooden door. The foyer was the same as when she had first visited the rabbi and Moskovitzky. Prayer books filled the shelves waiting for congregants to gather for the next service. A chest of black yarmulkes guarded the doors to the sanctuary. Prayer shawls were draped over a wooden rod. The rabbi kissed a yarmulke and placed it on his head, as did Moskovitzky, who handed one to Maddie together with a bobby pin for her to fasten it to her hair.

Inside the sanctuary under the back pew, she saw a bracelet. It reminded her of the identification bracelet engraved with her name she received as a First Communion gift. It was silver and shiny, that gift, and had a secret compartment where she kept a four-leaf clover rather than a family photo because she believed a four-leaf clover would bring her the luck of the Irish. She wore the bracelet day and night, everywhere but the shower. As she grew and the links became tighter it made a permanent indentation in the soft skin of her wrist until a link popped open and the bracelet fell from her wrist. Where, she did not know. Like life, one moment it had been there, the next it was gone.

Reaching under the pew, Maddie picked up the bracelet, examined it, then sealed it inside a stamped envelope she kept in her purse, a superstition she inherited from her ma who was always prepared in case she unexpectedly had to mail a letter.

"The *Torah*!" Rabbi ben Reuben shrieked. It had been unrolled down the aisle and a red swastika stenciled on each page. His body stiffened as if a bolt of lightning entered his body through his eyes and coursed through his nerves, then slackened as if the electricity had exited his nervous system. His arms flailed like high tension wires detached from their grounds.

"Epilepsy?" Maddie asked, but Moskovitzky shook his head.

The rabbi collapsed on the floor, gasping for breath like a man who would not survive without a respirator. He stared straight up, his eyes unseeing, the eyes of a blind man who no longer had memories of ever being sighted. Maddie put her purse under his head and loosened his belt and tie.

Moskovitzky replaced his yarmulke. The rabbi's lips quivered. He mumbled, a stutterer who choked on his words. His eyes widened. His eyelids withdrew inside his head. His face had the expression of a man witnessing something so horrific he could not turn away, something he had seen before but had erased from his memory.

"He needs a doctor," Maddie said. "Is there a payphone?"

The rabbi grabbed Maddie's arm. His fingers dug into her flesh. The tighter he gripped, the calmer he became. His face relaxed. The rabbi closed his eyes, then opened them. They focused, his eyes. Not on her. Not on Moskovitzky. Not on the ceiling above them. Not on anything in the sanctuary of the synagogue. In those eyes, Maddie now saw a clarity she had not seen before. Something had excised the cataracts that had blinded the rabbi to his past with a precision beyond the capability of any human hand. The rabbi's hand fell limply from her arm. With effort, he placed it flat against his chest, over his heart as if he were pledging loyalty to something known only to him. His change in demeanor transfixed Maddie.

"How could they have known?" The rabbi's voice sounded as if it were coming from somewhere else, another time, another place. He repeated his question, each repetition bringing his voice closer and closer until, at last, it was here and now. "How could they have known?"

Maddie held the rabbi's hands.

"So long ago. I was just ordained. Just married. A small apartment. Two rooms. A window overlooking *Gutenstrasse*."

The rabbi spoke softly and they had to bend over, their ears inches above his mouth.

"She made curtains. Blue and white. With flowers. Not much furniture. A table from my uncle. Two chairs. Didn't match. Sleeping. Hot. Windows open. Pounding at the door. Does the rabbi live here? More pounding, louder. *Schnell*. I was scared. Confused. Didn't know what to do. Gestapo. One had a riding crop. Drunk. Whiskey breath. Black shiny boots. I'm Otto Kempka.

"She came out of the bedroom. Soldiers went in. Tore apart the bedding. Pulled out drawers. Emptied closet. Smashed mirror. Kempka. Whiskey breath. Her wedding gown. She tried to save it. Kempka hit her with his riding crop. Cheek split open. Blood. Raised my hand. He hit me across the face and made her hold the gown. He forced a scissors into my hand. Cut into strips, he ordered. For my daughter, she begged. Kempka laughed. Never to be born, he said. It took forever. A pile of white at her feet. Like firewood at the feet of a person to be burned at the stake.

"The synagogue, Kempka said. Four stayed with her. An hour. Two blocks. An hour. Whiskey breath. The *Torah*. If you want to see your wife again . . . I unrolled it down the aisle. A bucket. Red liquid. Warm. Too thin to be paint. No paint smell. A brush. Stencil. Swastika. On every page, Kempka ordered. With each stroke I begged Hashem's forgiveness. An hour, two hours. How long? Don't know. Kempka drank whiskey. When I was done, I thought I had cut myself. They left me there. I ran home. She was gone. No clothes. No books. No furniture. No pictures. Nothing but strips of wedding gown. I went to the landlord. Out or I'll call the Gestapo. New tenants in the morning. I searched. Everywhere. Hospitals. Cemeteries. Jails. Morgues. The dump. The streets. The river. Never found. Never found. I was taken to the camps. I searched again. Survived. Came to America. Came to Chelsea. Never found."

The rabbi blinked. His eyes slowly focused as he returned from a distant place, a distant time.

"*Sie wäre wie alt?*" he asked. "Sixty-six? Did her eyes really sing? I don't have a picture. Is she dead? *Ist sie tot? Kann ich sicher sein Ich habe nie Kaddisch gesagt. Ich habe nie wieder geheiratet. Wie könnte ich?*

"Faces. I looked at faces. In crowds. On the streets. I didn't know why. Now, I do. *Vielleicht das nächste Gesicht. Einmal in einer Cafeteria. Essen Toast. Langsam. Sehr, sehr langsam.* Working girl's hands. Clean from a lifetime spent in other people's water. After every bite, wiped her lips with the napkin. *München, sagte ich. Pardon? Sie sagte. Aus der Tür. Die Straße entlang. Weg. Weg.*"

The rabbi was quiet now. Moskovitzky was crumpled on the floor beside him, his head bowed. Maddie wept. She wept for the rabbi. For the words she did not know, but understood. For the wife whose name he never spoke. For the *Torah* unrolled on the synagogue floor. For what was happening in Boston. She wept tears of bitterness and in her tears she forged a bond between herself and these two ancient Jews, and she knew, the way one knows a truth to be true precisely because it cannot be proven, that somewhere, beyond all the tears, walked a young Jewish bride, the rabbi's wife, in the company of young Master Devlin. She now appreciated the lesson of Elizabeth's death, that each death sires its own unique sadness, and she realized she now wept for the exception which proved the rule, that the sadness caused by the death of Master Devlin and the rabbi's wife was the same sadness, made bitter by being murdered out of hatred. The rabbi was quiet now, and still she wept.

The rabbi rose from the floor. Page by page, with great care, he rolled up the *Torah* while Moskovitzky searched for the finials, mantle, and silver breastplate. He found the *yad*, the silver pointer used by the reader to mark his place. Under the front row of pews, she found the stencil. A swastika like in the rabbi's story.

"Read a portion," Moskovitzky said.

The rabbi recited the blessing offered by those called to the *Torah*: "*Borchu es adonoi amvoroh . . .*,"

Maddie stared at the black letters glowing through the swastika's pale red. At the *seder* table that night, the rabbi had told her *Torah* was the tree of life to those who clung fast to it and now she saw how it revived him. He picked up the *yad*. She followed its tip across the page as he touched each word. The rabbi's voice strengthened word by word and filled the sanctuary. At the end of the passage, the rabbi recited the blessing after the reading of the *Torah*: "*Boruch ato adonoi . . .*,"

"It's from *Exodus*," the rabbi said, "the crossing of the Red Sea when Moses parted the waters and the Children of Israel passed safely but the Egyptians drowned.

"There is another version. When Moses led the Children of Israel to the Red Sea, it is said, he cried out to Hashem for help. Hear my prayers, Moses said. Hashem replied: This is not a time for prayer. This is a time for faith. Go forth into the Red Sea or suffer your fate at the hands of the Egyptians. Moses led the Children of Israel into the waters. The water rose to their ankles, their knees, their waists, their chests, their necks. Moses walked onward and the Children of Israel followed. When the water reached their noses, the sea churned and parted and Moses led them to safety."

Maddie thought of Yeats's poem, *Parnell's Funeral*. Her da cried whenever he read it. Yeats asked, "What is this sacrifice?" and lamented that Parnell's death was a useless sacrifice because his heart was eaten by his own people. Now, Yeats's question, What is this sacrifice? confronted her. She could not run from being Mary Ann Devlin any more than Jacob Moskovitzky could run from being Jacob Moskovitzky. For her, for the rabbi, for Moskovitzky, the answer to Yeats's question, sooner or later, had to be, I am this sacrifice.

Another thought formed in Maddie's mind, slowly co-alescing the way a memory does when the mind unexpectedly encounters a reminder of the past. Levy did not resist a plea bargain because he was a fatalist bound by God's will; nor did he resist a plea bargain because he was a fanatic on a mission. His resistance was a proclamation to her, to the rabbi, to Moskovitzky, of his innocence, a proclamation of his willingness to go to trial than plead guilty to something he did not do. It was an act of courage, his answer to Yeats's question. He, too, was that sacrifice.

She took Moskovitzky's hand in one of hers, the rabbi's in the other, resting her fingertips against his gnarled knuckles. In her mind's eye, she also held Levy's hands, convinced now beyond all reasonable doubt that he was innocent in fact.

As they, Maddie, Rabbi ben Reuben, Moskovitzky, exited the synagogue into the oven of a hot April night and passed through the handiwork of hate spread out on both sides of a dying, dead Chelsea street, she vowed to God to follow the bracelet from beneath the pew in the synagogue in Chelsea and to follow the stencil to wherever they may lead. And she vowed to God to become, if necessary, whatever sacrifice was demanded of her to prove Avram Levy innocent. On Elizabeth's soul, she did vow. And the souls of her namesakes and the souls of her ma and da and grand da and she wished they were all alive to share the moment.

And, they were.

-5-

Maddie escorted Rabbi ben Reuben and Jacob Moskovitzky through the gauntlet of destruction which once was a Chelsea street of Jewish shops, stepping over fire hoses snaking away from hydrants, stepping around fire engines and police cruisers and ambulances with their back doors open. A cop hustled them behind a police barrier that cordoned off a side street. A scrum of reporters demanding access, television and newspapers, swarmed around them, their way blocked by a wall of police. A reporter with a *The New York Times* press credential hanging around his neck tried to interview them, but Maddie brushed him aside, brushed all the reporters and cameramen aside. Breaking free of the scrum, she guided the rabbi and Moskovitzky away from the police barrier, down the side street, back to the rabbi's home.

That night, sleep did not come to Maddie Devlin. Television, radio, records, books, magazines, warm milk, a snifter of brandy, a bottle of Guinness, nothing quieted her mind nor quelled her anxieties. Her future, her escape from the sinkhole of legal aid, her liberation, now lay engulfed in the disemboweled innards of a pig greedily devoured by rats and feral cats on the floor of a kosher butcher; in the flakes of carbonized pages of sacred texts wafting in the fiery wind; in pale red swastikas desecrating the parchment of the Hebrew Bible; in an identification bracelet sealed in an envelope in her purse.

She tried to visualize what lay beyond, but a fog, thick and viperous, occluded her view. She was about to take her first step on a long journey; but she had no guide. Alone at the midpoint of her life, she would have to find her own way. She felt spikes being driven through her hands and feet, a crown of thorns being forced down on her head, wounds being gouged in her side.

The suffocating heat kindled memories Maddie now wished she did not have, memories of clients who had murdered but were acquitted because she had out-thought, out-prepared, out-lawyered the prosecution. How many had murdered again? Too many, but she had wrapped herself in the cliché of the Seventh Amendment; no sin committed, no sin confessed. Not according to Levy's Talmud test. That test she had failed. She had researched Catholic doctrine. It was more forgiving, teaching it was morally licit for an attorney to defend a client the attorney knows to be guilty as long as the attorney does not misrepresent facts to the court, such as allowing the client to commit perjury or presenting an alibi defense the attorney knew to be false. Being morally licit did not assuage her guilt. Outside her window, heat currents swarmed around the street-light like thugs waiting their turn to rape a young girl.

Maddie threw on some clothes and wandered the neighborhood. Bags of garbage awaiting the morning pickup lined the curbs. She smelled and tasted the heat-intensified stench. Lights from the twenty-four-hour convenience store at the corner beckoned. The bullet editions of the morning papers would be on the newspaper rack. A way to kill time until dawn. Maybe a better future was hidden in her horoscope.

"I saw you on the tube," the clerk said as she handed him a five-dollar bill to pay for two twenty-five-cent newspapers. He wore a leather sweat band on each wrist, laced with rawhide rather than buckled. The veins in his arms wiggled like blue earthworms burrowing beneath his skin. There were no needle marks. Maybe he injected between his toes. Many of her clients did. On his forehead above his right eye, a tattoo of a skull laughed when he raised his eyebrow. As he talked, its jaws opened and closed. None of the gang members she had defended over the years sported a tattoo like that. Maybe there was a new gang in town; or, maybe, it was a souvenir of too much hash, too much booze, too much cunt, while on R&R

in Saigon. She had never seen this clerk before; but, then, with the rapid turnover on the graveyard shift, she rarely saw the same person twice. His hand lingered over the button that opened the cash drawer. She asked for her change.

"I hear you fuck Jews. Darkies. Spics. Gooks. How 'bout me? War hero, I am."

She picked up three packages of hot dogs, $1.49 each, from the cooler. "I get off on these, pencil prick. Buy yourself a blow job with the change." His obscenities chased her down the street. He stood on the sidewalk outside the store. Its fluorescent lights made him look like a child's toy which glowed in the dark. From down the block, she shouted, "Your better half dripped down your mother's leg,"

He faked a move toward her. "At least I had a mother."

In her apartment, Maddie nibbled on the hot dogs, raw and uncooked, kosher, which she hadn't noticed when she grabbed them. The problem messages hidden in horoscopes was that, like beauty, their meaning was in the eye of the beholder. She might as well believe in the Oracle of Delphi.

She telephoned George Harriman. "Meet me at Behan's. It's about the Chelsea business."

"Christ, Maddie, do you know what time it is?"

"Time is of the essence, Uncle George."

Behan's was Southie's last all-night railroad diner and it didn't serve decaf. A "Sanka is for sissies" needlepoint made by one of the waitresses hung above the coffee urns. Sanka, as everyone in Southie knew, was packaged in orange, a color as welcome in Behan's as Maddie Devlin herself.

Maddie was on her third cup of coffee and the caffeine was beginning to infuriate her system as she waited for Harriman. People who traded day for night crowded the diner: cops and firefighters unwinding from the four to midnight shift; truck drivers on their way from delivering the bullet edition of the newspapers; donut makers relaxing before firing up the grease vats to prepare for the morning rush; janitors and cleaning ladies who moved into Boston's office towers after the secretaries, business executives, bankers, lawyers finished for the day; interns and residents recuperating from a seventy-two hour shift in the emergency rooms of the city hospitals. They all flocked to Behan's because Behan's specialized in truckburgers—shitburgers in impolite company—a hamburger grilled in butter with a slab of American cheese, topped by a fried egg, sunny side up, and thick slices of fresh onions pan fried in the butter and hamburger juices. Banished to the back booth by the door to the restrooms, Maddie sat alone with her coffee.

"Two truckburgers rare and a large milk," Harriman called to the counterman as he made his way the length of the diner to where Maddie waited. A "whole milk is holy" needlepoint by the same waitress decorated the milk dispenser. Harriman traded greetings, a handshake or slap on the back, a whisper, at every stool along the counter, every booth along the wall of windows.

"So, my rose upon the rood of time," he said when he reached her. "What witchery are you up to at this ungodly hour?"

"I found this in the Chelsea synagogue." She dropped the envelope with the identification bracelet in the middle of the table. "And the swastika stencil."

With a pencil, Harriman picked up the identification bracelet and held it to the light, then returned it to the envelope, sealing it. "Trojan horse," he said.

"Who's Badger?" Maddie asked. The name Badger Thomas was engraved beside the Trojan horse.

"Silvy Thomas's brother. She's Mabi's woman." The waitress brought the truckburgers and milk, sneering at Maddie as she set the order on the table.

Maddie ignored her. "This is why Ugolino wanted a change of venue. He figured out the connection."

Harriman filled his mouth with truckburger. He ripped a napkin from the dispenser and wiped his chin. "I thought it was Levy's absence from Capablanca."

Maddie continued, "The bracelet links Chelsea to the Trojans. I'm betting the stencil links the Trojans to Bumper's murder. I'm betting it's his blood on the stencil."

"Interesting theories."

"Worth investigating."

"By the police."

"I don't trust Ugolino," Maddie said, "especially after he handed off the case to Angelo the Sweeper."

"Why would Ugolino protect Mabi and the Trojans? A black, a Jew, one scalp's as good as the other for him."

"Not when the black is fat on drug money and the Jew indigent."

"Speculation."

"Often the first step toward the truth."

Harriman chewed his truckburger. His facial expression, earnest as if he were trying to solve a puzzle, told Maddie his mind was not on his food. His eyes snapped back into focus, fixing on her as if she were a fugitive, armed and dangerous

"If this is evidence," he said, "you can't withhold it. You could be disbarred. I could be fired and lose my pension. Your da would be the first to agree with me."

"If I'm right, and my gut tells me I am, you'll be a hero and Ugolino will be doing time for obstructing justice. As for my da, I think he'd back me on this one."

Maddie wanted to believe her da would. She had last seen him more than nine years before on a Friday afternoon in September, a month after she sat for the bar exam, two months

before the announcement of the results. Years of smoking cigarettes and inhaling the oily fumes of the punch press room
had killed him. The afternoon of his wake, a few private moments before the arrival of the mourners, she leaned forward
and kissed him on his forehead, leaving as their last tangible
link a smudge caused by her lipstick. She examined her da's
face, searching the hollows of his cheeks and the shadow of his
beard for clues as to the whereabouts of his soul. He looked so
serene, so much the gentleman in his burial suit. He had finally
escaped to the rural corner of his beloved Ireland, reunited in
heaven with all who loved him and with all whom he loved.

She had felt so abandoned that day nine years ago,
standing alone beside her da's open casket, greeting mourners,
accepting their platitudes with the kindness with which they
were offered. Being the only child of only children had never
bothered her before. She never thought about it. Yet, now, her
side of the Devlin family would go extinct like the dinosaurs
with herself eternally shamed by the lies of a false informer.
More than her da lay dead in the casket. She felt weightless,
without substance, buffeted like a milkweed in a strong wind.
The long line of mourners crowding the foyer of the funeral
home and filling the parlor did not dispel her loneliness. Soon,
these people would leave, go back to their own lives, their own
problems, reducing their connection to her to a polite hello,
how are you, on Sunday morning after Mass.

Her mind drifted as she greeted the callers, reserving
enough concentration to address each by name, to thank
them for their condolences. She had spent too much of her
life burying people, her ma, her daughter, her da. Who was left
to bury her? Love wasn't worth the sorrow it brought. Father
Curry told her to remember the happy times, but how could
she be truly happy knowing life was so ephemeral. Maybe the

nuns had it right. In high school she believed only women afraid of happiness hid inside the nun's habit. Maybe it wasn't fear, but wisdom to realize the only true happiness was eternal happiness which only came from falling in love with God's only begotten Son; but, the nuns didn't seem so happy either. She could tell by the way they walked, slowly as if life had already passed them by.

That day at her da's wake she had asked for a glass of water and Moynihan led her into a private parlor reserved for immediate family. The mourners waiting their turn grumbled at the interruption. By the window of the parlor another couple sat, their heads bowed in prayer. Maddie was grateful for their presence. She closed her eyes and rested her head on her hands, trying to merge into the silence. Clothes rustled, people rising, as quietly as possible, tiptoeing so they wouldn't disturb her. She raised her head out of politeness to acknowledge them.

"Duncan!"

"I'm sorry about your dad." He shifted his weight from foot to foot. "My wife, Natalie."

"I feel like I knew your father, the way Duncan talked about him," Natalie said. She had a soft, kind voice, the perfect voice to soothe a young child with a scraped knee or elbow.

"I heard about Elizabeth," Duncan said. "I was in California. I bought a card, but I couldn't bring myself to mail it. I was going to call, but . . . I guess I figured you didn't want to hear from me."

"I didn't want to hear from anyone," Maddie said. "When are you due?" she asked Natalie.

"Five weeks."

"Do you have a name?"

"James if it's a boy; Colleen for a girl."

Maddie wanted to keep her talking. The peacefulness of her voice, the soft, smooth flow of her words. "Are you here for a visit?"

"We're moving to Boston," Duncan said. "I have a grant to do blood research. Somehow I ended up in hematology."

"I pegged you as a pediatrician," Maddie said.

"Hon." Natalie leaned against the back of a couch.

"She tires easily in the heat," Duncan said.

Maddie offered her hand, first to Natalie, then to Duncan, keeping her arm stiff so he couldn't lean in and kiss her. "Thanks for coming. Good luck with the baby."

Maddie lingered in the parlor to give them a chance to leave. Something about Natalie's voice told Maddie they could become great friends, not acquaintances who made believe they were friends by playing bridge; but Maddie knew they never would. It wouldn't be fair to Duncan. Nor to herself.

College had divorced her and Duncan; Boston College for her, Notre Dame for him. Maddie had also been accepted at Notre Dame, but she needed a scholarship and Boston College offered her one. Three days before Duncan left for Notre Dame, he came over to fix her bike. When he had finished, she invited him in for lemonade. They cuddled on the living room couch while he finished his drink, then she kissed him, enjoying the taste of lemonade in his mouth. When he closed his eyes, she pulled up her top and pressed his hand against her breast. The feeling of his hand on her breast gave her the same sense of being connected, being anchored, as when they held hands and she wondered if this was the difference between sex and love. As they kissed, she saw herself, sixty years in the future, flabby and wrinkled, and she wondered if Duncan would be there for her.

Soon, they were naked, lying on the floor, and she could feel the summer breeze blowing against her skin. She guided him into her, the pain not as bad as the anticipation, and as he moved, she became wetter. She moved with him, answering each thrust with a thrust of her own until, like a flash of heat lightening in summer, he filled her with himself, then deflated, too limp to continue, and slipped out of her, his penis lying wet and shrunken against her thigh.

"I'm sorry," he mumbled.

She guided his hand to her, but he jerked it away as if her wetness repelled him. He stood up, saying it was getting late. She reached for him; but he had started dressing, slipping into his underwear, then his shorts and jersey. "Hold me. Please."

He left quickly and she lay there on the damp towel in the middle of her living room floor listening to the click of the reflector in the spokes of the front wheel of his bike as he pedaled away. She felt as if she had been widowed before being married.

Duncan neither phoned nor wrote from Notre Dame until President Kennedy's assassination when he called and tried to comfort her. She also tried to comfort him, but all they could do was cry and, for the first time when it really mattered, she realized Duncan would never comfort her again.

As that weekend unfolded, the weekend of Dallas and Oswald and Ruby and a new president being sworn in on an airplane flying toward Washington, Maddie sat in front of the television, feeling the grief of Carolyn and John John, adding it to her own; and when John John saluted his fallen father, she gathered her own personal grief around her like a winter coat, tied it around her throat like a scarf, and rode the Green Line into Park Street, walking down the stairs to Park Street Under where the Harvard Square-Ashmont line stopped, a true subway with a live third rail. She sat on a bench beneath a no-smoking sign pushing at cigarette butts with the toes of her shoes, buttoned up against the November cold, which came from within. Two, three, four trains, some for Harvard Square, some for Ashmont, arrived, stopped, departed. With each, she thought about jumping on the tracks, electrocuting herself, being crushed.

The day passed and the trains continued arriving, stopping, departing, mostly empty because everyone was home watching history on television. Soon, though it really wasn't soon, a police officer told her the station would be closing for the night, the last Green Line would be arriving in a few minutes. She caught the last train home where, still wrapped tightly in her coat and scarf, she climbed into bed, too numb to dream, too tired to sleep.

Sunrise, she tossed and turned, exhausted. Downstairs, over the soft sound of the television, she heard her da and Uncle George talking quietly about how worried they were at her reaction to Jack Kennedy's assassination, how it seemed so much more extreme than her reaction to her ma's death, and whether Father Curry should be asked to counsel her. Listening to their voices, Maddie realized her da, for all his silences, for all his solitude, for the way he dragged her hither and thither in Dublin, loved her in the special way fathers love daughters. She stripped off her winter coat and unwound the scarf from around her neck. She smelled from sleeping in her clothes and she wanted to shower for her da, then hug him and cry on his shoulder and tell him that she loved him and that she would be all right and to thank him for being her da. The shower felt good and, for the first time since Kilmainham, since Traitor's Hell, she felt clean.

As those memories retreated back into storage and memories of her da's wake replaced them, she remembered that Harriman had joined her in the sitting room on that day nine years earlier.

"You holding up okay?"

THE FIRE THIS TIME

"I saw Duncan Siward. He's married. His wife is pregnant."

"People are waiting."

She offered her hand so he could help her stand. "Have you chosen a reading?"

"I was leaning toward *The Second Coming*, but I wonder if it's too political. Would you prefer something else?"

"One of the early poems," she said. "Maybe *The Song of Wandering Aengus*. ' . . . the silver apples of the moon, the golden apples of the sun . . .'" She drew a deep breath. "The Christmas after ma died, we went to Ireland, Kilmainham, Traitor's Hell, Glasnevin. He made me promise . . . "

"He's finally free, Maddie." Harriman had placed his hand on her shoulder. "Don't take his place in the cell."

Now, nine years later, April of 1981, she had become her father's proxy in the prison of the past, a pariah to everyone for whom St. Patrick's Day was a holy day of obligation. Sitting across from Harriman in the back booth of Behan's, she said, "I want you to arrest Badger Thomas."

"Charges?" Yellow yoke dried on Harriman's chin.

"The bracelet is more than enough probable cause for an arrest. I should know."

"Not if the police don't know about it. Not if it's not logged into the evidence room." He bit into his second truckburger. "What's your theory?"

"It puts him at the scene the way the skull cap put Levy at the scene and you arrested him."

Harriman lowered his half-eaten truckburger.

"Keep the bracelet, but . . . "

"Chain of custody, Maddie," he interrupted. "How will I establish chain of custody?"

"I'm taking the stencil to Duncan Siward at Mass. General," Maddie continued, "so he can run blood grouping tests."

"You're playing a dangerous game, Maddie. A call from Ugolino and the DA will charge you with withholding evidence, tampering with evidence, interfering with a police investigation, God knows what else."

"What police investigation? Angelo the Sweeper's dog and pony show spoon fed to the press? Ugolino himself told me he had his man as soon as Charlie found the skull cap. No. I turn this in and Procaccino will make it disappear faster than the booze at a cop's retirement party."

"I'll have your back."

"Thanks, but no thanks. The DA will charge you as my co-conspirator. I don't want you to sacrifice your pension over something that's my responsibility."

Maddie twitched as the caffeine roiled her nervous system. She had scooped up the bracelet and sealed it in the envelope without showing it to the rabbi or Moskovitzky. She doubted they had seen her do it. The argument was so obvious: a plant, a frame, the same argument she planned to use to explain Levy's skull cap. She cursed the stupidity of her haste.

"Brand me a traitor, but I'm an honest traitor. Ugolino may lie to prove Levy guilty, but I won't lie to prove him innocent."

"I'll need to take your statement tonight because I'm leaving for Dublin after early Mass."

"Why now? I need you here."

"Ugolino. Some conference on international extradition procedures. I think he suspects something and wants me out of the way. I'll be a phone call and a five-hour flight away." Harriman covered her hands with his. "You'll have to sign off on it under the pains and penalties of perjury."

"Is my credibility that low?"

"Standard operating procedure."

"Not in any witness statements I've been given."

"Yes, your credibility's that low."

"With you, too?" When Harriman did not reply, she asked, "Who'll make the arrest?"

"If there's an arrest," he spoke slowly to emphasize the iffy nature of the situation, "the gang unit. It's their play whether I'm here or not. There's hell to pay if anyone trespasses into their jurisdiction."

"Will they?"

"I'll call in an IOU."

"They know what they're doing?"

"Ever overturn one of their collars?"

"Thank you, Uncle George."

For the first time since she could remember, Maddie didn't notice the heat.

PART II

MABI

Chapter 9

Easter Sunday, April 19, 1981

-1-

Mabi felt trapped inside a light bulb he couldn't turn off.

Chelsea had been perfectly executed. The Trojans had assembled at their home base in the cellar of the tenement where Gabe Tucker once lived. Mabi had stolen the name of the gang from a comic book Gideon, his old man but not his old head, had long ago thrown in his face. When Gabe Tucker lived there, a lily-white slumlord from lily-white Lexington owned the building, but now the Trojans owned it, trading it for a promise not to firebomb the slumlord's house or office. The gang had acquired several other buildings the same way. It held title to all in the names of straws, nominee realty trusts dreamed up by one of the lawyers the Trojans had on retainer, another scam like Ta-Kome Pizza, a store front that sold Sicilian pizza by the square or by the pie, to launder drug money. Lighting, plumbing, electrical work, carpentry, and building supplies to renovate the buildings were tithed by whites doing business in the black community. For the Trojans' chill pad, local merchants donated furniture, appliances, and assorted play-things such as pool tables, stereos, televisions, and video games. Cates for Carpets contributed floor covering, tile in the kitchen and bathroom, wall-to-wall in the other rooms; Bendet's Home Furnishings, couches, chairs, and accessories.

For Chelsea, the Trojans had worn light weight running shoes with black rubber soles, black dungarees, black jerseys decorated with the silhouette of a Trojan horse in a dusky shade of gray so dark it was invisible to anyone more than a few feet away, and black gloves. Lampblack smeared on their cheeks and foreheads absorbed the glare from their sweat. Theatrical make-up blackened their teeth. They costumed themselves to be as visible as ravens on a moonless night.

"Everything ready?" Mabi had asked.

"The pig it's gutted and iced, the blood bottled," Spider, Mabi's warlord, had said. "We jacked a truck-load of crystal glasses and they be smashed."

"Firebombs?"

"Three dozen," Spider replied.

"Explosives?"

"The sun be shining tonight," Scorpion, the explosives expert, replied.

"We need an hour inside," Mabi said. "Nothing goes down 'til we done and clear. Badger! Grab that shoe box and ride with me."

A half hour later, Mabi and Badger had vaulted the low wall behind the Chelsea synagogue, which housed the remnants of Rabbi Isaac ben Reuben's congregation, the congregation where Levy once made up a *minyan*, and lowered themselves into its tiny back-yard. Jimmying the lock on the back door, they entered the small social hall immediately beneath the sanctuary.

"Make sure the water's steam hot," Mabi ordered Badger.

THE FIRE THIS TIME

In the sanctuary, Mabi mounted the stage and located what Professor al-Saffah had called the Ark. From behind its curtain he removed a set of scrolls which he stripped of its silver ornaments and velvet cover. Untying the sash that bound the scrolls, he unrolled them down the aisle past rows of empty pews. The paper was thick and coarse, the pages sewn together by hand. The letters reminded him of the Hebrew letters on the graves in the cemetery he had vandalized, on the synagogue walls he had spray painted with swastikas, on the tablets beside the lions in the African Meeting House, page after page of tiny black letters. He ran his fingers over a few lines, feeling the texture of the ink. Fucking old, he thought, maybe as old as al-Saffah's chess set.

"Yo! Hot water," Badger said.

"I don't see no steam rising."

Badger's excitement drained from his face like life from a junkie swimming in the sweetness of another fix. Returning minutes later, he asked, "Steamy enough for you?"

"No, but we ain't got time to fuck around." Mabi gave him a brush and stencil. "Mix in the blood, then do like I said."

Mabi perched on a window sill and peeked through a curtain to check the street. He sensed a higher presence in the sound of the brush rubbing against the stencil. He felt as pumped, as invincible, as the night he'd killed Luke Shaw. From Luke Shaw to Bumper Sullivan, he had murdered, pushed drugs, led the Trojans, at first without regret, then with an occasional second thought, at last without guilt because it had been decreed, all he had done. The power lording over him, he now understood, was not the power of the book or the power of belief; it was the power of his name. When you name something, you own it; and Allah had soul-bought him by naming him Mabi. Gideon and Hannah, Silvy, the Trojans, they only made demands. He had given them a chance, hundreds of chances, but only his

247

name gave him what he needed, a past, a present, a future. Revelation's book was all. Its pages turned fast, faster than ever before. How many more to the end?

"Done," Badger said.

"The fire next time it's now, little bro, and you helped light the kindling."

Now, a few hours later, back at the crib, he and Spider had been tallying the week's drug receipts in the money room, stacking Hamiltons, Jacksons, Franklins, smoking dope, siggin' each other and everyone else in the fucking gang. The money room had been built to Mabi's specifications in the tenement basement where the coal bin had once been: cinderblock walls lined with sheets of lead, poured concrete floor and ceiling, solid core steel door with inside hinges, a keyless lock, an old-fashioned walk-in safe. Every Sunday, Mabi and Spider reviewed the books and divided the week's profit among the gang, equal shares for everyone, a double share for Mabi, a share for a rainy day fund.

"We're going to butter the bread real thick this week," Mabi said.

"Check out Brother Ambrose," Spider replied. "I think he's putting our cut into them fancy roller skates."

"Maybe we should have a sit down." The intercom buzzed and Mabi unlocked the door for Silvy Thomas, his woman, Badger's older sister.

"Badger's been arrested. Middle of the night. Six cops with a paper." Silvy slapped him across the face with it. "They busted him right in front of me and Cealy for that Chelsea shit." Cealy was Silvy's and Badger's mother. "Anything happen to Badger I'll kill you dead." Mabi put his arms around her and let her beat on him until she exhausted her anger. "That's why I won't never become Mrs. Mabi."

"Tell Cealy," Mabi said, "he be bailed when the courts open come morning. Trojans they take care for their own."

"He ain't your own to take care of." She spit in his face.

Later, after Silvy left, after Spider divided the week's green into shares, after the Easter morning sun rose on the desolation that once was a Jewish street in Chelsea, Mabi no longer felt pumped, no longer felt invincible. "Everything has a fixed term of life, an endpoint, an *ajal*," al-Saffah had preached. "Your life, my life, the life of the universe, the desecrations and corruptions of Christianity and Judaism, everything has its *ajal*." He feared Badger's arrest was the first page of his *ajal*, the first page of the Trojans' *ajal*. Alone, his *ajal* haunted him like the shadows in his bedroom and the noises made by the radiator that had kept him awake at night when he was a young child.

Hauling his doubts the way slaves once shouldered bundles of cotton, Mabi visited Badger at the Charles Street Jail. "What you doing here, you fucking punany?"

"I lost my bracelet. When I undressing at home, I seen it missing."

"You facing all kinds of juvie shit. Remember. Fifth Amendment. They can't make you talk."

"My grille be sealed tighter than a nun's cunt."

"It fucking better be or you'll be Mushi Badger at every chink joint in Chinatown."

-2-

The night of Badger's arrest was not the first time Mabi felt trapped inside a light bulb he couldn't turn off. He had felt the same way the night of Bumper Sullivan's murder as he made his way from Capablanca carrying plastic bags of Bumper's blood in a supermarket shopping bag to the apartment of his mullah, his sage, Professor Husam al din al-Saffah, an imam from the Disciples of Abraham Mosque who disguised his true identity by posing as a professor of Islamic studies at the Boston campus of the University of Massachusetts. That earlier night, the air, too hot to breathe, seared Mabi's lungs and boiled his brain. Visions of things not there obstructed his vision. The stink of rust, so strong he could taste it, wafted from the supermarket shopping bag and clung to the lining of his nose, souring his stomach. His sweat blackened the supermarket logo–"Purity Supreme As Fresh as Tomorrow"–and bonded the shopping bag to his arms and chest. His heartbeat sent waves pulsing through Bumper's blood. In his ears, the sound of those waves echoed. He struggled to open the door to the lobby of al-Saffah's apartment building. Inside the lobby, the heat, frenzied from being caged all day, feasted on him. As he climbed the stairs, the temperature climbed with him. With each step, with each vision of things not there, each smell of rust, each roar of waves crashing, he had relived Bumper Sullivan's murder and the chess game that preceded it.

At the Capablanca Chess Club, Mabi had maneuvered Bumper into a chess game by calling out Pete Kelly, the Club champion, for refusing to accept Mabi's challenge to a match. Kelly had urged Bumper to "put that damn nigger in his place," Kelly's voice loud enough for Mabi to hear. Mabi let the slur slide. The words of infidels mattered not.

Mabi knew Bumper had a key to Capablanca. He knew Bumper often lingered in the library after the Club closed at 9:00 p.m. to study the games of the international grandmasters. He knew because he had staked out the club several times that at eleven a cab chauffeured Bumper home, a cab, Bumper had bragged time after time that was owned by a company dependent on his dad for taxi medallions. He knew he had a window of about ninety minutes after Virgil, the janitor, locked up before the cab came. Ninety minutes. Enough time for two endgames, maybe three. He would only need one.

Mabi had worked the clock and ran a drag past the Club's 9:00 closing. As much as Bumper loved showing off, he knew Bumper would never risk losing in front of an audience, especially to him, an uppity black who, in Bumper's eyes, didn't know his place. If the game finished after hours Bumper would proclaim victory regardless of who won. No one would believe Mabi calling out Bumper for his bullshitting.

Now, in the penetrating heat in the stairwell of al-Saffah's apartment building, Mabi relived the last two hours of Bumper's life minute by minute. The clock had chimed the hour, 9:00, and he had said, "I guess Bumper man we be finishing our game some other time."

"Come to the service door after the janitor leaves," Bumper had whispered. "He's gone by nine-thirty."

Mabi had exited through Capablanca's heavy front doors into the heat. The soles of his shoes had stuck to the driveway blacktop. He slipped into the shrubs and bushes landscaping the perimeter of the Club grounds. His alibi depended on not being seen. Concealed by the foliage, he kept in the shadows as he worked his way to the far side of the building where thickets of leaves shielded him. Desperate for a drink, he wiped his forehead with a leaf, then sucked his own sweat. Its saltiness made him thirstier. He felt like Q roasting on the spit. Time slowed, its passage mired in the heat. Interior lights shining through windows in the apartment building adjacent to the Club chess-boarded the grounds. Sounds from those windows open to catch a night breeze irritated him—the Bruins playing the Canadiens in Boston Garden, a husband and wife arguing about the checkbook balance, another husband trying to wheedle his wife into sex, a bedtime story being read aloud, *Little Red Riding Hood.* He should be home, curled up with Silvy, sweet Silvy, making love 'neath the air conditioner. Why wasn't that written in Allah's book?

"Allah's book?" Mabi had asked the first time al-Saffah had mentioned it. "Not the Prophet's?"

"Did Moses write the Ten Commandments?" al-Saffah had replied. "It is not a book in the way the Koran is," al-Saffah had continued. "There are no pages, no words, no sentences, just your future. This future is revealed to you by what you do as you do it. You may think you have free will, but you do not. If you were to die tonight, it is because your death was written in Allah's book."

"Stop mind-playing me."

"Think of it this way," al-Saffah said. "What does a superstar athlete do after making a game-winning play? What does a movie star do after winning an Oscar? They praise God and thank Him for their victory. Why do they thank Him? Because they believe He ordained it. What do Jews pray on their new year? That their god inscribe them in the book of life for another year. The book what's called predestination."

Mabi furrowed his brow.

"Fate," al-Saffah said, "prescribed in advance of its revelation."

"God's will?" Mabi asked.

"When I say what you will do is written in Allah's book, I am saying it is fated to happen. You don't reveal your future by reading it in a book; you reveal it by what you do, when you do it."

"Action speaks louder than words."

"That's one way to put it."

"So, if I be offing you tonight," Mabi asked, "that be written in this book?"

Al-Saffah nodded.

"What if there be more than one book? Mine says I off you. Yours says I don't. Who be reading true?"

"We all read from the same book," al-Saffah said.

"I'm not sure I be taking this text."

Don't need to. Just do your thing and all will be revealed."

The muthafucka of all alibis, Mabi thought.

Now, a clock chimed the quarter hour, 9:15. The hockey game was between periods. The husband and wife now argued about who overdrew the checking account. The other husband yelled words like "frigid" and "cockteaser" at his wife. The mother reading *Little Red Riding Hood* now recited bedtime prayers. To take his mind off the heat, Mabi threw it into the future; first, a few weeks when the heat wave would break and his brain would stop cooking; then, two, three, four years when he'd have enough bank to live on for nine lives. But which life was he on? Six to go if three names, three identities—Leroy, Priam, Mabi—used up three lives. Which life would Silvy share? The ninth, he hoped. He'd cut the most bank for that one. What about four, five, six, seven, eight? What's that book say 'bout them? He wished he could skip them over, go straight to number nine.

The exterior lights of Capablanca went dark and Virgil's ride drove up to the service entrance. A clock chimed the half hour, 9:30. Mabi retrieved the supermarket grocery bag he had hidden in the bushes behind the Club and knocked on the service door, softly so no one in the apartment building would hear, once, then again, before Bumper opened it.

Bumper led him to the library on the second floor which housed the treasures of Capablanca, its antique chess sets, oil portraits of grand masters past and present, books on the theory and gamesmanship of chess-many rare and out of print-and two mahogany chess tables with inlaid chess boards, the black squares made of obsidian, the white of moonstone. He had never been in the library before because at the foot of the staircase the Club had posted a "Whites Only" sign that was visible to his eyes and no others. Bumper had reproduced the layout of the game with a hand-carved set of chess men whose white pieces were the army of King Richard Coeur de Lion and his crusaders and whose black pieces were Saracen and his Muslim believers. Mabi turned his white king to face Bumper's forces.

"What's in the bag?" Bumper asked.

"Potato chips. Hungry?"

"Starved."

32.   KR-QB1

Using standard chess notation, Bumper entered Mabi's move, the white rook on the king's side to the first rank of the queen's bishop file, in the spiral notebook in which he recorded each of his matches. The library clock chimed the quarter hour, 9:45. Bumper licked potato chip grease from his fingers, then moved his bishop in the King's file to the fourth rank.

32.   .....   B-K4
33.   K-Q3   R-R1

In his mind's eye, Mabi clapped his hands. You fucking blew it, he thought. If Bumper had moved his bishop to the fifth row of the bishop's file, he would have been forced into moving his rook to the second row of the bishop's file, permitting Bumper to capture his queen with a rook, eventually leading to his king being checked by Bumper's knight. He would be defenseless. Now, Mabi could force a draw with an elegant end game, maybe win if Bumper made another mistake.

"I gotta take a leak," Mabi said. He hastily toured the Club to make sure Virgil had closed the windows and drawn the curtains. After he returned, the next moves came quickly.

34.	R-Kt6 ch	Kt x R
35.	P x Kt ch	K-Q2
36.	Kt-B5 ch	K-K2

"Any more?" Bumper crunched the empty potato chip bag into a ball and tossed it at Mabi who swatted it away.

"Something tastier." Mabi positioned the shopping bag between his feet and pulled several lengths of rope from it. Bigger and stronger, a man overpowering a boy, Mabi lashed Bumper's left arm to the armrest of the chair. Bumper's legs kicked and flailed. Mabi easily sidestepped them. With his free hand, Bumper punched at Mabi, his fist sliding off Mabi's forearm. Mabi let him flail away, then pinned and lashed Bumper's right arm to the other armrest. Fear twisted Bumper's face into knots. Was this how black faces looked, Mabi wondered, as they were dragged to the lynching tree?

"I can't write a ransom note with my hands tied."

"Nothing to ransom."

Mabi skipped the gag. Let Bumper beg. Scream. Cry. Payback for all them blacks who begged and screamed and cried when whitey tightened the noose. Fuck Allah! Fuck al-Saffah. This be for Medgar Evers and Emmet Till, Dr. King and James Chaney, the Scottsboro boys and four little Birmingham girls in their Sunday finest, and for all the unknowns who got no tombs for laying on flowers. And for my brother Jim Ed, wher-ever his body may be.

Mabi dumped syringes, tubing, and ten plastic blood bags, all stolen from the Red Cross, on the floor. A person weighing one hundred thirty pounds would fill the ten bags. Bumper would fill five and part of a sixth. Shock would set in after the loss of about twenty percent of his blood. He would pass out while the second bag filled, die during the third. Not instan-taneous like in a lynching, but a slow fade into oblivion, his mind fearing, fearing, fearing. How'd whitey miss this trick? The clock chimed the hour, 10:00.

37. R-K1

Mabi entered his move in Bumper's spiral notebook. He wanted to have a complete record of the match, a souvenir, something to shove in al-Saffah's face the next time al-Saffah dissed his chess playing. Bumper inhaled and exhaled rapidly, then started to laugh.

"What's so funny?" Mabi asked.

"Your kind never win."

Mabi whipped the black queen at Bumper. Its crown caught the side of Bumper's head where a cushion of hair shielded his skin.

37. .....   R-R6 ch

Mabi connected the syringes to the plastic tubing and the tubing to the plastic bags, two complete systems, one to use, one for back up. He tied a length of elastic rubber around Bumper's right arm at the elbow. With his fingertips, he lo-cated a pulsing protruding blood vessel and inserted a needle, then taped it to Bumper's arm. He drew back on the syringe and watched the blood flow.

Bumper flexed his arm, but the cord bit into his flesh and held him tight. He leaned forward, straining against the rope, stretching, stretching, but couldn't reach the syringe with his mouth. He pushed against the chess table with his legs, but the chair was too close, too heavy, the carpet too plush, to give him the leverage he needed to topple over backwards.

"You as stuck as a pig on a spit." Mabi twirled his king, then moved it.

38.   K-B4

Like watery ketchup, Bumper's blood traveled through the plastic tubing, curving to the left and then to the right, flowing uphill and then sliding down, passing the arm and leg of the chair, up the leg of the table, until it reached the plastic bag where at first, drop by drop, then in a trickle, and finally in a slow, steady stream, it accumulated, puffing out the sides of the bag and rising like a tide, deep red and rich with oxygen. Bumper stared at his blood. He tried to rest his head on the palm of his hand, but the rope restrained him.

"What's your move?" Mabi asked.

38.   .....   R-B6 ch

Mabi piled the remaining plastic bags on the chess table.

39.   K-Kt 5

The red tide continued to rise. Bumper's head slumped forward, then to the side. His chin rested on his collarbone.

He jerked back suddenly, involuntarily, his nervous system taking control of his muscles. He struggled to free himself, but couldn't translate mental commands into action. He opened his mouth to scream, but couldn't find his voice. The clock chimed the quarter hour, 10:15. His mouth hung open, loose and slack.

39. .....   R-K6
40. R-QR1

"You the devil?" Bumper asked, his voice raspy.

"That what they teaching you in your church? Black folks be the devil? I ain't no devil. I's Mabi, the prophet, revealing the divine message of Allah, the one true God."

"Why?" Bumper's voice quivered as if it had aged one hundred years. His jaws moved sluggishly; his tongue lay heavily in his mouth; his chin wagged from side to side, distorting his words.

"For your blood."

"You drink blood?"

Mabi ignored Bumper's question. He looked around for Avram Levy's skull cap. It should have fallen out of the shopping bag when he dumped the syringes, tubing, and plastic blood bags on the floor. He checked the shopping bag, but it was empty. Had he forgotten it? How could he have? Without it, the mission would fail. Bumper would be a murder victim, killer unknown. Al-Saffah would crucify him. Sweat accumulated on his forehead. He burrowed in his back pocket for his handkerchief. The skull cap. Wrapped inside the handkerchief as neatly as an ounce of blow. Now he remembered: part of his precautions to make sure he did not touch it with his bare fingers.

Where to put it? Not on the chess table. Not at the foot of the bookcase. Unlikely Levy would miss seeing it either place. Under the chair? By the right front leg? The left back? Here, there, everywhere, he positioned and repositioned it, searching for the one true place written in the book. Left back, he decided. Likely Levy would miss seeing it there. He flipped it so the name stitched in the lining faced down, then up. Right side up, upside down, inside out, he never figured revelation would be so hard.

"How come?" Bumper's voice strained to escape his body.

"You not deserving any explaining the way you keep shittin' on me and Virgil."

Hours earlier before the Club had closed while Mabi and Bumper were in the opening stage of their chess match Virgil had limped into the game room carrying the butt pail for emptying the ashtrays. Hobbled by arthritis, he circled the room. Struggling, he pushed and pulled furniture out of his path, bending over and around people who didn't think it necessary to get out of the way of a black man hired as a sop to Boston's black voters. Required to perform his janitorial duties while dressed in a tuxedo, Virgil resembled a penguin warehoused in an uncaring zoo.

"Hey, boy, get me a soda," Bumper had shouted. "He'd be fired," Bumper bragged to Mabi, "if it weren't for civil service."

Mabi had sat paralyzed. Virgil despised him and that hurt. In Virgil, old and broken, forced to subsist on a wage earned pandering to whites, but still able to hold his head, if not his body, erect, Mabi observed the dignity of man and the resignation of defeat mixed like clay and water, fired in a kiln, and transmuted into a fine glaze. Virgil's eyes never ceased asking Mabi—*Why you here?*—and Mabi's thoughts never stopped replying—*You done paying your dues, old man.*

Several chess moves later, Virgil had returned to the game room struggling to carry a tray of sodas.

"Look who's finally back," Bumper said

"He's moving fast as he can," Mabi said.

"My grandpa Sean moves faster and he's five years in the grave."

Virgil gripped the tray with both hands and hobbled between the chess tables and around the chairs. His shoes scuffed the carpet and his face grimaced each time he placed weight on his knees.

"It better be cold," Bumper said.

"Why you so hard-assed?" Mabi asked.

"If he were white, you'd order him around the same. Don't like it, lump it."

"Lump it? What's 'lump it'?"

"Hey. You talk black. I talk white. You wanna understand me, learn white."

Virgil leaned forward, balancing the tray on his left hand, and handed Bumper a soda. "I said a cold one," Bumper sneered, "not hot like it just came from darkest Africa." Bumper slammed it back down on the tray, which crashed to the floor. Soda cans rolled under the tables and chairs.

"Let me help," Mabi said to Virgil.

"I not needin' help from a Sam like you."

Mabi saw *signifyin* sounding in Virgil's eyes, one putdown after another, each sharper than the previous one. Since he had joined Capablanca, Virgil had been siggin' him worse than any member. You be ridin' shotgun for the devil in a place like this, was Virgil's favorite. Calling him Mr. Shine was another.

Now, hours later in the library rather than the game room, Mabi glared at Bumper and thought, Virgil's dues just about paid up. How badass sweet it going to be. Bumper struggled to lift his head and look Mabi in the eye. Mabi squatted beside him. "Your pope he started a story in the way back days saying Jews baked Passover *matzoh* with the blood of Christian boys. Your church sold this story like it sold tickets to heaven. The Jew bakeries be baking *matzoh* soon. When you be found, your blood drained, a Jewcap on the floor, you be the next incarnation of the blood libel."

Bumper strained to open his mouth. His tongue filled the space between his teeth like a boulder blocking the opening of a cave.

"Your bloodless body," Mabi said, "will be inciting the first great pogrom in America right here in Boston. No place deserving it more."

"When I get to heaven," Bumper said, his words garbled, his voice so weak a person standing in the corner of the library would not have heard it, "I'll make God . . ."

"Allah don't heed the words of infidels."

Bumper opened his mouth, but nothing came out.

"Time's running," Mabi said. "What's your move?"

40.   .....   B x P

Mabi disconnected and sealed the first bag, fastening a new one in its place. Through the thick plastic, the blood warmed his hand.

41.   R-R7 ch

As the second bag filled, Bumper's head fell forward onto his chest, his eyes opening and closing, his vision blurring. Mabi kneeled beside him. "You hear me?" Bumper grunted. "The game it's over. Your best move, K-K1, leads to perpetual checks. Any other move gives me mate. I gonna be able to queen my sixth rank pawn. You had me beat, but let it slip away. You be doing no better than a draw and only if you play it perfect."

Bumper closed his eyes. His breathing slowed. The second bag continued to fill. Mabi picked up the crumpled potato chip bag, collected the chess pieces, and wiped them with a soft cloth dipped in cleaning fluid. He returned the chess set to the shelf beside the jade set from China and pushed the chairs against the table, rubbing out the indentations in the rug with the toe of his running shoe. No one would know a chess game was played in the library on the night Bumper Sullivan died. Mabi checked the position of Levy's skull cap. He lifted Bumper's head, released it. It flopped forward like the head of a brother broke-necked from being lynched. Bumper's breathing labored. Mabi changed the second bag for a third, a fourth, a fifth, the sixth and final bag. When the flow slowed to a trickle, he untied Bumper and carried him to the couch. The clock chimed the half-hour, 10:30. Plenty of time. He held a small mirror in front of Bumper's mouth. It didn't fog. Checkmate.

Hours later, burdened by a shopping bag weighed down with six plastic bags of Bumper Sullivan's blood, Mabi kicked al-Saffah's door.

"Welcome home, my son."

Mabi thrust the shopping bag into al-Saffah's arms and poured himself a glass of ice water while al-Saffah carefully lined up the bags of Bumper's blood on a plastic tray. Mabi stared into his empty water glass. Bumper's spiral notebook. Where was it? He thought he had put it in the shopping bag. He shoved his hands down his pockets, front and back. No notebook. Maybe he lost it. In some gutter somewhere along the way. What-if he forgot it in the library? He had sanitized the library, checked and double-checked to make sure he had left nothing behind, nothing that would point to anyone but Avram Levy. He couldn't go back now. He'd have to wait 'til morning, 'til the Club reopened. He wished he knew the janitor's hours, his cleaning schedule. Morning might be too late.

Al-Saffah made space in the refrigerator for Bumper's blood. Mabi put the water glass to his lips, then realized it was empty.

In the early morning hours following Bumper Sullivan's murder, Mabi, queasy from the heat, let himself into his crib. Visions of Bumper's spiral notebook danced before his eyes, ghost like, taunting and haunting. Maybe leaving it in the library wasn't so bad. Nothing tied it to him, him to it. Wrong, said the ghosts. Notations of the last few moves rose from the page and orbited his head. Shit! He felt like he'd been chuck chumped. How could he be so fucking stupid! Maybe the cops'll think Levy made that writing. Maybe.

Silvy slept on the couch. The strange white light of television snow from a station long signed off illuminated the room. Silvy twinkled like a star, her glow coming from within as if her soul had escaped her body and surrounded her in a cocoon. Her skin was brown and rich and sweet, maple syrup skin, such high color compared to his, which was darker than the Kenyan coffee beans he ground every morning. He shut off the television and she reabsorbed her cocoon. She stirred. He kissed the back of her hand, then gently massaged it. He felt royal. He stroked her forehead and cheeks and patted her lips with his fingertips. She kissed them. He drew her slowly toward himself and hugged her. No maybe 'bout this.

"Let me freshen up," she said. I'm tasting my sleep."

Mabi heard the radio over the running water. Silvy always played the radio in the bathroom. It was like she had wired it into the light switch. Mabi got two beers from the refrigerator. Silvy returned from the bathroom. "As God is my judge, radio says someone offed Mayor Charlie's kid."

"No shit." He handed her a beer.

"There's no more safety anymore."

"Plenty of safety here."

"What's that blood on your hand?"

"Trojan business. No worry of yours."

"You in another fight?"

Mabi's arm spasmed as if was strapped in Alabama's Yellow Mama and some honky executioner had zapped him with ten thousand million volts.

"When you gonna quit them Trojans? You sitting on a lifetime of money and the Trojans not a forever run."

"Stop acting like a kid roofing from building to building paying no mind." Mabi struggled to calm his voice. "You don't watch out you be missing the next roof."

"What you so upset about? God don't like ugly. One snap His fingers and He'll put you down so fast your soul be dead before your body."

"My body ain't dead yet," he said, caressing her neck, shoulder, breast.

"It ain't live neither." She pushed him away as she said good-bye.

From the rooftop of his building, Mabi watched Silvy home. The night heat wrapped itself around him like a curse. He curled up beneath the television antennas. His arm throbbed, synchronized to his pulse. His head ached with worry about the spiral notebook. Leroy. Priam. Mabi. So many names, so many lives–all his–all perched on the rods of the antennas like vultures in trees, quiet, patient, watching, waiting, readying to fight for the juiciest feeding spot. If I died right now, he asked himself, what name they be putting on my stone? On the rooftop of his building, sprawled under the spindly arms of the television antennas that extended over him as if in prayer, the specter of a blank marker guarding his bones beside Jim Ed's empty grave haunted Mabi. Tormented, he fell into a sleep, shallow and fitful like a heroin nod, his mind unsettled, craving something no addiction would cure, his pilgrimage from Leroy to Priam to Mabi passing before his eyes as if he were dying.

When he awoke, the blood on his hands seemed to ooze from his pores, while dawn's rosy fingers–a phrase Mabi remembered from the comic book–crept along the rooftop where he shivered in spite of the night's heat, heralding a new Boston, one that had not existed less than twelve hours before.

Now, days later, Bumper boxed and buried, Badger jailed because he had lost his ID bracelet on the Chelsea mission, Mabi, still unable to sleep, lay in bed counting sheep, black sheep. Soon, he thought, the courts be open, Badger be bailed, and the world no longer be spinning out of control.

Chapter 10

Monday, April 20, 1981

-1-

The blood had finally washed off Mabi's hands and he wasn't conjuring up blank grave markers or agonizing over *ajal*, his or the Trojans', as he waited with Silvy and Silvy's mother, Cealy Thomas, in the hallway outside the Boston Juvenile Court after Badger's arraignment to visit with Badger before he was remanded to the juvenile cell block of the Charles Street Jail. Badger's bail hearing had been continued one day so the prosecutor could present evidence that Badger should be held without bail because he was a danger to the community.

Cealy Thomas, named for a grandmother who died at eighty-seven in the bed in which she was born, had dressed for court in her church clothes: pill box hat with black mesh veil, black dress, black gloves, and black parasol. In the Ebenezer Baptist Church, the women wore their hats during the worship, but in the courtroom where the rules were different, she removed it because a court officer threatened to evict her if she didn't. "Ladies don't go bare head in public," she protested, but the court officer cowed her into obeying him by snarling an expletive. Now, with Badger remanded to custody to await his bail hearing, nagging Mabi was Cealy's only release. "How come they don't free him up right now?" She poked Mabi in the thigh with her parasol. "If you stood up and told that judge Badger been at the movies with you, he'd be coming home. In jail he ain't mixing with a high class of folk."

"Tomorrow he be bailed," Mabi said. "Then he comes back for trial and he'll be free forever."

"Trial?" Cealy put her hands to her cheeks as if she were feeling for a fever. "Only guilty people needin' trials. Oh, Lord, why You testing me so hard?"

Lawyers milling about waiting for the session to resume edged away from the bench where Cealy sat, pretending to ignore her but stealing glances as if she had a physical deformity, a wine spot on her face or frostbite scarred cheeks.

"Don't there be room for one more sinner in the Amen corner, Lord?"

Silvy pulled Mabi aside. "She won't last 'til tomorrow. She was wailing all night."

"Lord," Cealy shouted, silencing the hum of small-talk, "how come You banishing me from Your mercy seat."

"She's wasting a fit over shit," Mabi said.

"Lord! I deserve to be sipping the cup of salvation."

"Stop your wailing, woman," Mabi said. "Badger be home tomorrow."

"I hope you're sitting on the right side of the Lord," Cealy said.

"You can make book on it," Mabi replied.

-2-

Making book on it. Mabi had bet his life on making book on it, first on a comic book years before, then a policy book, more recently a holy text. He wished he had never learned how to read.

Livermore Place in Roxbury used to be an address, but now only one building remained on the block, the old Hotel Harvé which once rented rooms by the half-hour to sailors on liberty, husbands whose wives had perpetual headaches, and college students on a slut run, but was now a Single Room Occupancy where Massachusetts dumped welfare mothers and their children, one family to a room regardless of the number of kids. When Livermore Place was in its prime, the Hotel Harvé was surrounded by other buildings. Now, encircled by the rubble of vacant store-fronts vandalized years before, a jewelry store that used to be Siegel and Sons, a furniture store that used to be Goldfarb's Furniture, a travel agency that used to be Dimond Travel, and a fur store that used to be Nathan the Furrier, the ground floor of the Hotel Harvé was a bar, Blackbird's.

Iron grates, rusted and bent, barricaded the windows. Sheet metal covered with graffiti shielded the front door. Scorch marks marred the bricks, each a memorial to the white fire companies that refused to venture into Livermore Place, the black companies that did before the Boston Fire Department was desegregated. A small cardboard sign taped to the inside of the window and illegible behind the grime cautioned "Ladies welcome if accompanied by Gentlemen." Blackbird's looked like a fortress which had survived a long siege because its assailants retreated one attack too soon.

On this hot April afternoon, the afternoon after Badger's arraignment, the afternoon before his bail hearing, the sun bathed Livermore Place in a benign light that relegated to the shadows the fears of the neighborhood: the fear fire would gut another building and spread devastation to another block; the fear of bullets, drive-bys, and random deaths Mayor Charlie only acknowledged in election years; the fear their children would succumb to the lure of drugs and the street gangs that peddled them; the fear their sons would turn to crime and their daughters to prostitution to support their drug habits, the fear of the welfare being cut off; the fear of fear itself.

Out of this benevolent light, Scorpion, one the sources of those fears, entered the darkness of Blackbird's to stake out the inside. He shepherded four drinkers to tables near the front door, then sat at the head of the bar between the front door and the booth where Amelia "Beaujolais" Wine, the only black female police officer on the Boston police force, waited. Whenever direct communication between Mabi and Chief Ugolino was necessary, Mabi and Beaujolais met at Blackbird's. Ugolino didn't trust the telephone and Mabi didn't trust police stations. On Scorpion's signal, Mabi and Spider trucked in. Spider sealed the door, making the bar as impregnable as a union picket line thrown up around a Boston construction site to keep out black laborers. Five Trojans scattered themselves around the neighborhood.

Mabi paused inside the door to let his eyes adjust. Two TVs played behind the bar, a basketball game videotaped the previous evening on one, a game show on the other. Stilts, the afternoon bartender, pumped up the volume on both. Beaujolais wore street clothes rather than her police uniform, her blouse unbuttoned almost to the waist, no bra, her skirt slit three-quarters of the way up her thigh. In her late twenties, her thighs looked home to a baker's dozen of sweet potato pies, her ass to another baker's dozen. Black men want women of substance, she said to explain her girth. Her eyes weighed down with the glitter in her eye shadow, she sat with her arms spread wide, displaying herself like a piece of costume jewelry at a pawn shop or second-hand store. Mabi wasn't in the mood for no boosting.

Mabi led her to a back booth, then sat opposite her. The images on the nearer screen framed her dark face in the glare of television light. Over her right shoulder, Robert "Double O" Parish slam dunked over the Chocolate Thunder for two points. "Badger! By supper." Mabi slapped the table with the flat of his hand.

"Baby, you know the ribs they ain't free."

On the screen, Dr. J. pirouetted past Kevin McHale and sank an in-your-face lay-up.

"I's already buttering his bread so thick his arteries be blockaded."

"Something new needs something new."

"What am I buying?" Mabi demanded.

"Ugolino stays off your case and only Badger's baby black ass gets busted for Chelsea." Behind Beaujolais, Tiny Archibald completed a backdoor play off Larry Bird's outlet pass to Chris Ford.

"Listen up, marshmallow tits." Mabi leaned forward and yanked one of her breasts out of her blouse and squeezed it until she winced. "You deliver me Badger or I'll hack off your fucking tits, bronze 'em, and mount 'em on the grille of my ride." He released her breast with a half twist that brought tears to her eyes.

She massaged her bruise marks and tucked her breast inside her blouse, buttoning it to the neck. "Ugolino ain't offering a menu. You eat what he serves or you starve."

"Starvin' ain't healthy for fat asses like him. Or you."

Mabi fixed his eyes on Beaujolais until she looked away. On the television, Cedric "Cornbread" Maxwell took Caldwell Jones inside, made the basket and drew the foul. Gesturing toward the basket with his patented wave, he canned the foul shot to complete a three-point play.

"You tell Chief Stereo," Mabi said, "the North End, his North End, be the next Chelsea you don't deliver Badger to-night." When Beaujolais rose to leave, he grabbed the waistband of her skirt and pulled her toward him. "Don't get sucked in by all this affirmative action shit. Boston still a plantation and you nothing more than the plantation owner's fucking cunt."

-3-

If Beaujolais was nothing more than the plantation owner's fucking cunt, Mabi asked himself, what was he? A field hand? An overseer? Was he anything more than his name? Would he ever be?

Mabi. "Prophet" in Arabic, Aramaic, Hebrew. A soldier in the army of Allah, the one true God who had revealed His divine message and chosen him as His messenger. His birth name, Leroy Wallaca, was a slave name. After his brother died in the Nam and he started gang-leading the Trojans, he called himself Priam after an ancient king who died for his people. Jim Ed didn't die for his people; he died for whitey in a war against the yellow. At his brother's funeral, he vowed not to make the same mistake.

Two years earlier, 1979, when he was still Priam he first heard Allah's divine message from a guest preacher at the New

World Primitive Baptist Church, Professor Husam al din al-
Saffah, a mullah and a professor of Islamic studies. To this day
Mabi's flesh crept up and down his bones when he remembered how al-Saffah scanned the congregation and locked eyes
with him. Coal black, al-Saffah's eyes burned with the fury of
a Boston cop hunting bloods for sport.

"Listen, my children," al-Saffah had preached, "to Allah's
message, you Christians who go to Christian churches and
sing Christian hymns and chant Christian gospels. When your
grandparents struggled to break slavery's chains, who did they
pray to? The same God as the plantation owner who prisoned
them in those chains! Who do you think this God, this white
man's God, this Jesus Christ Superstar God, listened to? Your
grandparents or the Klan who carried his cross? Who burned
his cross into their yards? Into their flesh? So long as you pray
to this God who heeds only the prayers of white folk your souls
will remain in bondage. Your bodies may know the delusion
of freedom, but your souls know the truth of truths. When
you understand this, only then will you shatter the chains that
enslave you even as you sit here in your finery on this beautiful
Sunday morning."

In Mabi's memory of that morning, al-Saffah spoke directly to him.

"Abraham, father of Isaac, prayed that a community sub-
missive to Allah and taught by His messenger would arise out
of Abraham's seed. Muhammad is that messenger and the nations of Islam are that community, the only true descendants
of Abraham. Muhammad restored to the religion of Abraham
the purity destroyed by the blasphemies and corruptions of
Christians and Jews."

Al-Saffah lowered his hands and leaned forward as if he
were about to whisper a secret into the ear of each congregant.

"Do not follow Jesus the Slaver. Let Muhammad lead you to Allah the Liberator who will preach to you of *ajal.*"

Al-Saffah slowed his speech and softened his voice.

"Life is like water sent down from heaven. Men, animals, plants, insects, all living things drink the water of life. When the earth takes on the green glow and glitter of the water of life and man thinks he has dominion over the world, Allah stops the rainfall and the glow and glitter decays into desert dust. No afflictions befall man that are not first written in Allah's book. No one is born unless it is first written in the book. No one dies unless it is first written in the book. Jesus did not write this book. Nor did Yod. Heh. Vav. Heh.. Nor the Father or the Son or the Holy Spirit. No. Allah wrote this book. Only Allah. Everything you have done and will do is written in Allah's book, but the lines are not revealed to you except through your act of speaking them, your act of doing them. By the miracle of revelation, Allah makes you free."

Al-Saffah was calm, deliberate, emphasizing his points with a gesture of his hand, a nod of his head.

"Allah gave everyone, everything, *ajal,* a term of life. You have a term of life. Nations have a term of life. Races have a term of life. The debasement of Abraham's religion by Christians and Jews has a term of life. Only the final triumph of Islam is eternal and everlasting."

Al-Saffah stepped down from the pulpit and centered himself on the aisle separating the pews.

"The black man's bondage in Klan-white America has a term of life. Only when you accept the truth of *ajal* will you unshackle your chains and be truly free. Those who would be free, walk with me."

This text had intrigued Mabi and he followed al-Saffah down that aisle, out of that church, into the light of Sunday's sun. Al-Saffah had opened his eyes to how cracker devils bull-shitted black folk by suckering them with Jesus the White and by scheming them into kissing the feet of Superstar's cross. Al-Saffah had opened his eyes so that he understood Allah offered a religion where action not only spoke louder than words, but where action became Allah's divine revelation.

For two years, Mabi had lived by this text. Made book on it. Had he misread it?

At al-Saffah's home later that Sunday after church, al-Saffah had introduced him to chess. First, they had shared a meal of figs and olives, cubes of cheese, chunks of lamb flavored with spices he had never tasted before, and squares of pastry dripping with honey. After the meal, al-Saffah sat him on a small Oriental rug beside a low circular table decorated with a frieze of hand carved gargoyles. Al-Saffah reclined on a pillow across the table. On the wall above al-Saffah's head hung eight scimitars, seven circling the eighth, the largest. Jewels overlaid their hilts, red, green, blue, some as clear as glass. Beside the scimitars, a sword and leather scabbard hung vertically.

Al-Saffah stood and drew the blade from the scabbard. "From Spain. The Nasrid period, fifteenth century. Part of my heritage." He slid the sword back into its scabbard. "What is your heritage? A comic book?"

"Who squared you 'bout that?"

"A comic book salvaged by your father from the trash left behind by passengers on the Greyhound he drives? *Tales of the Trojan War* I believe it was called."

"How you know that?"

"And, thus, Leroy Wallaca became Priam."

"You been spying on me?"

"Allah does not spy. Allah knows and has decreed your *ajal* as Priam shall end."

"No one ending nothing but me."

Al-Saffah smiled, not a smile of joy or happiness, but a smile of satisfaction. He removed a lacquered box from a cabinet. "This chess set is from Iran, hand carved during the Seljuq period. Twelfth century." Sixteen pieces of pale green marble laced with white highlights and sixteen pieces of tan marble with dark brown and white highlights nested in a black velvet liner. Al-Saffah handed him a pawn.

"Teach me to play. With this set."

"You must earn the right to play with these."

That Sunday after church, he began first weekly, then daily, chess lessons with al-Saffah, each starting and finishing with a reading from the Koran. Interspersed in the lectures about the function and purpose of each chess piece—how they moved, how the moves were recorded in chess notation, isolated pawns and weak pawn structures, time and tempo, openings and endgames—were teachings on the religion and culture of Islam. "Chess is really a game of war," al-Saffah explained, digressing from the history of the Crusades and how Christians stole the Holy Land from Muslims. After a year, al-Saffah granted that he might play with the ancient marble set.

"How can this be twelfth century?" he asked. "It looks newer than today."

"The army of Allah is almost twice as old." Al-Saffah opened with the white king's pawn to the fourth rank, P-K4, and he responded in kind. "If you became a soldier in His army," al-Saffah said, "you will be ordained Mabi, which means "prophet" in the languages of Islam."

"I like my name."

"You discarded your birth name . . ."

"Leroy Wallaca a dumbass slave name. Priam the name of a warrior."

"A comic book name."

"A warrior's name earned in battle. I's proud of it."

"How much prouder would you be if Allah bestowed your name on you?"

"You always been called al-Saffah?" He moved the knight in his queen's bishop's file to the third rank, Kt-QB3, to counter al-Saffah's move of the knight in his king's bishop file to the third rank, Kt-KB3. He liked the way the knights hopped, skipped, and jumped, one square forward or backward, one square diagonally either to the right or the left. It allowed for sneak attacks, unlike the bishops or rooks which moved backward or forward in straight lines like battering rams or the pawns confined to moving forward, one square at a time except for the opening move when two squares were possible. He would master this game, not for the sake of the game itself but because he understood how its lessons would translate to the gang-wars fought on the streets of Boston.

Al-Saffah remained silent as they exchanged moves, until after thirty for each he captured Priam's queen and announced check.

"Why me that Sunday in church?" Priam asked as he captured al-Saffah's queen and moved out of check.

"It was written in Allah's book."

"Don't be so fucking bogue."

"Your choice of the language of the street imprisons you in the past. Liberate yourself from that past. The present is ephemeral. Leroy Wallaca and Priam are ephemeral. Only the future truly exists. Only Mabi is eternal."

"I'm no player piano and you no piano man."

"Mabi is a rare name reserved for special people."

"You a nickel slick and a nickel short."

"The riches of Allah are not measured in base coin."

"You talk like you're on the pipe."

Names had bedeviled Mabi for as long as he could remember, especially his own. Once again, he was six, an old six, his first day of school, when teach taught the class how to look up their names in the phone book and home-worked them to print out the name above, the name below. He found one, his old man Gideon, stooping between Wall and Wallace. He spent the rest of the day playing with the letters, arranging and rearranging them to form other names. "Alcawla" was his favorite because it was as mysterious as the frizzly chicken Gideon hung in the kitchen.

"Count them Walls and Wallaces," he said to his mother Hannah. He handed her the sheet of paper on which he had scrawled "Wallaca." The a's looked like o's and the upper case W filled as much space as the rest of the letters. "How come only one Wallaca?"

Hannah leaned against the door still wearing her nurse's whites. Her shoes hung in a plastic bag on the back-door knob waiting for morning. She smiled the automatic smile mastered in nursing school to appear cheerful when treating patients who would never see their next birthday as she reviewed her son's homework.

"How come there be only one?" he asked again.

Hannah shuddered. Fear still bewitched her. The immigration officer unable to pronounce or spell their surname had renamed them Wallaca after the Ethiopian village they had fled. If Leroy could find their name in the phone book, so could the Ethipian Emperor's militia, but Gideon refused to pay for an unlisted phone number. Waste of money, he said whenever she brought it up. Nothing but a hex protects against a hex.

After supper when Leroy came in from shooting baskets at the playground and Gideon returned from driving the Greyhound, he asked his father what "Wallaca" meant.

"What do you mean, 'mean'?" his father replied, hiding behind a comic book he had scavenged from trash left on the bus.

"Where's our name from?"

Gideon looked up, his eyes puffy and bloodshot from a day on the road. "Names don't come from nowhere."

Leroy shifted the basketball from one hip to the other. "Billy Sunshine says it a slave name."

Hannah stepped in from the kitchen, wearing her fruit and vegetable apron, green apples, green tomatoes, green summer squash. "Slavery ended long before we . . ."

"Hush up, woman." Gideon rolled the comic book into a rod and slapped it against his leg.

"Billy Sunshine says we're off the plantation," Leroy continued. "Says we white-blooded."

Gideon threw the comic book at Leroy. "Tell Jim Ed to read you this 'fore bed."

Hannah slumped against the wall. Her apron wrinkled. The fruits and vegetables drooped as if they were spoiled rotten. "With all President Johnson's doing," she said to Gideon, "life's going to be different for Jim Ed and Leroy. They have to be ready to live in the new world."

"You can bleach your talk, woman, but you can't bleach your skin." He held up that day's *New York Daily News*. Two headlines framed a front-page picture of blacks looting Rothstein's Furniture on West 125th Street during the power black-out that darkened the entire East coast two nights earlier. "Top Cop: Shoot to Kill," read the headline above the photograph. "Cong. Powell: We're not Animals," read the lower headline.

"Shoot who?" Leroy asked.

Gideon scowled. "You, you ninny. You."

Hannah picked the comic book off the floor and handed it to Leroy. "Go upstairs."

"Go upstairs." Gideon elevated his voice to mock his wife. "There be more truth in that comic book than in that new world she always taking text on."

Hannah nudged Leroy toward the stairs, then retreated to the kitchen. Gideon bunkered himself inside the *Daily News*.

That night, Leroy asked his older brother, Jim Ed, "What you know 'bout our name?"

"Nothing but a name same as Russell," Jim Ed said.

On the ceiling, Jim Ed had tacked a poster of Bill Russell, center for the Boston Celtics, which Gideon had bought Leroy at a Celtic-Knicks game in Boston Garden where they celebrated Leroy's sixth birthday. First in line at the souvenir stand, last to be helped, had so angered Gideon they left before the end of the third quarter. Still, Leroy liked the poster's smiling leprechaun, the fierceness of Russell's eyes, and the straight line of his body from fingertips to toes as he leaped to block a shot. Leroy jumped off the bed, mimicking Russell's shot-blocking leap. His fingertips brushed against the poster.

"I bet Russell knows where his folks be from," Leroy said.

"Don't take Billy Sunshine's slave-name shit so serious," Jim Ed said. "He's so backwards he brushes his teeth with toilet paper and wipes his ass with a toothbrush." Jim Ed sat down on the edge of Leroy's bed, the comic book on his lap.

"How come the old man gets so mad when I ask him?"

"He's just tired from driving." Jim Ed opened the comic book so Leroy could see the drawings. "This called *Tales of the Trojan War*, written in way back years by some dude named Homer."

Leroy marveled at the warrior's muscular arms and legs, their rectangular chests, square jaws. Flat on the page, the drawings came alive as Jim Ed weaved a spell of Achilles, Odysseus, Hector, Greeks and Trojans, gods and goddesses, a wooden horse hundreds of hands high–a spell finer than any fairy tale ever told by Hannah or hex pronounced by Gideon. That night, Leroy dreamed he was racing across the Trojan plain in a chariot at the head of an army of thousands. Above the thunder of the horses, the warriors, his warriors, shouted Wallaca! so loud the voices reached up to the mountain top where the gods and goddesses covered their ears. King of kings, he led Achilles, Odysseus, Agamemnon and the rest of the Greeks into battle. He fought Hector. He breached the gates of Troy. He scrawled his name on the walls and ramparts of the city with the blood of dead Trojans. 'Wallaca.' Everyone worshipped the name. But in the morning, at school with Billy Sunshine teasing him again about being white-blooded Leroy knew it was only the dream of a kid pissed off because his old man answered his questions with a comic book instead of straight talk.

Dreaming kept Leroy happy for a while; but, as he grew older, he realized dreaming was no more real than Wallaca. Night after night, he nagged Gideon. No matter how tired his old man was or how rested, he either booted him away with "It's just a name," or threatened to call down some voodoo curse if he didn't shut up. Once Gideon whupped him, counting out the blows like a slave master counting lashes. Jim Ed knew no more and Hannah, fearing Gideon might beat on her instead if she interceded, never betrayed whatever secrets she held. "Make a name of Leroy Wallaca," Jim Ed said; but, as time passed, the questions about his name burrowed deep into his heart, where they incubated, a virus of hate waiting to be triggered. Keep your fucking secrets, Leroy decided. Someday I'll be creating my own name and it won't be Leroy Wallaca.

By his eighth birthday, Leroy had learned to read well enough to read the comic book himself and by the summer of 1967, the summer Boston burned with race riots, he knew *Tales of the Trojan War* by heart.

That spring, the spring of 1967, the city's whites concentrated on the Red Sox, who had not sported a winning record since 1957 and in 1966 finished ninth, a half game out of last place. Boston loved the 1967 Red Sox lead by Yastrzemski, Conigliaro, Petrocelli, Lonborg, Waslewski, Osinski, a team easily embraced by a bleached white city that elevated baseball to a religion. If Negroes like Foy and Scott in the infield, Smith and Tartabull in the outfield, Santiago and Wyatt on the pitcher's mound, stained the roster, the fans tolerated their presence as penance for winning after so many losing seasons. Few Negroes attended Red Sox games, boycotting an ownership that had refused to sign Mays, Robinson, or Aaron because of the color of their skin and hired an alcoholic racist manager with a colorful nickname so the owner would have a drinking buddy. Ownership didn't care. The seats were full of hungry whites who gorged themselves on overpriced hot dogs and beer, peanuts and popcorn, and Cracker Jacks. Boston's crackers, a sizable minority many of whom professed otherwise, loved their Cracker Jacks. And the prize inside.

One Friday afternoon in June, welfare mothers barricaded themselves inside the Grove Hall welfare office in the heart of Roxbury, one of Boston's Negro neighborhoods, to protest changes in welfare eligibility rules. Soon, the Tactical Police Force gathered outside, milling about like a street gang ready to rumble. When the order to liberate the building came, the police, wearing riot gear with helmets, face masks, leather jackets, gloves, protective cups, and knee-high boots and armed with riot clubs–longer, thicker and harder than the standard billies–charged the front doors while a second squad stormed the building from the back, clubbing the welfare mothers into submission. The police action escalated into warfare, four nights of rioting, four nights of occupation by the police. Boston's Blue Hill Avenue became a street like so many in Watts, Detroit, Newark. Furniture stores, shoe stores, hardware stores, variety stores, liquor stores, dry cleaners, all the stores along a fifteen-block stretch of Blue Hill Avenue between Grove Hall and Quincy Street burned, Boston's contribution to the looting, vandalism and arson that plagued American cities during Lyndon Baines Johnson's presidency.

After four nights of sirens, tear gas, burglar alarms that rang unanswered, fires that burned unchecked, four nights of bloody heads and broken bones, four nights of mommas wailing and daddies bailing, calm did not so much return as rise out of the smoldering ashes of Blue Hill Avenue, spreading like mold on the rotting fruit sold by Roxbury supermarkets.

June dragged on. The Red Sox continued winning, giving the police something to talk about as they patrolled the streets of Roxbury. Slowly, the ashes cooled. Negroes began meeting secretly in small groups behind closed doors. Gabe Tucker organized such a meeting in the basement of his tenement. Jim Ed, then seventeen, Leroy, eight, and sixteen others, crowded into a basement lit by a twenty-five-watt bulb hanging from the ceiling. Police brutality obsessed everyone. Twenty injuries became two hundred. The news reported no casualties; rumors claimed twenty, thirty, forty, more.

"Hear me, brothers," Gabe Tucker said. "Last night two honky pigs cornered me in the alley and did their business on my face."

"On his face!" shouted Nate Garvy, a burly kid standing in the middle of the room.

"On my face. We're a new generation. No pushing us around no more. We need be showing them honkies a real burn."

Jim Ed said, "Whose backyard we burning?"

Nate Garvey said, "Them muthafucks who busted heads at Grove Hall."

"How come they never bust heads in Southie or Bunker Hill?" Gabe swayed like he was taking a text. "'Cause no brothers living in them places." Calls of Right on! rolled around the room until Gabe clapped his hands. "Now on, we be the Zuluz," and he spelled it for them. "Them be our brothers in Africa," Gabe said.

"Fucking diesel mouth," Jim Ed said, "with shit for brains and brains for shit." Everyone knew Jim Ed had been taking fighting lessons in Chinatown, learning things with names no one could pronounce. Rumors flew 'round the 'hood Jim Ed could kill with either hand, either foot, take out five men at once. No one believed it, but no one dared challenge him. "Hear me good. What's a gang gonna do? Rip off booze from the packy? The only work we getting these days is in Nam. When does Uncle call us nephew? When he needs bodies to ship out to replace them he's shipping back. Zuluz gonna make that right?"

"Study long, study wrong," Gabe said. "If we don't fight our fight, who will?"

"Fighting your fight only the funeral makers be rolling in Franklins." Jim Ed took Leroy by the hand and walked him up the stairs and out the door.

"Why you go and do that?" Leroy asked when they reached the street.

"We don't need no gang."

"If this be revolution, we should be swinging, not singing."

"Since when you quoting Malcom X?"

"I's as deep as you is shallow."

"Dried-up piss be deeper than you."

"Someday I'll be leading them Zuluz. I'll make me a name so great people they'll call you Leroy's big bro'!"

Jim Ed slapped him upside the head. "And Ed Brooke he'll be living in the White House." Brooke, a black man married to a white woman, had been elected to the United States Senate as a Republican in 1966 in a landslide victory–61 per cent to 39 per cent–over his Democratic opponent, a former Massachusetts governor.

That night while Jim Ed worked out in Chinatown Leroy again dreamt about Troy; but this time, for the first time, he was a Trojan, fighting beside Hector to protect his home, his turf; sitting with Priam, king of Troy; plotting strategy; killing Achilles to avenge Hector's death and the mutilation of his body; becoming leader of the Trojans. In his dream, he figured out the trick of the Trojan horse and roasted alive the Greeks inside, then raced down Blue Hill Avenue in a chariot, acknowledging the cheers of the 'hood. He knew then someday the Zuluz would become the Trojans, his Trojans, and that he would no longer be Leroy Wallaca. In his dream, he stopped in front of his house where Jim Ed, never Gideon, never Hannah, waited. I got me a name, he shouted, saluting Jim Ed with a clenched fist, Priam, leader of the Trojans. In his dream, Jim Ed never saluted back.

-4-

An hour had passed, then a second, since Mabi had sent Beaujolais on her merry way to deliver his ultimatum to Ugolino.

Now Mabi waited for the phone to ring. He tried to read the ticks of the clock. Juries that decided things quick, he knew from experience, always returned guilty verdicts. The longer the delay, the greater the chance for a not-guilty or a hung jury. If Ugolino intended to say no, he'd say no in an instant. Yes might take a while. He had time; not forever time, but time.

His mind wandered, but always came back to one thing. His name. Mabi. This name, his name, still intrigued him. He never thought he'd give up Priam; but al-Saffah had offered him a past, a history, a heritage, a past where Allah, not Leroy, killed Billy Sunshine; a past where Allah, not Priam, killed Luke Shaw, a past where Allah, not Mabi, killed Bumper Sullivan. And a future. The turn of a page away. If he was a long way from Priam, he was a longer way, much longer, from Leroy Wallaca.

Until Mabi strode through the front door of the Capablanca Chess Club in South Boston, no blacks had crossed the Club's threshold other than Virgil or an occasional tradesman, delivery person, or waiter or waitress employed by a caterer working a private function. Those blacks entered and exited through the service entrance, which led to a labyrinth of cobwebbed basement hallways and a staircase to the kitchen. Their presence on the first and second floors was limited to the performance of their duties.

Programmed by al-Saffah, Mabi had marched up the Club's circular drive and through a front door so solid older members needed help opening it, past the coatroom to the right, through the foyer and into a living room whose centerpiece was an antique standing globe of the world at the time of Magellan. In each corner and behind each occasional table the broad green leaves of a supernal ficus pointed toward the nearest window. To the left, through double doors of dark

polished wood with polished brass doorknobs, doors so perfectly balanced and precisely hinged they opened, so it seemed,
with a mere breath, was the chess room where peaceful games
of war descended from violent games of peace were played
with an intensity bordering on the frenzy of actual combat. Yet,
the only sound was the barely audible brush of felt pad against
lacquered chessboard.

At the reception desk, Brian Cairns, the club manager,
glanced up from his newspaper, *The Irish Times* air-shipped
daily from Dublin by Aer Lingus for the many emigrants and
their children and grandchildren living in and around Boston.
"Deliveries through the service entrance."

"I's here to sign up."

"Army recruiting office on Union corner of Williams."

Cairns folded his paper, the sports section on top, a photo
of Seamus 'Sam Bam' Cunningham dragging three defenders
across the goal line to score the winning points for Leinster
against Connacht in the Irish Rugby Union Cup finals.

"For Capablanca Chess Club," Mabi said.

"No vacancies."

"This be a city place and the law says anyone living in
Boston free to join." He slapped his driver's license with its
Boston address down on Sam Bam's muddy, bloody legs.

"Law says building capacity is one-fifty and we're full up."

"Millie Moran she still a member?"

Cairns fidgeted with his left sideburn, curling, then un-
curling its coarse hairs.

"Poor Millie," Mabi continued, "went to her eternal reward yesterday. Seen it in the obits. Her board, it's now mine."

The laws forcing Capablanca to extend a membership to
Mabi did not compel its members to play chess with him. Everyone except Avram Levy, a rabbinical student who recently

relocated from Crown Heights in New York to Chelsea, refused whenever he talked up a game.

"How they let you in?" Mabi asked Levy during their first match.

"I'm the exception that proves the rule."

"They calling you Jewboy, kike, Christ killer, behind your back."

"And to my face."

"That be one fancy little hat."

"It's called a *yarmulke*. I wear it as a sign of respect for Hashem. My father gave me a set of twelve for my *bar mitzvah*."

Mabi slapped the button on the chess clock. "Levy, man. Let's fray and frazzle these lace curtains by trying out for the chess team."

Capablanca competed in the Boston Metropolitan League and the United States Chess Federation New England League. All members were eligible to vie for the six positions on the team.

"The city games are Friday nights when I go to *shul*."

"Where?"

"Sabbath services."

"Play me into shape and I'll try out for both of us."

Mabi won his first four matches, one victory away from clinching a place on the team. "No," al-Saffah said when Mabi bragged to him. "It will interfere with your mission."

"What you be meaning?"

"It is not what's written in the book."

"How you know? If doing be revealing, how you know before it be done?"

Submitting to al-Saffah, Mabi eliminated himself by intentionally losing in the fifth and final round. In spite of his skill at chess, his good manners at the chess board, he still could not arrange matches other than with Levy.

-5-

The clock ticked. The phone did not ring. Mabi waited. His mind continued to wander.

Mabi understood hatred. It was instinctive, his understanding, the way prey knew its predator must kill it, must eat it, to live. His realization that he could reverse the prey/predator relationship by being the hater rather than the hated was also instinctive. He was too young to understand, much less read, the dictionary definition of the word "instinct" when he started hating whites. It was on his sixth birthday when Gideon, first in line, was last served at that Boston Garden souvenir stand. The police response to the 1967 race riots gave him a second reason. Whites stoning school buses carrying black children into white neighborhoods after the federal court desegregated Boston's public schools in 1974, a third. The murder of his brother in Vietnam by the collusion of a white cop, white prosecutor, white judge, white cunt legal aid attorney, the fourth and final reason. Jim Ed's death killed any possibility that reason, rather than instinct, would control Mabi's response to what happened around him, what happened to him.

It was December, 1971. Jim Ed was a sophomore at Northeastern University studying electrical engineering and computer science, paying his way by janitoring nights and weekends in Boston's office towers, cleaning toilets, polishing floors, emptying trash cans. One hawk-day Friday when gullies of snow made the unplowed streets in Boston's black neighborhoods impassable, the intersections inaccessible to pedestrians because of the mountains of snow tossed up by traffic, Jim Ed boy-scouted an elderly woman across the street, carrying her groceries in one arm, supporting her with his other. Half-way across, the traffic light turned green. Horns blaring, cars and trucks surged forward, careened around them, drivers rolling down their windows to swear, shout racial epithets. Rather than stop traffic, rather than help them across, the cop on the beat ticketed them for jaywalking. "Fifty dollar fine," he said, the joy of the holiday season dripping from each word.

"The lady's old with arthritis in her knees," Jim Ed tried to explain, but the cop, Sean Meagher, Jr. according to his name tag, prodded Jim Ed with his billy. By instinct, Jim Ed raised his hands into a martial arts position, lowering them quickly. Meagher jabbed him again. "A & B on a police officer. You're under arrest."

The sound of sirens in the distance mixed with the tinny music of *Jingle Bells* escaping from the supermarket whenever the door opened.

Meagher poked him again, pushing him back. "Resisting arrest. Flight. How high you want me to pile these charges?"

"High as your momma's jelly." Jim Ed grabbed the end of the billy and yanked Meagher forward, then laid him out with a punch to the jaw. "That's A & B on a police officer."

Meagher's partner, Patrick Turley, jumped out of the police cruiser and aimed his service revolver at Jim Ed. "Make your move. Save the taxpayer the cost of prosecuting and jailing your sorry black ass."

"You ain't got the balls," Jim Ed said.

Up against the wall with his legs spread-eagled, Jim Ed knew he could take down Turley by slowly pushing back to create slack, then collapsing forward and kicking back with his heel, breaking Turley's shin bone half way between his knee and foot.

That night after Jim Ed's arrest, Hannah said to Gideon, "The Emperor's militia, they going to find us." Stress fouled her diction, coloring her speech white to black. "The police will send his fingers to the FBI and one night the Emperor be kicking down our door." The Emperor was the dictator who ruled Ethiopia.

Leroy eavesdropped at the top of the stairs, standing where he wouldn't cast a shadow on the living room floor. Who be the Emperor? Leroy wondered.

"If the newspaper prints our name," Hannah said, "they be writing up our death notices 'fore this done. We should've gone to court for the name change, like I begged."

Leroy snuck out the back door and hid in the alley behind the candy store, huddling on a box deep in the alley's shadows. The cold numbed his feet, his feelings. He wished he could fall asleep and wake up in a land where there were no emperors and everyone knew the meaning of their names. The reds and greens of Christmas reflected off the brick wall above his head. They crooks? Escaped cons hiding from the man? Something worse? At his age he couldn't imagine what could be spooking his folks. Gusts of wind swirled around him. Other people's garbage piled up around his legs, newspapers, plastic wrappings from the supermarket, empty brown paper bags damp with the booze that dripped from the wino's lips as he slurped his supper. Wallaca, he thought, it means no more than this garbage.

Unable to make bail, Jim Ed passed the weekend asking everyone in the lockup how much time he'd have to serve, how large a fine he'd have to pay. He figured he'd have to drop out of school for a year, maybe two or more if the judge came down hard.

"No fucking fine," said one of the guards escorting him to court Monday morning. Cuffed and chained, paraded like a caged gorilla in a circus parade, Jim Ed felt the humiliation of a slave being led to the trading block. "Your ass's doing time," the guard said, "telephone number time."

Sitting in a small interview room handcuffed to a radiator too hot to touch, Jim Ed saw his future melting away. A criminal record would freeze him out of computers and electronics where a government security clearance was as necessary as a college degree. He might as well go to television repair school, but what white woman would believe Sears had sent him and open her door?

A man preceded by the stink of a cigar and trailed by a white woman entered. "I'm Claudius J. Antenor, but people call me C. J. Ant. This here's Maddie Devlin, law student extraordinaire."

Balding, his head a rounded ovoid like a watermelon, C. J. Ant dressed in shades of green—a lime green sports jacket with a white vest over a pastel green shirt, dark green slacks—and white accessories, tie, belt, shoes, vest pocket handkerchief. A cigar bobbed up and down in his mouth as if it had a life of its own. Maddie Devlin wore a loose fitting jumper that flattened her figure. She stood in the doorway, half inside, half outside, holding a briefcase in front of her breasts like a shield.

"Why'd they chain me to this hot box?" Jim Ed asked.

C. J. Ant knocked the cigar ash to the floor. The heat in the room magnified the cigar's stink and Jim Ed tasted it with every breath. "No Boston jury will acquit you for beating up a white cop, no matter how justified."

"What I need you for then?" Jim Ed asked.

"I'm going to build so much reversible error into your trial the conviction's guaranteed to be reversed on appeal. Sooner or later, the DA will have bigger fish to fry and I'll cut a deal, maybe time served before trial, maybe a fine and a walk away." He turned to Maddie, still standing in the doorway. "Can he afford me?"

"He's paying his way through college, electrical engineering and computer science at Northeastern."

"I can get you a nice little plea bargain for a thousand. Thirty days tops."

"Those trials you mentioned," Jim Ed said.

"Twenty-five hundred. Each."

"I don't have that kind of scratch. Can you cut me a break on the plea bargain?"

"Nine hundred 'cause I like your kind with the brains to try and make something of themselves. Give me your phone number so I can arrange for someone to bring down my fee." C. J. Ant pointed his cigar at Maddie. "She's going to ask you some questions. She's only a third year law student, but she's better than ninety per cent of the lawyers you'll see in court this morning."

"I didn't hire no law student," Jim Ed said.

"We're a package deal." C. J. left, taking his cigar, leaving its odor.

As Maddie questioned him, education, job history, priors, Jim Ed wondered if Gabe Tucker had been right. Johnson's Great Society wasn't working out so great.

Later that morning, C. J. Ant returned, cigar smoke garlanding his head. "Your lucky day. Judge Wayne John Webster's handling dispositions. He's a general in the Marine reserves."

Maddie added, "Volunteer for a four-year hitch. He'll drop all charges and seal your record. You can legally tell people you have no record when they ask."

"No record?" Jim Ed asked.

"Like it never happened," C. J. Ant replied.

"Security clearance?"

C. J. Ant shrugged. "Depends what level."

"Don't sound like volunteering to me."

"You're the client," C. J. Ant said. "You want to reject my best advice, be my guest."

Jim Ed wondered how many cases C. J. Ant knocked off a day, how many blacks he smart-talked into going to war. Slavery in a different uniform. At a thousand a pop, his wallet must be fatter than cheap bacon was greasy. The cunt's pocket-book, too.

Maddie handled the disposition, emphasizing Jim Ed was coming to the defense of an elderly woman, that he misinterpreted the intentions of the police officer, conceding that he shouldn't have lost his temper. "A perfect candidate for the Marines," she concluded. Judge Webster agreed.

Several days later, after a physical and a battery of tests administered by the Marines under the watchful eyes of Suffolk County prison guards, Jim Ed having taken the oath at the courthouse before he was released from custody, he and Leroy stood by the plate glass window in one of the terminals at Logan Airport, watching planes land and take off while they waited for his flight to Parris Island.

"Gabe Tucker had it right," Leroy said.

"If I was convicted," Jim Ed said, "I'm out of electronics and computers 'cause I can't get a security clearance with a record. With the charges dropped and a good behavior in the Marines, maybe it's like it never happened."

"And the cop gets a medal. It's not like you choosing 'tween steak and lobster. You fell for the ol' okee-dokee." Leroy watched the trains of baggage cars snaking around the airport tarmac. "Gideon tell you the meaning of Wallaca?"

"He gave me a hang dog out of hell look and Hannah just turned away and sucked on her handkerchief."

Leroy leaned against the plate glass window, warming his backside with the air rising from the baseboard heater. "Gideon, he may be hiding from the law. Hannah's fearing some emperor see our name in the paper 'cause of you."

"Why didn't you say something?"

"Gideon would only make your leaving twice as sour as that buttermilk he drinks." Leroy squatted over the radiator. The warm air felt good on his crotch.

"When it's your turn to sing," Jim Ed said, "I want you singin' a new song."

"Zuluz."

"Fuck them."

Leroy turned away as a line of passengers entered the terminal from an incoming flight, tanned and dressed for summer in January, shirts red and blue and bright with flowers. They carried string bags of grapefruit and oranges. Men and women both sported Woburn Lions Club baseball caps–a gang of old folks displaying their colors. A metallic voice sounding like it was from another world announced Jim Ed's flight.

Jim Ed hugged Leroy. "Don't run with the Zuluz. You're all the folks got now."

"They get you back in twelve months."

"Sixteen. Marines rotate out after thirteen months, plus three months of boot camp." Jim Ed picked up his duffel bag, then walked down the boarding ramp toward the waiting plane, one of an army of blacks dressed in green, fighting yellows in the jungles of Vietnam for the red, white and blue. The rainbow dream.

After Jim Ed's departure, Gideon withdrew so deeply into the constants of his life that the shadow of his former self became a black hole. Five days a week, including two weekends out of three, he sagged into the driver's seat of a Greyhound in the Boston terminal at sunrise, arrived in New York, where he wolfed down a hot dog and a warm orange soda while the bus was refueled, and left for the return trip with lunch still sloshing around his stomach, arriving home for a late supper he was too tired to eat. Ten hours a day, sometimes eleven or twelve depending on weather or traffic, five days a week, fifty weeks a year, he jockeyed for lane space with double-hitched tractor trailers and watched his outside mirrors for tiny sports cars that sneaked into his blind spot while passing on the right. Three months into Jim Ed's tour of duty marked Gideon's tenth year without an accident. The company gave him a certificate torn off a pad of certificates bought at an office supply store, as well as both Thanksgiving and Christmas off in the same year.

Whenever Leroy approached him to talk about the family name the talk exploded into a tirade.

"You being tricked by the two-headed lady saying one thing out one mouth, opposite out the other," Gideon liked to say. Half way through Jim Ed's fourth month in Vietnam, Gideon started talking in circles about two-headed ladies, double-sighted persons and practitional doctors. He dismissed Hannah's prayers for Jim Ed's safe return as conjuring. He demonized the preachers who gave her solace as root doctors. When she persisted, he dragged her to a shield man to break the "spell." For one hundred dollars cash money, the shield man mixed a potion of disturbment powder, confusion oil, poke root, and blood plant leaves, poured it into the cupped palm of a talking hand, and watched for the quivers as Gideon asked it questions. The talking hand didn't even tremble. As a last resort, Gideon hung a frizzly chicken from the jamb of the kitchen doorway to ward off demons and evil spirits. The chicken hung by the neck, head bent as if it had been lynched, snatching appetites from everyone who sat at the kitchen table.

Still, Hannah persevered, rejecting Gideon's voodoo, surviving on prayers. As time passed, Leroy came to envy his mother's strength, so much so he approached her with his questions; but, as in the past, she responded only with silence or evasion. Angry, frustrated, Leroy turned to the Zuluz to re-place the family that departed with Jim Ed to Vietnam. When he wrote Jim Ed about his attempt to join the gang, Jim Ed wrote Luke Shaw, head blood in charge of the Zuluz, that if the gang made Leroy a member, when he, Jim Ed, returned to Boston from Nam he would waste every fucking gang member starting with Shaw himself. Shaw so feared Jim Ed that one letter from the other side of the world was enough to black-ball Leroy. In a phone call home while on leave in Saigon, Jim Ed cussed Leroy out, putting down the Zuluz for trashing its 'hood rather than helping its own. Leroy trashed his brother for fighting a war on the other side of the world instead of being home to stand up to Billy Sunshine when Billy Sunshine teased him Wallaca was a slave name. "That's the name stitched on my uniform," Jim Ed said to Leroy. "It's all the name I'm ever going to have."

As the war escalated, the hate and resentment festering in-side Leroy convinced him if he didn't join the Zuluz, he would end up a loner without family, without gang colors to protect him, a loner whose life wasn't worth dried dog shit. Being Chinatowned only offered so much protection. When he ap-proached the Zuluz a few months later, Luke Shaw offered a deal: "Take down Billy Sunshine and maybe we let you hang."

Leroy had never thought about killing before. Jim Ed killed people every day, not for his country which didn't need defending from the Viet Cong, but to stay alive. Self-defense. Killing Billy Sunshine the same. The more he thought about it, the more he realized real life was no different than the comic book. It was his choice whether he killed or be killed. America was as much a battlefield as some jungle halfway around the world, Boston's streets as much a battlefield as the flat, dusty plain outside an ancient walled city.

"Want me to nine him?" Leroy asked Luke Shaw.

"Coward's way. Hand to hand."

"If we're lucky," Spider, Luke's warlord said, "maybe you and him you'll waste each other."

"Better double check your fortune cookie," Leroy replied.

Later that week on the way to shoot hoops, Leroy detoured to the candy store where Billy Sunshine hung out.

"Hey, slave boy," Billy said.

"I hear your momma spreads her jelly over white bread by the loaf." Leroy stood with his weight toward the front of his feet, trying to look nonchalant so Billy wouldn't see how his legs and feet were positioned to spring forward or dodge to the side. Billy, he figured, would lead with his right, being right-handed. He eyed that hand while he let Billy squeeze his shoulder. He faked a cry of pain, until Billy, laughing, relaxed, then rammed the heel of his palm into the bottom of Billy's nose, pushing his head back against the iron grating that covered the window in the door. When Billy straightened out, Leroy gave him a shot to the groin that shoved his balls into his guts, followed by a stiff arm to the eye.

"Man," Leroy said, "you bleeding like your momma's pussy after she comes home from work." Blood gushed from Billy's nose and leaked from his eye socket. When he reached for the gun he kept in the holster in the small of his back, Leroy straight-armed him again, angling upwards this time, shoving the bone in his nose back into his brain. Billy Sunshine died before his head hit the cement.

Time slowed to a crawl as Leroy waited for Jim Ed's letter and Luke Shaw's invite to join the Zuluz. Somehow, Jim Ed always found out what was going down back home and would write Leroy letters preaching like a Sunday sermonizer about schooling, about not doing drugs, about not running with the

Zuluz, sermons that didn't mean shit because Jim Ed, with all his schooling, with all his hard working, was still LBJ's slave boy in Vietnam. As much as he hated those sermons, Leroy welcomed them because letters were now his only connection to his brother. Time passed without word and Leroy worried Jim Ed was dead or missing or a prisoner of war. On the streets, the Zuluz avoided him and the talk was that Luke Shaw feared him the way elderly white folk feared blacks. People who never talked to him before warned him about being jumped. Still, he worried too much about Jim Ed to gangsta limp 'round the 'hood like the new HNIC. He had the sugar from knowing people feared him, but the novelty wore off faster than a two-minute brotha. He'd trade it for having Jim Ed home.

Weeks after Billy Sunshine's murder, Jim Ed called from Saigon sounding like he was no farther away than the phone booth at the candy store. "Leroy," he said, "you so dumb I wonder if you dump rainwater out your boots 'fore you put 'em on."

"Billy Sunshine don't got the tongue to put me down no more. People step aside when I stroll the street." Leroy tried to visualize his brother. Was Jim Ed in some bar surrounded by gook pussy looking to make a day's pay? Wherever he was, he was no longer the man in dress blues in the photograph on the mantle.

"When I done whipping you," Jim Ed said, "people be thinking Sonny Liston looked good and Joe Louis looked bad. Know what I'm saying?"

Leroy started to respond, but static swallowed his words and the overseas operator disconnected them.

On March 4, 1973, Gideon and Hannah received the telegram: 'President Nixon shares your grief at the loss of a son, but is comforted in knowing he died answering his country's call.' Later that month, the Marines confessed they could not identify a body as being Jim Ed's, but, nonetheless, promised a coffin, a flag, and a funeral with full military honors. In mid-April, two weeks after Leroy's fourteenth birthday, Hannah and Gideon buried an empty coffin, dull gray like a sardine tin, dented in one corner where it was dropped in transit. Leroy mourned Jim Ed and the way their brotherhood ended in static, static on a telephone line, static between their hearts. With Jim Ed dead, Gideon drifting around the house like he was under a spell, Hannah serving detention in the amen corner, Leroy figured it was time to make the Zuluz his own.

On a Friday night in late April when the first south wind of the season blanketed the 'hood with a summery heat, Leroy crashed a gang-only party at the Zuluz crib. As soon as Luke's posse seen him, someone pulled the jukebox plug and flipped on the overhead lights. On Luke's signal, the Zuluz retreated to the side, leaving Luke and his girl, Becky Hawkins, in the center of the room. "By the Zuluz code," Leroy said to Luke Shaw, "I challenge you here and now, winner be HNIC, loser be dead."

"Your ass frontin' your mouth," Luke said, "the way you jaw jackin' like a house boy praising his master."

"You as good at handfighting as lipfighting?" Leroy asked.

"You sure wanting to wear our colors bad."

"Fuck your colors. You soon be wearing mine."

"We Zuluz now and we Zuluz forever."

"And your momma's pussy backs up worse than the Southeast Expressway at Friday rush hour. I hear she sells monthly passes to commuters."

Luke told Becky to join the rest of the gang and dispatched Spider, his warlord, to lock the outside door. "Where you want the body shipped, boy?"

"Fire up the jukebox. *Dancing with Mr. D.*, dedicated to the late, great Luke Shaw."

"You talk a good fight, but I ain't Billy Sunshine."

"You soon be setting all the same."

The strident vocal filled the room as Luke and Leroy circled each other. When Luke plunged forward, Leroy grabbed his wrist and flipped him to the floor. They circled again. Leroy's leg shot out, catching Luke flush on the nose and knocking him off his feet.

Luke licked blood off his lips. "I'm gonna close my hands 'round your neck tighter than white on rice." He rocked from side to side. When Luke lunged, Leroy yanked his arm and snapped his elbow. Luke backed away, the blood from his nose tracking his retreat on the floor. Leroy stalked him. As they moved, Luke reached for his blade, custom made with a cutting edge sharpened and ground to a fine point so he could either slice or plunge. Thrown hard enough, it would stick in a bone like an arrow shot from a crossbow. "Suck on this, slave boy!"

"Your blade's made of Jell-O same as your cock."

Luke swung the knife in wide arcs. Leroy figured Luke wouldn't risk throwing it, wouldn't risk losing the one thing that gave him half a chance. Leroy also figured Luke had to get in tight enough to gut him. Leroy saw fear in Luke's eyes as Luke maneuvered to get close, but with each step forward, Leroy stepped back, avoiding the corners, daring Luke to attack. They moved in lockstep until Luke charged. Leroy slide-stepped, then broke Luke's cheekbone with one punch. The knife fell, vibrating as it stuck in the floor. Luke looked to the Zuluz for help.

"You eating at a table for one," Spider said, holding back the gang.

Luke edged toward the stairs, his right arm hanging down like an empty sleeve. Leroy pulled the knife from the floor, measured his target, and flung it. End over end it whirred until it entered Luke's neck and lodged in his windpipe, killing him so fast his soul didn't have time to escape. The beat of his body tumbling down the stairs became part of the beat of the music until, with a final thud like a final drum roll, Luke came to rest against the locked door. The room was as silent as a bitch who cock-teased and got raped.

Leroy stood before the Zuluz, demanding the respect they gave Luke. "My name it's Priam and now we be the Trojans."

"This some trickeration?" Spider asked.

"You challenging me or you wanna be my warlord?" If Spider was still warlord, Priam figured, he'd only have to earn Spider's respect.

"From appetite to asshole I'll call you Muhammad Ali if it gets you on." Spider pointed to the bitches lining the wall. "Leader chooses his woman."

"The biddy." Priam pointed to Silvy Thomas, the only one who looked close to him in age.

-6-

Stilts knew when to give Mabi space, when to make small talk, when to crack jokes, when to talk serious. Space was what Mabi needed as he waited for Beaujolais's telephone call. Blackbird's was empty now, the other drinkers having suddenly lost their thirst. Still, Mabi's mind wandered, back now to the first dawn after Bumper Sullivan's murder. Mabi had watched the eastern sky begin to lighten on the rooftop of his building trembling like an addict suffering withdrawal. He had watched Silvy home from that rooftop, then dreamed again the dream, another comic book dream, he first had the night he offed Luke Shaw. In that dream, he had climbed the fire escape to the roof of his building and leaned against the chimney watching the fog settle on the rooftops. Jim Ed had appeared among the television antennas. Mabi had tried to speak, but Jim Ed held out one hand and the words stuck in his throat.

"Listen up," Jim Ed said. "Two gates link our worlds, a gate of horn providing easy passage for true souls and a gate of ivory providing escape for false dreams."

Two gates materialized among the rooftop antennas, one bone yellow like a ram's horn, the other alabaster white like an elephant's tusk. He moved toward the yellow, but Jim Ed blocked his way and pushed him through the white, off the roof-top, back into the bedroom where in his dream he awoke, his bedding so damp he wondered if he'd pissed the bed. Layers of fat engulfed his heart, so heavy it pinned him to the mattress.

Priam, as Mabi called himself at the time, tried to escape this heaviness by making the Trojans the most powerful street gang in Boston. Block by block, they expanded their turf, doubling it once, then again. When he decided to drive competing drug pushers out of business, he used *Tales of the Trojan War* for inspiration, slaying one pusher with a bow and arrow, another with a spear through the heart, stoning a third to death, dragging a fourth through the streets tied to the bumper of a car. Still, the nightmare continued, night after night, Jim Ed pushing him through the ivory gate, the fall further and further each time, until he awoke, sweating, pinned to wet bedding by a heaviness that centered in his heart and spread throughout his body as if it circulated with his blood.

At home, he and Gideon and Hannah argued about school and calls from the truant officer. "School didn't save Jim Ed from dying in Nam," he told his parents.

"There's a witch riding that boy," Gideon said to Hannah. "You should tie his shirt to his underwear with black thread."

Mabi, then Priam, punched the frizzly chicken hanging from the door jamb. Feathers drifted to the floor. "Leroy's dead. Buried in Jim Ed's empty grave. All your praying and conjuring won't resurrect him."

"Maybe," Gideon said, "the devil what stole his body should be moving on. Leroy he'll always have a home here, Priam never. Your things in boxes by the curb."

He fought the impulse to attack his father. He gasped for words, but had none. Gideon drank coffee as if he weren't there and Hannah, erect in her chair, lips frozen shut, stared at him as hard as anyone ever had. He searched her face for some sign she'd take his side. He bent to kiss her, but she turned away and his lips brushed her hair. "Someday," he said, "you'll be sorry you let him do this."

"Satan's a liar," she said, "a conjurer, too. You better watch out, 'cause he's conjurin' you."

Through the fall and winter after he had moved out, he didn't see Hannah or Gideon except from a distance or scoping out the house to make certain things were right. He slept on the floor of Trojan headquarters, dubbed Ilion from the comic book, that was still in the basement of the tenement where Gabe Tucker once lived. Somewhere in that basement, rolled in a tube, stored in an unpacked box, was the Bill Russell poster, a relic waiting for someone to hang it on a ceiling or garbage it away. The nightmares continued. The Trojans did not raise up the weight off his heart; nor did seizing control of the drug trade throughout the city. The money, the power, the fear, the respect—nothing lifted the heaviness.

Winter dragged, hanging on like a child clinging to its mother's leg. That April he tried to make peace with Hannah on the anniversary of the burial of the empty coffin in Jim Ed's grave. He arrived first, accompanied by the Trojans, bearing flowers stolen from a fay florist. Hannah ignored him, them. She removed sewing shears from her purse and clipped the tall grass around the stone.

Dead grass surrounded all the graves in Nigger Heaven as white municipal workers called that section of the cemetery, which languished as unkempt and uncared for as when it was a potter's field except for a few neat, well-trimmed sites tended by families who cared. Although a federal judge ordered Boston to desegregate its cemeteries, most of Boston's blacks were still buried among the remains of anonymous white paupers that had accumulated during the city's three hundred fifty years. For all the unmowed weeds in summer, unraked leaves in fall, unshoveled snow in winter, unwatered shrubs in spring, the gravestones themselves, shining in the hot sun like bleached-white bones, survived, vandalized only by rain, wind, hail, and snow.

Blade by blade, Hannah cut the grass and piled it in neat mounds, then wiped dust from the recessed letters chiseled into the granite with a threadbare cleaning rag. She took a flower, the delicate violet edges of its petals tinged brown, and placed it above where Jim Ed's head should have been. Doubled over by the weight of her memories, the strength of her fears, she seemed old and weak and abandoned by God. She mustered enough strength to say some words.

"Almighty and eternal Father . . . "

"All right!" the Trojans chanted in reply.

" . . . source of all life . . . "

"Yea, Lord."

" . . . we love those summonsed away unto Thee . . . "

"Be with us, O Lord!"

" . . . and we thank Thee for their memories . . . "

"You be truth telling."

" . . . which comfort us earthbound mourners . . . "

"We listening."

" . . . and keep us trusting in thy righteous wisdom . . . "

"Gawd, she testifying."

" . . . we mourners lift up our heads to Thee . . . "

"Again."

" . . . yea, we do lift up our heads to Thee . . . "

"Bring me over!"

" . . . and we do consecrate our lives to Thee . . . "

"Our lives."

" . . . in tribute to our dead who are bound to Thee . . . "

"Have mercy."

" . . . He do have mercy . . . "

"Sing out!"

" . . . if we magnify . . . "

"Preach it."

" . . . and sanctify . . . "

"I swear I do."

" . . . our faith in His love . . . "

"His sweet love."

" . . . Yea, His sweet love which links one generation to the next . . . "

"I'm over! I'm over!"

" . . . so Lord, we praise Your holy name and I say amen . . . "

"Say it again."

" . . . Amen! I say amen!"

Like a pilgrim who knew her age would keep her from the Promised Land, Hannah walked at a pall-bearer's pace, head erect, eyes forward, out of Nigger Heaven toward the distant gates of the Nigger Hell known as Boston.

Kneeling, Priam gathered the dead grass as if he were harvesting it. I ain't got no more roots than this grass, he thought. He placed the longest stalk along the top edge of the stone for the bro he lost, the next longest for his nameless self. He added two more for Hannah and Gideon, whether they were his real blood or not, and another for Silvy, sweet Silvy. A short stalk for Silvy's bro Badger, a handful for the Trojans. He laid a solitary stalk across the top. He struck a match against the side of the grave. The grass leaped into flames, flared, then blackened into ashes, coloring the bright white of the stone the way Boston's blacks colored the city. His entire life was trapped inside that stain.

Spitting into his hands, he tried to scrub it away, spitting and scrubbing, spitting and scrubbing, until his spit came out dry and a gray smudge remained. He rose and walked toward the gates of the cemetery, past the graves of Boston's anonymous white paupers, past the graves of Boston's blacks, out of Nigger Heaven, into Nigger Hell.

-7-

In Blackbird's, the phone remained silent. Spider and Scorpion, like Stilts, gave Mabi his space. Mabi's mind continued to wander. Again, he was on the rooftop of his building on the morning after Bumper Sullivan's murder.

As the eastern sky continued to brighten that morning, the city began to stir and awakened Mabi from his dream and he thought about the last time he had gone to church. It was the Sunday of al-Saffah's guest sermon when he accompanied Silvy and Badger to the New World Primitive Baptist Church where Silvy taught the preschool class in Bible studies and Badger, when forced, attended a scripture class. Black children, shouting, singing, laughing, some whining, some fighting over toys, filled the classroom.

"Priam! Priam!" A small boy, Jesse, tugged at his leg. "Let's make a clay man." He gripped Mabi's baby finger and led him to the clay table.

He gouged out a hunk of clay and rounded it into a ball, flattening the top with his thumb. "This the head," he said. He rolled four pieces into thick snakes. "The arms and legs." He molded a torso from a large chunk, pinching it at the middle to create a waist, and joined the limbs to the torso. Three spitballs of red clay became the eyes and a nose and three thin snakes, two short and one long, became a grin and a pair of eyebrows. "What you naming him?"

"Trojan," Jesse said. "He can save my place 'til I be growed."

"Better take Trojan home then."

"You made him," Jesse said. "You take him."

"I be standing him right 'side my bed."

A bell rang and one of the aides led the children upstairs to the sanctuary.

"You're poisoning these kids," Silvy said.

"I'm awe inspiring 'em."

"Only the good Lord awe inspiring."

"You saw how the good Lord awe inspired my brother. And what's sweet Jesus done since then? No change in Boston. Shit, no change anywhere. The man still lynching us. He just not using rope no more. No awe inspiring in that."

"You want inspiring, come to the service. There's a guest sermon. A mullah."

He did attend that service, did become al-Saffah's disciple, did allow al-Saffah to circumcise him, did allow al-Saffah to change his name from Priam to Mabi, and, under al-Saffah's thrall, did carry out mission after mission to fulfill al-Saffah's goal of creating a holy war in Boston.

"How I get away with so much so fast?" Mabi asked when al-Saffah explained the missions, each escalating up the ladder of hatred. "Heavy jail time I be caught."

"Have faith," al-Saffah replied.

The first mission occurred the night before the first Thanksgiving after Mabi's conversion when he used fertilizer to burn a cross into the grass of a Jewish cemetery. When Mayor Charlie denounced anti-Semitism at a news conference on Thanksgiving morning, Mabi replied that night by burning a Star of David into the lawn of a Catholic cemetery. When this produced nothing more than a flurry of ecumenical statements from politicians and religious leaders, Mabi heisted five gallons of blood from a slaughter house and defaced the white marble expanse of Temple Israel with gargantuan swastikas; then, later that night, he vandalized the crèche in front of St. Patrick's and decorated its gray gothic curves with three bloody Ks.

Quickly, the soft voices of ecumenism rose into angry demands for justice. Fingers pointed. Catholic and Jews asked, first privately, then publicly, whether the other might not be responsible. Late on a Saturday night in February after a blizzard drove the temperatures into negative numbers and wind-drifted snow buried the streets, Mabi firebombed the homes of Rabbi Joseph Esrael and Father Dominic Ponichtera. Both burned to death because the fire engines and ambulances could not overcome the weather conditions and the unplowed streets.

"You are a true disciple," al-Saffah had said at the time, his voice reverential; and at the time Mabi had felt truly blessed.

-8-

Later that day, no longer able to wait for Beaujolais's phone call at Blackbird's, Mabi left a message for her with Stilts and returned to the Trojans' crib where he sat in judgment over Brother Ambrose for stealing from the Trojans. Ambrose was a mule, a courier who delivered drugs to the addicts, collected payments, and remitted the money to the gang. Spider prosecuted. Two Trojans wrestled Ambrose into the defendant's chair in front of Mabi's desk and stationed themselves on either side like police officers guarding a convict appearing in court on a habe. "Where them skates with the orange wheels?" Mabi asked.

"They's my first Tuesday skates," Ambrose said. "Purple's my today color."

"How many colors you got?"

"One for each day of the month."

"Didn't know the rainbow had so many colors. How you paying for them fancies when you ain't paid the Trojans in . . . how long, Spider?"

"From the jump."

"That long." Mabi said.

"Longer."

"Man," Ambrose said, "you know I'm good for the green."

"If you're so good for the green, where's it be?" Mabi nodded at Spider.

"You into Quall for almost ten large," Spider said. "Horses, dogs, football, numbers, the works. Quall ready to tan your black ass."

"Man, the eagle it fly tomorrow," Ambrose said.

"How about it flying right now? I don't want Quall thinking he eats first."

"No bird flies so high so fast. Two hours."

"By ripping off the packy?" Mabi asked.

"One hour."

"If the bloods see you fucking with us, they'll fuck with us and before you change your skates only old lady whites be fearing the Trojans."

Scorpion rushed in. "Beaujolais waiting downstairs real authority looking."

"Spider. Dance Ambrose with Mr. D., then spread his fancy skates 'round the hood. Kids deserving easy rides."

"I ain't no sell-out," Ambrose cried.

"Say what?" Spider said. He turned to Mabi. "Hangin' him from a streetlight send the message real clear."

"Fuck shit no!" Mabi snarled. "Too many lynchings of too many of our people for us to be lynching each other. OD him so he go out smiling."

Beaujolais, sporting the gang colors of a Boston cop, marched in and replaced Brother Ambrose in the defendant's chair.

"Badger's too good a collar and Ugolino he ain't dealing. 'Less you pay extra, he's busting you too."

"For what?"

"For what he fucking busted Badger for."

Mabi removed a nine and a Glock from the desk's center drawer and laid them on the desk pointing at Beaujolais. "Tell Ugolino if Badger ain't home for supper tomorrow he'll be celebrating summer eulogizing at police funerals, starting with yours. Come September he'll be starring in his own. Tell him I'll fuck him so bad he'll go down in a closed coffin. Tell him it's the fire this time." He waved her out of the room.

"We should do a cop now," Spider said, "so they know we're serious."

"I said home for supper tomorrow. Give her a chance to deliver the message."

Outside, Cealy and Silvy intercepted Mabi on the tenement's front stoop. "Where's my baby?" Cealy demanded. "How come he ain't freed yet?"

"Tomorrow," Mabi said. "I said he be bailed tomorrow. It's still fucking today."

"Don't be talking to Cealy like that." Silvy slapped at his face, but he deflected her hand with his forearm.

"The Lord's giving me no inducement to serenity until my Badger comes home," Cealy said. "I always thought you were right with the Lord the way you cared for my Badger after his daddy sent off, but now I can't help but think you a Satan sent man. I'm not budging 'till Badger be brought forward."

"Make the stoop your bed for all I care. Just don't shit on the stairs."

Maybe, Mabi thought as he retreated back inside, I shouldn't have used Badger on no missions. He recalled the night he had sent Badger to intercept Rabbi ben Reuben on the overpass above the Charles Street rotary near the Charles Street Jail. Mabi had fidgeted that night, waiting for Badger's safe return on a stool in Ta-Kome Pizza's back room, hidden behind two stacks of cardboard take-out boxes.

Demand for pizza had wilted in the Afric heat and the ovens at Ta-Kome Pizza, which sold Sicilian pizza by the square operated by the Trojans to launder drug money, were turned off to save the cost of electricity. Mabi didn't nickel and dime, but he counted pennies. If he saw one on the sidewalk, he stooped to pick it up. Bad luck to pass it by, he said. Or, never too rich, never too proud. Hexed up like your father, Silvy said. If it was from his birth year, he saved it in a piggy bank Gideon gave him on his fourth birthday, a rocket launcher which shot coins at a slot in a sphere sporting the bumps and bruises of the moon's craters and mountains. Dimes easily made it through the slot into the sphere's hollow interior, quarters rarely, nickels and pennies about half the time. The slot was too narrow for half dollars. Mabi didn't know Gideon had stolen it from the bus company Lost and Found, but there were a lot of things he didn't know about his folks. That's one reason why he was now Mabi, formerly Priam, no longer Leroy Wallaca. No easy pages in Allah's book.

The stench of tomato sauce baked into Ta-Kome's back room's linoleum floor and sheetrock walls fouled the air. He had skipped supper. He never ate when he worried about people he loved and he loved Silvy's brother as the kid brother he never had. When Judge "Send 'em South" Sadowski sentenced Badger's dad to ten to twenty to be served in Walpole on trumped up charges of armed robbery and criminal mayhem, Mabi became Badger's surrogate father. Together they grooved on Boston Celtic basketball games, cheering for Jo Jo, Tall Paul, and Charlie Scott, but never Big Red or Hondo. The Celtics, he told Badger, were the first NBA team to break the color line, first to start five brothers, first to have a black coach. He missed those Celtics, the Celtics of his boyhood, the Jones boys, Satch, Russ, some afterthought white-asses. He missed his Bill Russell poster, rolled in a cardboard tube, stored in a box he'd never unpack, but it was a poster from a different lifetime, a different person's lifetime, a lifetime which had reached its *ajal*. He resented today's Celtics and its reliance on great white hopes to win championships. The advent of Larry Bird as their next super star savior hardened his attitude. Beauty in his mind was not skin deep.

Mabi cradled a can of root beer, fiddling with the straw, trapping soda, releasing it, trapping, releasing, trapping, releasing. Knowing Spider and Scorpion were riding shotgun for Badger did not calm his worries. His fingertips beat on the lid of the can as if possessed by Shaytān. Fucking al-Saffah, he thought. I'm as controlled as this fucking soda. He sucks me in when he wants to suck me in, blows me out when he wants to blow me out. Mabi didn't understand why the soda didn't drain from the straw when he sealed it with his fingertip any more than he understood why he became Mabi or how his life became trapped inside the pages of some book like a bookmark abandoned by an itinerate preacher who'd lost interest in the text. If he could skip to the end of the story . . . , but he didn't have no one to turn the pages. He flung the can across the storeroom, a storm of root beer raining down everywhere.

"Shit," Bugle, the counterman, said. "That soda be 'sugaring a carpet of ants."

Mabi sat stone still while Bugle wiped up the root beer with a towel, then sponged down the floor with a mop.

"Yo, Mabi!" Badger had duck-walked into the storeroom after intercepting the rabbi. "When I told rabbi man our eyes burning holes in his back . . ."

"Any trouble?" Mabi asked Spider.

"Just the trouble we made," Spider said. "Seen this?" He handed Mabi a copy of the first edition of Saturday's *Herald-American*. MATZOH MURDER! in block letters headlined the front page. Above the masthead, the paper claimed an exclusive: Why Bumper Sullivan had to die! Spider opened to page two. "Al-Saffah says Jews needing Bumper's blood to bake shit called *matzoh*."

"Sweet to the tongue, sour to the stomach," Bugle said.

"Home time for you," Mabi told Badger.

"Better let me wheel this baby home," Spider said.

"When Silvy heard I doing Trojan business," Badger said, "she told me she not keeping your company no more. You're so deep inside her shit your head sticking out her butt crack."

313

Mabi grabbed Badger and lifted him off the floor. "Don't fucking talk like that 'bout your sister." He dropped Badger who crumbled to the floor like a carcass that had been deboned. He kneeled and glared down at Badger. "Rats be lapping up your blood I hear you talk that way again."

Silvy's put-down stung him worse than fire crawling up and down his cock. The last time he was so deep in Silvy's shit was after al-Saffah sliced and diced his cock and it was too sore, the wound too raw, to take care of her needs. She pouted about his loss of interest in her, accusing him of fucking snow bunnies or sack chasers or going fag. The way she lowered her eyes and puffed up her lips aroused him; but erections still ached and he knew making love would hurt worse than a steel wool rubdown.

"Why you let him do you like that?" she had asked.

"To get holy. How many years you been begging me to get holy?"

"Nobody but Jews gets their cocks cut up like that."

"And Muslims." Maybe, he had thought at the time, Silvy's *ajal* had come. Maybe she had been written out of the pages of his book. Maybe she was nothing but head hunting, keeping him in trim because it meant something to be his woman.

"I don't see the rest of the Trojans getting holy."

"How many Trojan cocks you seen lately?"

"Their pussies ain't pouting."

"Maybe heaven ain't in their plans."

"How many virgins you been promised in that heaven?"

"None but you."

Shadowboxing with his regrets in Ta-kome Pizza's storage room, al-Saffah's words again filled Mabi's head. "There is an ancient rite," al-Saffah had said, "a religious duty, one of the most important events in the life of a Muslim male. No male can enter heaven who has not undergone this rite. You must be immersed into the Mashriq ritual of circumcision. In simpler times, there was a festival. You would be dressed in special raiment, decorated with flowers and led around the village in a procession. Afterwards, there would be a feast and gifts, many, many gifts. Fathers would betroth their daughters as part of the ceremony."

Mabi recalled how al-Saffah had whetted a dagger with a watered steel blade against a pumice stone, the way it glowed and hissed, how he covered his groin, how al-Saffah's eyes bored into him and pinned him to the couch and disconnected his hands from his mind so he himself undid his belt and opened his zipper and lowered his pants, how he laid back. The circle of scimitars rose from the wall above his head, rotated, faster, faster, a guillotine that would sever his head like a chicken being slaughtered if he attempted to stand. Something cool and wet touched his cock. Al-Saffah chanted words in a language he did not understand. Pain is ephemeral, was the translation, salvation eternal. Forceps, cold and metallic, clamped the tip of his cock, stretched his skin, held it taut. The slice, once, twice, a third time. He bit hard on the wooden dowel al-Saffah had placed in his mouth. How much he wanted to scream. At last, something soft cradled his cock, swathing it like a newborn freshly birthed.

"Welcome you to your heritage," al-Saffah said. "Let us pray for deliverance."

Supporting himself on al-Saffah's shoulder, he limped to the prayer rug spread before the *mihrab*. The pattern of the prayer rug, diamonds whose different colors formed larger diamonds, mirrored the ceramic tiles of the *mihrab*. The glow of the glass mosque lamp hanging from the ceiling—delicate red inscriptions enameled into the neck, a blazon of blue bands,

315

interlaced like snakes, Arabic inscription in gold leaf around the circumference, Syrian, first half of the fourteenth century–bathed the rug in a soft yellow light. Al-Saffah lowered him and faced him toward Mecca, then knelt beside him and forced him forward until his forehead touched the floor. Al-Saffah touched his forehead to the floor as well, then raised him to a kneeling position. For the first time al-Saffah called him Mabi.

The pain between Mabi's legs throbbed. Al-Saffah, the chess men, the scimitars, the dust of hundreds of pasts, all crowded in on him and, in the presence of so many old things, he felt newborn and nowborn out of the ashes of Leroy Wallaca, the ashes of Priam; newborn and nowborn out of the dust of Jim Ed; newborn and nowborn out of the hexes and hoaxes of Gideon, the silences of Hannah; newborn and nowborn out of the unknown into the known. He took a deep breath and willed away the pain and forced himself to bend forward until his forehead touched the floor. Yes, he thought. Mabi. Blood bought. A soldier in the army of Allah. As Mabi prayed, the pain between his legs subsided, disappeared, and with its disappearance he felt his being merge into the ancient artifacts surrounding him, merge into the chess set, merge into the sword and scabbard, merge into the mosque lamp, merge into al-Saffah, merge into the holiness of the book, and with this merger he immersed himself in the heritage, the history, the name he so badly wanted, so badly needed. If only Jim Ed were here to join me, he wished.

That night, as Silvy pouted he said, "Maybe you don't understand what growing up's about. Leroy he's a zero. Priam he's a punk. Mabi he's a man. There's this book and everything going down be already written into it and every day we turn another page and read what's up 'cept we don't read it, but do it all at once if you know what I mean."

"I liked it better when you thought you was a comic book hero."

"I'm hero of a better book now."

"Is this in your book?" She reached for him and filled her mouth with him.

Mabi, his cock swollen, still bleeding, pushed her away. "We be skipping sex 'til I heal up."

"How long?"

"Two weeks, maybe three; then we fuck our brains out."

She rested her head on his chest. "I want to have your baby," she said as they cuddled. "I don't want him growing up with no father. I want you to stop gang-leading, stop jigging with al-Saffah. I want you to live regular and normal."

"Drugs too good a hustle."

"Al-Saffah he the source?"

"You got brains behind that beauty. We his Boston outlet. He's got gangs dealing for him in Chicago, New York, L.A., other big cities. Financing his crusade."

"You being Murphied, you know."

"Al-Saffah he's no match for the Trojans."

"I know a hustle when I see one. Don't be blinded by the green."

"Green's like a traffic light, Silvy. It says when to go, when to stop. My traffic light it's still green." He held her tight that night, silent when she pressed him about fathering her child.

Now, while Spider drove Badger home, Mabi hightailed it from Ta-Kome Pizza to confront al-Saffah. "No more missions for Badger no matter what's written in that fucking book."

"Please. Among my people, our people, there is a ceremony of friendship." Al-Saffah removed a hookah from the shelf over the Koran bookstand, lifted the bowl from the slender neck of its glass vase, and poured a quart of water from a silver pitcher into it. He inserted a piece of flexible tubing covered with woven cloth into a hole in the side of the vase. The tubing had a pipe bit at one end. He filled the pipe with tobacco, pinch by pinch, tamping it down with the flat end of a pipe tool. When it was full, he rotated the hookah so the stem faced Mabi and passed him a box of wooden matches. Mabi lit the hookah and drew the smoke through the water, inhaling deeply. The tobacco in the pipe bowl glowed.

"You shall attend Bumper Sullivan's funeral," al-Saffah said. "The members of Capablanca will be there. Your absence will be noticed."

"Not as much as my presence."

"Your presence will not engender suspicions."

"What's that mean? 'Engender'?"

"Make people suspicious. Make them think maybe you had something to do with Bumper Sullivan's murder."

"Why didn't you say so in the first place?" Mabi reclined on his side and let the water-cooled smoke mellow him. The smoke rose in a column, collected under the ceiling, spread throughout the room until it hung like a fog bank. He wondered what the Jews had done to al-Saffah to make him hate so much. He wanted to hear about the scar on his face, the missing fingers. He imagined stories of torture and persecution. He felt at home with this man who hated as much as he did. The smoke eddied around the room, ethereal like a spirit at a séance. "Why Allah write Jew hating in His book?"

"I do not hate. I believe. I believe in the missions written in the book and revealed to me, to us, through our actions. Hatred is irrational; but belief, true belief, is divine." Al-Saffah scraped the ashes of the burned tobacco out of the bowl and cleaned the wet nicotine from the stem with a pipe cleaner, then refilled the bowl. "I do not hate Jews. I believe in the destiny chosen for me. For us."

Mabi's soul bubbled like the water in the hookah. He never thought hating and believing could be brother and sister. To him, hating was hating and believing was for Sunday morning fools. He understood now that believing took the hate out of hating, made something positive out of something negative, something good out of something bad, something black out of something white. This was better than some book making a religion out of alibiing.

Al-Saffah rose from his cushion and led Mabi to the prayer rug. "Come. Let us pray."

-9-

Al-Saffah, Mabi now recalled, had demanded that Mabi send Badger on the mission to intercept Rabbi ben Reuben on the bridge over the Charles Street rotary. It is inscribed in the book, pre-ordained, al-Saffah had said. Despite Badger's safe return, that night Mabi suffered another sleepless night in which Jim Ed appeared in his dreams speechifying on gates of ivory and gates of horn, blocking his path through the yellow, shoving him through the white. Morning brought no relief. At the top of Silvy's shit list, now more than ever he felt the need to get Hannah to answer his questions. How? He couldn't beat the answers out of her, nor flood her with dead presidents. Too much disapproval, too much disappointment, raged within her. She signified about the Trojans like a street corner preacher engaging in the dozens, calling him down, Spider, Scorpion, and everything he done since he shitcanned his birth name. Typical was, You need to get right with the Lord. Or, Leroy he'll always have a home, but Mabi he never will. Or, If Leroy

319

be dead, maybe the devil which stole his body should be moving on. Mabi endured these outbursts because of his need to have his questions answered.

As bad as it was with Hannah, it was worse with Gideon. The last time he saw his old man was the previous January when he bought a round-trip bus ticket for New York on Gideon's Greyhound. From Boston to Providence, they made small talk like distant cousins groping for a common background, discussing the weather, the Celtics, whatever. From Providence to New London, they reminisced about his childhood, birthday parties for himself or Jim Ed, their one and only trip to Boston Garden to see the Celtics because of the way Gideon was treated at the souvenir stand. From New London to New Haven, Mabi maneuvered the conversation to Gideon's childhood, stabbing in the dark with questions about his growing up during the Depression; but Gideon responded with grunts, when he responded at all. As the bus entered New Haven, Mabi asked about grandparents, aunts, uncles, other relatives. Gideon's silence shouted louder than loud. By the time the bus arrived at the New Haven bus station, their conversation had exploded into an argument which carried to the back of the bus where a nervous passenger begged a black Marine to intercede and make peace.

"Say what," the soldier said, coming forward. "Why you two boiling over?"

"What kind of name Dillard Smitherman?" Eyeing him up and down, Mabi figured him for a chocolate chip likely to melt if the temperature warmed.

"No cause for you to be dissing me."

"No cause for you to be butting in between my old man and me."

"He your boy?" Smitherman asked Gideon.

"So he says. My real son a Marine like you. Died in the Nam. They never found his body. Buried an empty casket. Flags and shit, but no body."

"Sorry it so," Smitherman said. "Just the same, this isn't the place to be going ten. Lady in back real nervous. Afraid of a hijacking or something."

"He's the hijacker." Mabi gestured at Gideon.

After the rest stop at the terminal, Gideon refused to let Mabi re-board, so he caught the next bus back to Boston, sulking in the last row like a child told he couldn't have a piece of candy.

That April, the April of Bumper Sullivan's murder, Mabi had joined Hannah in her kitchen, ducking his head to avoid the frizzly chicken still hanging from the door jamb.

"When you be tossing this?" he asked.

"You got your superstitions. Your father has his."

He poured himself a glass of soda, then sat down opposite his mother. Hannah sipped a soft drink. She wore a cloth housecoat decorated with a faded floral design, its colors bleached out from years of washing. .

"Don't be waking your father. He's not driving today."

"When's he ever going to take a hike from driving?" Mabi had tried convincing Gideon to quit the bus company, had offered to pay the bills; but Gideon said he'd pick cotton before living off drug money. Mabi played with a tear in the oil cloth covering the table. "You should be eating off fine white cloth."

"Won't change the way the food tastes." She stared over the rim of her glass at the place where the wall met the ceiling, ignoring him the way she ignored the hex bird.

"That smelly thing not shielding you from nothing but company at supper."

"Smells sweeter than any perfume your drug money buys."

"It's time you told me what Wallaca means."

"Since when Mr. Mabi caring 'bout that?"

"Never stopped."

"Ask him." She gestured toward the bedroom where Gideon napped.

"You shamed we polluted with white blood?"

"Not a drop."

"So why the vow of silence?"

"What's all the noise out there?" Gideon stepped into the kitchen, still stuffing his shirttail into his pants. "Our name it don't mean nothing more than Smith or Jones. I could see a six-year old not understanding that, but a smart-assed gang banger like you?"

"Gideon!"

"Hush up, woman. This world it's full of demons. Nothing helps demons more than a mouth too wide open."

"Nothing traps demons more," Hannah said, "than a mind too wide shut."

"Speak on it, Momma."

"Nothing to speak on," Gideon said. The doorbell rang. "Shut yourself in the bathroom." He squinted through the peep hole and saw a whitey in a suit holding up a badge and a cop ID.

"I'm Detective George Harriman. Please open the door."

"I hear you fine enough," Gideon said.

Mabi knew Harriman from the police file the Trojans compiled–round face, balding with a fringe of rust colored hair, razor burn on his cheeks and throat, a gold crown on one of his molars, top left side.

"We needing to be knowing all this shit?" Spider once asked.

Mabi shook his head. "Fact we can get it is what counts."

For a few dollars and some occasional blow or smack, Beaujolais Wine fed Mabi inside information about the police department and acted as an intermediary between Mabi and Ugolino when money had to change hands. Someday, to keep her honest, he would have to fuck her; but, if he was lucky, she'd be killed in the line of duty and he'd be rescued.

"Ever see one of these before?" Harriman held one of Levy's skull caps in front of the peep hole. "Jews wear them to their church."

"No Jews here," Gideon said.

"You could see better if you opened the door."

"Listen. If I tell you a hen it dip snuff, you'll be finding the box 'neath its wing."

"Is Mabi here?"

"No Mabi here."

"If you see him, ask him to give me a call." Harriman stuck his card into the crack between the screen door and its frame.

"Don't be holding your breath." Gideon watched him down the stoop, across the sidewalk, and into his car.

"How come you lied?" Hannah asked. "No frizzly chicken going to shield you if the man finds out you lied."

"You messed up in that Sullivan business, boy?" Gideon said to Mabi.

"Nothing but a game of chess."

"A real shame the way he grabbed the cross," Hannah said.

Gideon said, "If the Jew gets off, they be hunting in the hood."

"No worry," Mabi said. "I'm alibied up with al-Saffah."

"When you going to outgrow that foolishness?" Hannah asked.

"At least I know the meaning of my name," Mabi said.

Gideon shoved Mabi toward the back door. "Your gang it's calling."

"Your son he's answering."

Chapter 11

Tuesday, April 21, 1981

-1-

Hannah Wallaca, Silvy Thomas, and Cealy Thomas waited in the Wallaca kitchen for Mabi to telephone from the court-house. They marked time like generations of black women before them who awaited word on the outcome of court proceedings before white judges involving their men-folk. Nothing distracted them. Not the game shows on the television flickering in the corner. Not the magazines, *Ebony* and *Jet* and *Essence*, neatly stacked in chronological order, strips of paper bookmarking Hannah's place in each. Not the heat seeping through the window screens. Not the frizzly chicken hanging in the door and swaying when the fan rotated in its direction.

"Why Lord are You taking so long?" Cealy wailed.

"Can't be rushing Him," Hannah said.

"I'm blessed you two not pacers," Silvy said, "but you better lace up your patience shoes 'cause it's only ten twenty-five and Mabi said court don't start 'til ten o'clock assuming the judge shows up on time which he usually don't. Mabi says they do arraignments first, then plea bargains, and bail hearings last. He won't be calling 'til 'round one o'clock."

"How you figure that?" Cealy asked.

"They lunch-break at one and white judges don't fancy working after lunch."

"Get respect," Hannah said.

"Only for what's deserving it," Silvy said.

Which now excluded Mabi. Silvy blamed him and only him for Badger being arrested, but in front of Cealy and Hannah she praised him to the heavens to ease their hearts and minds.

The way Badger was growing up sickened Silvy. At first, Mabi was a big brother to him; but, by letting him run with the Trojans, he was just another ass-bad influence. Coming home full of bragging about this, bragging about that, Badger was more and more like Spider who still scared her dry in the middle of her period. We should move back south, she begged her mother, but she couldn't convince Cealy who still prayed every day her man's conviction would be reversed and he'd be released. As the morning ticked on, Silvy, Cealy, and Hannah settled into silence, afraid to speak out loud because, as Cealy put it, their voices might wake the devil and turn him against Badger.

"Who's going there?" Hannah yelled from the kitchen when the doorbell rang.

"Hush up!" Cealy whispered. "Maybe they'll go 'way."

Silvy peeked. "Some Betty Crocker."

"Satan sent." Cealy clasped her hands and shook them.

The woman knocked on the screen door, which was locked against the outside world by a latch-key hanging loose in the wooden frame. "I'm Maddie Devlin." She held her Board of

Bar Overseers card up to the screen. "I'm an attorney with Suffolk County Legal Services."

Silvy gripped the edge of the inside door which had been left open to catch a breeze. "You whites slower than two mules pulling opposite ways. Badger's hearing it be this morning."

"I'm looking for Mabi," Maddie said. "Is one of you Hannah Wallaca?"

"No Mabi here," Silvy said before Hannah could speak. "Why you looking for him anyhow?"

"I'd rather not say."

"If cat ate your tongue, it sure ate mine." Silvy started to close the inside door.

"Wait." Maddie said. "I'm defending Avram Levy and I need to find Mabi."

Silvy said, "If you want Mabi so bad, go see Stilts, the daytime barkeep at Blackbird's."

Hannah slapped Silvy's hand off the doorknob. "Why you needing to see Mabi?"

"This about my baby?" Cealy swayed in small arcs. Hannah steadied her with an embrace and held her up. Silvy slammed the door, then walked Cealy back to the kitchen, sat her down in a chair, and put her feet up. Hannah gave her a glass of cold water and Silvy wiped the sweat off her forehead with a damp paper towel. Hannah looked at Silvy with mournful eyes that sagged with a lifetime of tears.

"Bumper Sullivan and Chelsea, they linked," Hannah said.

"No more than sausages after they eaten," Silvy said.

"A mother knows."

"Hush up," Silvy said. "Too many blacks been killed by suspicions. Let's save judgment 'til we get some true facts."

The phone rang and Silvy rushed into the pantry.

"What's he saying?" Cealy leaned her head in close.

Silvy turned away, holding the receiver flat against her ear, staring at the kitchen cabinet where Jim Ed had carved his initials, JEW, when he was a kid. "We had company name of Maddie Devlin," she told Mabi. "She was looking for you, but I sent her to see Stilts."

Silvy hung up the phone. "Judge recessing so it'll be a while yet."

No one spoke. No one moved. In their stillness, each prayed God would hear and respond.

An hour later Mabi phoned to say Badger was denied bail.

-2-

Professor al-Saffah welcomed each new incident of anti-Semitism as a revelation of the *jihad* inscribed in the book. Boston's African-American community ignored the implications of Bumper's Brigade, happy to watch whites beat up on each other for a change. Mabi, however, understood sooner or later the public would blame the police for not stopping the violence and the cops would scapegoat the city's street gangs, especially the black gangs, for crimes committed by the Brigade. Boston worked that way. A lynching with due process and Mayor Charlie weeping on the TV was still a lynching.

"Lay your ear on the street," he told Scorpion. "Learn who them muthas be."

Scorpion reported back there was no Bumper's Brigade. "People just cherry-picking the name. Copy-catting. You better educate Detective Harry-man the Trojans not Bumper's Brigade."

"He too dumb to be educated." Mabi preferred more direct communication. He decided to send word to Ugolino through Beaujolais Wine. She hadn't passed on any interesting police gossip lately and he was tired of paying her for nothing more than her tongue hanging out her mouth whenever she saw him.

That evening, the six o'clock news reported several new incidents, swastikas burned on lawns or painted on synagogues, cemeteries vandalized, each one as original as what came out of a Xerox machine. After dinner, Mabi night-aired it on a neighborhood stoop, holding court, the steps his throne, the street his throne room. Two pairs of eyes, Spider's on the roof above, Scorpion's across the street, stood lookout as the neighborhood paraded before him: Jerry Keller, called Jerry the Juicer because he squeezed every last penny out of people who owed him money, and Frankie Lions, nicknamed Hathaway when he started wearing a black eye patch after losing an eye when his fixings flamed up unexpectedly, arguing because each claimed the right to book policy in the E Street housing projects; Sweet Cassie, a skeezer who'd been trying to raw dog it with Mabi since he was Priam; Jesse dribbling a basketball he could slam dunk even though he was only thirteen. A ball of crumpled newspaper landed on the stoop. Mabi glanced at Scorpion who gave him the finger with his left hand, a signal the man was coming. "Yo!" Mabi announced. "High five ol' blue dick, Harry-man the Singing Detective."

"Is there someplace we can talk?" Harriman asked.

Mabi spread his arms railing to railing across the stoop.

"Ever see this before?" Harriman showed him Levy's skull cap.

"Show it 'round."

"In New Orleans," Jerry the Juicer said. "When my granddaddy died, the horn players who funeralized him wore little hats like that."

Harriman dangled the skull cap in Mabi's face. "Ever see it?"

Mabi laughed. "You ain't jive-assing me into confessing I seen what you found at the murder scene before you just showed it to me. I ain't no ship's fool."

"See anyone at Capablanca wearing one the night Bumper was murdered?"

"The Jew."

"Where'd you go after you left Capablanca?"

"Asked and answered."

"I'm asking again."

"I'm not answering again."

"Humor me."

"Say something funny."

"A ride downtown funny enough?"

"Split my ribs laughing."

"We can talk here or we can talk downtown."

"Television cop shows, that where you get your training? *Hill Street Blues*? Nah. You more the *Kojak* type. Without the lollipop. If you watched them shows you'd know you take me downtown I can false arrest your ass so bad I'll be buying head with your pension."

"How do you think this skull cap ended up in the Capablanca library?"

"It crawled in through the bathroom window."

"Levy says he's missing one like this."

"Shit, if he told you some brother snatched it off his head on the Red Line, would you fucking arrest every black who rides the T?"

"Every last fucking one," Harriman said. "What's the street say about Bumper's Brigade?"

"When Chief Stereo tells you to round up the usual suspects, we ain't them." No need funneling the word through Beaujolais Wine, Mabi thought.

"Stay visible. I may want to talk to you again."

"Us darkies melt into the night."

Jesse dribbled away from the stoop, gathering speed with each stride. The others followed, Cassie snapping her fingers, Jerry the Juicer and Hathaway still arguing.

"You and Spider go ahead," Mabi said to Scorpion. "I'll catch you up at Blackbird's."

Alone on the stoop, Mabi closed his eyes to the neighborhood parade. Grandmas, none; grandpas, none; aunts and uncles, none; cousins, none; brothers and sisters, none; parents, none. The Trojans, not enough; memories of Jim Ed, not enough; Silvy, sweet Silvy, not enough. Allah, not enough. He wished he could read Hannah's mind, wiretap her brain. Maybe she'd 'fess up to Silvy, but he couldn't go knee-walking back to Silvy for help, not while he was so deep in her shit. Thinking strung him out like he was skanked. He felt as boxed and buried as Bumper Sullivan.

Mabi took a back route through alleys and yards to the block where Gideon and Hannah lived, to their building. He pounded on their door.

"Why you raisin' the dead?" Hannah asked.

"Where's Gideon?"

"Show your father some respect."

"Who says he's my old man?"

"The devil's in you, boy," Gideon said from the living room.

Mabi barged past Hannah. "You be the one full of nothing but demons and devils. Me? My life's full of nothing but nones. Grandmas, none; grandpas, none; aunts and uncles, none; cousins, none. Brothers, none. Moms and dads, none."

"Gideon!" Hannah shouted.

"Talk's the devil's work, woman," Gideon said.

"Stop hiding behind voodoo shit," Mabi said, fronting Gideon.

"You going to blow me away if I don't talk?" Gideon shaped his fingers into the profile of a gun. "Shit, you nothing but a once upon a time comic book super hero who never had no fucking super powers."

"Gideon!"

"Boy's got a quivering hand stuck up his ass."

-3-

Later that night, Mabi dispatched Spider to Silvy. "Tell her I been jumped by six cops who pistol-whipped the life out of my ass. Tell her I beat up worse than you ever seen. Tell her I dying and crying for her like a baby for its momma."

Mabi waited. If Silvy drove, she'd be there any minute. If she ran, maybe five or six; walked, eight or ten. He glanced at his watch. Three minutes. Traffic on the street, trucks, horns, car doors slamming, brakes screeching, rubber peeling, always traffic. Four minutes. People arguing over a parking space. He wiped his forehead on his pillowcase. Five minutes. Maybe she had to dress. Maybe her old lady's siggin' about the hour. Maybe she tripped down the stairs and busted up her head. Six minutes. A cunt came on TV reviewing some fly movie. Her skin darkened. Her long blonde hair kinked up into tight black curls. Freestyling, she morphed into a horse, bust out big with Silvy's face pulling a beer wagon. If you're not fucking sadder but wiser by now, the voice-over said, this one's not for you. Six minutes, eight minutes, twelve minutes, fifteen, he lost track. The second hand moved round and round, from the one to the two to the three, now past the four and five, over the six, seven and eight, then 'cross the nine and ten, to the eleven, back to the beginning.

Cops surrounded him, hundreds, each with Silvy's face. He punched at them, right, left, right, left, until one punched back so hard his eyes popped out of his head and he fell back on the bed. All the faces vanished except one which stood over him like Achilles over Hector in the fucking comic book which once upon a time was his yesterday, today, and tomorrow.

"You ain't started dying yet." Silvy slipped her belt off her jeans and looped it around her hand. "You gonna wish you were jumped by every white-ass black-ass-hating cop in Boston."

She whipped him, grunting each time the belt cracked his head or shoulders. The leather abraded his skin, the buckle lacerated it. He covered his eyes and gritted his teeth so he wouldn't bite off his tongue. He timed the rhythm of the blows, shifting his arms to free up his hands, and waited. Finally, when Silvy's fury spoiled her aim so the belt glanced off his arm, he grabbed it and ripped it away so fast the buckle tore open the palm of her hand. She screamed and he took her wrist and pressed hard against the veins and wrapped her hand in a bandage to stop the bleeding.

"I needing your help," he said.

"Badger he rotting in jail and you asking for my help. Fuck you!"

"Don't stretch my strings. They 'bout ready to snap."

"Crackle and pop."

"I need to take Hannah somewhere and she's not likely to go without you."

"Fuck you!"

"African Meeting House. Tomorrow."

"Fuck you!"

"To learn her some history."

"If you're fixing on raping me, rape me already; but stop your jive." "I ain't no fucking rapist."

"You something worse."

"When I was a kid, I asked Gideon and Hannah what 'Wallaca' meant and they said nothing. I asked why I have no grandmas, no grandpas, no aunts, no uncles, no cousins, and Gideon gave me that goddamn comic book. I went out and made me a name and I made me a family. Then, I met al-Saffah and Allah and I made me a Father, too. But, that ain't enough. Hannah she's holding back some truth Gideon won't let her tell me. I figure if I take her where it's full of black history, I can break into her mind. She won't go if you don't and she won't talk if you not there. You owe me this much."

"I owe you nothing. You owe me Badger."

"You want to shit me out your ass, fine. Leave if you're burning to. Badger be staying where he be. Life be going on."

"That the price for you helping Badger?"

"Cheap enough."

"What guarantee I got?"

Mabi opened the drawer in the night table beside the bed. "Take my nine." He tapped his chest over his heart with his fist, then the side of his temple with his fingertips. "Guarantee enough for you?"

The muscles in Silvy's face relaxed. The glare in her eyes softened. She took a deep breath, a cleansing breath, and exhaled slowly, silently, a gentle breeze compared to the previous storms. She reached out and turned Mabi's head toward her so she could look him directly in the eye. "Learning this secret, it make you Leroy again?"

Mabi put his arms around her and they swayed gently. He loved her and couldn't stomach her acting so Miss Ann. If he could make her understand, maybe he could melt her down a little. He felt like one of the children in her Sunday school class needing comfort after being scared awake from a nap

by dreaming the devil. Feeling her against him, listening to
her breathing, smelling her sweat, that's all he needed, that's
all he wanted. Later, she could decide if her life lay with his.
If it didn't, he'd rewrite that fucking book 'til it said what he
wanted.

Chapter 12

Wednesday, April 22, 1981

-1-

Wednesday morning, the seventh or seventeenth or seventieth day of the heat wave, Boston had lost count, Silvy phoned Hannah and suggested she join her and Mabi walking the Black Heritage Trail.

"In this weather," Hannah said. "Don't see the point."

"History's the point."

"Not my history."

"All black history's your history," Silvy said.

"All black skin's not the same shade," Hannah said before she relented.

Later that morning, Mabi, Hannah, and Silvy, climbed the north slope of Nigger Hill, so named by proper nineteenth-century Bostonians because it was Boston's first black ghetto. By 1981, the National Park Service had whited out the epithet of Nigger Hill from the history of African-Americans in Boston by referring to Beacon Hill in its pamphlet on the Black Heritage Trail. The pamphlet sanitized Boston's black history in other ways. It did not inform tourists that a nineteenth century missionary society dismissed Nigger Hill as a "horrid sink of pollution," for example, or that an eminent Harvard historian writing in the middle of the twentieth century characterized its black population as not being "of high order". As a result, the few tourists who wandered the Black Heritage Trail were as ignorant of Beacon Hill's past as Mabi, Silvy, and Hannah.

With its narrow streets, narrower even than the narrow streets of the south slope, with its four- and five-story walk-ups crowded together like slum tenements, with its base bordering on the miasma of Cambridge Street rather than the sylvan elegance of Beacon Street, Boston Common, and the Public Garden, Nigger Hill was clearly the less desirable side of Beacon Hill. Yet, because it was walking distance to the new office towers being erected in Mayor Charlie's Boston, the elites, predominately white, now lusted after homes abandoned decades earlier by Boston's blacks when they moved to Roxbury.

If tourists who wandered the Black Heritage Trail in 1981 paid attention to what they saw, they would notice that the buildings on the north side of Pinckney Street, the street dividing the north slope from the south, stretched in an unbroken barrier from West Cedar Street near the base of Beacon Hill on the west to Joy Street on the east with one cross street, Anderson Street, to provide north/south passage for the nineteenth-century blacks who walked over the crown of the hill to work as servants or hired hands, cleaning houses and stables, cooking and serving meals, for the rich whites living on the sunny south slope.

If those tourists read the plaques installed here and there on exterior walls, they would learn that Massachusetts was the only state that recorded no slaves in the Federal Census of 1790; that as Boston's black population grew after the War of Independence and the War of 1812, it moved into the area of seventeen oddly shaped West End blocks bounded by Pinckney, Charles, Cambridge, and Joy Streets; that in this enclave, the barber, John J. Smith, gained fame as an abolitionist and the shopkeeper, Lewis Hayden, stored gunpowder in his cellar to blow up his house rather than return the fugitive slaves he sheltered to their southern owners, as required by the Fugitive Slave Act of 1850. They would learn as well that Boston's first school desegregation suit occurred in 1850 when Sarah Roberts, age five, was denied admission to five schools convenient to her home on Nigger Hill because in nineteenth-century Boston blacks, if they went to school at all, went to all black schools, an arrangement blessed by Chief Justice Lemuel Shaw of the Massachusetts Supreme Judicial Court in his 1850 opinion upholding the segregation of Boston's public schools.

As the nineteenth-century advanced toward the Civil War, Boston's growing population of "colored persons, the descendants of Africans," as Chief Justice Shaw labeled Boston's black population in his 1850 opinion, continued to concentrate on Nigger Hill, caring for each other and sheltering southern blacks who survived the trip north on the underground railroad. Tourists who were both students of history and well attuned to present-day Boston would appreciate that the more Boston changed, the more it stayed the same.

The emotional and geographic heart of Nigger Hill was the snub nosed alley known as Smith Court, the location of the African Meeting House, journey's end for Mabi, Silvy, and Hannah in 1981 as it had been for thousands of Boston's blacks in the nineteenth century. Number 3, a double house built of wood, which survived every Beacon Hill fire since 1799.

Number 5 where the deacon of the African Meeting House lived on the second floor with his nine children so he could rent out the first floor. Number 7A, a double house built in the backyard of Number 7 in 1799 and connected to Smith Court by Holmes Alley, one of many pedestrian alleys connecting the backyards of south slope homes to streets on the north slope. Number 10, built as rental income property in 1853 by a black chimney sweep. Number 8, the African Meeting House, dedicated on December 6, 1806, as the home of the First African Baptist Church, the Abolition Church. From an engraved wall plaque, Silvy read aloud the story of Cato Gardner and the building of that church.

"What's abolition?" Hannah asked in a frail voice.

"How can you live here and not know abolition?" Silvy asked.

Hannah threw the Black Heritage Trail Guide to the pavement. "This place used to be a Jew prayer house. I got no interest."

Mabi knocked on the door.

"No interest," Hannah repeated.

Slowly, it opened. Its hinges, rusty with neglect, creaked and groaned. "We're closed." Virgil's ancient voice was barely audible above the rasp of the hinges.

"We came to see the African Meeting House," Silvy said.

"It's not fit for visiting."

"We came special," Silvy said. "Just a fast look-see."

Virgil eyed them with suspicion. "What for?"

Silvy whispered something in his ear.

"Be quick. I'm working Capablanca tonight."

Mabi helped Hannah into the foyer. Age and decay surrounded them. The paint on the window frames, yellowed by time, had the dried, cracked appearance of stream beds in

THE FIRE THIS TIME

a drought, their many layers of thickness still puffy with the humidity of past rainy seasons, the puffiness made soft to the eye, hard to the touch, by the desiccation of time. As they climbed the staircase to the meeting room on the second floor, vibrations dislodged paint chips from the railing and motes of paint rained down. Water stains discolored the ceiling and walls of the stairwell and the central meeting room, which was filled with pews. A balcony of pews encircled it on three sides. A raised platform jutted out of the back wall. In an arch recessed into that back wall two lions on their hind legs faced each other, each holding a tablet with two columns of strange letters carved into them. A lectern, its wood cracked open wide enough to insert a coin, graced the front edge of the platform.

"Them lions look fierce enough to eat them tablets," Mabi said.

"The lions of Judah," Hannah said. "Been a lifetime since I seen them." She sat in the front pew, struggling to hold herself erect. "They holding the tablets of the Lord and opening their mouths to proclaim His word." She moved her lips, silently mouth-reading the words on the tablets. She had a distant look in her eyes as if she were seeing beyond the walls of the African Meeting House. Mabi had seen that look before when Hannah prayed for Jim Ed's return, when she lit memorial candles to Jim Ed's memory on the anniversary of the telegram, when she made her annual pilgrimage to tend an empty grave.

"Heat after you?" Silvy put her purse in the corner of the pew. "Lie down. Use this for a pillow."

"No need for lying down."

A small cloud crossed the sun. The room darkened. The shadow paused on Hannah's face. Her eyes regained their focus. Their distant look dissolved as if the shadow had unlocked something deep within her and brought it to the surface. The cloud moved on, dragging its shadow with it. Hannah's eyes glowed with a light that was not there before. She gripped Mabi's arm.

"I was born in Africa like that Cato Gardner," Hannah said. "Gideon and I we born in a small village in Ethiopia name of Wallaca. When we came into this country, the immigration couldn't speak our names so they wrote down Wallaca instead."

Mabi bit his tongue. He was skeptical like the Leroy Wallaca of his dream when the leprechaun on the Bill Russell poster tacked to the ceiling of the bedroom he shared with his brother, Jim Ed, came to life and whispered in his ear that he was descended from a thousand generations of leprechauns. He wanted to believe, but belief required letting go and he wasn't ready.

"What's Ethiopia like?" Silvy asked.

"Mud huts with thatched roofs shaped like upside down ice cream cones. No windows. One low door. Called *tekels*. My folks next to Gideon's."

"How'd you come into this country?" Silvy asked.

"Italian soldiers they occupied our village and stole all the food so everyone was starving and the children were dying and they brang in priests from Rome telling us we should all pray Jesus and those who did ate and the rest of us hungered."

All those childhood dinner hours when Hannah forced him and Jim Ed to finish their suppers so they could belong to the clean plate club crystallized in Mabi's mind. Not wasting food was one of Hannah's religions. He understood, now, why Gideon and Hannah gave each other food on their birthdays, their anniversary, other special occasions.

"How'd you escape?" Silvy asked.

"My poppa, Gideon's poppa, they good at working metal so they earned money making things for the soldiers. They saved up for the bribes and when they had enough they sent us into this country. Nineteen hundred and thirty-eight. I was twelve and Gideon fifteen."

A door slammed in the balcony. "I'm fixing to leave," Virgil called down. "You done poking 'round?"

"Go up with him," Mabi said to Silvy. "Distract him into storytelling 'bout this place." He took Silvy's place on the pew. "What about the rest of the family?"

"War came and the mail stopped. After the war our letters were never replied."

From the balcony, Silvy's sing-song voice asked questions about the history of the African Meeting House, oohing and aahing when Virgil told her about the black barber, John J. Smith, the abolitionist, the black storekeeper, Lewis Hayden, and his gunpowder.

Hannah paused. Her eyes flitted back and forth from Mabi's face to the lions of Judah, to the ceiling, to other places. It was as if she were confronting things that frightened her and she was looking for a way to escape. She closed her eyes, then slowly opened them. Calm now, her eyes anchored on Mabi's face, Mabi's eyes.

"Gideon and me we belong to a tribe called Falashas. That's a word meaning stranger or people who got no land. We lived in Ethiopia long before people been writing history books." Her eyes held steady, never wavering from Mabi's. "Once there were millions of us, but now hardly none. We be persecuted by preachers taking texts teaching everyone to hate us because some say Falasha blacksmiths made the nails for the Cross and Falasha carpenters hewed the wood and made the Cross itself. All lies, but Christian folk taught lies be the gospel truth."

Jesus Christ Superstar, Mabi thought. "Where them Falashas from?"

"My great-grandpapa he told stories about how we descended from Abraham."

Hannah recited Falasha history like Silvy telling Bible stories to her Sunday school class, beginning with the reign of Moses and continuing through the marriage of Solomon and Sheba, the conquests of Yehudit, the slow decline over the last thousand years, the virtual extinction of the entire tribe in the last decade.

Mabi wondered if this was the same Abraham as al-Saffah's. "You tell Jim Ed any of this shit?" She sobbed quietly and shook her head. "Why not?"

"Same reason we never told no one." Hannah paused and Mabi sensed she was gathering her strength, or her courage. "There's a lot of Falasha kings name of Gideon," she continued, "and he thinks he be descended. He's fearing someone come from there to kill us if the Emperor know we here."

"You say I'm descended from kings?"

"In name if not in blood."

Mabi sensed Hannah's relief at finally telling him the secret of his heritage. Now, he believed because he needed to believe. He believed because he needed a past, a real past that went further back in time than the Trojans, a past which came out of real history, a history of people who once lived, not some comic book history of make-believe. He believed because he believed it had been pre-ordained by being written in Allah's book that Hannah would make these revelations to him in this place on this day at this time. He believed because it made sense out of all the arguments he had overheard between Gideon and Hannah, because it explained the frizzly chicken and Gideon's obsession with hexes and being hexed, and, most of all, why there was only one Wallaca in the Boston telephone book, why he had no grandparents, aunts or uncles, cousins.

For all these reasons, he believed and because Hannah was his momma and his momma wouldn't tell him things if they weren't God's holy truth.

"Someday real soon," Mabi said, "you and me we have a talk long and hard 'bout this Falasha tribe so's I feel connected. When me and Silvy have a son, I want him to be a Wallaca and be told the story of Ethiopia as soon as he old enough to understand." The words slipped out of his mouth as if Silvy had decided to come back to his bed.

Hannah unzipped her purse. "I don't want no gang-leading grandson so don't be naming no son of yours Wallaca unless you be calling yourself Wallaca, and don't be calling yourself Wallaca as long as you're leading that gang. Between this gang business and this Allah business and this grandson business you night riding me to the grave."

She unzipped an inner compartment and withdrew an envelope cat-faced with wrinkles. "This came a few days after Jim Ed's funeral."

Mabi withdrew a letter from the envelope. The writing scrawled across the pages, rising as it went from left to right.

Dear Wallacas:

I just back from the bush and if I don't make sense it's because I'm still too buzzed by what I seen which is why I's writing you to explain how your son be dead.

My name Roadkill, not my Christian name but my bush name. We all have new names here in the bush. It's like our real selfs somewhere in the real world doing real world things while our other selfs in the bush fighting the NVA. If our other selfs be killed, maybe our real selfs still be alive in the real world. If this sounds insane, things be so insane here the only way to stay sane is to be insane youself. Jim Ed said that's a Catch 22. His bush name Shanghai because of the way he ended up in this man's Marines.

Shanghai he was one righteous splib. Not many like him at the snuff level. Most of us snuffs, chuck and splib alike, too dumb or poor to evade Uncle Sam. That made Shanghai different, his going to college and all.

Corporal Dickhead being a chuck from 'Bama didn't like me and Shanghai because we city splibs. And we's black. We called him Corporal Dickhead because that's where his brains be sitting. A real gunjy, the corporal. A lifer, too. Nothing worse for us snuffs, splib or chuck, than being lorded over by a gunjy lifer looking to make sergeant.

No need to tell you who Corporal Dickhead picked first to walk point or man the Loco Pocos outside the perimeter. Splibs like me and Shanghai and the other brothers. High body count for Loco Pocos being we out there with nothing but a radio and our ears listening for the gooks. That's not how Shanghai got killed. Would have been his good luck if it were.

We's in the jungle. Lot of jungle. Real tropical. And the bamboo, thicker than . . . well, I won't say because it ain't decent talk for decent folk like you. Cheddar's in the forward Loco Poco. Cheddar from Wisconsin and a big Packer fan. Not a bad guy for a chuck. Got along with us splibs which is why

Corporal Dickhead assigned him point and forward listening post duty.

Very dark night. Most nights dark because the jungle blocks out the sky 'cept when firefights or mortars or tracers firework things up. Me and Shanghai resting in our holes, too tired to build hooches when we hear screams so God awful we could barely recognize Cheddar's voice. Come daylight, Corporal Dickhead sends Shanghai out to investigate. Shanghai comes back with a lower leg, boot still on the foot, flesh all torn up like it was eaten. A tiger, Corporal Dickhead says. Who knew there was tigers here in the bush.

Dickhead and Shanghai get into a big argument about going out to find the rest of Cheddar because Marines never never never leave their dead behind. Dickhead tells Shanghai if he wants to red dog it he can take volunteers, but not so many to deplete the squad. I volunteer and some other splibs, but none of the chucks because Cheddar nothing but a Mr. Shine to them.

We hacking our way through the jungle with our K-bars finding pieces of Cheddar here and there, collecting them when Shanghai suddenly motions us down. Up ahead be this tiger munching on Cheddar the way you and me munch on ribs at the Q.

Shanghai disperses us so we surround the tiger. Whichever way it runs, it be shot. Shanghai wormed his way forward looking so hard at the tiger he didn't see the trip wire. The landmine so close it shredded Shanghai. A few of us inside its range was also wounded.

Before we can retrieve Shanghai we hear tubing and the mortars come raining down bull's eye on our position. They could have been 60 mike mikes, maybe 120's, none of us experienced enough to tell the difference. We dee-deed it. God must've been awake because we all made it out. Except for Shanghai. Night came before we could go back. Damn if we didn't hear that tiger all night long. Might have been two of them. Next morning, not a trace of Shanghai. Not even a scrap of uniform. And Cheddar, none of him neither.

That's why you buried an empty coffin.

Semper Fi,
Roadkill

Mabi folded the letter as neat as he could and gave it back to Hannah, who returned it to the inner compartment of her purse. He didn't know what to say, didn't know what to think. It didn't seem real, Jim Ed eaten by a tiger. Maybe the letter was a fake, a forgery conjured up by the Marines to hide the truth. Maybe this Corporal Dickhead fragged Jim Ed. Mabi wished he had real names, names he could hunt down, names he could talk to.

Hannah touched a tissue to the corners of her eyes.

Another door opened, then closed. "I'm locking up now," Virgil said.

"Take Hannah home," Mabi said to Silvy. "I got some heavy thinking to do."

As Silvy led Hannah out of the sanctuary of the African Meeting House down the front staircase through the decaying foyer on to Smith Court and into the heated heart of Nigger Hill, a sour feeling spread through Mabi's body. Hannah was Leroy's mother, he said to himself, not Mabi's. Who be at fault he was Mabi? Not Jim Ed who did his damnedest to steer him away from the gangs. Not Hannah or Gideon because he would've become Priam, then Mabi, whether he knew what Wallaca meant or not. Al-Saffah. Who else but al-Saffah. He wished he was Leroy again when the holiest book he read was a comic book.

-2-

Later that afternoon, Mabi telephoned Silvy every five minutes, but no one answered and the ringing haunted him as if each ring set free evil spirits to prey upon his soul. He wished he had a frizzly chicken hanging over the phone. On the twentieth try, Cealy answered. After wailing about Badger, she said, "She's daycaring. At the church. Hiding behind kids and crayons."

The door to the daycare center was locked and no one answered the bell so Mabi jimmied it open and let himself in. The center was empty. Toys and games and craft materials sat neatly on the shelves. Midget chairs were tucked under low tables like children put to bed for the night. Mabi slouched on a chair so low to the floor his knees bumped up against his chin. He opened the alphabet blocks and piled them on top of each other, a tower of letters. The letters became word fragments; the word fragments, phrases; the phrases, sentences. No paragraphs. No pages. If the blocks hid a message, he could not read it. He telephoned al-Saffah.

"I'm quitting." He pressed the phone against his chin and spoke quickly.

"My son, my son." Al-Saffah spoke slowly with a lowered voice.

"Don't son me none."

"Your work is not done."

"Find someone else to make your *jihad*."

"You were chosen because of the way your brother was stolen from you."

"Stop gaming me."

"Does the name Mary Ann Devlin mean anything to you?"

"The Jew's lawyer."

"She was the law student working for Claudius J. Antenor who railroaded your brother into the Marines. She was the instrument of his death. You were not chosen blindly. *Jihad* is the gift to you to avenge your brother."

Thoughts of *jihad* piled up inside Mabi's head, then tumbled down like the alphabet blocks at his feet. The thoughts made no more sense than the jumble of letters.

"What you doing here?" Silvy sounded like she came home and found a process server in her living room. "Kids coming back from their field trip and I need you to be leaving." She herded the blocks together with her feet.

Mabi rushed his words before his courage to say them disappeared. "I need you. I love you. I want you to have my baby."

Silvy faced a block with the letter X toward him. "I see Badger growing up without a father and I don't want that for my children. I see my momma growing old without a husband and I don't want that for me. You great for summer days, but no good for winter nights."

"Money's no worry."

"You as dumb as a piece of charcoal is black. If you seriously talking marriage, I'm willing to become Mrs. Leroy Wallaca, not Mrs. Mabi or Mrs. Priam. I want my husband working an honest job with us living off honest pay even if it means we buying our furniture at the Goodwill and our ride be a Chevy shitbox. When you fit that description, phone me up. If I ain't Mrs. Somebody Else, we can talk."

The outside door opened and the hallway filled with children, shouting, singing, laughing.

"You better move on. People see you here I may lose this job."

"Silvy . . ."

"Go! Now!"

At home, the unseasonable heat wearied Mabi; his fatigue made him light-headed. He was angry with himself the same way he was with Hannah when she wouldn't let him take down the frizzly chicken poisoning her kitchen. Shit. Silvy wanted downtown cooking from an uptown menu. He was Mabi. It took him how many years to become Mabi. He couldn't fall asleep and wake up Leroy. Be easier for the sun to rise at night and Jim Ed to return from the dead. The phone rang and when Mabi answered it he heard Gideon's voice competing with a PA system announcing a bus leaving for Philadelphia with stops in Newark, Trenton, and Atlantic City.

"Don't put too much meaning into that Falasha shit your momma shined you with. Sometimes she talks delirious, the heat and all."

Mabi slammed down the phone. Hannah, Silvy, Gideon, all wanting Leroy, none willing to break a sweat to get him, no one finger lifting for him but al-Saffah. Fuck! Shit! I be Mabi, he thought, as long as I be in god damn book and I be in that book as long as I be Mabi. The book filled his mind. He wanted to turn its pages, see how the story ended; but the pages were too heavy and he didn't have the strength. Give me the rainbow sign, he prayed. No more water, the fire this time.

PART III

THE FIRE THIS TIME

Chapter 13

Thursday, April 23, 1981

-1-

Out of deference to Jacob Moskovitzky's age, Maddie Devlin visited him at his home to show him the blood grouping test results and to explain her strategy for using them in court. Stalled in traffic on Storrow Drive, she worked through her presentation in her mind, trying to decide what to tell Moskovitzky, what to leave out. She knew Duncan Siward would be cross-examined. Relentlessly. Absent a prosecutorial misstep, what she didn't want disclosed would come out, namely how the stencil came into Siward's possession. She could not base her strategy on the chance Bonturo would make a mistake. She needed Moskovitzky's opinion. She had to tell him everything.

She had gone to Duncan Siward's lab the previous Monday, the 20th, and had not been welcomed.

"Dr. Siward's in his lab and he's not to be disturbed under any circumstances," his technician, a post-doc who felt more at home in the lab than in an office treating patients, had said. Her voice had been as sour as her lab greens.

"Disturb him. It's an emergency."

"What business could Dr. Siward possibly have with you?"

Maddie had smiled. She was beginning to take perverse pleasure in the way people treated her. Being a pariah had its advantages. It liberated her from the constraints of socially acceptable behavior and freed her to be more aggressive, less ladylike, in pursuit of her goals. She had pushed through the swinging doors behind the desk where the technician wrote up her lab results, ignoring the 'Staff Only' sign, and forced her way into the hematology lab, evading the technician's grasp.

"What . . . Maddie!"

"I'll call security," the technician said.

"No," Duncan said. "It's all right."

"I tried to stop her."

"Not to worry. I was about to break for coffee."

Maddie waited for the technician to leave, then placed the stencil and slide on the lab bench with the care of a paleontologist handling an unclassified fossil. "I need a blood grouping."

He picked up the stencil by its edges. "Chelsea?"

"The slide is from Bumper Sullivan's autopsy."

"How . . . "

"Privileged information." What he didn't know wouldn't come back to bite her.

He held the slide up to the light. "I've never done a blood grouping without live blood. I don't even know if it's possible. There's more involved than blood typing. Categories you've never heard. Gm factors, five altogether, and two Kp factors. Thirty-nine factors in a complete test."

"I want all thirty-nine. How long?"

"No idea."

"Tomorrow. I'll bring lunch."

"I'd prefer you call."

"See you then."

"The director may not approve," Duncan said. "I'll come to you."

She missed the teenager who made out with her on her back porch. She felt a twinge of the happiness she once knew, the happiness of a high school girl who thought life was an endless summer; but, only the heat had come true. Except for Michelle Furey who had melted like a candle in a conflagration.

Now, Maddie sounded her horn at the car in front of her which had stopped, afraid to merge into traffic. One opening passed; then a second, a third. Maddie sighed. Siward's visit to her office with the test results had also been problematic.

She had cleared a seat for him in her cubicle at the offices of Suffolk County Legal Services by taking a mountain of files from her extra chair and stacking them on the floor: Sanchez for breaking and entering, Figone for assault and battery on a police officer, O'Leary for possession of a controlled substance, Goralla for larceny over, Lombard for driving to endanger, and Ferraro for being a common nightwalker. People whose lives intersected hers–some once, others many times–so briefly she couldn't associate their names with their faces and, without first names, she did not remember which were men, which were women. She made space on her desk for the lunch Duncan had picked up at the Bread Loaf Deli. He placed the napkins and plastic forks on a copy of Warren Bixler's treatise *Defending the Juvenile*.

Maddie had reached for her purse.

"My treat," he had said.

"I insist." She had stuffed a ten dollar bill in his shirt pocket.

A calendar featuring an advertisement for an insurance agency hung on the partition behind her desk, its blocks black with tiny printing. The third week of June with a single entry, "Levy trial, Suffolk Sup.", stood out like empty squares in a nearly completed crossword puzzle.

"Quiche isn't good for you," Siward said, "cholesterol and all."

"Better than a hot pastrami sandwich."

"Both samples may come from the same person."

"May? Is that the best you can do?"

"I don't have live blood."

"Can you testify in court?"

"Would I survive cross-examination?"

"Are the results more probable than not?"

"Don't know. I've never seen it referenced in the literature."

"It'll be a first. Write it up."

"If this were peer reviewed, it would probably be rejected."

"You doctors are all alike. You'll say anything to avoid going to court."

"I'm being honest with you, Maddie. I'm sorry if it doesn't fit your agenda. Both samples may come from the same person. Or may not. If I had live blood, I could give you a more definitive answer."

"Guilt and innocence may turn on this."

"It's the best I can do."

She gave him another dollar. "Now that you've been paid by the defense, it's privileged as attorney work product and you have to keep it confidential."

Because of the way Ugolino had curtailed the police investigation, Maddie knew what would happen if word leaked out. The police pathologist would discover a labeling mistake on the slide. The stencil would now match a bag lady found dead in an abandoned subway station. What Rabbi ben Reuben had said after finding the defaced *Torah* unrolled on the floor of the sanctuary on the night of the *seder* now roiled her mind: "When I was done, I thought I had cut myself."

Now, after several additional openings in the traffic, the car in front of her still hesitated. Maddie leaned on her horn. She was tempted to inch forward and kiss bumpers, anything to get that car to move. An oncoming driver, so unlike the typical Boston driver, slowed and waved for the car to merge ahead of him. About fucking time, Maddie thought. About fucking time.

Jacob Moskovitzky's home health aide showed her to a room on whose walls hung dozens of photographs, old, soft focus, many sepia-toned from the era of big boxy cameras, hoods that draped the photographer, additional light not always synchronized with the opening and closing of the shutter. The photographs were of people, not places, all posed against a plain backdrop in a studio where conditions could be controlled. Photographs of men and women alone, men and women in couples, couples surrounded by a horde of children, multi-generational groupings, Moskovitzky's family tree, Maddie assumed. She studied each photograph with children, searching for the one small child who had aged into the attorney who now told her that in his opinion Duncan Siward's blood grouping test results were inadmissible into evidence at trial.

"I think I can coax Dr. Siward into testifying more probable than not."

"If the judge did admit it, in this climate no juror would believe it." Moskovitzky had said the same thing when Maddie told him Levy denied he had made the notations of the chess game in Bumper Sullivan's spiral notebook.

"You only need one for a mistrial," Maddie reminded him.

"The Messiah will return before someone open-minded enough to consider Avram innocent is seated on that jury."

"Which is why I say a plea bargain . . . "

"Avram will not plead guilty to a crime he did not commit."

Maddie detected a hitch in his voice. Chelsea had not persuaded him of Levy's innocence as it had her. She decided to let it pass. Every difficult case needed to be leavened by the yeast of skepticism.

Moskovitzky struggled to lift himself out of his chair, refusing Maddie's offer of help. Supporting himself with his cane, he walked over to a photograph of a man and woman and young child, a boy, wearing a dress as young boys often did in that era. A tear drained from his eye. In that tear, Maddie suddenly understood the symmetry between Levy and her grand da Michael, both victims of someone who bore false witness for profit. She wondered what her grand da would have done if the IRB had offered exile and banishment rather than death on the condition he admit being an informer, a traitor. Would he have confessed guilt to a crime he did not commit to save his life? Logic said he should, the same logic she had urged upon Moskovitzky moments ago, the same logic she had urged on the rabbi, the same logic both had rejected and rejected again, the same logic Levy had also rejected.

She had spent her career defending people for whom lying was as ordinary as jaywalking or running a stop sign, people for whom the truth was as disposable as a used condom or a wad of chewed gum. She wanted to believe her grand da was not one of those people. Levy's courage, made it possible for her to do so. That was Levy's gift to her. And what was her gift to him? A plea bargain born of cowardice, rationalized by cowardice. No, her gift to him would be to transform what she knew to be true into admissible evidence so strong, so persuasive, that beyond a reasonable doubt it would convince the most Jew-hating juror, the most ardent member of Bumper's Brigade, that Levy did not murder Bumper Sullivan.

Or to die trying.

-2-

Maddie Devlin drove around Roxbury, unable to locate the streets on her map because the street signs had been stolen from most of the intersections. When she asked for directions, people delighted in misleading her, if they responded at all. After an hour, she found Livermore Place and parked across from Blackbird's. All neighborhoods had local bars, she thought, recalling how her da had frequented O'Driscoll's several nights a week, always after dinner because her da insisted the family gather around the table at least once a day to share a meal. Small talk grew into large talk as conversation about what had happened in school or at work expanded into discussions of the difficulties of the Irish assimilating in nineteenth century Boston, the current troubles in Northern Ireland, and politics, always politics, Boston's favorite blood sport.

Named for a poem by Yeats, O'Driscoll's was her da's local bar. Trish's side of the family went to Mangan's, opposite side of the street one block down. Although her da threw second darts for O'Driscoll's, the team captain substituted for him when they threw at Mangan's. Charlie, before he was mayor and still had time, never threw at O'Driscoll's. Neither team agreed to throw against the other at a neutral site unless those substitutions were made. When Maddie came of age, she occasionally accompanied her da on Thursdays when O'Driscoll's welcomed women. She drank her first Guinness there and remembered how everyone laughed when she spit up her first mouthful. She knew she would not be welcome now.

But, O'Driscoll's wasn't surrounded by vacant lots over-flowing with bricks and cinder blocks, sheet rock and lumber, shingles and tar paper, the skeletons of so many buildings. And trash. Garbage. The decomposing bodies of dead household pets. The rats those decomposing bodies attracted. It reminded her of the South Bronx which as a child she had gawked at through the windows of the elevated subway on the way to the Bronx Zoo during the family's one and only visit to New York. "America's Dresden," her da had said. She didn't know what he meant then; she did now.

Like O'Driscoll's, Blackbird's had booths along the walls and tables in the center. A tall black man behind the bar polished glasses. Two customers, sat in a corner booth in the back, one in his late teens, the other in his early or middle twenties. Maddie doubted the alcohol police ran sting operations for underage drinkers in a bar like Blackbird's. Nor did they have the balls to barge in and demand a bribe. She walked the length of the bar to where the bartender stood. "You Stilts? I'm looking for Mabi." She handed him her business card which he discarded without a glance.

She placed a ten-dollar bill on the bar. Toying with her, the bartender poached a beer glass from a sink of soapy water, rinsed it, and wiped its inside with the ten spot, then tossed the soggy wad of green back at her. "Ask them boots in the corner."

Maddie's heartbeats played tag with each other as she walked over to the booth. Her heart had not fibrillated like this since the one and only time she had appeared before the United States Supreme Court to argue a search and seizure case. The Justices had done nothing to put her at ease, flame-throwing questions at her before she had finished introducing herself, silencing her in mid-sentence when her allotted time was up. She had maintained her composure then, she would maintain it now. "I'm looking for Mabi. I'm with Suffolk County Legal Services, the public defender."

"He don't need no defendin'," one said. His voice crackled like the radio during a summer thunderstorm.

The other sipped coffee, holding the mug with both hands. "Stilts don't brew it as good as my momma. Her coffee grinder broke down yesterday, but I was able to get it grinding again this morning."

"I starvin' for some sweet jelly roll," the first one said. "I been living on stale dry cornbread all week."

"Like sucking cardboard," the other said. He turned to Maddie. "If you looking for Mabi, this the place. He holds calling hours downstairs."

"I'll wait here," Maddie said.

"He don't take meetings in public."

"I's Scorpion," the first one rasped. "He's Spider. You Devlin? The Jew's attorney? I seen you on the tube. You real fly in the flesh." Maddie intuited the unspoken "for a white cunt."

Spider unlocked a door along the back wall. Scorpion grabbed her wrist, dragging her through it before she had a chance to resist. The lock clicked. They descended, one behind her, one in front. The stairwell was warm, like a furnace room, and narrow, built at a time when people were shorter and thinner. Her right arm brushed one wall, her left shoulder the other. Their footsteps echoed, the three of them sounding like six.

In her mind, Maddie ran through the various judo techniques she had learned in the women's self-defense class her da had insisted she take. They were always taught and practiced on flat surfaces, floors with mats. Never on stairs. *Nagi-Wazi* or throwing techniques, *Te-Waza* or hand techniques, *Ashi-Waza* or foot techniques, with any of these the three of them were likely to tumble into a pile-up at the bottom of the stairs. If there were *Tachi-Waza* or standing techniques that could be used on stairs, she had not learned them. Her da was right when he scolded her for not enrolling in the advanced class.

A landing at the bottom of the stairs, too small, too cramped, to extend her arms or legs. It would be like trying judo moves in an over-crowded elevator. Another door opened with the squeal of metal rubbing against metal. Behind her, a door closed with the slam of wood against wood. Again, metal screeched on metal and a light revealed a small room, sparsely furnished, but crowded by a double bed against the wall opposite the door covered with a ratty olive-green blanket, a chest of drawers, and a rocking chair. Scuff marks wore a path in the linoleum from the door to the bed.

"This the place where Stilts blows the blues when his old lady's locked him out," Spider said.

Before she could attack, Spider kicked her legs out from under her and slammed her on to the bed. His knee nose-dived to her chest between her breasts, pinning her to the mattress. Panting, she struggled to suck air into her lungs. When her breathing returned to normal, she scissor-kicked, then swung her legs, first to the right, then to the left, but lacked the leverage needed to free herself. She went limp to give herself time to regain her strength and think through the situation. Let them think they've won was one of the lessons she learned in her self-defense class. They'll relax, get careless, give you an opening. Unlike judo moves, this strategy could not be practiced in the gym.

"Sing the lady some verses," Scorpion said. A lifetime of cigarettes had turned Scorpion's larynx into a chip of hickory charcoal. He ran a few scales up and down a harmonica, then blew the plaintive wail familiar to whites who went to college

when Maddie did and prided themselves on being able to identify the bluesmen who influenced the Rolling Stones.

Spider started singing:

> I got a sweet woman;
> She lives right back the jail.
> She's got a sign on her window,
> Good cabbage for sale.

"That the 'Low Down Blues'," Scorpion said. "Jelly Roll
Morton. Bessie Smith she's my favorite."

Again, Spider sang:

> He boiled my first cabbage,
> And he made it awful hot.
> When he put in the bacon
> It overflowed the pot.

"'Empty Bed Blues,'" Spider said, "but we got no call singing
them now."

The heating pipes lining the ceiling clanged. The air,
heated and dried by those pipes, smelled musty from the evaporated sweat of a multitude of people baked into the mattress,
the blanket, the chair's upholstery.

Moving like a flash of summer lightening, Spider wadded
his handkerchief into a ball and stuffed it in Maddie's mouth,
gagging her with a piece of rope before she could spit it out.
She tried to counter with an *obi tori gaeshi* or belt grab reversal,
but her fingers slipped before she could close them around his
belt. She reached out to attempt a *kata guruma* or shoulder

wheel, but he twisted her arm and pinned her in a full-nelson before she could complete the move.

Spider whistled while Scorpion stripped her blouse off. As he fumbled with the hook of her bra, his long fingernails scratched the small of her back. With his belt, he bound her wrists behind her. Maddie had studied *Ma-Sutemi-Waza* or back sacrifice techniques and *Yoko-Sutemi-Waza* or side sacrifice techniques in her self-defense class, but none with her hands bound behind her at the wrists. Still pinned to the mattress, she lacked the leverage to use her legs for *Kansetsu-Waza* or joint locking techniques.

Judo had never failed Maddie. Never. Not even the time she was attacked by the brothers and cousin of a prostitute sentenced to hard time for murdering her john. Her best efforts could not negate the DNA evidence found on the prostitute and the victim. They weren't seeking revenge, these men, because they loved and cared for their sister and cousin; but, rather, because they had lost their meal ticket. Years later, whether released after serving her sentence or due to the leniency of the parole board, she'd be so old, so haggard, she wouldn't turn enough tricks to pay for a light snack for one of them, much less three. Judo had not failed her then even though she was out-numbered three-to-one.

She searched her catalog of *wazas*, desperate to find one that might work, but her mind had gone blank as if her subconscious had accidentally hit the delete key, erasing all she had learned in her self-defense class. Out of breath, Maddie attempted to roll over to cover herself, but Scorpion grabbed her shoulder and flipped her on her back. The stink of his sweat gagged her. She blamed herself, not because of the single-mindedness that brought her to Blackbird's; but because she failed to translate their language into her language. For years she had defended street blacks, listened to their talk without trying to understand what they said, assumed they were saying nothing worth hearing. Now her ignorance, her racism, as quiet and concealed as it was, condemned her.

Spider rolled two blunts, lit them with a wooden kitchen match, and handed one to Scorpion. Maddie hated dope heads, especially the rapists she defended who claimed they were too high to know what they were doing. When Spider turned to face her, his crotch bulged. She struggled to pull her hands apart.

Scorpion took a penny from his pocket and flipped it. "Call it, man." His voice grated like a dull hand saw scraping against a piece of green hardwood.

"Heads."

The coin hung in the air, then landed in Scorpion's palm. He slapped it on the back of his other hand and showed it to Spider. Maddie studied their faces for a clue as to heads or tails. When Scorpion asked Spider to roll him another, she knew.

She wished she could dull her nerve endings until her whole body felt like it was shot through with Novocain, but there was nothing to distort her senses except fear and fear was an ineffective anesthetic. Her arms ached from the weight of her body. The acrid smoke irritated her eyes and nose.

Scorpion unbuckled her slacks. His knuckles scraped her abdomen as he unzipped her pants. He curled his fingers around the elastic band of her underpants and lifted her off the bed. "Never seen pussy that color before."

"'Member when Edwina dyed her hair that color?" Spider asked. "She dyed her pussy to match."

"Ugly cunt that woman had."

Spider laughed. "Fucking ugly."

"But not too ugly to fuck."

Scorpion rolled Maddie onto her stomach and spread her legs. A spring sticking out of the mattress scratched her. He took off his pants. The zipper sounded like one of Boston's trolleys scraping the side of the tunnel. She thought she heard another sound, footsteps on the stairs or someone walking around in the bar upstairs. The heating pipes clanged. Scorpion grabbed the inside of her thighs and forced her legs apart until she felt she was being split open like a lobster claw by a man ravenous with hunger. Did she hear the sound again? She no longer trusted her senses. Too many sensations assaulted her, the feel of hands on her thighs, the smell of sweat, the sight of stains on the mattress, the smell of the dope, the taste of the handkerchief in her mouth, and a sound her mind might have created, or if it were real, the sound of a rat scurrying through the cellar, knocking something over.

The mattress shook. Scorpion knelt between her legs. He yanked her ass upwards by her hip bones. Spider slipped a pillow under her stomach.

"Get it on, man," Spider said. "I expected home for supper."

"Tell her you already ate."

"Shit to pay if I don't feed her right."

The noise again. Closer. More distinct. Am I hallucinating? Maddie wondered. Is this how women react while being raped? She wanted to scream, but the handkerchief gagged her. Panic triggered new urges, strange urges, urges she had never had before, the urge to take a knife and castrate Spider and Scorpion and dump their balls into a toilet and flush them into the sewers to be eaten by rats. If she had a gun, she'd blow their heads off without hesitation. Her impacted rage ran wild. The benefits of years of therapy, of cognitive restructuring, of practicing impulse control, vanished as if she had never been to Dr. Przystas. For her mind to survive, provided her body did, she would have to begin again at the beginning, a new twelve session protocol, group and individual. This angered her as much as the horror of being raped by Spider and Scorpion.

This new urge, this urge to hurt, to maim, to kill, over-whelmed her. This sudden blood lust to kill lifted her mind out of her body to places she had not anticipated.

A recidivist once told her only the first killing was hard. All the others were fun. His words echoed through her mind like a refrain. She willed her mind away from thinking about the pillow under her stomach or the hands on her buttocks or the mattress spring grinding into her skin or the sweaty smell clinging to her like a wet film. All the others were fun.

Instead, she visualized cutting off their manhood, Spider's and Scorpion's. She visualized the blood flowing down their legs, a scalpel peeling the skin off their faces. She heard their screams. She reveled in the writhing of their death dances, the grinding gears of their death rattles. Yet, she felt neither guilt, nor remorse. No one would condemn her act of vengeance.

If she killed tonight, she knew she would kill again to-morrow. All blacks, young and old, male and female, would, for her, now be Spider or Scorpion. Now she understood how the blood lust of hatred began. From her deepest fears floated a thought, a solitary frightening thought, the thought that, yes, all the others would be fun. She doubted she would be the same person again. She would not want to be.

A new sound. Familiar. A spring, rusty, being stretched. Metal against metal. Louder. More persistent. How much time since the footsteps. Two seconds? Five? Ten? Time had stopped. Metal against metal again. Over her shoulder. A man as large as he was black. His body filled the door frame. His head ex-tended to the lintel.

"She ready for riding," Spider said. "You want firsts?"

"Cut her loose."

"Fucking A I will."

"Do it."

Spider unknotted the belt, untied the gag, pulled the handkerchief from her mouth. Maddie wiggled her jaw back and forth and wrapped herself in the blanket. She itched as the coarse cloth scratched her. The inside of her mouth felt stuffed with cotton. Mabi rummaged through her purse and tossed her car keys to Spider. "Move her ride to the Government Center garage."

"Ain't no Cadillac," Scorpion said.

"All you riding today."

"Shit, man," Spider said. "Pussy for one, pussy for all."

"She's Badger's ticket."

"No reason we can't punch it first," Spider said.

"Give damaged goods, get damaged goods. Now move your asses."

"Little fucking never damaged nobody."

Mabi stood before her. An ebony statue. She hated racist metaphors, but once again she was a prisoner of language. She didn't know any other way to phrase her thoughts. He was blacker than any black she had ever seen. Coal on ice. She felt so illiterate. A drop of saliva, the first, moistened her mouth. Her tongue felt lumpy against her teeth. The blanket irritated her skin. She wanted to scratch–her sides, her thighs, her back, her breasts; but she refused to open the blanket, refused to expose herself. Her calves were falling asleep under the weight of her body, but stretching her legs would uncover her vaginal area. She craved a damp cloth to wipe between her breasts, along her thighs, her crotch. She yearned to stand, to extend her arms and legs so no part of her skin touched any other. She drew her cocoon closer. Mabi victimized her with his silence as she had hundreds of witnesses during her legal career. "Why'd you stop them?" she asked at last.

She felt like a trial attorney facing a surprise witness. Strategies scrolled through her mind. She searched for one that would allow her to regain control. She had to out-think him, she realized. She was too drained, physically, emotionally, to try and out-muscle him. She saw no percentage in being trade bait. Ugolino might refuse the trade; Mabi might double cross him. She understood, now, how her da survived Guadalcanal, how her namesakes endured Kilmainham, how her grand da had the courage to stand before the firing squad. If the Trojans were going to gangbang her to death, fuck 'em. If she had any control, it derived from knowing Mabi or some other Trojan had killed Bumper and used his blood to desecrate the Torah. How else would Bumper's blood get from his body to the stencil to the swastikas? What other Trojan? It was Mabi who played chess with Bumper that night. Coincidence? Unlikely. Circumstantial? Probably, but circumstantial evidence was a weak foundation to build a defense on. If she could convince Mabi that she shared this knowledge with others, that her disappearance would finger him, maybe he'd free her. Bullshit, she thought; but what choice did she have? None but to go for the jugular. And, if it were hers, well, bleeding to death was an honorable way to die as long as the wound was not self-inflicted.

"Why'd you kill Bumper Sullivan?"

His hand surrounded the base of her throat. His fingers encircled her neck. He squeezed and she realized he could break her neck as easily as a child could snap a twig. She had lost at Russian roulette. She now faced the same choice Ann Devlin had faced in Kilmainham when she suffered years of torture without betraying Robert Emmet. It was her turn to answer Yeats's question—"What is this sacrifice?"—and the answer would have to be the same in the basement of Blackbird's as it was on a dead street in Chelsea or in the street in front of the Dublin post office in 1916 or when her grand da faced the IRB firing squad. No wonder skulls on old grave stones always laughed.

-3-

As the white hot sun melded into early evening red, Silvy, Cealy, Mabi, and Dr. John Obeah waited in the Thomas's kitchen for Beaujolais Wine to deliver Badger. Obeah's presence quieted the bickering between Mabi and Silvy. Every few minutes as if set off by some internal alarm, Cealy shook her hands at the ceiling and begged the good Lord to hurry home her Badger.

"You giving us fits, Cealy Thomas," Silvy said.

"The Lord don't listen to them who don't talk."

Twilight deepened to the moment between day and night when there were no shadows. At last, Beaujolais arrived with Badger. Dr. Obeah administered a thorough physical, poking Badger's abdomen, chest, and the fleshy parts of the neck with his fingers, listening to his heart and lungs, examining his teeth, eyes, ears and throat, inspecting his groin and scrotum, taking his pulse, blood pressure, and temperature and checking his skin for bruises, welts, or other abrasions.

"How you feeling, son?"

"I ain't your son."

"Answer the man," Mabi said.

"Like when I popped my first cherry."

"You ain't popped no cherries," Mabi said.

"He's prime," Dr. Obeah said.

Mabi telephoned Stilts at Blackbird's. "Tell Spider to scare shit into Devlin's pants, but no hurts. Not even a bruise." He turned to Silvy. "I kept my promise, so let's go where we won't be intruding on this mother and child reunion."

"Only 'cause Hannah gave me words for you and I promised to deliver them."

"That all I'm worth, second-hand words?"

"You wish."

At his place, Mabi tried to put his arms around her.

"My love's not coming down for you no more."

"Fuck why?"

"For the way you making Badger your legacy. I'm taking him down home." She paused. "And for what you done to Mayor Charlie's kid."

"I done nothing to that kid."

She returned his gaze, even up and twice as hard. "Hannah knows. She's not deaf, dumb, and blind, your momma."

"What she know?"

"And them Falashas from the African Meeting House. You know what they be?"

"Some African tribe."

"Some Jew African tribe. Shit! You as Jewish as that fucking Levy."

"You lying lying or lying true?"

"Lying true."

"Jim Ed?"

"Never knowed." Silvy paused. "What goes 'round comes 'round."

-4-

Maddie did not sleep that night. After her release from Blackbird's, she took a bus to a neighborhood where she could hail a cab that would take her to the Government Center parking garage. When the garage elevator opened at the seventh floor, Spider jumped in and pushed the emergency stop button. Without saying a word, he crouched over her, pinning her shoulders with his knees. Like a drunken barber, he sheared her hair. She refused to scream, resolved not to give him the satisfaction. She lay as still as she could while he pulled her hair away from her scalp and chopped it off at the roots. More than once he drew blood.

At home, with an envelope of hair mixed with dirt and debris from the elevator floor, she felt like an escaped prisoner of war. Mabi had not confessed, at least not verbally, but she felt confident she had solved Bumper Sullivan's murder. If she died before sharing her information, Mabi would fly free and Levy would be convicted. Reaching for a tissue, she knocked Elizabeth's hospital photograph off the night table. "Baby Girl Gloucester." Her eyes were closed, her skull misshapen, her skin wrinkled. Indentations from the forceps distorted the sides of her head. It had taken a month for the indentations to fill in. Maddie righted the photo.

At her make-up table, she looked herself in the eye, a stare-down with her soul to see who blinked first. When neither did, line by line she filled one page after another in a legal pad with a detailed statement of the information she had gathered and the inferences she drew from it. She explained the link between Bumper Sullivan's murder and the desecration of the synagogue and why she concluded Mabi and the Trojans had committed both crimes. She recounted seeing al-Saffah's name in Ugolino's guest register and his testifying at the bail hearing, facts that in her mind established he was part of the plot. She described what had happened in the basement of Blackbird's, recreating what Mabi had said almost verbatim. She included a paragraph on Spider's assault in the parking garage elevator. She explained why she did not take this information to Ugolino, his attempt to bribe her with a Superior Court judgeship. She listed the physical evidence—the slide with the blood, the blood-stained stencil, Duncan Siward's report, Badger's identification bracelet, a remnant of olive blanket from Blackbird's, the plastic bag with her hair and debris from the elevator floor, the photocopy of the last page of Bumper's spiral notebook—and where she hid it all. The more she wrote, the calmer she felt, calm enough to end her statement with Yeats's epitaph:

> Cast a cold eye
> On life, on death.
> Horseman, pass by!

Come morning, she would mail copies to Rabbi ben Reuben, Moskovitzky, Duncan Siward, Uncle George, and Trish Sullivan. She thought about adding a note to Trish's copy, but what would she say? That jail no longer ran in the Devlin blood? But it did. More than ever. Their past may have been rewritten, revised, corrected, but it was still the death row within which they were imprisoned.

In the bathroom, Maddie moistened her head with a hot towel and shaved her scalp, not a fashion statement but an act of defiance, a battle scar she would wear proudly, exposed to the world rather than hidden beneath a scarf or wig. And if people mistook her for a cancer victim undergoing radiation or chemotherapy, let them; in a sense a cancer had lived within her since birth and now, at long last, she was vanquishing her disease.

Too charged up to sleep, she poured herself a Guinness, emptying the bottle straight down the center of the glass. Her father scolded her the first time she poured Guinness that way, but she liked to watch the brown foam rise to the rim, then recede as the black liquid rose in its place. The clock on the wall chimed the half-hour, 3:30 a.m.

She telephoned Michelle Furey. "I need a will."

"At this hour?"

"Can you come here? I don't want to go out."

"You all right?"

"I will be when I have a will."

"What about witnesses? I need two witnesses."

"Please."

While Maddie waited, she dumped the contents of her purse on the kitchen table and rifled through the mess, looking for the scrap of paper with the name of Uncle George's Dublin hotel. It was among the food coupons in her supermarket envelope.

When Harriman came on the line, Maddie said, "Mabi killed Bumper." The echo of her voice and the slight time lag in his response unnerved her.

"You sound in an awful way."

She read him her statement.

"Prepare a second original in your own handwriting. Sign each page and hide it with the evidence so I can find it."

Minutes later the front door buzzer sounded and Maddie let Michelle Furey into the building. "Christ, Maddie." Furey recoiled. "What happened to you?"

Maddie led her to the kitchen table, offered her a Guinness, which Furey refused. "I need a will."

"Come to my office in the morning. We'll do it right. Witnesses. All the formalities."

"I need it now." Maddie patted the side of her head to straighten strands of hair that were no longer there. "Morning may be too late."

"Chemotherapy? Is that why you shaved your head?"

"Read this." Maddie gave Furey her statement.

"My folks have a cabin up country. Middle of nowhere. We can hide out there."

"I'm done hiding out. Never again."

Furey gazed at Maddie with the resignation, the understanding, of someone visiting a beloved relative on her deathbed. The sadness in Furey's eyes comforted Maddie, told her that Furey cared.

"We could do a holographic will," Furey said. "It's better than nothing. It has to be in your handwriting. I'll dictate the language."

Maddie wrote as Furey spoke, then signed each page as well as the signature line on the last page attesting that she intended this holographic will to be her "last will and testament signed freely and voluntarily for the purposes set forth therein and with full knowledge and understanding of its contents." Peace veiled Maddie in an inner calm. "Kiss me," she said.

"I love you," Maddie said after they made love. "Now, skedaddle."

"I want to stay."

"No. If it's to be my fate, it's my fate alone."

Chapter 14

Friday, April 24, 1981

-1-

While Maddie Devlin prepared for Yeats's horseman, Mabi paced the floor of his bedroom like a death row prisoner awaiting his last meal. His encounter with Silvy haunted him. Her words assailed him like the evil spirits that vexed Gideon. If Gideon's hexing don't make me a witch doctor, Mabi thought, and Hannah's praying don't make me a holy roller, being Falasha don't make me Jew bait. Fear feasted on his innards like maggots on the dead. After all the years and all the training and all the chess games and all the missions and all the praying to Allah, after being sliced and diced–his manhood in al-Saffah's hands and under al-Saffah's knife–after turning page after page in that god damn book, after all this, was being Jew bait his fucking *ajal*? If al-Saffah found out who he was by blood, he, like every other fucking Jew, would be the enemy.

He knew what it meant to be black in the Birmingham of the North and he knew what it meant to be a Trojan; but to be Jew bait? His head spun like the wheels of Brother Ambrose's skates. What was Falasha? A word. A fucking word. Because of this word and for no other reason, al-Saffah would now hate him. Fuck! He pounded his thigh with his fist. I ain't had me no soul transplant. An hour after Friday's dawn, he barged in on Hannah.

"Falashas, Momma. Speak on it."

"No forgiving for Bumper Sullivan or Chelsea."

"I'm not asking forgiving."

"Knowing the meaning of your name don't raise the dead."

On his way out the door, Mabi paused at the photograph of Jim Ed in his Marine dress uniform. Jim Ed's deep brown eyes stared out at him and suddenly he was eight years old again and swaggering in Jim Ed's shadow as his brother faced off against Gabe Tucker while the embers of Boston burning still glowed; eight years old again and feeling his brother's manhood surging through him, eight years old again and dreaming of being the crown prince to Jim Ed's king. He turned away from the judgment in those eyes and their unanswered question: Whose backyard I be burning?

Friday's rush hour clogged the streets as Mabi inched his way toward Copley Square and the Boston Public Library. He felt anxious, eager, scared all at the same time, like he did fronting Billy Sunshine outside the candy store. He didn't like them old feelings.

Copley Square was a desert paved in brick. The Hancock Tower rose above it like a bronze totem that trapped in its mirrored face all who ventured into the brick desert. People, like camel caravans, snaked across its glass surface. Mabi searched for himself in the reflection. On the far side of the square, opposite Trinity Church, the library shimmered in the heat's convection currents. Four black wrought iron light fixtures crowned with seven spikes hung above the Dartmouth Street entrance, one on each corner of a hexagon and the seventh in the center. Fall on them, Mabi thought, and you meat on a fork. He wished they were hanging over the front door of the Trojans' chill pad. Above the fixtures, names were carved into the façade, Dvrer, Plavtvs, Theorcitvs, Clavd, Povssin. He had never seen so many V's. Plavtavs. Plavitivis. He hesitated on the steps. The spikes were now spears, comic book spears impaling so many Greeks, so many Trojans, the agony of death frozen on their faces. He searched the façade for a name he knew. Homer. The comic book dude. At the top of the first block to the right of the entrance. Seeing that almost made him feel welcome.

"I want to study up on Falashas," Mabi told the lobby attendant, Prudence according to her name tag, which also identified her as a Friend of the Library volunteer.

Prudence closed her book, *An Illustrated History of Paul Revere Silver and Pewter*, bookmarking her page with her thumb. Her eyes brimmed with skepticism. "Falashas?"

"Them's a black tribe in Africa."

"A school project?" Prudence raised her head so that she appeared to be looking down her nose at Mabi even though she was sitting and he was standing.

"You pointing me in the right direction or no?"

"Listen carefully for I shall not repeat myself. For reference, follow the hallway to my right, past the souvenir desk, which is closed, through the open court yard, to the lobby of the new wing; then, go up the staircase to the second floor, not the mezzanine, mind you, but the second floor, and a reference librarian will help you."

Mabi wanted to haul Prudence to the roof and drop her on the spikes. Her and the rest of Wonder Bread white-assed Boston, white-assed America. He passed through a pair of swinging doors into a courtyard with an open roof. Sunlight streamed in, reflecting off walkways of crushed stone, illuminating potted plants and miniature trees. A fountain with a waterfall sprayed mist. Wooden chairs lined the walls, stone benches the walkways. Fuckin' Mayor Charlie don't clean garbage from black gutters, don't plow snow off black streets, don't trim weeds 'round black graves, but eagles for this shit he's got. Mabi grabbed a handful of stones and hurled them at a cherub spouting water. In the new wing, the lobby rose like the inside of a hollow pyramid. The arrow directing patrons to the reference librarian pointed straight up. He circled the perimeter, then climbed the stairs, ninety-five steps from the lobby to the second floor, almost twice as many as from the basement of the Trojans' crib to the rooftop. Two of them tenements standing on each other's shoulders would fit inside this place with room for most of another.

"I'm here to read up on Falashas," he announced at the reference desk. "Them's a black tribe in Africa."

The reference librarian, an Asian-American wearing a shapeless, colorless smock, smiled at him. She had straight black hair and no visible curves. "Books published before 1975 are listed in those volumes against the wall. Books published after 1975 are catalogued on microfilm. The readers are against the windows behind me. Everything's alphabetical."

Volume 20, Fah-Fam. He doubted Fam meant the same as in the hood. Two pages of Fal entries, but none under Falasha. Maybe I not reading it right, he thought. He wished Silvy were with him. He closed, then reopened the book. Still, two pages of entries beginning with Fal, but none for Falashas. After twenty minutes, a microfilm reader became available. He twisted around to the reference librarian. "How's this work?"

"Shhh! Read the instructions."

Mabi played with the switches until he found one that lit up the screen. Min. He turned the wheel and letters scrolled by in front of him, Min, Mil, Mih, blurring as they went faster. He slowed down at Est, then scrolled back. Fac, Fag, Fai, Fal. "You got three books on Falashas," he shouted. "Bring me what you got."

"We have an open stack system." With a rubber tipped finger, she pointed to the catalog numbers. "Go to the DS shelves to your left inside the wall. The books are arranged in order. DS135 is between DS134 and DS136. The numbers are on the spines."

No wonder brothers and sisters not using this place. He found the DS shelves, books about Jews, hundreds and hundreds of books about Jews; but the numbers went from DS135. E70 to DS135.E80, no E75's.

"No books with them numbers," he told the reference librarian.

"If you want to borrow them, submit a reserve request and we'll notify you by mail in four to eight weeks. If you want to read them here, there are duplicate copies in the research library in the old wing. Upstairs opposite the main entrance. Do you have a library card?"

Mabi flashed his driver's license. "That good enough ID for you?"

She copied the information from his license on to a form. "Here's a temporary card. Your permanent card should arrive in four to eight weeks."

Mabi retraced his path to the front entrance, shoved his temporary library card under Prudence's nose, then followed the signs to the research library. He resented going to white places to find his past, search for his future. Falasha books should be with black books, not Jew books. Black books should be in black libraries where blacks would be welcomed instead of treated like gangbangers who can't read past "See Spot run." He felt his heritage being bleached out by whites squeezing it dry.

"I here to look up Falashas," he told the librarian, a white woman whose velvety lips were designed for one thing. Between the legs of white pussy was one place he figured he'd always be welcome.

She gestured toward the card catalogue. He found the drawer labeled Fah-Fal. Eleven entries. Some in English. Others in a bunch of other languages. "All eleven." He stood so his arm touched hers while she jotted numbers down on scrap paper. He felt her muscles move against his. He regretted not fucking Devlin. Next time. The librarian wrote down a twelfth number.

"Take this to the kiosk in the Abbey Room across the hall." She stepped back and looked him in the eye. Her eyes were steel gray, like cement, like Jim Ed's empty coffin. He didn't believe in the evil eye, but he felt himself weakening as her look battered the fortress he had built around himself. He felt as exposed as the time al-Saffah sliced him and diced him. She blinked and he felt pain between his legs as if her eyelids guillotined what al-Saffah had missed.

"What about stuff too new for books?"

"We have *The New York Times* Index. Under Falashas you'll find the dates and page numbers. The papers are in the microfilm room."

He took refuge in the microfilm room. The twelfth number was a phone number, a challenge he would never accept. Black pussy castrated their men. He'd be damned if he'd let this white pussy do the same. Pages of *The New York Times* passed before him until he reached the front page of the edition he wanted, a Sunday paper. He had the jitters of a person about to meet his grandparents for the first time and was afraid they wouldn't like him.

He dawdled over the articles, reading each closely. In the Pantanal region of Brazil, poachers imperiled wild life, jaguars, capybaras, otters and alligators. Why did people care more about that shit than blacks in Boston? He lingered at the lingerie ads, beautiful women, all white, modeling frilly bras and slinky slips, their tits jutting out as if their bodies were for sale rather than the underwear. News stories passed before him like scenery outside a car window: authors disputing over what really happened leading up to Pearl Harbor, Turks asking for increased aid from Western Europe, Polish dairy workers threatening strikes, archeological discoveries under the streets of Sofia, a scientist finding a fossil of the world's oldest bird, one hundred forty million years old. He wished his past were as long. The articles wearied him, and he realized he was avoiding doing what he had come to the library to do. He didn't give a fuck about military unrest in Spain or labor problems in Singapore or who would be the next ruler of Tunisia.

He scrolled to the next page and a headline yanked his eyes out of his head: "Torture Reported of Ethiopian Jews." His heart skipped a beat at the first line of the story: "Falashas, as the black Jews of Ethiopia are called . . ." He put his head inside the hood of the microfilm machine to read the small print in the dim light. The Ethiopian government, the article said, was arresting Falashas and torturing them, closing their schools, denying them exit visas to Israel, and barring them from decent farm land. He felt queasy at the description of the torture suffered by the Falashas, tied hand and foot to long poles, suspended upside down, beaten with clubs; flesh sliced open, the wounds becoming infested with worms; broken bones which were never set. ODing Brother Ambrose was God's mercy compared to this shit. The more he read, the more he understood what Gideon and Hannah feared, why they covered up their past, his past, and why they never told him or Jim Ed what their name meant. He wondered how much of this shit was still happening.

He filled out a request for a copy of the article and paid the fee.

While he waited, a library volunteer delivered a book to him, one of the three in English. He sat on a bench in the court yard. It was a quiet morning and there were no other readers. The sound of the water calmed him. He leafed through the book, too scared to read it. Sentences about the slaughter of children caught his eye. A youth named Yonatan, the youngest son of Azariah Gette, escaped the slaughter of village students because the security police mistook him for a teacher. After the massacre, the government returned the children's clothes, shredded by bullet holes. The security police demanded bribes of $50.00 per bullet hole before releasing a child's corpse to its parents for burial. One child, four children; bullets, a bomb; Ethiopia, Alabama. And in Boston outside Mayor Charlie's city hall a black man attacked with the American Flag. Mabi read until, again, he wished he had never learned how to read.

In the middle of the book, photographs. Faces, black faces, faces with the same noses and lips and hair he saw every day on Blue Hill Avenue; but they were the faces of Falashas from Ethiopia. A caption: "School children in the Falasha village of Wallaca." Wallaca. He thought his eyes were tricking him, making him see things that weren't. He rubbed them, closed them, opened them; but the words did not change. The village of Wallaca. Before or after the massacre? he wondered. He counted the children. Twenty-nine. Twenty-nine pairs of eyes looked sadly at the camera, wishing they could climb inside the magic box and go wherever the picture went. One boy, a gap between his front teeth and a mouth shaped like an egg lying sideways, reminded him of Badger. Is Silvy Falasha? He rubbed his fingertips across their cheeks as if he could comfort them across time and space. If this picture be old enough, he thought, maybe Gideon and Hannah be in it; but if it be too new, these kids may all be massacred. He held the book to his chest as if his heartbeat could transmit life to nameless children from another world, another time, nameless children who lived his past, nameless children who never would have been massacred if Wallaca was part of the Trojans' turf. He wished he could wish them all back to life.

-2-

By sunrise Friday morning, Maddie had prepared and mailed photocopies of her statement to Rabbi ben Reuben, Moskovitzky, Duncan, Harriman, and Trish, two copies to each, one mailed from her neighborhood post office, the other from the post office in the first floor lobby of the Federal Court-house; then, with her mind at ease knowing neither Mabi's fate nor hers depended on whether the horseman stopped or passed her by, she walked to Pemberton Square where the Single Justice Session of the Supreme Judicial Court convened daily at 10:00 a.m. on the fourteenth floor of the New Court-house. Maddie didn't care for the New Court-house. Nor did she care for appellate courtrooms. They lacked jury boxes.

In the courtroom, a court officer interrupted his reading about the launch of the first space shuttle to peek at her from behind a page of the morning paper. Bonturo tried to cover up his shock at her appearance by playing tic-tac-toe at the counsel table. A young reporter from the press pool dozed on a back bench, his eyes closed. Maddie wished he had a camera so she could flaunt her new hairless style to the world.

"I heard you were going to Washington," Bonturo said with a hitch in his voice.

"Bald is beautiful. You should try it." She arranged her files on the table designated for appellant's counsel, positioning the papers so the lectern and microphone blocked Bonturo's view. Paranoia was one of the more endearing qualities of trial attorneys.

The royal blue curtain behind the bench parted and Justice Alexandra Pallas, the second woman appointed to the Supreme Judicial Court, ascended the bench. A month shy of fifty, she was still attractive, her eyes icy blue with a hint of the softness that would be brought out by candlelight. During oral argument, her smile disarmed attorneys. Neither her gender nor her beauty preoccupied her. A black robe is not high fashion, she replied to a television reporter who asked if she thought she was too glamorous for the Supreme Judicial Court.

"Is an interlocutory matter like this ripe for appeal?" Justice Pallas asked.

"Judge Gomita certified a question of law to this court," the clerk replied.

"I will hear you, Ms. Devlin."

"Thank you, Your Honor." Maddie rested her arms lightly on the lectern but stood erect so she would not appear to be leaning. "Judge Gomita denied bail because he thought there was a high probability Mr. Levy would flee before trial. He arrived at this conclusion . . ."

"Do you disagree with the proposition the likelihood of flight is a sufficient legal basis to deny bail?"

"No, and that's why I request you remand this matter to Judge Gomita so I may present additional evidence to prove Mr. Levy will not flee."

"What type of evidence?"

"Evidence which establishes Mr. Levy's innocence and the guilt of someone else."

Out of the corner of her eye, Maddie saw motion, but she did not look in Bonturo's direction. She did not want to break eye contact with Justice Pallas. She needed to sustain it. Eye contact transformed the hearing from an audience to a dialogue.

"Do you know who murdered Charles F. Sullivan, III?"

"I believe I do."

"You harbor some doubt?"

"A scintilla's worth."

"Shouldn't you present your evidence to the police or the district attorney?"

"I have made it available to Detective George Harriman of the Boston Police Department." Maddie adjusted the gooseneck microphone. "The *Torah* desecrated in the Chelsea synagogue was desecrated with Charles Sullivan's blood. The rampage in Chelsea was perpetrated by the Trojans, one of Boston's street gangs. I have personally received death threats from two people at the top of their leadership structure."

Justice Pallas poured herself a glass of water and Maddie felt the inside of her mouth go dry. "You are asking me to take a lot on faith."

"I am not asking you to bail Mr. Levy. I am only requesting a remand so I can present my evidence to Judge Gomita. Avram

Levy is a very devout Jew, Your Honor, and is studying to become a rabbi. He is also a member of the synagogue in Chelsea and regularly attends services there. It is inconceivable he, either acting alone or with the aid of a street gang, would murder Charles Sullivan and use Charles's blood to perpetrate such a heinous anti-Semitic act, especially one directed at his own congregation whose members will testify he is well liked and well respected. Mr. Levy does not have the criminal pathology necessary to commit such a crime. The persons who utilized Charles Sullivan's blood to desecrate the *Torah* must be the same persons who killed him. It is the only conclusion that makes sense. This is the essence of the evidence I wish to present under oath on remand. Mr. Bonturo will, of course, have an opportunity to cross-examine."

"I have some trouble with a blanket accusation directed against a large group even if you characterize that group as a street gang."

"I have identified the individual who, in my opinion, killed Charles Sullivan to Detective Harriman, but I prefer not doing so at this hearing because the press is present."

Justice Pallas swiveled her chair sideways, leaned back, and looked up at the ceiling. "What do you have to say, Mr. Bonturo?"

Bonturo rose and began speaking before he reached the lectern. "Thank you, Judge. Everything Ms. Devlin said sounds plausible on the surface, but she has not presented one scintilla of independent evidence to corroborate any of her statements. If she is concerned about the press, I request you close this hearing and require her to present her evidence here and now."

"I do not countenance banning the public from my courtroom, Mr. Bonturo."

"It will take some time for the police to corroborate these allegations," Bonturo said. "Mr. Levy must be retained in custody until the investigation is complete."

Justice Pallas stood and paced behind the bench. "I'm not being asked to release Mr. Levy. I'm being asked to remand this matter to the Superior Court for further hearing. Please focus your argument accordingly."

Bonturo's hand accidentally bumped the microphone and a hollow sound echoed throughout the courtroom. "Sorry, Judge. The presentation of evidence on remand may prejudice future proceedings in this case, deprive Mr. Levy of a fair trial, and fabricate an issue to obtain a reversal of his conviction on appeal."

Justice Pallas leaned on the back of her chair and peered down at Bonturo. "I find it comforting the prosecution is so solicitous of the legal rights of the defendant. You may avoid those problems, Mr. Bonturo, by assenting to Mr. Levy's release on bail?" Justice Pallas rapped her gavel twice.

"But, Judge . . ."

"This matter is remanded to Judge Gomita for further proceedings." She was off the bench before Bonturo could register his objection.

"Attorney Devlin." The reporter leaned over the railing separating public seating from the enclosure reserved for attorneys. "What's your evidence?"

"Come to the bail hearing," Maddie replied. "If you're lucky, it may be this afternoon."

"I want next Monday," Bonturo said. "The police need time to investigate your allegations."

"An innocent man shouldn't be kept in prison one extra second." Maddie had not expected it to be so easy to finesse Bonturo into a confrontation in front of a reporter.

"If your evidence is made public," Bonturo said, "he'll be freed at the expense of arresting and convicting the real killer. You've got to consider the public interest."

"Believe me," Maddie said, "not even Maddie Devlin could find a loophole in the case against the real killer." She smiled at the reporter. "What did you say your name was?"

"Scott Dunleavy."

"I'll be watching for your by-line."

Judge Gomita scheduled the remand hearing for the following Tuesday afternoon at 2:00 which mollified Bonturo because it meant the district attorney's office would have time to conduct its investigation. The police wanted to sequester Maddie in a hotel where it would be easier to maintain tight security, but she refused. Death had passed her by and would not return, not for a while at least, because she had important work still unfinished. This was how her da must have felt on Guadalcanal. Nevertheless, she allowed C. J. Ant to be appointed associate counsel to handle routine court appearances prior to the remand hearing.

Saturday morning's *Boston Globe* would carry Scott Dunleavy's by-line on the front page in a story so exclusive the *Globe* managed to keep it from the broadcast media, but not from the *Herald-American* which quoted Rabbi ben Reuben praising Maddie as the Ruth of Boston's Jewish community.

Outside, the heat refused to abate.

-3-

Boston's heavy traffic, especially its double-parked delivery vans, jaywalking suits and skirts racing from one important meeting to the next, cabbies who usurped all lanes of traffic, and busses that lumbered in and out of traffic from stop to stop, slowed Mabi's rush to share his discovery with Silvy. He might as well have been on the Central Artery or Storrow Drive inbound at 5:00 p.m. On Blue Hill Avenue, a bus driver not intimidated by his horn, cut him off, then stopped in the middle of the street to pick up and discharge passengers. His car's air conditioner sucked in exhaust fumes, bringing tears to his eyes as had the photo of the children of Wallaca now hidden inside his shirt. Their somber faces, the sadness of their eyes, their stolen childhood, the premature finality of their *ajal*, burned against his skin like a slaver's hot branding iron. They were dead but he was alive because Hannah and Gideon had escaped and the parents of these children had not. He knew why he lived and Billy Sunshine died, why he lived and Luke Shaw died, why he lived and Mayor Charlie's kid did not; but he didn't understand the luck, the fate, the accident of circumstance, that spared him but not the children of Wallaca. So he could become a blood-bought soldier in the army of Allah? Fuck that.

At the corner, the traffic light turned red. There had to be more to it than blind fate. The bus driver shifted into neutral and gunned the engine. Mabi's car filled with fumes. He cried, but his tears did not wash away the sting. He felt close to the twenty-nine children of Wallaca, closer than to Badger or Spider or any of the Trojans, closer than to Silvy. He wished Jim Ed were there to share the moment. Fucking tiger. They were his bloods, Jim Ed's bloods, not street bloods, but true bloods, blood of his blood, blood of Jim Ed's blood, bonded to him by more than skin color or neighborhood or any fucking book. He pulled over to the curb. The more he cried, the more his eyes stung. He was them, they were him, his past, his present and, now, his future.

-4-

Mabi found Silvy in a park down the street from the day-care center taking a late lunch break. The back slats of the park bench where she sat were split and splintered. Someone had knocked off the cement arms; chunks of cement bouldered the ground. Broken glass, green and brown and clear, mostly wine or beer bottles, sparkled in the sunlight. Years earlier during election season, Mayor Charlie had had the benches repaired. The wooden slats had been painted deep green and the grounds cleaned up. New grass had been planted, as well as flowers, shrubs; but the city never repaired the vandalism of kids in the 'hood trying to prove they were tough enough to be Trojans. *Whose backyard I be burning?*

"Silvy? Something to show you." She chewed her sandwich like he wasn't there. He slipped the photograph out from his shirt. It had puckered from his sweat. "The kid on the far right, he look like Badger. Maybe you Falasha."

"My people are from Alabama." She ignored the photograph.

"Those kids are from a village called Wallaca."

She folded the wax paper from her sandwich and put it in her lunch bag. She peeled an orange, collecting the rind on a napkin.

"I'm asking for help, Silvy. You making me beg for it?"

"I once said I'd give Leroy Wallaca every ounce of help I had; but Mabi, well I wouldn't spare him a drop of water in the middle of the Sahara Desert." She sat erect and in her bearing he saw a queen every bit as regal as the Falasha queen Yehudit he had read about in the library that morning.

"Changing from Mabi to Leroy ain't like switching on-off."

"What comes easy goes easier."

"Why you turning white on me, bitch?"

"Turning white? Some things don't have colors. Right and wrong for one. Good and evil for another. Go. Do whatever you think be written in that fucking book. I'll keep my future to myself, thank you."

Mabi's shoulders sagged as he returned to his car. He no longer knew what to believe. He understood now the truth of *ajal.* You're born, you live, you die, life goes on. Life goes on. It didn't for the children of Wallaca, but who gave a rusty fuck? Sure as shit no one in Boston or anywhere else in the fucking universe other than the village of Wallaca except maybe himself, maybe Hannah and Gideon, maybe Jim Ed if he had lived. He felt as spaced out as if he had shot up pure grade. He hoped when he crashed he'd land in a righteous place.

-5-

Later that afternoon, clearheaded and clear-eyed, Mabi landed at al-Saffah's.

"Welcome, my son," al-Saffah greeted him. "You look in mourning. Perhaps my hookah will cheer you. I have a fresh tin of Sobranie Black and Gold."

"You ever hear of a black tribe called Falashas?"

Al-Saffah's eyes narrowed to a squint. "Who told you about the Falashas?"

"Trojans used to be Zuluz. We into African tribes. Study up on them."

"A pitiful tribe. Blacks masquerading as Jews."

"Suppose a Falasha comes saying he's a true believer in Allah, you treat him same as me?"

Al-Saffah bowed his head as if he were praying Allah would reveal the right answer. "No. I wouldn't. Let me ask you a question. Would you permit a Caucasian to join the Trojans if he said he was black but for the color of his skin?" Al-Saffah paused to let Mabi ponder the question. "There are preconditions which must exist for true belief to be present. If we don't insist on them, we'd be misled by every charlatan who mouthed the words we wanted to hear."

Preconditions. Mabi hadn't considered preconditions. He had just believed. Just acted out of faith. Silvy believed in Jesus. He believed in Allah. He thought she was wrong. She thought he was. She had faith. What did he have? If everything in the universe had its unique *ajal*, did Allah?

Al-Saffah rested his fingers on Mabi's forearm. "A Jew, whether raised a Jew or not, could never embrace the purity of Islam just as a Caucasian, even if raised by blacks, could never be black. A human raised by wolves does not a wolf become. It's the Tarzan myth, one of the oldest in the world; but it overlooks one elemental truth: you are what you are, not what you say you are."

Mabi leaned against the Koran bookstand. "If I said I was Falasha, would that put me on the wrong side of your *jihad*?"

"Your true name would not have been revealed to be Mabi if you were Falasha. No. If you were Falasha, you would be struck down as an infidel who corrupted the religion of Abraham to undermine, to halt, to eradicate the purification process we have begun."

Mabi felt trapped between faith and whatever its opposite was. It was a feeling he didn't have words for. Either he believed in that book or he didn't. Either he believed he had been chosen or believed he hadn't. Chosen. Everybody wanted to be chosen. Trick was who's doing the choosing.

Al-Saffah set up the chess board. "Let us put aside childish talk of Falashas and share the hookah over a game of chess."

Mabi thought of the eight centuries of history embodied in the chess set, eight fucking centuries. Once, it seemed an eternity compared to his past, but now it seemed a split second compared to the thousands of years of Falasha history. If I am what I am, he thought, how can I be different from what I was this morning? If everything be written in some fucking book, this must have been. And if it wasn't, this book must be as bogue as Gideon's comic book.

Unable to concentrate, he lost in fewer than thirty moves. Declining al-Saffah's offer of a rematch, he drove home where he locked the door and disconnected the phone. He had thinking to do, hard thinking, much too much for his liking.

-6-

Late Friday afternoon as the evening rush hour clogged the tunnels leading to and from Boston's Logan Airport, Maddie paced back and forth in front of the doors through which passengers exited after clearing customs. George Harriman's plane circled thousands of feet above her. Before departing Shannon, he had arranged for two detectives in plain clothes to shadow her wherever she went. At the airport, in addition to the detectives a policewoman in uniform wandered through the crowd. Two hours late, Harriman's plane landed and, after another hour, he cleared customs.

"Maddie. Maddie." He dropped his suitcase. "Your hair."

"I had a close shave."

"Ah, my rose in the rood of time." They hugged like father and daughter. On the drive back to police headquarters, he reviewed the file.

"We have more than enough for a search warrant," she said. "Get me a stenographer. I'll dictate the application."

Rush hour had ended, the only consolation for the plane's late arrival, and the tunnel backed up to the toll booths rather than the airport access road. As they inched along, Maddie relaxed, her hand in Uncle George's. At District 1, they drafted affidavits with exhibits and applications for search warrants for Mabi's apartment, the Trojans' headquarters, Blackbird's, Silvy Thomas's home, and the home of Gideon and Hannah Wallaca. Several hours later, the stenographer had finished typing them.

"Who's the emergency judge?" Maddie asked.

"We should wait 'til morning," Harriman said. "At this hour, you'd have to be twice as persuasive."

"Suppose Mabi disappears?"

"He's in his apartment, which is under surveillance. If he takes one step outside, he'll be arrested."

"Don't wait. Arrest him now. You don't need a warrant to search his apartment if it's incident to a lawful arrest."

"This case is much too big for a warrantless search." Harriman leaned back in his chair and rubbed his eyes.

"Long day," Maddie said.

"I owe you an apology, Maddie, for all the shit I gave you for defending the Jew."

"His name is Avram Levy."

"For defending Avram Levy."

"Why? Because he's innocent?"

"No. Because you did the right thing."

"Don't make me into something I'm not."

-7-

While Maddie dozed, Harriman, on a hunch, checked the duty roster to see which black police officers were on duty, when their shifts started, where they were assigned. There were only a handful and it took him less than twenty minutes. One of them, he figured, was on the Trojans' payroll. Several he eliminated because they would not go on duty until after the morning edition of the *Herald-American* hit the newsstands. He had fed the newspaper information and they promised front-page coverage in return for the scoop. Others he eliminated because they were stationed in districts other than District 1. That left three possibilities: Amelia Wine whose shift started at 4 a.m., Joe Ladeira whose shift ended at 8 a.m., and Dick Remillard who always seemed to be on duty. Harriman made sure each of them learned about the applications for the search warrants. He wished he knew for certain which one of them was Mabi's spy. If Irish eyes weren't smiling, it would be none of the above.

Saturday's headline in the *Herald-American* asked, DID THE TROJANS FRAME AVRAM LEVY? It seems more than a coincidence, the paper editorialized, that Mabi, leader of the notorious black street gang known as the Trojans, played chess with Bumper Sullivan within hours of his murder. How many of Mabi's fingerprints would have been found on Avram Levy's skull cap if the police had properly tested it that night instead of assuming Mr. Levy's guilt?

"Didn't they call for his execution?" Maddie asked.

"That's what I love about that rag," Harriman said.

Chapter 15

Saturday, April 25, 1981

-1-

By sunrise, Mabi's mole at police headquarters had informed him that the police were applying for search warrants for his crib, the Trojans', Silvy's place, Hannah's and Gideon's apartment, and Blackbird's. On the street he counted two, no three, stake-out teams in unmarked cars. He waved at one from his kitchen window, laughing as the driver covered his face with that morning's *Herald-American*. Down the street beyond the lines the police had set up, television trucks from the local network affiliates waited. Mabi plugged in the phone and called Spider at the Trojans' crib. "My place surrounded by cops and the TV."

"Here, too."

"You know what to do."

"It done."

"Silvy taken care of?"

"She's played out about it. Catch al-Saffah on the tube? He makes you the second coming."

Mabi hung up, then telephoned one of the lawyers the gang had on retainer, a Jew named Greenberg, because Mabi was color blind when the stakes were high enough.

"How long can you tie up them warrants?"

"A day, two tops with an appeal," Greenberg said.

"Go the distance."

"Stay in and you're safe. The police are scared shitless about violating your rights and blowing up the case on a constitutional nicety. Otherwise, they'd have busted you and searched your place incident to the arrest."

The cops didn't worry Mabi. Cops never did. Boston cops were always on sale and he had access to enough dollars to buy his way out of anything. Still, he had planned for the day his dollars would be worthless, mapping back doors into other buildings, escapes routes over rooftops, through passageways in basements. Let the cops think they had him trapped. When the time came, he would Houdini them but good.

He lay down on his bed to think. He was inside a shrinking triangle, a triangle with al-Saffah on one side, his being Falasha on the second, and his doing what he'd done to Mayor Charlie's kid on the third. It rested on his shoulders like a slave's collar, this triangle, shrinking 'til it crushed his windpipe, snapping his neck. He felt dizzy, angry, stupid, for letting al-Saffah con him.

The clay man Jesse had crafted for Mabi in the Sunday school playroom frowned. Mabi rubbed his eyes. The rest of the room—Silvy's photo on the bureau, the wallpaper, the Bill Russell poster, the chair at the foot of his bed—was in sharp focus. Jesse's clay figure now sat in the chair at the foot of his bed. Life size. Familiar. At the figure's feet, a tiger. A hand reached out and grabbed Mabi's in a soul shake. Flesh, not clay.

"It's traveling time." Jim Ed placed his hand on Mabi's shoulder. Mabi trembled at its warmth. "Close your eyes." Later, "You can look now."

They were on a fire escape in the 'hood. Night. Hot. On the street, the Trojans marched as if to the funereal music of a dirge, Silvy, who was seven months pregnant, and Spider in the lead. The gang carried a glass coffin on their shoulders. Inside, wrapped partially in a winding sheet with the head exposed, a corpse. Candles bathed the glass coffin in a halo.

As the procession passed, windows in the tenements opened. Hannah and Gideon joined the march when it reached their corner, as did Cealy Thomas. Children played hide and seek among the adults. Jesse, wearing denim coveralls and pajama tops, was always "it."

"Who made him a little kid again?" Mabi asked. No reply.

Jesse wrapped his arms around Silvy's thighs, rubbing the top of his head against the bottom of her belly. "Let's sing a lullaby," she said.

Jesse wiped his eyes with balled-up fists. Silvy handed him to Stilts and began singing:

> Hush, little baby, don't you cry
> You know your momma was born to die
>
> All my trials, Lord, soon be over.

Her voice, pure, strong, cleansed the street. Others sang with her.

> River Jordan is muddy and cold,
> Well, it chills the body, but not the soul
>
> All my trials, Lord, soon be over.

Scorpion played a blues harp. Like a trumpet, it poured forth notes so rich they could be tasted, so sweet they dissolved the grief. Silvy's soprano caressed these notes, made love to them, point and counterpoint, melody and harmony, voice and blues harp, competing, complementing, merging, then separating to begin the cycle again.

>Too late my brothers, too late but never mind

>All my trials, Lord, soon be over.

>If living were a thing that money could buy,
>You know, the rich would live and the poor would die.

>All my trials, Lord, soon be over.

The funeral became a parade, the mourning a spiritual celebration. Everyone rejoiced in life as the traditional black lament escorted Mabi in death.

>There grows a tree in paradise,
>And the pilgrims call it the tree of life

>All my trials, Lord, soon be over.

Jesse joined in, his falsetto rising above Silvy's soprano.

>Too late my brothers, too late but never mind
>All my trials, Lord, soon be over.

>All my trials, Lord, soon be over.

Silvy raised her head. On the fire escape, Mabi felt her eyes burn into him. He saw what she saw, a scroll unrolled along the aisle of a synagogue in Chelsea, a red swastika stenciled on each page. She repeated a verse.

> There grows a tree in paradise,
> And the pilgrims call it the tree of life
>
> All my trials, Lord, soon be over.

She held the last note until everyone stopped singing, until Scorpion stopped blowing, until her voice reached beyond the fire escape into the heavens, fading only when the sun edged above the horizon, washing the mourners in the red glow of first light, coloring the glass coffin with a scarlet burnish so it looked like it was filled with hot coals. As the funeral procession marched east toward the new day, Mabi slumped on the steps of the fire escape.

"Take me home," he begged Jim Ed. He blinked and it was as if they had never left his bedroom.

"I'm here to challenge you," Jim Ed said. "Same terms you gave Luke Shaw." Jim Ed scratched the head of the tiger between its ears. The tiger yawned, eyeing Mabi with calm solemnity, unconcerned about where its next meal was coming from.

Mabi led with a quick jab, but Jim Ed parried it, catching Mabi's fist and flipping him onto the bed like a wet do-rag. Jim Ed pinned him with a forearm to the neck. Mabi thrashed around like a woman being raped, kicking, flailing, unable to get the leverage he needed to throw Jim Ed off. He grabbed Jim Ed's jawbone and tried to break it with brute force, but Jim Ed bit his fingers to the bone. They rolled around the room. The tiger moved from one corner to another, content to watch.

"Mabi!" A voice, high-pitched, screaming. Jim Ed evaporated. The tiger dissolved. Another shriek, then silence. Mabi's head cleared. In his arms, he cradled Silvy. Bruises disfigured her face. He fetched a wash-cloth, wrung it out with cold water, and gently bathed her face. Her eyelids flickered and he looked deep into her pupils to make sure she could focus. His fingers massaged her scalp, searching for fractures, her nose to see if it was broken. Balls of paper, crushed and crumbled, and bits and pieces of clay littered the floor. Only one corner of the Bill Russell poster remained tacked to the wall.

Silvy shifted in his arms.

"The cops?" Mabi asked.

"Walked right in the front door."

"Why?"

"Because I haven't turned white on you."

He kissed the top of her head.

"When I walked in you were shaking like a kid having a nightmare so I tried waking you but when I grabbed your shoulders you screamed and hollered, Jim Ed! Jim Ed! and throwed me 'cross the room like I was a Raggedy Ann doll."

He unbuttoned her blouse to search for more bruises. Her skin was unbroken, soft, supple, still the color of fresh maple syrup. He examined her breasts for contusions, arousing his sex to the flash point. He caressed her and kissed her nipples and when she whispered Please, made love to her with a gentleness that magnified their passion until, exhausted, they both fell asleep. When he awoke, she was spreading pieces of the poster on the floor to try and patch them together, but the edges would not line up. She returned to bed and hugged him tightly, drawing strength from him as they made love on a bed bathed with sunbeams. In the afterglow, she felt a twinge and she knew the way a woman knows things a man will never understand that his seed had impregnated her.

"It's time," he said.

"Don't go."

"No choice."

"There's always a choice," she said.

He hugged her and buried his face in her hair to imprint her scent in his memory.

"I'm scared," she said.

"The next time you see me, you be seeing Leroy Wallaca."

"I love you."

"I love you."

-2-

An hour later Mabi sat across the chessboard from al-Saffah waiting for al-Saffah's next move. He did not mention the morning papers because he didn't want his confrontation with al-Saffah to be over the wrong thing.

When al-Saffah showed him Scott Dunleavy's piece in the *Globe* and told him about the television interviews, he nonchalanted it. Smoke from al-Saffah's hookah saturated the room, settling on al-Saffah's shoulders like rings circling a peg, veiling his harsh features in a cloud. The thickness of the atmosphere diffused the light; the *mihrab* looked like a torch barely visible in a heavy fog. The Islamic-style chess pieces cast multiple silhouettes. He had broken whatever linkage chained him to eight centuries of unknown chess players. He no longer envied the chess set for its past, but he understood how it had become a part of his, as much a part as a poster of Bill Russell or a comic book or a photo of the children of Wallaca razored out of a library book.

Playing the Majdorf variation of the Sicilian Defense, al-Saffah held a two-point advantage, two pawns. Mabi unfolded the photocopy of *The New York Times* article about the torture of the Falashas in Ethiopia and fanned at the smoke. The paper rattled. "Chess should be played in the silence of the desert dawn," al-Saffah said. "It's a game for that quiet moment before the sun breaks the plane of the horizon, when the desert air still chills the body."

"If my noise be your bother, you should be resigning."

"Not with a two pawn advantage."

Al-Saffah's bravado belied the position of his pieces. His king cowered at QR1. Mabi's rooks patrolled the knight's and bishop's files on the queen's side and his queen attacked the isolated pawn guarding al-Saffah's king. Mabi's knight was the trigger that would spring the final trap. There was no escape. If al-Saffah moved his queen's rook to K-B2, then Q-B2 would force mate in two moves. If al-Saffah attacked with his bishop to K-Kt5, Q-R1 would give Mabi refuge in his own corner where al-Saffah could not pin him. Al-Saffah lacked the tempo or time to start the sequence of moves necessary to checkmate him. Mabi recalled Bumper Sullivan's taunt: The average player would become world champion if he could make two successive moves once each game.

Al-Saffah reclined his king, conceding the game. "Now we've completed this child's game, let us plan the Trojans' next mission."

"How come it ain't no child's game when you win?"

"Don't be petulant, my son. It is written that the blood of Jews and Catholics will flow freely until they become extinct, first in Boston, then in America, then throughout the world. Jerusalem will become a charnel house for all but the followers of Allah. Out of this divine inferno the phoenix of Islam shall rise triumphant from the ashes. You shall be the warrior who starts the blood flowing."

"I remember you readin' me from that Koran," Mabi said, "about how them who wage war against God be executed and suffer heavy in the next world."

"An eye for an eye."

Mabi's past welled up and burst forth from his eyes, fixing al-Saffah with a stare fed by the power of memories, memories of Jim Ed, memories of the children of Wallaca, memories of Leroy and Priam. Belief powered Mabi's stare, not belief in hatred or the corruption of the religion of Abraham by Christians and Jews, not belief in some *jihad* supposedly ordained by Allah, not belief in al-Saffah as Allah's messenger, but rather a belief Allah had ordained *ajal* to the enmity between the children of Abraham to be replaced by brotherhood. Allah, Mabi now understood, had chosen him to fulfill the destiny of his name, to be His prophet, to be His instrument to rid the world of al-Saffah and those who would prostitute Allah and the holy precepts of the Koran for their own unholy and ungodly purposes. The fire next time burned in Mabi's eyes, spreading holy flames throughout the room.

"I've been heaven sent," Mabi said. The softness of his voice did not mute its thunder.

Al-Saffah leaped, aiming for the soft, fleshy part of Mabi's throat. Mabi rolled to his side, then to the floor, then pinned al-Saffah with a knee to the back, grinding it against al-Saffah's spine at the base of his neck. He pulled back on al-Saffah's arms until the bones of his upper arms popped out of the shoulder sockets. Al-Saffah kicked wildly, pummeling Mabi with his heels. Mabi secured al-Saffah's hands; then, immobilized his legs, and tied his wrists against the small of his back.

"Kill me and you honor me with martyrdom," al-Saffah said. "In the next world eternal victory will be mine."

"Be no thousand virgins waiting to fuck you." With a knife, Mabi cut open al-Saffah's sleeves. He inserted plastic tubing into al-Saffah's nose and snaked it down his throat into his stomach, taping it to his neck and arm. He connected a syringe to the plastic tubing and plunged the needle deep into a vein in al-Saffah's forearm and taped it in place. He turned al-Saffah on to his side so gravity would pull the blood through the tubing. "The prophecy of your name it's coming true at last."

Blood from al-Saffah's veins distended his stomach. He struggled and as he did his heartbeat accelerated, pumping the blood faster, filling his stomach. He felt weak, chilled. His muscles quivered, but the syringe remained in place, drinking his blood with an unslaked thirst. "Why?" he grunted. His breathing was labored. Blood overflowed his stomach and backed up in his gullet, drooling from his mouth.

Mabi held up *The New York Times*. "I am Falasha."

Al-Saffah's lips shivered. He tried to respond, but only spoke gibberish. His eyes began to glaze, the pupils to dilate. He could not focus. "Jew," he hissed as death froze his face. Still, the blood flowed and his body twitched with the kinetic energy of death. Blood streamed from his mouth and pooled at Mabi's feet. Death eternally froze al-Saffah's lips in the shape of the word "Jew."

Mabi thought again about the children of Wallaca, about the Falashas, about four girls in Birmingham, about Martin and Medgar, about all who had been lynched, known and unknown, about the six million. Leading the Trojans was such a fucking waste. Doing time for killing Bumper Sullivan and trashing Chelsea was such a fucking waste. His time as Mabi had achieved *ajal*. The Falashas needed him. He needed them. More. He needed them more. Going to Ethiopia, he would atone for burning his own backyard. He would avenge the men, women, children hung upside down from poles like animals, avenge the open wounds where worms were allowed to breed, the broken bones left unset, the mothers and fathers who paid bounties for the corpses of their children. Atone and revenge.

It was written in the book, his book, the only book worth reading.

-3-

Later that night, at the Gulf station at the Charles Street rotary, Mabi filled several five-gallon cans with gasoline. At al-Saffah's, he built a pyre in the living room–furniture, books, magazines, paper, whatever he could find that would burn. He centered al-Saffah's body on the top. He put the box of ancient chess pieces on the floor beside the door and phoned Silvy.

"It's me, Leroy. I needing one last favor. Lay me next to Jim Ed and put Leroy Wallaca on the stone." He hung up before she could say anything and dialed the *Boston Globe*.

"City desk. Crocker."

"You got true confessions on the line, baby." He heard clicks, beeps. "You're talking to Leroy Wallaca, who used to be Mabi way back when. I killed Bumper Sullivan and spread his blood 'round Chelsea. Tonight, I, Leroy, offed al-Saffah. Rabbi Esrael. Me. Father Dominic. Me. The Jew houses, churches, grave yards. Me! Me! Me!" He ripped the telephone out of the wall and tossed it on the pyre and chanted

"I ain't needing
  no rainbow sign
  'cause tonight I lighting
  the fire this time,"

as he doused the room with gasoline, saving some to make a Molotov cocktail. In the kitchen, he snuffed out the pilots in the gas stove and turned on the jets. A calmness he had never before experienced descended on him. He was going to a better place. It was his destiny, his *ajal*. Saluting the circle of scimitars, he ignited the Molotov cocktail and hurled it on the pyre. The explosion cooked his face and singed his hair. The heat dried his tears while they were still in his eyes. The flames danced as fire consumed the pyre and peeled al-Saffah's flesh from the bones. As the fire consumed Mabi's past, laid bare his future, he shouted his name: *Leroy Wallaca, Leroy Wallaca, Leroy Wallaca!* He opened the door. The air flow sent a column of flames through the ceiling. As he picked up the box of ancient chess pieces, the gas accumulating in the kitchen exploded and hurled a fireball into the star-filled sky, a fireball so high, so bright, night was day. Later, people would say it was as if the sun had risen at midnight.

It took several hours and multiple alarms to bring the fire under control and another twenty-four hours to extinguish it. Nothing remained but soggy debris and ash, which clung to the rubber boots of the arson squad who sifted through the debris for clues of the fire's origins. As April turned into May, the sun dried the ash and swirls of wind scattered the gray dust, first around the 'hood, then around Boston. The fire this time was no more.

Chapter 16

Tuesday, April 28, 1981

-1-

At the Tuesday afternoon remand hearing, Judge Gomita, acting on a motion brought by Bonturo and assented to by Maddie, dismissed all charges against Levy. In a statement of political pettifoggery, Mayor Charles Sullivan wasted several hundred words begging the citizens of Boston to let the healing begin.

Boston's Jewish community would not heal for several generations. Disguising their true feelings in unctuous lip service, they were loath to repeat the mistake made a generation earlier by their German brethren. They closed the spigot of campaign contributions to Mayor Charlie's Senate campaign. Applications pending before the Boston Redevelopment Authority for major construction projects throughout the city were withdrawn as Jewish developers decided other cities provided a more hospitable environment and a better return on investment. Corporations being wooed to relocate to the greater Boston area sought cities where their Jewish employees would not feel threatened, or worse.

The militants in Boston's African-American community challenged the authenticity of the recording of Mabi's confession. To them and their agenda, the evidence of Mabi's guilt was just another noose of white dollars around the neck of a black man. If the more moderate members of that community harbored the same doubts, they hid them behind platitudes and denunciations of anti-Semitism.

Boston's Irish community was conflicted, unable to decide who most deserved its opprobrium, a Jew or an African-American. Both, equally, was the final consensus.

In this volcanic heat wave, Boston's veneer of civility, its patina of liberalism, had melted and its true nature had erupted. It would take a cold wave of ice age duration to still the flames. Well into the twenty-first century they would flicker, flare up, die down but never die out, ever ready for new fuel to reignite the conflagration.

-2-

On Tuesday afternoon, Maddie resigned from Suffolk County Legal Services. Steve Frohling, ever in character, squeezed her too tightly for a good-bye hug, resting his hands on the curve of her ass in what Maddie knew was not a sign of respect and affection. She did not return the hug.

At the Aer Lingus office in Government Center, she bought two tickets to Ireland, one for herself, the other for Michelle Furey, both one way, both open return. Maud O'Donnell consented to meet with them as did the leadership of the IRA to discuss the wording on the plaque it intended to mount on her grand da's marker identifying him as a hero of the Republic. The future Maddie had deferred for so many years, the past she had avoided, she was now eager to embrace.

-3-

That evening, Maddie joined Rabbi ben Reuben, Moskovitzky, and Levy at services. The streets around the *shule* were still scarred and Maddie knew the scars would never heal. The streets would be rebuilt, glossy new buildings, home to chain stores and fancy retailers and franchises, all intended to create a new Chelsea. For years into the future, descendants of the original community would bring their children to Chelsea and show them where the butcher shop had been, the bookseller, the ritual bath, the tenements where sewing machines once whirred. It was as much a part of the legacy of the Jews of Boston as the *Pesach* of these hot April days.

After services Maddie accompanied the rabbi, Moskovitzky, and Levy to the rabbi's home. It was a subdued celebration, not really a celebration, the rabbi said, more like a *shiva*–a ritual of mourning.

Maddie did not feel comfortable. These men had seen her at her worst; yet, they accepted her with grace and a generosity of spirit.

"*Schnapps?*" The rabbi filled four shot glasses half way. "*L'chaim.* To life."

Maddie marveled at this man who could offer a toast to life after all he had lived through. She felt something she had not felt in years, a simple elemental feeling she had not enjoyed since the last time she nursed Elizabeth on the morning of her death. She felt good, not guilty, about being alive. She felt good, not guilty, about being Irish. She felt good, not guilty, about being her grand da's granddaughter. Now, when she visited the cemetery to place flowers on Elizabeth's grave, on the graves of her ma and da, she would still cry; but she would also offer the Rabbi's toast, *L'chaim.* To life.

Slowly, day by day, Maddie's hair began to grow back. By the time she and Michelle Furey left for Ireland, she was more beautiful than ever.

Epilogue

-1-

Monday, May 17, 2004

In Trish Sullivan's living room, in the presence of immediate family both *in corpus* and *in spiritus*, Trish, acting under the authority of a one-day license issued by the Commonwealth of Massachusetts, officiated at the marriage of Maddie Devlin and Michelle Furey. After Trish pronounced them married, she asked what surname they wished to adopt. Maddie said Furey-Devlin and Michelle said Devlin-Furey so they flipped a coin which, miraculously, landed on its edge. When everyone stopped laughing, they kissed with the love only newlyweds share as their families, both *in corpus* and *in spiritus*, cheered.

"Who carries who over the threshold?" Charlie Sullivan asked.

"Neither," Maddie said.

"We're too old for that," Michelle added.

Boston's newspapers refused to publish their wedding announcement.

-2-

Thursday, October 9, 2008

The image of the two tombstones lingered in the mind of Leroy Wallaca, Jr. as he, his wife Miranda, his mother Silvy Thomas, his grandparents Cealy Thomas and Hannah and Gideon Wallaca, and his Uncle Badger Thomas walked toward the gates of Nigger Heaven. It was a warm, sunny October afternoon and Nigger Heaven was as overgrown with weeds as ever. Miranda pushed a stroller carrying Leroy Wallaca, III. It was Yom Kippur, after the Sabbath the holiest day on the Jewish calendar. Hannah insisted they visit Leroy's and Jim Ed's graves that day. The leaves on the maple trees bordering the footpath were tinged with hints of yellow and scarlet. Birds darted from branch to branch, chirping in the autumnal air. Squirrels scampered from tree to tree, playing rather than gathering food for the winter.

"I don't remember Indian summer lasting so long," Silvy said.

Age had rounded Silvy's cheeks and swollen her feet so she could only wear oversized slippers. On her good days, she used a cane; on this day, a walker. Her stomach bulged under her loose-fitting dress. Her eyes were puffy.

"As God's in His heaven," Cealy said, "first frost will come soon enough."

As they approached Nigger Heaven, the dates on the tombstones receded deeper into the past, headstones of people who never saw the twentieth century, the nineteenth, some the eighteenth, headstones carved with images of cherubic angels or laughing death heads, headstones where the 's' looked like an 'f', headstones from the time when more people died before the age of ten than after the age of fifty.

At Jim Ed's and Leroy's graves, Silvy asked Hannah to say some words, and Hannah did, the same words she said every visit, the same words she had said years earlier when the Trojans flanked Jim Ed's grave and an empty coffin was lowered into the earth. When Hannah finished, Silvy said, as she always did, how nice a prayer it was, and they bowed their heads in silence.

Now, as they passed through Nigger Heaven and approached the rusted iron fence that separated the dead from the living, Silvy asked her mother, "How can you be thinking of frost on a day like this?" As she spoke, a gust of wind blew some trash against her legs.

"It's in the air," Cealy said. "Always is."

Silvy kicked at the trash and Barack Obama and Joe Biden smiled at her from a campaign poster. Someone had blackened their front teeth and crayoned Hitler-style mustaches under their noses. A spider crawled across Obama's cheek, stopped for a second on Biden's right eye, then scurried into the grass at the edge of the cemetery. Silvy folded the poster, her hands shaking too much to square the corners of the creases, and placed it in the basket hanging from the railing of her walker. As the four of them continued past the headstones, past the hedges, past the shrubs and birds and squirrels, out of Nigger Heaven into Nigger Hell, the spider, hungry to snare its dinner, weaved its web in the tall grass beside an ancient and anonymous grave while, in his stroller, Leroy III shook his baby rattle and scared the songbirds from the trees.

Acknowledgments

In the past 40 to 50 years there have been a number of academic studies which argue that Black English is neither a non-standard form of English nor a dialect spoken primarily by African-Americans, but rather a unique language with its own grammatical structure and its own vocabulary. In crafting the dialogue spoken by the African-American characters, I relied upon two of these studies: Geneva Smitherman, *Talkin and Testifyin – The Language of Black America*, Wayne State University Press (1986); Geneva Smitherman, *Black Talk*, Houghton Mifflin (1994, 2000).

With respect to the Falashas, I am indebted to Louis Rapoport, *The Lost Jews: Last of the Ethiopian Falashas*, Stein and Day (1980) as well as *'Fact Sheets'* issued by the Ethiopian Jewry Committee of the Jewish Community Council of Metropolitan Boston (1982) Additional information may be found by searching the Index of *The New York Times*.

The prayer that Hannah Wallaca recites over her son's grave is the *Mourner's Kaddish*, the traditional Jewish prayer for the remembrance of the dead. It is based on an English translation in common use in Reform Jewish congregations in the 1970's and 1980's. Central Conference of American Rabbis, *Gates of Prayer* (1975)

The Vietnam war generated a great deal of slang and jargon much of which was created by the troops on the ground in country. There are numerous websites devoted to this slang and jargon. Another fertile source is Karl Marlantes, *Matterhorn: A Novel of the Vietnam War*, Atlantic Monthly Press (2010). This material proved invaluable in crafting the letter Roadkill sent to the Wallacas regarding Jim Ed's death in Vietnam.

The song that Silvy sings when Mabi views his imagined funeral procession is *All My Trials*, a traditional American folk song that became popular during the folk revival of the 1950's and 1960's. Like many traditional American folk songs, its origins are murky at best. According to *The Joan Baez Songbook*, Ryerson Music Publishers (1964), it is an American Southern gospel song that predates the Civil War. It has also been argued that some of the phrases in the lyrics can be found on a 1798 English gravestone. The lyrics sung by Silvy were adapted from the Joan Baez recording.

I am indebted to three individuals whose keen editorial eyes enabled me to see things I would have otherwise missed. While I did not always agree with them and did not adopt all of their suggestions, their input greatly improved *The Fire This Time* and my gratitude to them is unbounded. Thank you, Pamela Painter, Beverly Swerling, and Ted Gilley.

Lastly, I greatly benefited from the encouragement and moral support I received over the years from Albert J. Gowan for my writing in general and this novel in particular. I deeply regret Al did not live to share this moment with me.

About the Author

Liss, a multiple Pushcart Prize nominee, a nominee for the sto-rySouth Million Writers Award, and a finalist for the Flannery O'Connor Short Fiction Prize sponsored by University of Georgia Press, the St. Lawrence Book Award sponsored by Black Lawrence Press, and the Bakeless Prize sponsored by Breadloaf Writers' Conference and Middlebury College, has published more than 50 short stories. He has received numerous awards and other forms of recognition for individual short stories including *The Florida Review* Editor's Award for Fiction; .James Still Prize for Short Fiction sponsored by *Wind*; Midnight Sun Award for Fiction sponsored by *Permafrost*; Third prize in the Arthur Edelstein Prize for Short Fiction; Finalist for the Raymond Carver Award for Short Fiction sponsored by *Carve Magazine*; and Honorable Mention in the *New*

Letters Literary Award for Fiction and the *Glimmer Train* June, 2014 Fiction Open. Liss has also been published in *The Saturday Evening Post*, *Alfred Hitchcock Mystery Magazine*, *The South Dakota Review*, *The South Carolina Review*, *Dogwood*, *The Worcester Review*, *Fifth Wednesday Journal*. He earned a BA from Amherst College, Amherst, MA; a JD from Columbia University School of Law, New York, NY; and an MFA from Emerson College, Boston, MA. He was the recipient of a Grant-in-Aid in Literature from the St. Botolph Club Foundation, Boston, MA where he leads a workshop in writing fiction.